CONAN THE BERSERKER

ROBERT E. HOWARD

The right of Robert E. Howard to be identified as the author
of this work has been asserted by him in accordance with
the Copyright, Designs and Patents Act 1988.

This edition first published in Great Britain in 2011 by
Gollancz
An imprint of the Orion Publishing Group
Orion House, 5 Upper St Martin's Lane, London WC2H 9EA
An Hachette UK Company

This edition published in Great Britain in 2011 by Gollancz

1 3 5 7 9 10 8 6 4 2

A CIP catalogue record for this book
is available from the British Library.

ISBN 978 0 575 11502 6

Typeset by Deltatype Ltd, Birkenhead, Merseyside

Printed and bound by CPI Group (UK) Ltd, Croydon, CR0 4YY

The Orion Publishing Group's policy is to use papers that
are natural, renewable and recyclable products and made
from wood grown in sustainable forests. The logging and
manufacturing processes are expected to conform to the
environmental regulations of the country of origin.

www.orionbooks.co.uk

CONTENTS

The People of the Black Circle   1

The Slithering Shadow   86

Drums of Tombalku (Draft)   122

The Pool of the Black One   148

Red Nails   179

Jewels of Gwalhur   265

Beyond the Black River   311

COPYRIGHT AND PUBLICATION DETAILS

THE PEOPLE OF THE BLACK CIRCLE

1

Death Strikes a King

The King of Vendhya was dying. Through the hot, stifling night the temple gongs boomed and the conchs roared. Their clamor was a faint echo in the gold-domed chamber where Bunda Chand struggled on the velvet-cushioned dais. Beads of sweat glistened on his dark skin; his fingers twisted the gold-worked fabric beneath him. He was young; no spear had touched him, no poison lurked in his wine. But his veins stood out like blue cords on his temples, and his eyes dilated with the nearness of death. Trembling slave-girls knelt at the foot of the dais, and leaning down to him, watching him with passionate intensity, was his sister, the Devi Yasmina. With her was the *wazam*, a noble grown old in the royal court.

She threw up her head in a gusty gesture of wrath and despair as the thunder of the distant drums reached her ears.

'The priests and their clamor!' she exclaimed. 'They are no wiser than the leeches who are helpless! Nay, he dies and none can say why. He is dying now – and I stand here helpless, who would burn the whole city and spill the blood of thousands to save him.'

'Not a man of Ayodhya but would die in his place, if it might be, Devi,' answered the *wazam*. 'This poison—'

'I tell you it is not poison!' she cried. 'Since his birth he has been guarded so closely that the cleverest poisoners of the East could not reach him. Five skulls bleaching on the Tower of the Kites can testify to attempts which were made – and which failed. As you well know, there are ten men and ten women whose sole duty is to taste his food and wine, and fifty armed warriors guard his chamber as they guard it now. No, it is not poison; it is sorcery – black, ghastly magic—'

She ceased as the king spoke; his livid lips did not move, and there was no recognition in his glassy eyes. But his voice rose in an eery call, indistinct and far away, as if called to her from beyond vast, wind-blown gulfs.

'Yasmina! Yasmina! My sister, where are you? I can not find you. All is darkness, and the roaring of great winds!'

'Brother!' cried Yasmina, catching his limp hand in a convulsive grasp. 'I am here! Do you not know me—'

Her voice died at the utter vacancy of his face. A low confused moan waned from his mouth. The slave-girls at the foot of the dais whimpered with fear, and Yasmina beat her breast in anguish.

In another part of the city a man stood in a latticed balcony overlooking a long street in which torches tossed luridly, smokily revealing upturned dark faces and the whites of gleaming eyes. A long-drawn wailing rose from the multitude.

The man shrugged his broad shoulders and turned back into the arabesque chamber. He was a tall man, compactly built, and richly clad.

'The king is not yet dead, but the dirge is sounded,' he said to another man who sat cross-legged on a mat in a corner. This man was clad in a brown camel-hair robe and sandals, and a green turban was on his head. His expression was tranquil, his gaze impersonal.

'The people know he will never see another dawn,' this man answered.

The first speaker favored him with a long, searching stare.

'What I can not understand,' he said, 'is why I have had to wait so long for your masters to strike. If they have slain the king now, why could they not have slain him months ago?'

'Even the arts you call sorcery are governed by cosmic laws,' answered the man in the green turban. 'The stars direct these actions, as in other affairs. Not even my masters can alter the stars. Not until the heavens were in the proper order could they perform this necromancy.' With a long, stained fingernail he mapped the constellations on the marble-tiled floor. 'The slant of the moon presaged evil for the king of Vendhya; the stars are in turmoil, the Serpent in the House of the Elephant. During such juxtaposition, the invisible guardians are removed from the spirit of Bhunda Chand. A path is opened in the unseen realms, and once a point of contact was established, mighty powers were put in play along that path.'

'Point of contact?' inquired the other. 'Do you mean that lock of Bhunda Chand's hair?'

'Yes. All discarded portions of the human body still remain part of it, attached to it by intangible connections. The priests of Asura have a dim inkling of this truth, and so all nail trimmings, hair and other waste products of the persons of the royal family are carefully reduced to ashes and the ashes hidden. But at the urgent entreaty of the princess of Khosala, who loved Bhunda Chand vainly, he gave her a lock of his long black hair as a token of remembrance. When my masters decided upon his doom, the lock, in its golden, jewel-encrusted case, was stolen from under her pillow while she slept, and another substituted, so like the first that she never knew the difference. Then the genuine lock travelled by camel-caravan up the long, long road to Peshkhauri, thence up the Zhaibar Pass, until it reached the hands of those for whom it was intended.'

'Only a lock of hair,' murmured the nobleman.

'By which a soul is drawn from its body and across gulfs of echoing space,' returned the man on the mat.

The nobleman studied him curiously.

'I do not know if you are a man or a demon, Khemsa,' he said at last. 'Few of us are what we seem. I, whom the Kshatriyas know as Kerim Shah, a prince from Iranistan, am no greater a masquerader than most men. They are all traitors in one way or another, and half of them know not whom they serve. There at least I have no doubts; for I serve King Yezdigerd of Turan.'

'And I the Black Seers of Yimsha,' said Khemsa; 'and my masters are greater than yours, for they have accomplished by their arts what Yezdigerd could not with a hundred thousand swords.'

★

Outside, the moan of the tortured thousands shuddered up to the stars which crusted the sweating Vendhyan night, and the conchs bellowed like oxen in pain.

In the gardens of the palace the torches glinted on polished helmets and curved swords and gold-chased corselets. All the noble-born fighting-men of Ayodhya were gathered in the great palace or about it, and at each broad-arched gate and door fifty archers stood on guard, with bows in their hands. But Death stalked through the royal palace and none could stay his ghostly tread.

On the dais under the golden dome the king cried out again, racked by awful paroxysms. Again his voice came faintly and far away, and again the Devi bent to him, trembling with a fear that was darker than the terror of death.

'Yasmina!' Again that far, weirdly dreeing cry, from realms immeasurable. 'Aid me! I am far from my mortal house! Wizards have drawn my soul through the wind-blown darkness. They seek to snap the silver cord that binds me to my dying body. They cluster around me; their hands are taloned, their eyes are red like flame burning in darkness. *Aie*, save me, my sister! Their fingers sear me like fire! They would slay my body and damn my soul! What is this they bring before me?—*Aie!*'

At the terror in his hopeless cry Yasmina screamed uncontrollably and threw herself bodily upon him in the abandon of her anguish. He was torn by a terrible convulsion; foam flew from his contorted lips and his writhing fingers left their marks on the girl's shoulders. But the glassy blankness passed from his eyes like smoke blown from a fire, and he looked up at his sister with recognition.

'Brother!' she sobbed. 'Brother—'

'Swift!' he gasped, and his weakening voice was rational. 'I know now what brings me to the pyre. I have been on a far journey and I understand. I have been ensorcelled by the wizards of the Himelians. They drew my soul out of my body and far away, into a stone room. There they strove to break the silver cord of life, and thrust my soul into the body of a foul night-weird their sorcery

4

summoned up from hell. Ah! I feel their pull upon me now! Your cry and the grip of your fingers brought me back, but I am going fast. My soul clings to my body, but its hold weakens. Quick – kill me, before they can trap my soul for ever!'

'I cannot!' she wailed, smiting her naked breasts.

'Swiftly, I command you!' There was the old imperious note in his failing whisper. 'You have never disobeyed me – obey my last command! Send my soul clean to Asura! Haste, lest you damn me to spend eternity as a filthy gaunt of darkness. Strike, I command you! *Strike!*'

Sobbing wildly, Yasmina plucked a jeweled dagger from her girdle and plunged it to the hilt in his breast. He stiffened and then went limp, a grim smile curving his dead lips. Yasmina hurled herself face-down on the rush-covered floor, beating the reeds with her clenched hands. Outside, the gongs and conchs brayed and thundered and the priests gashed themselves with copper knives.

2

A Barbarian from the Hills

Chunder Shan, governor of Peshkhauri, laid down his golden pen and carefully scanned that which he had written on parchment that bore his official seal. He had ruled Peshkhauri so long only because he weighed his every word, spoken or written. Danger breeds caution, and only a wary man lives long in that wild country where the hot Vendhyan plains meet the crags of the Himelians. An hour's ride westward or northward and one crossed the border and was among the Hills where men lived by the law of the knife.

The governor was alone in his chamber, seated at his ornately carven table of inlaid ebony. Through the wide window, open for the coolness, he could see a square of the blue Himelian night, dotted with great white stars. An adjacent parapet was a shadowy line, and further crenelles and embrasures were barely hinted at in the dim starlight. The governor's fortress was strong, and situated

5

outside the walls of the city it guarded. The breeze that stirred the tapestries on the wall brought faint noises from the streets of Peshkhauri – occasional snatches of wailing song, or the thrum of a cithern.

The governor read what he had written, slowly, with his open hand shading his eyes from the bronze butterlamp, his lips moving. Absently, as he read, he heard the drum of horses' hoofs outside the barbican, the sharp staccato of the guards' challenge. He did not heed, intent upon his letter. It was addressed to the *wazam* of Vendhya, at the royal court of Ayodhya, and it stated, after the customary salutations:

'Let it be known to your excellency that I have faithfully carried out your excellency's instructions. The seven tribesmen are well guarded in their prison, and I have repeatedly sent word into the hills that their chief come in person to bargain for their release. But he has made no move, except to send word that unless they are freed he will burn Peshkhauri and cover his saddle with my hide, begging your excellency's indulgence. This he is quite capable of attempting, and I have tripled the numbers of the lance guards. The man is not a native of Ghulistan. I cannot with certainty predict his next move. But since it is the wish of the Devi—'

He was out of his ivory chair and on his feet facing the arched door, all in one instant. He snatched at the curved sword lying in its ornate scabbard on the table, and then checked the movement.

It was a woman who had entered unannounced, a woman whose gossamer robes did not conceal the rich garments beneath them any more than they concealed the suppleness and beauty of her tall, slender figure. A filmy veil fell below her breasts, supported by a flowing head-dress bound about with a triple gold braid and adorned with a golden crescent. Her dark eyes regarded the astonished governor over the veil, and then with an imperious gesture of her white hand, she uncovered her face.

'Devi!' The governor dropped to his knees before her, surprise

6

and confusion somewhat spoiling the stateliness of his obeisance. With a gesture she motioned him to rise, and he hastened to lead her to the ivory chair, all the while bowing level with his girdle. But his first words were of reproof.

'Your Majesty! This was most unwise! The border is un-settled. Raids from the hills are incessant. You came with a large attendance?'

'An ample retinue followed me to Peshkhauri,' she answered. 'I lodged my people there and came on to the fort with my maid, Gitara.'

Chunder Shan groaned in horror.

'Devi! You do not understand the peril. An hour's ride from this spot the hills swarm with barbarians who make a profession of murder and rapine. Women have been stolen and men stabbed between the fort and the city. Peshkhauri is not like your southern provinces—'

'But I am here, and unharmed,' she interrupted with a trace of impatience. 'I showed my signet ring to the guard at the gate, and to the one outside your door, and they admitted me unannounced, not knowing me, but supposing me to be a secret courier from Ayodhya. Let us not now waste time.

'You have received no word from the chief of the barbarians?'

'None save threats and curses, Devi. He is wary and suspicious. He deems it a trap, and perhaps he is not to be blamed. The Kshatriyas have not always kept their promises to the hill people.'

'He must be brought to terms!' broke in Yasmina, the knuckles of her clenched hands showing white.

'I do not understand.' The governor shook his head. 'When I chanced to capture these seven hillmen, I reported their capture to the *wazam*, as is the custom, and then, before I could hang them, there came an order to hold them and communicate with their chief. This I did, but the man holds aloof, as I have said. These men are of the tribe of Afghulis, but he is a foreigner from the west, and he is called Conan. I have threatened to hang them tomorrow at dawn, if he does not come.'

'Good!' exclaimed the Devi. 'You have done well. And I will

tell you why I have given these orders. My brother—' she faltered, choking, and the governor bowed his head, with the customary gesture of respect for a departed sovereign.

'The king of Vendhya was destroyed by magic,' she said at last. 'I have devoted my life to the destruction of his murderers. As he died he gave me a clue, and I have followed it. I have read the *Book of Skelos*, and talked with nameless hermits in the caves below Jhelai. I learned how, and by whom, he was destroyed. His enemies were the Black Seers of Mount Yimsha.'

'Asura!' whispered Chunder Shan, paling.

Her eyes knifed him through. 'Do you fear them?'

'Who does not, Your Majesty?' he replied. 'They are black devils, haunting the uninhabited hills beyond the Zhaibar. But the sages say that they seldom interfere in the lives of mortal men.'

'Why they slew my brother I do not know,' she answered. 'But I have sworn on the altar of Asura to destroy them! And I need the aid of a man beyond the border. A Kshatriya army, unaided, would never reach Yimsha.'

'Aye,' muttered Chunder Shan. 'You speak the truth there. It would be fight every step of the way, with hairy hillmen hurling down boulders from every height, and rushing us with their long knives in every valley. The Turanians fought their way through the Himelians once, but how many returned to Khurusun? Few of those who escaped the swords of the Kshatriyas, after the king, your brother, defeated their host on the Jhumda River, ever saw Secunderam again.'

'And so I must control men across the border,' she said, 'men who know the way to Mount Yimsha—'

'But the tribes fear the Black Seers and shun the unholy mountain,' broke in the governor.

'Does the chief, Conan, fear them?' she asked.

'Well, as to that,' muttered the governor, 'I doubt if there is anything that devil fears.'

'So I have been told. Therefore he is the man I must deal with. He wishes the release of his seven men. Very well; their ransom shall be the heads of the Black Seers!' Her voice thrummed with

8

hate as she uttered the last words, and her hands clenched at her sides. She looked an image of incarnate passion as she stood there with her head thrown high and her bosom heaving.

Again the governor knelt, for part of his wisdom was the knowledge that a woman in such an emotional tempest is as perilous as a blind cobra to any about her.

'It shall be as you wish, Your Majesty.' Then as she presented a calmer aspect, he rose and ventured to drop a word of warning. 'I can not predict what the chief Conan's action will be. The tribesmen are always turbulent, and I have reason to believe that emissaries from the Turanians are stirring them up to raid our borders. As your majesty knows, the Turanians have established themselves in Secunderam and other northern cities, though the hill tribes remain unconquered. King Yezdigerd has long looked southward with greedy lust and perhaps is seeking to gain by treachery what he could not win by force of arms. I have thought that Conan might well be one of his spies.'

'We shall see,' she answered. 'If he loves his followers, he will be at the gates at dawn, to parley. I shall spend the night in the fortress. I came in disguise to Peshkhauri, and lodged my retinue at an inn instead of the palace. Besides my people, only yourself knows of my presence here.'

'I shall escort you to your quarters, Your Majesty,' said the governor, and as they emerged from the doorway, he beckoned the warrior on guard there, and the man fell in behind them, spear held at salute.

The maid waited, veiled like her mistress, outside the door, and the group traversed a wide, winding corridor, lighted by smoky torches, and reached the quarters reserved for visiting notables – generals and viceroys, mostly; none of the royal family had ever honored the fortress before. Chunder Shan had a perturbed feeling that the suite was not suitable to such an exalted personage as the Devi, and though she sought to make him feel at ease in her presence, he was glad when she dismissed him and he bowed himself out. All the menials of the fort had been summoned to serve his royal guest – though he did not divulge her identity – and he stationed a squad of spearmen before her doors, among them the warrior who had guarded his own chamber. In his preoccupation he forgot to replace the man.

The governor had not been long gone from her when Yasmina suddenly remembered something else which she had wished to discuss with him, but had forgotten until that moment. It concerned the past actions of one Kerim Shah, a nobleman from Iranistan, who had dwelt for a while in Peshkhauri before coming on to the court at Ayodhya. A vague suspicion concerning the man had been stirred by a glimpse of him in Peshkhauri that night. She wondered if he had followed her from Ayodhya. Being a truly remarkable Devi, she did not summon the governor to her again, but hurried out into the corridor alone, and hastened toward his chamber.

Chunder Shan, entering his chamber, closed the door and went to his table. There he took the letter he had been writing and tore it to bits. Scarcely had he finished when he heard something drop softly onto the parapet adjacent to the window. He looked up to see a figure loom briefly against the stars, and then a man dropped lightly into the room. The light glinted on a long sheen of steel in his hand.

'Shhhh!' he warned. 'Don't make a noise, or I'll send the devil a henchman!'

The governor checked his motion toward the sword on the table. He was within reach of the yard-long Zhaibar knife that glittered in the intruder's fist, and he knew the desperate quickness of a hillman.

The invader was a tall man, at once strong and supple. He was dressed like a hillman, but his dark features and blazing blue eyes did not match his garb. Chunder Shan had never seen a man like him; he was not an Easterner, but some barbarian from the West. But his aspect was as untamed and formidable as any of the hairy tribesmen who haunt the hills of Ghulistan.

'You come like a thief in the night,' commented the governor, recovering some of his composure, although he remembered that there was no guard within call. Still, the hillman could not know that.

'I climbed a bastion,' snarled the intruder. 'A guard thrust his head over the battlement in time for me to rap it with my knife-hilt.'

'You are Conan?'

'Who else? You sent word into the hills that you wished for me to come and parley with you. Well, by Crom, I've come! Keep away from that table or I'll gut you.'

'I merely wish to seat myself,' answered the governor, carefully sinking into the ivory chair, which he wheeled away from the table. Conan moved restlessly before him, glancing suspiciously at the door, thumbing the razor edge of his three-foot knife. He did not walk like an Afghuli, and was bluntly direct where the East is subtle.

'You have seven of my men,' he said abruptly. 'You refused the ransom I offered. What the devil do you want?'

'Let us discuss terms,' answered Chunder Shan cautiously.

'Terms?' There was a timbre of dangerous anger in his voice. 'What do you mean? Haven't I offered you gold?'

Chunder Shan laughed.

'Gold? There is more gold in Peshkhauri than you ever saw.'

'You're a liar,' retorted Conan. 'I've seen the *suk* of the gold-smiths in Khurusun.'

'Well, more than an Afghuli ever saw,' amended Chunder Shan. 'And it is but a drop of all the treasure of Vendhya. Why should we desire gold? It would be more to our advantage to hang these seven thieves.'

Conan ripped out a sulfurous oath and the long blade quivered in his grip as the muscles rose in ridges on his brown arm.

'I'll split your head like a ripe melon!'

A wild blue flame flickered in the hillman's eyes, but Chunder Shan shrugged his shoulders, though keeping an eye on the keen steel.

'You can kill me easily, and probably escape over the wall afterward. But that would not save the seven tribesmen. My men would surely hang them. And these men are headmen among the Afghulis.'

'I know it,' snarled Conan. 'The tribe is baying like wolves at my heels because I have not procured their release. Tell me in plain words what you want, because, by Crom! if there's no other way, I'll raise a horde and lead it to the very gates of Peshkhauri!'

Looking at the man as he stood squarely, knife in fist and eyes glaring, Chunder Shan did not doubt that he was capable of it. The governor did not believe any hill-horde could take Peshkhauri, but he did not wish a devastated countryside.

'There is a mission you must perform,' he said, choosing his words with as much care as if they had been razors. 'There—'

Conan had sprung back, wheeling to face the door at the same instant, lips asnarl. His barbarian ears had caught the quick tread of soft slippers outside the door. The next instant the door was thrown open and a slim, silk-robed form entered hastily, pulling the door shut – then stopping short at sight of the hillman.

Chunder Shan sprang up, his heart jumping into his mouth.

'Devi!' he cried involuntarily, losing his head momentarily in his fright.

'*Devi!*' It was like an explosive echo from the hillman's lips. Chunder Shan saw recognition and intent flame up in the fierce blue eyes.

The governor shouted desperately and caught at his sword, but the hillman moved with the devastating speed of a hurricane. He sprang, knocked the governor sprawling with a savage blow of his knife-hilt, swept up the astounded Devi in one brawny arm and leaped for the window. Chunder Shan, struggling frantically to his feet, saw the man poise an instant on the sill in a flutter of silken skirts and white limbs that was his royal captive, and heard his fierce, exultant snarl: '*Now* dare to hang my men!' and then Conan leaped to the parapet and was gone. A wild scream floated back to the governor's ears.

'Guard! *Guard!*' screamed the governor, struggling up and running drunkenly to the door. He tore it open and reeled into the hall. His shouts re-echoed along the corridors, and warriors came running, gaping to see the governor holding his broken head, from which the blood streamed.

'Turn out the lancers!' he roared. 'There has been an abduction!' Even in his frenzy he had enough sense left to withhold the full truth. He stopped short as he heard a sudden drum of hoofs outside, a frantic scream and a wild yell of barbaric exultation.

Followed by the bewildered guardsmen, the governor raced for the stair. In the courtyard of the fort a force of lancers stood by saddled steeds, ready to ride at an instant's notice. Chunder Shan led his squadron flying after the fugitive, though his head swam so he had to hold with both hands to the saddle. He did not divulge the identity of the victim, but said merely that the noblewoman who had borne the royal signet-ring had been carried away by the chief of the Afghulis. The abductor was out of sight and hearing, but they knew the path he would strike – the road that runs straight to the mouth of the Zhaibar. There was no moon; peasant huts rose dimly in the starlight. Behind them fell away the grim bastion of the fort, and the towers of Peshkhauri. Ahead of them loomed the black walls of the Himelians.

3

Khemsa Uses Magic

In the confusion that reigned in the fortress while the guard was being turned out, no one noticed that the girl who had accompanied the Devi slipped out the great arched gate and vanished in the darkness. She ran straight for the city, her garments tucked high. She did not follow the open road, but cut straight through fields and over slopes, avoiding fences and leaping irrigation ditches as surely as if it were broad daylight, and as easily as if she were a trained masculine runner. The hoof-drum of the guardsmen had faded away up the hill before she reached the city wall. She did not go to the great gate, beneath whose arch men leaned on spears and craned their necks into the darkness, discussing the unwonted activity about the fortress. She skirted the wall until she reached a certain point where the spire of the tower was visible above the battlements. Then she placed her hands to her mouth and voiced a low weird call that carried strangely.

Almost instantly a head appeared at an embrasure and a rope came wriggling down the wall. She seized it, placed a foot in the loop at the end, and waved her arm. Then quickly and smoothly she was drawn up the sheer stone curtain. An instant later she scrambled over the merlons and stood up on a flat roof which covered a house that was built against the wall. There was an open trap there, and a man in a camel-hair robe who silently coiled the rope, not showing in any way the strain of hauling a full-grown woman up a forty-foot wall.

'Where is Kerim Shah?' she gasped, panting after her long run.

'Asleep in the house below. You have news?'

'Conan has stolen the Devi out of the fortress and carried her away into the hills!' She blurted out her news in a rush, the words stumbling over one another.

Khemsa showed no emotion, but merely nodded his turbaned head. 'Kerim Shah will be glad to hear that,' he said.

'Wait!' The girl threw her supple arms about his neck. She was panting hard, but not only from exertion. Her eyes blazed like black jewels in the starlight. Her upturned face was close to Khemsa's, but though he submitted to her embrace, he did not return it.

'Do not tell the Hyrkanian!' she panted. 'Let us use this knowledge ourselves! The governor has gone into the hills with his riders, but he might as well chase a ghost. He has not told anyone that it was the Devi who was kidnapped. None in Peshkhauri or the fort knows it except us.'

'But what good does it do us?' the man expostulated. 'My masters sent me with Kerim Shah to aid him in every way—'

'Aid yourself!' she cried fiercely. 'Shake off your yoke!'

'You mean – disobey my masters?' he gasped, and she felt his whole body turn cold under her arms.

'Aye!' she shook him in the fury of her emotion. 'You too are a magician! Why will you be a slave, using your powers only to elevate others? Use your arts for yourself!'

'That is forbidden!' He was shaking as if with an ague. 'I am not one of the Black Circle. Only by the command of the masters do I dare to use the knowledge they have taught me.'

'But you *can* use it!' she argued passionately. 'Do as I beg you! Of course Conan has taken the Devi to hold as hostage against the seven tribesmen in the governor's prison. Destroy them, so Chunder Shan can not use them to buy back the Devi. Then let us go into the mountains and take her from the Afghulis. They can not stand against your sorcery with their knives. The treasure of the Vendhyan kings will be ours as ransom – and then when we have it in our hands, we can trick them, and sell her to the king of Turan. We shall have wealth beyond our maddest dreams. With it we can buy warriors. We will take Khorbhul, oust the Turanians from the hills, and send our hosts southward; become king and queen of an empire!'

Khemsa too was panting, shaking like a leaf in her grasp; his face showed gray in the starlight, beaded with great drops of perspiration.

'I love you!' she cried fiercely, writhing her body against his, almost strangling him in her wild embrace, shaking him in her abandon. 'I will make a king of you! For love of you I betrayed my mistress; for love of me betray your masters! Why fear the Black Seers? By your love for me you have broken one of their laws already! Break the rest! You are as strong as they!'

A man of ice could not have withstood the searing heat of her passion and fury. With an inarticulate cry he crushed her to him, bending her backward and showering gasping kisses on her eyes, face and lips.

'I'll do it!' His voice was thick with laboring emotions. He staggered like a drunken man. 'The arts they have taught me shall work for me, not for my masters. We shall be rulers of the world – of the world—'

'Come then!' Twisting lithely out of his embrace, she seized his hand and led him toward the trap-door. 'First we must make sure that the governor does not exchange those seven Afghulis for the Devi.'

He moved like a man in a daze, until they had descended a ladder and she paused in the chamber below. Kerim Shah lay on a couch motionless, an arm across his face as though to shield his sleeping eyes from the soft light of a brass lamp. She plucked Khemsa's arm and made a quick gesture across her own throat. Khemsa lifted his hand; then his expression changed and he drew away.

'I have eaten his salt,' he muttered. 'Besides, he can not interfere with us.'

He led the girl through a door that opened on a winding stair. After their soft tread had faded into silence, the man on the couch sat up. Kerim Shah wiped the sweat from his face. A knife-thrust he did not dread, but he feared Khemsa as a man fears a poisonous reptile.

'People who plot on roofs should remember to lower their voices,' he muttered. 'But as Khemsa has turned against his masters, and as he was my only contact between them, I can count on their aid no longer. From now on I play the game in my own way.'

Rising to his feet he went quickly to a table, drew pen and parchment from his girdle and scribbled a few succinct lines.

'To Khosru Khan, governor of Secunderam: the Cimmerian Conan has carried the Devi Yasmina to the villages of the Afghulis. It is an opportunity to get the Devi into our hands, as the king has so long desired. Send three thousand horsemen at once. I will meet them in the valley of Gurashah with native guides.'

And he signed it with a name that was not in the least like Kerim Shah.

Then from a golden cage he drew forth a carrier pigeon, to whose leg he made fast the parchment, rolled into a tiny cylinder and secured with gold wire. Then he went quickly to a casement and tossed the bird into the night. It wavered on fluttering wings, balanced, and was gone like a flitting shadow. Catching up helmet, sword and cloak, Kerim Shah hurried out of the chamber and down the winding stair.

The prison quarters of Peshkhauri were separated from the rest of the city by a massive wall, in which was set a single iron-bound door under an arch. Over the arch burned a lurid red cresset, and beside the door squatted a warrior with spear and shield.

This warrior, leaning on his spear, and yawning from time to time, started suddenly to his feet. He had not thought he had dozed, but a man was standing before him, a man he had not heard approach. The man wore a camel-hair robe and a green turban. In the flickering light of the cresset his features were shadowy, but a pair of lambent eyes shone surprisingly in the lurid glow.

'Who comes?' demanded the warrior, presenting his spear. 'Who are you?'

The stranger did not seem perturbed, though the spear-point touched his bosom. His eyes held the warrior's with strange intensity.

'What are you obliged to do?' he asked, strangely.

'To guard the gate!' The warrior spoke thickly and mechanically; he stood rigid as a statue, his eyes slowly glazing.

'You lie! You are obliged to obey me! You have looked into my eyes, and your soul is no longer your own. Open that door!'

Stiffly, with the wooden features of an image, the guard wheeled about, drew a great key from his girdle, turned it in the massive lock and swung open the door. Then he stood at attention, his unseeing stare straight ahead of him.

A woman glided from the shadows and laid an eager hand on the mesmerist's arm.

'Bid him fetch us horses, Khemsa,' she whispered.

'No need of that,' answered the Rakhsha. Lifting his voice slightly he spoke to the guardsman. 'I have no more use for you. Kill yourself!'

Like a man in a trance the warrior thrust the butt of his spear against the base of the wall, and placed the keen head against his body, just below the ribs. Then slowly, stolidly, he leaned against it with all his weight, so that it transfixed his body and came out between his shoulders. Sliding down the shaft he lay still, the spear jutting above him its full length, like a horrible stalk growing out of his back.

The girl stared down at him in morbid fascination, until Khemsa took her arm and led her through the gate. Torches lighted a narrow space between the outer wall and a lower inner one, in which were arched doors at regular intervals. A warrior paced this enclosure, and when the gate opened he came sauntering up, so secure in his knowledge of the prison's strength that he was not suspicious until Khemsa and the girl emerged from the archway. Then it was too late. The Rakhsha did not waste time in hypnotism, though his action savored of magic to the girl. The guard lowered his spear threateningly, opening his mouth to shout an alarm that would bring spearmen swarming out of the guardrooms at either end of the alleyway. Khemsa flicked the spear aside with his left hand, as a man might flick a straw, and his right flashed out and back, seeming gently to caress the warrior's neck in passing. And the guard pitched on his face without a sound, his head lolling on a broken neck.

Khemsa did not glance at him, but went straight to one of the arched doors and placed his open hand against the heavy bronze lock. With a rending shudder the portal buckled inward. As the girl followed him through, she saw that the thick teakwood hung in splinters, the bronze bolts were bent and twisted from their sockets, and the great hinges broken and disjointed. A thousand-pound battering-ram with forty men to swing it could have shattered the barrier no more completely. Khemsa was drunk with freedom and the exercise of his power, glorying in his might and flinging his strength about as a young giant exercises his thews with unnecessary vigor in the exultant pride of his prowess.

The broken door let them into a small courtyard, lit by a cresset. Opposite the door was a wide grille of iron bars. A hairy hand was visible, gripping one of these bars, and in the darkness behind them glimmered the whites of eyes.

Khemsa stood silent for a space, gazing into the shadows from which those glimmering eyes gave back his stare with burning intensity. Then his hand went into his robe and came out again, and from his opening fingers a shimmering feather of sparkling dust sifted to the flags. Instantly a flare of green fire lighted the enclosure. In the brief glare the forms of seven men, standing motionless behind the bars, were limned in vivid detail; tall, hairy men in ragged hillmen's garments. They did not speak, but in their eyes blazed the fear of death, and their hairy fingers gripped the bars.

The fire died out but the glow remained, a quivering ball of lambent green that pulsed and shimmered on the flags before Khemsa's feet. The wide gaze of the tribesmen was fixed upon it. It wavered, elongated; it turned into a luminous greensmoke spiraling upward. It twisted and writhed like a great shadowy serpent, then broadened and billowed out in shining folds and whirls. It grew to a cloud moving silently over the flags – straight toward the grille. The men watched its coming with dilated eyes; the bars quivered with the grip of their desperate fingers. Bearded lips parted but no sound came forth. The green cloud rolled on the bars and blotted them from sight; like a fog it oozed through the grille and hid the men within. From the enveloping folds came a strangled gasp, as of a man plunged suddenly under the surface of water. That was all.

Khemsa touched the girl's arm, as she stood with parted lips and dilated eyes. Mechanically she turned away with him, looking back over her shoulder. Already the mist was thinning; close to the bars she saw a pair of sandalled feet, the toes turned upward – she glimpsed the indistinct outlines of seven still, prostrate shapes.

'And now for a steed swifter than the fastest horse ever bred in a mortal stable,' Khemsa was saying. 'We will be in Afghulistan before dawn.'

4

An Encounter in the Pass

Yasmina Devi could never clearly remember the details of her abduction. The unexpectedness and violence stunned her; she had only a confused impression of a whirl of happenings – the terrifying grip of a mighty arm, the blazing eyes of her abductor, and his hot breath burning on her flesh. The leap through the window to the parapet, the mad race across battlements and roofs when the fear of falling froze her, the reckless descent of a rope bound to a merlon – he went down almost at a run, his captive folded limply over his brawny shoulder – all this was a befuddled tangle in the Devi's mind. She retained a more vivid memory of him running fleetly into the shadows of the trees, carrying her like a child, and vaulting into the saddle of a fierce Bhalkhana stallion which reared and snorted. Then there was a sensation of flying, and the racing hoofs were striking sparks of fire from the flinty road as the stallion swept up the slopes.

As the girl's mind cleared, her first sensations were furious rage and shame. She was appalled. The rulers of the golden kingdoms south of the Himelians were considered little short of divine; and she was the Devi of Vendhya! Fright was submerged in regal wrath. She cried out furiously and began struggling. She, Yasmina, to be carried on the saddle-bow of a hill chief, like a common wench of the market-place! He merely hardened his massive thews slightly against her writhings, and for the first time in her life she experienced the coercion of superior physical strength. His arms felt like iron about her slender limbs. He glanced down at her and grinned hugely. His teeth glimmered whitely in the starlight. The reins lay loose on the stallion's flowing mane, and every thew and fiber of the great beast strained as he hurtled along the boulder-strewn trail. But Conan sat easily, almost carelessly, in the saddle, riding like a centaur.

'You hill-bred dog!' she panted, quivering with the impact of shame, anger, and the realization of helplessness. 'You dare – you *dare*! Your life shall pay for this! Where are you taking me?'

'To the villages of Afghulistan,' he answered, casting a glance over his shoulder.

Behind them, beyond the slopes they had traversed, torches were tossing on the walls of the fortress, and he glimpsed a flare of light that meant the great gate had been opened. And he laughed, a deep-throated boom gusty as the hill wind.

'The governor has sent his riders after us,' he laughed. 'By Crom, we will lead him a merry chase! What do you think, Devi – will they pay seven lives for a Kshatriya princess?'

'They will send an army to hang you and your spawn of devils,' she promised him with conviction.

He laughed gustily and shifted her to a more comfortable position in his arms. But she took this as a fresh outrage, and renewed her vain struggle, until she saw that her efforts were only amusing him. Besides, her light silken garments, floating on the wind, were being outrageously disarranged by her struggles. She concluded that a scornful submission was the better part of dignity, and lapsed into a smoldering quiescence.

She felt even her anger being submerged by awe as they entered the mouth of the Pass, lowering like a black well mouth in the blacker walls that rose like colossal ramparts to bar their way. It was as if a gigantic knife had cut the Zhaibar out of walls of solid rock. On either hand sheer slopes pitched up for thousands of feet, and the mouth of the Pass was dark as hate. Even Conan could not see with any accuracy, but he knew the road, even by night. And knowing that armed men were racing through the starlight after him, he did not check the stallion's speed. The great brute was not yet showing fatigue. He thundered along the road that followed the valley bed, labored up a slope, swept along a low ridge where treacherous shale on either hand lurked for the unwary, and came upon a trail that followed the lap of the left-hand wall.

Not even Conan could spy, in that darkness, an ambush set by Zhaibar tribesmen. As they swept past the black mouth of a gorge that opened into the Pass, a javelin swished through the air and thudded home behind the stallion's straining shoulder. The great beast let out his life in a shuddering sob and stumbled, going headlong in mid-stride. But Conan had recognized the flight and stroke of the javelin, and he acted with spring-steel quickness.

As the horse fell he leaped clear, holding the girl aloft to guard her from striking boulders. He lit on his feet like a cat, thrust her into a cleft of rock, and wheeled toward the outer darkness, drawing his knife.

Yasmina, confused by the rapidity of events, not quite sure just what had happened, saw a vague shape rush out of the darkness, bare feet slapping softly on the rock, ragged garments whipping on the wind of his haste. She glimpsed the flicker of steel, heard the lightning crack of stroke, parry and counter-stroke, and the crunch of bone as Conan's long knife split the other's skull.

Conan sprang back, crouching in the shelter of the rocks. Out in the night men were moving and a stentorian voice roared: 'What, you dogs! Do you flinch? In, curse you, and take them!'

Conan started, peered into the darkness and lifted his voice.

'Yar Afzal! Is it you?'

There sounded a startled imprecation, and the voice called warily.

'Conan? Is it you, Conan?'

'Aye!' the Cimmerian laughed. 'Come forth, you old war-dog. I've slain one of your men.'

There was movement among the rocks, a light flared dimly, and then a flame appeared and came bobbing toward him, and as it approached, a fierce bearded countenance grew out of the darkness. The man who carried it held it high, thrust forward, and craned his neck to peer among the boulders it lighted; the other hand gripped a great curved tulwar. Conan stepped forward, sheathing his knife, and the other roared a greeting.

'Aye, it is Conan! Come out of your rocks, dogs! It is Conan!'

Others pressed into the wavering circle of light – wild, ragged, bearded men, with eyes like wolves, and long blades in their fists. They did not see Yasmina, for she was hidden by Conan's massive body. But peeping from her covert, she knew icy fear for the first time that night. These men were more like wolves than human beings.

'What are you hunting in the Zhaibar by night, Yar Afzal?' Conan demanded of the burly chief, who grinned like a bearded ghoul.

'Who knows what might come up the Pass after dark? We Wazulis are night-hawks. But what of you, Conan?'

'I have a prisoner,' answered the Cimmerian. And moving aside he disclosed the cowering girl. Reaching a long arm into the crevice he drew her trembling forth.

Her imperious bearing was gone. She stared timidly at the ring of bearded faces that hemmed her in, and was grateful for the strong arm that clasped her possessively. The torch was thrust close to her, and there was a sucking intake of breath about the ring.

'She is my captive,' Conan warned, glancing pointedly at the feet of the man he had slain, just visible within the ring of light. 'I was taking her to Afghulistan, but now you have slain my horse, and the Kshatriyas are close behind me.'

'Come with us to my village,' suggested Yar Afzal. 'We have horses hidden in the gorge. They can never follow us in the darkness. They are close behind you, you say?'

'So close that I hear now the clink of their hoofs on the flint,' answered Conan grimly.

Instantly there was movement; the torch was dashed out and the ragged shapes melted like phantoms into the darkness. Conan swept up the Devi in his arms, and she did not resist. The rocky ground hurt her slim feet in their soft slippers and she felt very small and helpless in that brutish, primordial blackness among those colossal, nighted crags.

Feeling her shiver in the wind that moaned down the defiles, Conan jerked a ragged cloak from its owner's shoulders and wrapped it about her. He also hissed a warning in her ear, ordering her to make no sound. She did not hear the distant clink of shod hoofs on rock that warned the keen-eared hillmen; but she was far too frightened to disobey, in any event.

She could see nothing but a few faint stars far above, but she knew by the deepening darkness when they entered the gorge mouth. There was a stir about them, the uneasy movement of horses. A few muttered words, and Conan mounted the horse of the man he had killed, lifting the girl up in front of him. Like phantoms except for the click of their hoofs, the band swept away up the shadowy gorge. Behind them on the trail they left the dead horse and the dead man, which were found less than half an hour later by the riders from the fortress, who recognized the man as a Wazuli and drew their own conclusions accordingly.

Yasmina, snuggled warmly in her captor's arms, grew drowsy in spite of herself. The motion of the horse, though it was uneven, uphill and down, yet possessed a certain rhythm which combined with weariness and emotional exhaustion to force sleep upon her. She had lost all sense of time or direction. They moved in soft thick darkness, in which she sometimes glimpsed vaguely gigantic walls sweeping up like black ramparts, or great crags shouldering the stars; at times she sensed echoing depths beneath them, or felt the wind of dizzy heights blowing cold about her. Gradually these things faded into a dreamy unwakefulness in which the clink of hoofs and the creak of saddles were like the irrelevant sounds in a dream.

She was vaguely aware when the motion ceased and she was lifted down and carried a few steps. Then she was laid down on something soft and rustling, and something – a folded coat perhaps – was thrust under her head, and the cloak in which she was wrapped was carefully tucked about her. She heard Yar Afzal laugh.

'A rare prize, Conan; fit mate for a chief of the Afghulis.'

'Not for me,' came Conan's answering rumble. 'This wench will buy the lives of my seven headmen, blast their souls.'

That was the last she heard as she sank into dreamless slumber.

She slept while armed men rode through the dark hills, and the fate of kingdoms hung in the balance. Through the shadowy gorges and defiles that night there rang the hoofs of galloping horses, and the starlight glimmered on helmets and curved blades, until the ghoulish shapes that haunt the crags stared into the darkness from ravine and boulder and wondered what things were afoot.

A band of these sat gaunt horses in the black pitmouth of a gorge as the hurrying hoofs swept past. Their leader, a well-built man in a helmet and gilt-braided cloak, held up his hand warningly, until the riders had sped on. Then he laughed softly.

'They must have lost the trail! Or else they have found that Conan has already reached the Afghuli villages. It will take many riders to smoke out that hive. There will be squadrons riding up the Zhaibar by dawn.'

'If there is fighting in the hills there will be looting,' muttered a voice behind him, in the dialect of the Irakzai.

'There will be looting,' answered the man with the helmet. 'But first it is our business to reach the valley of Gurashah and await the riders that will be galloping southward from Secunderam before daylight.'

He lifted his reins and rode out of the defile, his men falling in behind him – thirty ragged phantoms in the starlight.

5

The Black Stallion

The sun was well up when Yasmina awoke. She did not start and stare blankly, wondering where she was. She awoke with full knowledge of all that had occurred. Her supple limbs were stiff from her long ride, and her firm flesh seemed to feel the contact of the muscular arm that had borne her so far.

She was lying on a sheepskin covering a pallet of leaves on a hard-beaten dirt floor. A folded sheepskin coat was under her head, and she was wrapped in a ragged cloak. She was in a large room, the walls of which were crudely but strongly built of uncut rocks, plastered with sun-baked mud. Heavy beams supported a roof of the same kind, in which showed a trap-door up to which led a ladder. There were no windows in the thick walls, only loop-holes. There was one door, a sturdy bronze affair that must have been looted from some Vendhyan border tower. Opposite it was a wide opening in the wall, with no door, but several strong wooden bars in place. Beyond them Yasmina saw a magnificent black stallion munching a pile of dried grass. The building was fort, dwelling-place and stable in one.

At the other end of the room a girl in the vest and baggy trousers of a hill-woman squatted beside a small fire, cooking strips of meat on an iron grid laid over blocks of stone. There was a sooty cleft in the wall a few feet from the floor, and some of the smoke found its way out there. The rest floated in blue wisps about the room.

The hill-girl glanced at Yasmina over her shoulder, displaying a bold, handsome face, and then continued her cooking. Voices boomed outside; then the door was kicked open, and Conan strode in. He looked more enormous than ever with the morning sunlight behind him, and Yasmina noted some details that had escaped her the night before. His garments were clean and not ragged. The broad Bakhariot girdle that supported his knife in its ornamented scabbard would have matched the robes of a prince, and there was a glint of fine Turanian mail under his shirt.

'Your captive is awake, Conan,' said the Wazuli girl, and he grunted, strode up to the fire and swept the strips of mutton off into a stone dish.

The squatting girl laughed up at him, with some spicy jest, and he grinned wolfishly, and hooking a toe under her haunches, tumbled her sprawling onto the floor. She seemed to derive considerable amusement from this bit of rough horse-play, but Conan paid no more heed to her. Producing a great hunk of bread from somewhere, with a copper jug of wine, he carried the lot to Yasmina, who had risen from her pallet and was regarding him doubtfully.

'Rough fare for a Devi, girl, but our best,' he grunted. 'It will fill your belly, at least.'

He set the platter on the floor, and she was suddenly aware of a ravenous hunger. Making no comment, she seated herself cross-legged on the floor, and taking the dish in her lap, she began to eat, using her fingers, which were all she had in the way of table utensils. After all, adaptability is one of the tests of true aristocracy. Conan stood looking down at her, his thumbs hooked in his girdle. He never sat cross-legged, after the Eastern fashion.

'Where am I?' she asked abruptly.

'In the hut of Yar Afzal, the chief of the Khurum Wazulis,' he answered. 'Afghulistan lies a good many miles farther on to the

26

west. We'll hide here awhile. The Kshatriyas are beating up the hills for you – several of their squads have been cut up by the tribes already.'

'What are you going to do?' she asked.

'Keep you until Chunder Shan is willing to trade back my seven cow-thieves,' he grunted. 'Women of the Wazulis are crushing ink out of *shoki* leaves, and after a while you can write a letter to the governor.'

A touch of her old imperious wrath shook her, as she thought how maddeningly her plans had gone awry, leaving her captive of the very man she had plotted to get into her power. She flung down the dish, with the remnants of her meal, and sprang to her feet, tense with anger.

'I will not write a letter! If you do not take me back, they will hang your seven men, and a thousand more besides!'

The Wazuli girl laughed mockingly, Conan scowled, and then the door opened and Yar Afzal came swaggering in. The Wazuli chief was as tall as Conan, and of greater girth, but he looked fat and slow beside the hard compactness of the Cimmerian. He plucked his red-stained beard and stared meaningly at the Wazuli girl, and that wench rose and scurried out without delay. Then Yar Afzal turned to his guest.

'The damnable people murmur, Conan,' quoth he. 'They wish me to murder you and take the girl to hold for ransom. They say that anyone can tell by her garments that she is a noble lady. They say why should the Afghuli dogs profit by her, when it is the people who take the risk of guarding her?'

'Lend me your horse,' said Conan. 'I'll take her and go.'

'Pish!' boomed Yar Afzal. 'Do you think I can't handle my own people? I'll have them dancing in their shirts if they cross me! They don't love you – or any other outlander – but you saved my life once, and I will not forget. Come out, though, Conan; a scout has returned.'

Conan hitched at his girdle and followed the chief outside. They closed the door after them, and Yasmina peeped through a loophole. She looked out on a level space before the hut. At the farther end of that space there was a cluster of mud and stone huts, and she saw naked children playing among the boulders, and the slim erect women of the hills going about their tasks.

Directly before the chief's hut a circle of hairy, ragged men squatted, facing the door. Conan and Yar Afzal stood a few paces before the door, and between them and the ring of warriors another man sat cross-legged. This one was addressing his chief in the harsh accents of the Wazuli which Yasmina could scarcely understand, though as part of her royal education she had been taught the languages of Iranistan and the kindred tongues of Ghulistan.

'I talked with a Dagozai who saw the riders last night,' said the scout. 'He was lurking near when they came to the spot where we ambushed the lord Conan. He overheard their speech. Chunder Shan was with them. They found the dead horse, and one of the men recognized it as Conan's. Then they found the man Conan slew, and knew him for a Wazuli. It seemed to them that Conan had been slain and the girl taken by the Wazuli; so they turned aside from their purpose of following to Afghulistan. But they did not know from which village the dead man was come, and we had left no trail a Kshatriya could follow.

'So they rode to the nearest Wazuli village, which was the village of Jugra, and burnt it and slew many of the people. But the men of Khojur came upon them in darkness and slew some of them, and wounded the governor. So the survivors retired down the Zhaibar in the darkness before dawn, but they returned with reinforcements before sunrise, and there has been skirmishing and fighting in the hills all morning. It is said that a great army is being raised to sweep the hills about the Zhaibar. The tribes are whetting their knives and laying ambushes in every pass from here to Gurashah valley. Moreover, Kerim Shah has returned to the hills.'

A grunt went around the circle, and Yasmina leaned closer to the loop-hole at the name she had begun to mistrust.

'Where went he?' demanded Yar Afzal.

'The Dagozai did not know; with him were thirty Irakzai of the lower villages. They rode into the hills and disappeared.'

'These Irakzai are jackals that follow a lion for crumbs,' growled

Yar Afzal. 'They have been lapping up the coins Kerim Shah scatters among the border tribes to buy men like horses. I like him not, for all he is our kinsman from Iranistan.'

'He's not even that,' said Conan. 'I know him of old. He's an Hyrkanian, a spy of Yezdigerd's. If I catch him I'll hang his hide to a tamarisk.'

'But the Kshatriyas!' clamored the men in the semicircle. 'Are we to squat on our haunches until they smoke us out? They will learn at last in which Wazuli village the wench is held. We are not loved by the Zhaibari; they will help the Kshatriyas hunt us out.'

'Let them come,' grunted Yar Afzal. 'We can hold the defiles against a host.'

One of the men leaped up and shook his fist at Conan.

'Are we to take all the risks while he reaps the rewards?' he howled. 'Are we to fight his battles for him?'

With a stride Conan reached him and bent slightly to stare full into his hairy face. The Cimmerian had not drawn his long knife, but his left hand grasped the scabbard, jutting the hilt suggestively forward.

'I ask no man to fight my battles,' he said softly. 'Draw your blade if you dare, you yapping dog!'

The Wazuli started back, snarling like a cat.

'Dare to touch me and here are fifty men to rend you apart!' he screeched.

'What!' roared Yar Afzal, his face purpling with wrath. His whiskers bristled, his belly swelled with his rage. 'Are you chief of Khurum? Do the Wazulis take orders from Yar Afzal, or from a low-bred cur?'

The man cringed before his invincible chief, and Yar Afzal, striding up to him, seized him by the throat and choked him until his face was turning black. Then he hurled the man savagely against the ground and stood over him with his tulwar in his hand.

'Is there any who questions my authority?' he roared, and his warriors looked down sullenly as his bellicose glare swept their semicircle. Yar Afzal grunted scornfully and sheathed his weapon with a gesture that was the apex of insult. Then he kicked the fallen agitator with a concentrated vindictiveness that brought howls from his victim.

'Get down the valley to the watchers on the heights and bring word if they have seen anything,' commanded Yar Afzal, and the man went, shaking with fear and grinding his teeth with fury.

Yar Afzal then seated himself ponderously on a stone, growling in his beard. Conan stood near him, legs braced apart, thumbs hooked in his girdle, narrowly watching the assembled warriors. They stared at him sullenly, not daring to brave Yar Afzal's fury, but hating the foreigner as only a hillman can hate.

'Now listen to me, you sons of nameless dogs, while I tell you what the lord Conan and I have planned to fool the Kshatriyas.' The boom of Yar Afzal's bull-like voice followed the discomfited warrior as he slunk away from the assembly.

The man passed by the cluster of huts, where women who had seen his defeat laughed at him and called stinging comments, and hastened on along the trail that wound among spurs and rocks toward the valley head.

Just as he rounded the first turn that took him out of sight of the village, he stopped short, gaping stupidly. He had not believed it possible for a stranger to enter the valley of Khurum without being detected by the hawk-eyed watchers along the heights; yet a man sat cross-legged on a low ledge beside the path – a man in a camel-hair robe and a green turban.

The Wazuli's mouth gaped for a yell, and his hand leaped to his knife-hilt. But at that instant his eyes met those of the stranger and the cry died in his throat, his fingers went limp. He stood like a statue, his own eyes glazed and vacant.

For minutes the scene held motionless; then the man on the ledge drew a cryptic symbol in the dust on the rock with his forefinger. The Wazuli did not see him place anything within the compass of that emblem, but presently something gleamed there – a round, shiny black ball that looked like polished jade. The man in the green turban took this up and tossed it to the Wazuli, who mechanically caught it.

'Carry this to Yar Afzal,' he said, and the Wazuli turned like an automaton and went back along the path, holding the black jade ball in his outstretched hand. He did not even turn his head to the renewed jeers of the women as he passed the huts. He did not seem to hear.

The man on the ledge gazed after him with a cryptic smile. A girl's head rose above the rim of the ledge and she looked at him with admiration and a touch of fear that had not been present the night before.

'Why did you do that?' she asked.

He ran his fingers through her dark locks caressingly.

'Are you still dizzy from your flight on the horse-of-air, that you doubt my wisdom?' he laughed. 'As long as Yar Afzal lives, Conan will bide safe among the Wazuli fighting-men. Their knives are sharp, and there are many of them. What I plot will be safer, even for me, than to seek to slay him and take her from among them. It takes no wizard to predict what the Wazulis will do, and what Conan will do, when my victim hands the globe of Yezud to the chief of Khurum.'

Back before the hut, Yar Afzal halted in the midst of some tirade, surprised and displeased to see the man he had sent up the valley, pushing his way through the throng.

'I bade you go to the watchers!' the chief bellowed. 'You have not had time to come from them.'

The other did not reply; he stood woodenly, staring vacantly into the chief's face, his palm outstretched holding the jade ball. Conan, looking over Yar Afzal's shoulder, murmured something and reached to touch the chief's arm, but as he did so, Yar Afzal, in a paroxysm of anger, struck the man with his clenched fist and felled him like an ox. As he fell, the jade sphere rolled to Yar Afzal's foot, and the chief, seeming to see it for the first time, bent and picked it up. The men, staring perplexedly at their senseless comrade, saw their chief bend, but they did not see what he picked up from the ground.

Yar Afzal straightened, glanced at the jade, and made a motion to thrust it into his girdle.

'Carry that fool to his hut,' he growled. 'He has the look of a lotus-eater. He returned me a blank stare. I – *aie!*'

In his right hand, moving toward his girdle, he had suddenly felt movement where movement should not be. His voice died away as he stood and glared at nothing; and inside his clenched right hand he felt the quivering of *change*, of *motion*, of *life*. He no longer held a smooth shining sphere in his fingers. And he dared not look; his tongue clove to the roof of his mouth, and he could not open his hand. His astonished warriors saw Yar Afzal's eyes distend, the color ebb from his face. Then suddenly a bellow of agony burst from his bearded lips; he swayed and fell as if struck by lightning, his right arm tossed out in front of him. Face down he lay, and from between his opening fingers crawled a spider – a hideous, black, hairy-legged monster whose body shone like black jade. The men yelled and gave back suddenly, and the creature scuttled into a crevice of the rocks and disappeared.

The warriors started up, glaring wildly, and a voice rose above their clamor, a far-carrying voice of command which came from none knew where. Afterward each man there – who still lived – denied that he had shouted, but all there heard it.

'Yar Afzal is dead! Kill the outlander!'

That shout focused their whirling minds as one. Doubt, bewilderment and fear vanished in the uproaring surge of the blood-lust. A furious yell rent the skies as the tribesmen responded instantly to the suggestion. They came headlong across the open space, cloaks flapping, eyes blazing, knives lifted.

Conan's action was as quick as theirs. As the voice shouted he sprang for the hut door. But they were closer to him than he was to the door, and with one foot on the sill he had to wheel and parry the swipe of a yard-long blade. He split the man's skull – ducked another swinging knife and gutted the wielder – felled a man with his left fist and stabbed another in the belly – and heaved back mightily against the closed door with his shoulders. Hacking blades were nicking chips out of the jambs about his ears, but the door flew open under the impact of his shoulders, and he went stumbling backward into the room. A bearded tribesman, thrusting with all his fury as Conan sprang back, overreached and pitched head-first through the doorway. Conan stopped, grasped the slack of his garments and hauled him clear, and slammed the door in the faces of the men who came surging into it. Bones snapped under the impact, and the next instant Conan slammed the bolts into place and whirled with desperate haste to meet the man who sprang from the floor and tore into action like a madman.

Yasmina cowered in a corner, staring in horror as the two men fought back and forth across the room, almost trampling her at times; the flash and clangor of their blades filled the room, and outside the mob clamored like a wolf-pack, hacking deafeningly at the bronze door with their long knives, and dashing huge rocks against it. Somebody fetched a tree trunk, and the door began to stagger under the thunderous assault. Yasmina clasped her ears, staring wildly. Violence and fury within, cataclysmic madness without. The stallion in his stall neighed and reared, thundering with his heels against the walls. He wheeled and launched his hoofs through the bars just as the tribesman, backing away from Conan's murderous swipes, stumbled against them. His spine cracked in three places like a rotten branch and he was hurled headlong against the Cimmerian, bearing him backward so that they both crashed to the beaten floor.

Yasmina cried out and ran forward; to her dazed sight it seemed that both were slain. She reached them just as Conan threw aside the corpse and rose. She caught his arm, trembling from head to foot.

'Oh, you live! I thought – I thought you were dead!'

He glanced down at her quickly, into the pale, upturned face and the wide staring dark eyes.

'Why are you trembling?' he demanded. 'Why should you care if I live or die?'

A vestige of her poise returned to her, and she drew away, making a rather pitiful attempt at playing the Devi.

'You are preferable to those wolves howling without,' she answered, gesturing toward the door, the stone sill of which was beginning to splinter away.

'That won't hold long,' he muttered, then turned and went swiftly to the stall of the stallion.

Yasmina clenched her hands and caught her breath as she saw him tear aside the splintered bars and go into the stall with the maddened beast. The stallion reared above him, neighing terribly, hoofs lifted, eyes and teeth flashing and ears laid back, but Conan leaped and caught his mane with a display of sheer strength that seemed impossible, and dragged the beast down on his forelegs. The steed snorted and quivered, but stood still while the man bridled him and clapped on the gold-worked saddle, with the wide silver stirrups.

Wheeling the beast around in the stall, Conan called quickly to Yasmina, and the girl came, sidling nervously past the stallion's heels. Conan was working at the stone wall, talking swiftly as he worked.

'A secret door in the wall here, that not even the Wazuli know about. Yar Afzal showed it to me once when he was drunk. It opens out into the mouth of the ravine behind the hut. Ha!'

As he tugged at a projection that seemed casual, a whole section of the wall slid back on oiled iron runners. Looking through, the girl saw a narrow defile opening in a sheer stone cliff within a few feet of the hut's back wall. Then Conan sprang into the saddle and hauled her up before him. Behind them the great door groaned like a living thing and crashed in, and a yell rang to the roof as the entrance was instantly flooded with hairy faces and knives in hairy fists. And then the great stallion went through the wall like a javelin from a catapult, and thundered into the defile, running low, foam flying from the bit-rings.

That move came as an absolute surprise to the Wazulis. It was a surprise, too, to those stealing down the ravine. It happened so quickly – the hurricane-like charge of the great horse – that a man in a green turban was unable to get out of the way. He went down under the frantic hoofs, and a girl screamed. Conan got one glimpse of her as they thundered by – a slim, dark girl in silk trousers and a jeweled breast-band, flattening herself against the ravine wall. Then the black horse and his riders were gone up the gorge like the spume blown before a storm, and the men who came tumbling through the wall into the defile after them met that which changed their yells of blood-lust to shrill screams of fear and death.

6

The Mountain of the Black Seers

'Where now?' Yasmina was trying to sit erect on the rocking saddle-bow, clutching her captor. She was conscious of a recognition of shame that she should not find unpleasant the feel of his muscular flesh under her fingers.

'To Afghulistan,' he answered. 'It's a perilous road, but the stallion will carry us easily, unless we fall in with some of your friends, or my tribal enemies. Now that Yar Afzal is dead, those damned Wazulis will be on our heels. I'm surprised we haven't sighted them behind us already.'

'Who was that man you rode down?' she asked.

'I don't know. I never saw him before. He's no Ghuli, that's certain. What the devil he was doing there is more than I can say. There was a girl with him, too.'

'Yes.' Her gaze was shadowed. 'I can not understand that. That girl was my maid, Gitara. Do you suppose she was coming to aid me? That the man was a friend? If so, the Wazulis have captured them both.'

'Well,' he answered, 'there's nothing we can do. If we go back, they'll skin us both. I can't understand how a girl like that could get this far into the mountains with only one man – and he a robed scholar, for that's what he looked like. There's something infernally queer in all this. That fellow Yar Afzal beat and sent away – he moved like a man walking in his sleep. I've seen the priests of Zamora perform their abominable rituals in their forbidden temples, and their victims had a stare like that man. The priests looked into their eyes and muttered incantations, and then the people became the walking dead men, with glassy eyes, doing as they were ordered.

'And then I saw what the fellow had in his hand, which Yar Afzal picked up. It was like a big black jade bead, such as the temple girls of Yezud wear when they dance before the black stone spider which is their god. Yar Afzal held it in his hand, and he didn't pick up anything else. Yet when he fell dead, a spider, like the god at Yezud, only smaller, ran out of his fingers. And then, when the Wazulis stood uncertain there, a voice cried out for them to kill me, and I know that voice didn't come from any of the warriors, nor from the women who watched by the huts. It seemed to come from *above*.'

Yasmina did not reply. She glanced at the stark outlines of the mountains all about them and shuddered. Her soul shrank from their gaunt brutality. This was a grim, naked land where anything might happen. Age-old traditions invested it with shuddery horror for anyone born in the hot, luxuriant southern plains.

The sun was high, beating down with fierce heat, yet the wind that blew in fitful gusts seemed to sweep off slopes of ice. Once she heard a strange rushing above them that was not the sweep of the wind, and from the way Conan looked up, she knew it was not a common sound to him, either. She thought that a strip of the cold blue sky was momentarily blurred, as if some all but invisible object had swept between it and herself, but she could not be sure. Neither made any comment, but Conan loosened his knife in his scabbard.

They were following a faintly marked path dipping down into ravines so deep the sun never struck bottom, laboring up steep slopes where loose shale threatened to slide from beneath their feet, and following knife-edge ridges with blue-hazed echoing depths on either hand.

The sun had passed its zenith when they crossed a narrow trail winding among the crags. Conan reined the horse aside and followed it southward, going almost at right angles to their former course.

'A Galzai village is at one end of this trail,' he explained. 'Their women follow it to a well, for water. You need new garments.'

Glancing down at her filmy attire, Yasmina agreed with him.

Her cloth-of-gold slippers were in tatters, her robes and silken under-garments torn to shreds that scarcely held together decently. Garments meant for the streets of Peshkhauri were scarcely appropriate for the crags of the Himelians.

Coming to a crook in the trail, Conan dismounted, helped Yasmina down and waited. Presently he nodded, though she heard nothing.

'A woman coming along the trail,' he remarked. In sudden panic she clutched his arm.

'You will not – not kill her?'

'I don't kill women ordinarily,' he grunted; 'though some of the hill-women are she-wolves. No,' he grinned as at a huge jest. 'By Crom, I'll *pay* for her clothes! How is that?' He displayed a large handful of gold coins, and replaced all but the largest. She nodded, much relieved. It was perhaps natural for men to slay and die; her flesh crawled at the thought of watching the butchery of a woman.

Presently a woman appeared around the crook of the trail – a tall, slim Galzai girl, straight as a young sapling, bearing a great empty gourd. She stopped short and the gourd fell from her hands when she saw them; she wavered as though to run, then realized that Conan was too close to her to allow her to escape, and so stood still, staring at them with a mixed expression of fear and curiosity.

Conan displayed the gold coin.

'If you will give this woman your garments,' he said, 'I will give you this money.'

The response was instant. The girl smiled broadly with surprise and delight, and, with the disdain of a hill-woman for prudish conventions, promptly yanked off her sleeveless embroidered vest, slipped down her wide trousers and stepped out of them, twitched off her wide-sleeved shirt, and kicked off her sandals. Bundling them all in a bunch, she proffered them to Conan, who handed them to the astonished Devi.

'Get behind that rock and put these on,' he directed, further proving himself no native hill-man. 'Fold your robes up into a bundle and bring them to me when you come out.'

'The money!' clamored the hill-girl, stretching out her hands eagerly. 'The gold you promised me!'

Conan flipped the coin to her, she caught it, bit, then thrust it into her hair, bent and caught up the gourd and went on down the path, as devoid of self-consciousness as of garments. Conan waited with some impatience while the Devi, for the first time in her pampered life, dressed herself. When she stepped from behind the rock he swore in surprise, and she felt a curious rush of emotions at the unrestrained admiration burning in his fierce blue eyes. She felt shame, embarrassment, yet a stimulation of vanity she had never before experienced, and a tingling when meeting the impact of his eyes. He laid a heavy hand on her shoulder and turned her about, staring avidly at her from all angles.

'By Crom!' said he. 'In those smoky, mystic robes you were aloof and cold and far off as a star! Now you are a woman of warm flesh and blood! You went behind that rock as the Devi of Vendhya; you come out as a hill-girl – though a thousand times more beautiful than any wench of the Zhaibar! You were a goddess – now you are real!'

He spanked her resoundingly, and she, recognizing this as merely another expression of admiration, did not feel outraged. It was indeed as if the changing of her garments had wrought a change in her personality. The feelings and sensations she had suppressed rose to domination in her now, as if the queenly robes she had cast off had been material shackles and inhibitions.

But Conan, in his renewed admiration, did not forget that peril lurked all about them. The farther they drew away from the region of the Zhaibar, the less likely he was to encounter any Kshatriya troops. On the other hand he had been listening all throughout their flight for sounds that would tell him the vengeful Wazulis of Khurum were on their heels.

Swinging the Devi up, he followed her into the saddle and again reined the stallion westward. The bundle of garments she had given him, he hurled over a cliff, to fall into the depths of a thousand-foot gorge.

'Why did you do that?' she asked. 'Why did you not give them to the girl?'

'The riders from Peshkhauri are combing these hills,' he said. 'They'll be ambushed and harried at every turn, and by way of reprisal they'll destroy every village they can take. They may turn westward any time. If they found a girl wearing your garments, they'd torture her into talking, and she might put them on my trail.'

'What will she do?' asked Yasmina.

'Go back to her village and tell her people that a stranger attacked her,' he answered. 'She'll have them on our track, all right. But she had to go on and get the water first; if she dared go back without it, they'd whip the skin off her. That gives us a long start. They'll never catch us. By nightfall we'll cross the Afghuli border.'

'There are no paths or signs of human habitation in these parts,' she commented. 'Even for the Himelians this region seems singularly deserted. We have not seen a trail since we left the one where we met the Galzai woman.'

For answer he pointed to the northwest, where she glimpsed a peak in a notch of the crags.

'Yimsha,' grunted Conan. 'The tribes build their villages as far from the mountain as they can.'

She was instantly rigid with attention.

'Yimsha!' she whispered. 'The mountain of the Black Seers!'

'So they say,' he answered. 'This is as near as I ever approached it. I have swung north to avoid any Kshatriya troops that might be prowling through the hills. The regular trail from Khurum to Afghulistan lies farther south. This is an ancient one, and seldom used.'

She was staring intently at the distant peak. Her nails bit into her pink palms.

'How long would it take to reach Yimsha from this point?'

'All the rest of the day, and all night,' he answered, and grinned. 'Do you want to go there? By Crom, it's no place for an ordinary human, from what the hill-people say.'

'Why do they not gather and destroy the devils that inhabit it?' she demanded.

'Wipe out wizards with swords? Anyway, they never interfere with people, unless the people interfere with them. I never saw one of them, though I've talked with men who swore they had. They say they've glimpsed people from the tower among the crags at sunset or sunrise – tall, silent men in black robes.'

'Would you be afraid to attack them?'

'I?' The idea seemed a new one to him. 'Why, if they imposed upon me, it would be my life or theirs. But I have nothing to do with them. I came to these mountains to raise a following of human beings, not to war with wizards.'

Yasmina did not at once reply. She stared at the peak as at a human enemy, feeling all her anger and hatred stir in her bosom anew. And another feeling began to take dim shape. She had plotted to hurl against the masters of Yimsha the man in whose arms she was now carried. Perhaps there was another way, besides the method she had planned, to accomplish her purpose. She could not mistake the look that was beginning to dawn in this wild man's eyes as they rested on her. Kingdoms have fallen when a woman's slim white hands pulled the strings of destiny. Suddenly she stiffened, pointing.

'Look!'

Just visible on the distant peak there hung a cloud of peculiar aspect. It was a frosty crimson in color, veined with sparkling gold. This cloud was in motion; it rotated, and as it whirled it contracted. It dwindled to a spinning taper that flashed in the sun. And suddenly it detached itself from the snow-tipped peak, floated out over the void like a gay-hued feather, and became invisible against the cerulean sky.

'What could that have been?' asked the girl uneasily, as a shoulder of rock shut the distant mountain from view; the phenomenon had been disturbing, even in its beauty.

'The hill-men call it Yimsha's Carpet, whatever that means,' answered Conan. 'I've seen five hundred of them running as if the devil were at their heels, to hide themselves in caves and crags, because they saw that crimson cloud float up from the peak. What in—'

They had advanced through a narrow, knife-cut gash between turreted walls and emerged upon a broad ledge, flanked by a series of rugged slopes on one hand, and a gigantic precipice on the other. The dim trail followed this ledge, bent around a shoulder and reappeared at intervals far below, working a tedious way downward. And emerging from the cut that opened upon the ledge, the black stallion halted short, snorting. Conan urged him on impatiently, and the horse snorted and threw his head up and down, quivering and straining as if against an invisible barrier.

Conan swore and swung off, lifting Yasmina down with him. He went forward, with a hand thrown out before him as if expecting to encounter unseen resistance, but there was nothing to hinder him, though when he tried to lead the horse, it neighed shrilly and jerked back. Then Yasmina cried out, and Conan wheeled, hand starting to knife-hilt.

Neither of them had seen him come, but he stood there, with his arms folded, a man in a camel-hair robe and a green turban. Conan grunted with surprise to recognize the man the stallion had spurned in the ravine outside the Wazuli village.

'Who the devil are you?' he demanded.

The man did not answer. Conan noticed that his eyes were wide, fixed, and of a peculiar luminous quality. And those eyes held his like a magnet.

Khemsa's sorcery was based on hypnotism, as is the case with most Eastern magic. The way has been prepared for the hypnotist for untold centuries of generations who have lived and died in the firm conviction of the reality and power of hypnotism, building up, by mass thought and practise, a colossal though intangible atmosphere against which the individual, steeped in the traditions of the land, finds himself helpless.

But Conan was not a son of the East. Its traditions were meaningless to him; he was the product of an utterly alien atmosphere. Hypnotism was not even a myth in Cimmeria. The heritage that prepared a native of the East for submission to the mesmerist was not his.

He was aware of what Khemsa was trying to do to him; but

he felt the impact of the man's uncanny power only as a vague impulsion, a tugging and pulling that he could shake off as a man shakes spider-webs from his garments.

Aware of hostility and black magic, he ripped out his long knife and lunged, as quick on his feet as a mountain lion.

But hypnotism was not all of Khemsa's magic. Yasmina, watching, did not see by what roguery of movement or illusion the man in the green turban avoided the terrible disembowelling thrust. But the keen blade whickered between side and lifted arm, and to Yasmina it seemed that Khemsa merely brushed his open palm lightly against Conan's bull-neck. But the Cimmerian went down like a slain ox.

Yet Conan was not dead; breaking his fall with his left hand, he slashed at Khemsa's legs even as he went down, and the Rakhsha avoided the scythe-like swipe only by a most unwizardly bound backward. Then Yasmina cried out sharply as she saw a woman she recognized as Gitara glide out from among the rocks and come up to the man. The greeting died in the Devi's throat as she saw the malevolence in the girl's beautiful face.

Conan was rising slowly, shaken and dazed by the cruel craft of that blow which, delivered with an art forgotten of men before Atlantis sank, would have broken like a rotten twig the neck of a lesser man. Khemsa gazed at him cautiously and a trifle uncertainly. The Rakhsha had learned the full flood of his own power when he faced at bay the knives of the maddened Wazulis in the ravine behind Khurum village; but the Cimmerian's resistance had perhaps shaken his new-found confidence a trifle. Sorcery thrives on success, not on failure.

He stepped forward, lifting his hand – then halted as if frozen, head tilted back, eyes wide open, hand raised. In spite of himself Conan followed his gaze, and so did the women – the girl cowering by the trembling stallion, and the girl beside Khemsa.

Down the mountain slopes, like a whirl of shining dust blown before the wind, a crimson, conoid cloud came dancing. Khemsa's dark face turned ashen; his hand began to tremble, then sank to his side. The girl beside him, sensing the change in him, stared at him inquiringly.

The crimson shape left the mountain slope and came down in a long arching sweep. It struck the ledge between Conan and Khemsa, and the Rakhsha gave back with a stifled cry. He backed away, pushing the girl Gitara back with groping, fending hands.

The crimson cloud balanced like a spinning top for an instant, whirling in a dazzling sheen on its point. Then without warning it was gone, vanished as a bubble vanishes when burst. There on the ledge stood four men. It was miraculous, incredible, impossible, yet it was true. They were not ghosts or phantoms. They were four tall men, with shaven, vulture-like heads, and black robes that hid their feet. Their hands were concealed by their wide sleeves. They stood in silence, their naked heads nodding slightly in unison. They were facing Khemsa, but behind them Conan felt his own blood turning to ice in his veins. Rising, he backed stealthily away, until he could feel the stallion's shoulder trembling against his back, and the Devi crept into the shelter of his arm. There was no word spoken. Silence hung like a stifling pall.

All four of the men in black robes stared at Khemsa. Their vulture-like faces were immobile, their eyes introspective and contemplative. But Khemsa shook like a man in an ague. His feet were braced on the rock, his calves straining as if in physical combat. Sweat ran in streams down his dark face. His right hand locked on something under his brown robe so desperately that the blood ebbed from that hand and left it white. His left hand fell on the shoulder of Gitara and clutched in agony like the grasp of a drowning man. She did not flinch or whimper, though his fingers dug like talons into her firm flesh.

Conan had witnessed hundreds of battles in his wild life, but never one like this, wherein four diabolical wills sought to beat down one lesser but equally devilish will that opposed them. But he only faintly sensed the monstrous quality of that hideous struggle. With his back to the wall, driven to bay by his former masters, Khemsa was fighting for his life with all the dark power, all the frightful knowledge they had taught him through long, grim years of neophytism and vassalage.

He was stronger than even he had guessed, and the free exercise of his powers in his own behalf had tapped unsuspected reservoirs of forces. And he was nerved to super-energy by frantic fear and desperation. He reeled before the merciless impact of those hypnotic eyes, but he held his ground. His features were distorted into a bestial grin of agony, and his limbs were twisted as on a rack. It was a war of souls, of frightful brains steeped in lore forbidden to men for a million years, of mentalities which had plumbed the abysses and explored the dark stars where spawn the shadows.

Yasmina understood this better than did Conan. And she dimly understood why Khemsa could withstand the concentrated impact of those four hellish wills which might have blasted into atoms the very rock on which he stood. The reason was the girl that he clutched with the strength of his despair. She was like an anchor to his staggering soul, battered by the waves of those psychic emanations. His weakness was now his strength. His love for the girl, violent and evil though it might be, was yet a tie that bound him to the rest of humanity, providing an earthly leverage for his will, a chain that his inhuman enemies could not break; at least not break through Khemsa.

They realized that before he did. And one of them turned his gaze from the Rakhsha full upon Gitara. There was no battle there. The girl shrank and wilted like a leaf in the drought. Irresistibly impelled, she tore herself from her lover's arms before he realized what was happening. Then a hideous thing came to pass. She began to back toward the precipice, facing her tormentors, her eyes wide and blank as dark gleaming glass from behind which a lamp has been blown out. Khemsa groaned and staggered toward her, falling into the trap set for him. A divided mind could not maintain the unequal battle. He was beaten, a straw in their hands. The girl went backward, walking like an automaton, and Khemsa reeled drunkenly after her, hands vainly outstretched, groaning, slobbering in his pain, his feet moving heavily like dead things.

On the very brink she paused, standing stiffly, her heels on the edge, and he fell on his knees and crawled whimpering toward her, groping for her, to drag her back from destruction. And just before his clumsy fingers touched her, one of the wizards laughed, like the sudden, bronze note of a bell in hell. The girl reeled suddenly and, consummate climax of exquisite cruelty, reason and understanding flooded back into her eyes, which flared with awful fear. She screamed, clutched wildly at her lover's straining hand, and then, unable to save herself, fell headlong with a moaning cry.

Khemsa hauled himself to the edge and stared over, haggardly, his lips working as he mumbled to himself. Then he turned and stared for a long minute at his torturers, with wide eyes that held no human light. And then with a cry that almost burst the rocks, he reeled up and came rushing toward them, a knife lifted in his hand.

One of the Rakhshas stepped forward and stamped his foot, and as he stamped, there came a rumbling that grew swiftly to a grinding roar. Where his foot struck, a crevice opened in the solid rock that widened instantly. Then, with a deafening crash, a whole section of the ledge gave way. There was a last glimpse of Khemsa, with arms wildly upflung, and then he vanished amidst the roar of the avalanche that thundered down into the abyss.

The four looked contemplatively at the ragged edge of rock that formed the new rim of the precipice, and then turned suddenly. Conan, thrown off his feet by the shudder of the mountain, was rising, lifting Yasmina. He seemed to move as slowly as his brain was working. He was befogged and stupid. He realized that there was a desperate need for him to lift the Devi on the black stallion and ride like the wind, but an unaccountable sluggishness weighted his every thought and action.

And now the wizards had turned toward him; they raised their arms, and to his horrified sight, he saw their outlines fading, dimming, becoming hazy and nebulous, as a crimson smoke billowed around their feet and rose about them. They were blotted out by a sudden whirling cloud – and then he realized that he too was enveloped in a blinding crimson mist – he heard Yasmina scream, and the stallion cried out like a woman in pain. The Devi was torn from his arm, and as he lashed out with his knife blindly, a terrific blow like a gust of storm wind knocked him sprawling against a rock. Dazedly he saw a crimson conoid cloud spinning up and over the mountain slopes. Yasmina was gone, and so were the four men in black. Only the terrified stallion shared the ledge with him.

7

On to Yimsha

As mists vanish before a strong wind, the cobwebs vanished from Conan's brain. With a searing curse he leaped into the saddle and the stallion reared neighing beneath him. He glared up the slopes, hesitated, and then turned down the trail in the direction he had been going when halted by Khemsa's trickery. But now he did not ride at a measured gait. He shook loose the reins and the stallion went like a thunderbolt, as if frantic to lose hysteria in violent physical exertion. Across the ledge and around the crag and down the narrow trail threading the great steep they plunged at breakneck speed. The path followed a fold of rock, winding interminably down from tier to tier of striated escarpment, and once, far below, Conan got a glimpse of the ruin that had fallen – a mighty pile of broken stone and boulders at the foot of a gigantic cliff.

The valley floor was still far below him when he reached a long and lofty ridge that led out from the slope like a natural causeway. Out upon this he rode, with an almost sheer drop on either hand. He could trace ahead of him the trail and made a great horseshoe back into the riverbed at his left hand. He cursed the necessity of traversing those miles, but it was the only way. To try to descend to the lower lap of the trail here would be to attempt the impossible. Only a bird could get to the river-bed with a whole neck.

So he urged on the wearying stallion, until a clink of hoofs reached his ears, welling up from below. Pulling up short and reining to the lip of the cliff, he stared down into the dry river-bed that wound along the foot of the ridge. Along that gorge rode a motley throng – bearded men on half-wild horses, five hundred strong, bristling with weapons. And Conan shouted suddenly, leaning over the edge of the cliff, three hundred feet above them.

At his shout they reined back, and five hundred bearded faces were tilted up towards him; a deep, clamorous roar filled the canyon. Conan did not waste words.

'I was riding for Ghor!' he roared. 'I had not hoped to meet you dogs on the trail. Follow me as fast as your nags can push! I'm going to Yimsha, and—'

'Traitor!' The howl was like a dash of ice-water in his face.

'What?' He glared down at them, jolted speechless. He saw wild eyes blazing up at him, faces contorted with fury, fists brandishing blades.

'Traitor!' they roared back, wholeheartedly. 'Where are the seven chiefs held captive in Peshkhauri?'

'Why, in the governor's prison, I suppose,' he answered.

A bloodthirsty yell from a hundred throats answered him, with such a waving of weapons and a clamor that he could not understand what they were saying. He beat down the din with a bull-like roar, and bellowed: 'What devil's play is this? Let one of you speak, so I can understand what you mean!'

A gaunt old chief elected himself to this position, shook his tulwar at Conan as a preamble, and shouted accusingly: 'You would not let us go raiding Peshkhauri to rescue our brothers!'

'No, you fools!' roared the exasperated Cimmerian. 'Even if you'd breached the wall, which is unlikely, they'd have hanged the prisoners before you could reach them.'

'And you went alone to traffic with the governor!' yelled the Afghuli, working himself into a frothing frenzy.

'Well?'

'Where are the seven chiefs?' howled the old chief, making his tulwar into a glimmering wheel of steel about his head. 'Where are they? Dead!'

'What!' Conan nearly fell off his horse in his surprise.

'Aye, dead!' five hundred bloodthirsty voices assured him.

The old chief brandished his arms and got the floor again. 'They were not hanged!' he screeched. 'A Wazuli in another cell saw them die! The governor sent a wizard to slay them by craft!'

'That must be a lie,' said Conan. 'The governor would not dare. Last night I talked with him—'

The admission was unfortunate. A yell of hate and accusation split the skies.

'Aye! You went to him alone! To betray us! It is no lie. The Wazuli escaped through the doors the wizard burst in his entry, and told the tale to our scouts whom he met in Zhaibar. They had been sent forth to search for you, when you did not return. When they heard the Wazuli's tale, they returned with all haste to Ghor, and we saddled our steeds and girt our swords!'

'And what do you fools mean to do?' demanded the Cimmerian.

'To avenge our brothers!' they howled. 'Death to the Kshatriyas! Slay him, brothers, he is a traitor!'

Arrows began to rattle around him. Conan rose in his stirrups, striving to make himself heard above the tumult, and then, with a roar of mingled rage, defiance and disgust, he wheeled and galloped back up the trail. Behind him and below him the Afghulis came pelting, mouthing their rage, too furious even to remember that the only way they could reach the height whereon he rode was to traverse the riverbed in the other direction, make the broad bend and follow the twisting trail up over the ridge. When they did remember this, and turned back, their repudiated chief had almost reached the point where the ridge joined the escarpment.

At the cliff he did not take the trail by which he had descended, but turned off on another, a mere trace along a rock-fault, where the stallion scrambled for footing. He had not ridden far when the stallion snorted and shied back from something lying in the trail. Conan stared down on the travesty of a man, a broken, shredded, bloody heap that gibbered and gnashed splintered teeth.

Impelled by some obscure reason, Conan dismounted and stood looking down at the ghastly shape, knowing that he was witness of a thing miraculous and opposed to nature. The Rakhsha lifted his gory head, and his strange eyes, glazed with agony and approaching death, rested on Conan with recognition.

'Where are they?' It was a racking croak not even remotely resembling a human voice.

'Gone back to their damnable castle on Yimsha,' grunted Conan. 'They took the Devi with them.'

'I will go!' muttered the man. 'I will follow them! They killed Gitara; I will kill them – the acolytes, the Four of the Black Circle, the Master himself! Kill – kill them all!' He strove to drag his mutilated frame along the rock, but not even his indomitable will could animate that gory mass longer, where the splintered bones hung together only by torn tissue and ruptured fibre.

'Follow them!' raved Khemsa, drooling a bloody slaver. 'Follow!'

'I'm going to,' growled Conan. 'I went to fetch my Afghulis, but they've turned on me. I'm going on to Yimsha alone. I'll have the Devi back if I have to tear down that damned mountain with my bare hands. I didn't think the governor would dare kill my headmen, when I had the Devi, but it seems he did. I'll have his head for that. She's no use to me now as a hostage, but—'

'The curse of Yizil on them!' gasped Khemsa. 'Go! I am dying. Wait – take my girdle.'

He tried to fumble with a mangled hand at his tatters, and Conan, understanding what he sought to convey, bent and drew from about his gory waist a girdle of curious aspect.

'Follow the golden vein through the abyss,' muttered Khemsa. 'Wear the girdle. I had it from a Stygian priest. It will aid you, though it failed me at last. Break the crystal globe with the four golden pomegranates. Beware of the Master's transmutations – I am going to Gitara – she is waiting for me in hell – *aie, ya Skelos yar!*' And so he died.

Conan stared down at the girdle. The hair of which it was woven was not horsehair. He was convinced that it was woven of the thick black tresses of a woman. Set in the thick mesh were tiny jewels such as he had never seen before. The buckle was strangely made, in the form of a golden serpent-head, flat, wedge-shaped and scaled with curious art. A strong shudder shook Conan as he handled it, and he turned as though to cast it over the precipice;

then he hesitated, and finally buckled it about his waist, under the Bakhariot girdle. Then he mounted and pushed on.

The sun had sunk behind the crags. He climbed the trail in the vast shadow of the cliffs that was thrown out like a dark blue mantle over valleys and ridges far below. He was not far from the crest when, edging around the shoulder of a jutting crag, he heard the clink of shod hoofs ahead of him. He did not turn back. Indeed, so narrow was the path that the stallion could not have wheeled his great body upon it. He rounded the jut of the rock and came upon a portion of the path that broadened somewhat. A chorus of threatening yells broke on his ear, but his stallion pinned a terrified horse hard against the rock, and Conan caught the arm of the rider in an iron grip, checking the lifted sword in midair.

'Kerim Shah!' muttered Conan, red glints smoldering luridly in his eyes. The Turanian did not struggle; they sat their horses almost breast to breast, Conan's fingers locking the other's sword-arm. Behind Kerim Shah filed a group of lean Irakzai on gaunt horses. They glared like wolves, fingering bows and knives, but rendered uncertain because of the narrowness of the path and the perilous proximity of the abyss that yawned beneath them.

'Where is the Devi?' demanded Kerim Shah.

'What's it to you, you Hyrkanian spy?' snarled Conan.

'I know you have her,' answered Kerim Shah. 'I was on my way northward with some tribesmen when we were ambushed by enemies in Shalizah Pass. Many of my men were slain, and the rest of us harried through the hills like jackals. When we had beaten off our pursuers, we turned westward, toward Amir Jehun Pass, and this morning we came upon a Wazuli wandering through the hills. He was quite mad, but I learned much from his incoherent gibberings before he died. I learned that he was the sole survivor of a band which followed a chief of the Afghulis and a captive Kshatriya woman into a gorge behind Khurum village. He babbled much of a man in a green turban whom the Afghuli rode down, but who, when attacked by the Wazulis who pursued, smote them with a nameless doom that wiped them out as a gust of wind-driven fire wipes out a cluster of locusts.

'How that one man escaped, I do not know, nor did he; but I knew from his maunderings that Conan of Ghor had been in Khurum with his royal captive. And as we made our way through the hills, we overtook a naked Galzai girl bearing a gourd of water, who told us a tale of having been stripped and ravished by a giant foreigner in the garb of an Afghuli chief, who, she said, gave her garments to a Vendhyan woman who accompanied him. She said you rode westward.'

Kerim Shah did not consider it necessary to explain that he had been on his way to keep his rendezvous with the expected troops from Secunderam when he found his way barred by hostile tribesmen. The road to Gurashah valley through Shalizah Pass was longer than the road that wound through Amir Jehun Pass, but the latter traversed part of the Afghuli country, which Kerim Shah had been anxious to avoid until he came with an army. Barred from the Shalizah road, however, he had turned to the forbidden route, until news that Conan had not yet reached Afghulistan with his captive had caused him to turn southward and push on recklessly in the hope of overtaking the Cimmerian in the hills.

'So you had better tell me where the Devi is,' suggested Kerim Shah. 'We outnumber you—'

'Let one of your dogs nock a shaft and I'll throw you over the cliff,' Conan promised. 'It wouldn't do you any good to kill me, anyhow. Five hundred Afghulis are on my trail, and if they find you've cheated them, they'll flay you alive. Anyway, I haven't got the Devi. She's in the hands of the Black Seers of Yimsha.'

'*Tarim!*' swore Kerim Shah softly, shaken out of his poise for the first time. 'Khemsa—'

'Khemsa's dead,' grunted Conan. 'His masters sent him to hell on a landslide. And now get out of my way. I'd be glad to kill you if I had the time, but I'm on my way to Yimsha.'

'I'll go with you,' said the Turanian abruptly.

Conan laughed at him. 'Do you think I'd trust you, you Hyrkanian dog?'

'I don't ask you to,' returned Kerim Shah. 'We both want the Devi. You know my reason; King Yezdigerd desires to add her kingdom to his empire, and herself in his seraglio. And I knew you, in the days when you were a hetman of the *kozak* steppes; so I know your ambition is wholesale plunder. You want to loot Vendhya, and to twist out a huge ransom for Yasmina. Well, let us for the time being, without any illusion about each other, unite our forces, and try to rescue the Devi from the Seers. If we succeed, and live, we can fight it out to see who keeps her.'

Conan narrowly scrutinized the other for a moment, and then nodded, releasing the Turanian's arm. 'Agreed; what about your men?'

Kerim Shah turned to the silent Irakzai and spoke briefly: 'This chief and I are going to Yimsha to fight the wizards. Will you go with us, or stay here to be flayed by the Afghulis who are following this man?'

They looked at him with eyes grimly fatalistic. They were doomed and they knew it – had known it ever since the singing arrows of the ambushed Dagozai had driven them back from the pass of Shalizah. The men of the lower Zhaibar had too many reeking bloodfeuds among the crag-dwellers. They were too small a band to fight their way back through the hills to the villages of the border, without the guidance of the crafty Turanian. They counted themselves as dead already, so they made the reply that only dead men would make: 'We will go with thee and die on Yimsha.'

'Then in Crom's name let us be gone,' grunted Conan, fidgeting with impatience as he started into the blue gulfs of the deepening twilight. 'My wolves were hours behind me, but we've lost a devilish lot of time.'

Kerim Shah backed his steed from between the black stallion and the cliff, sheathed his sword and cautiously turned the horse. Presently the band was filing up the path as swiftly as they dared. They came out upon the crest nearly a mile east of the spot where Khemsa had halted the Cimmerian and the Devi. The path they had traversed was a perilous one, even for hill-men, and for that reason Conan had avoided it that day when carrying Yasmina, though Kerim Shah, following him, had taken it supposing the

Cimmerian had done likewise. Even Conan sighed with relief when the horses scrambled up over the last rim. They moved like phantom riders through an enchanted realm of shadows. The soft creak of leather, the clink of steel marked their passing, then again the dark mountain slopes lay naked and silent in the starlight.

8

Yasmina Knows Stark Terror

Yasmina had time but for one scream when she felt herself enveloped in that crimson whirl and torn from her protector with appalling force. She screamed once, and then she had no breath to scream. She was blinded, deafened, rendered mute and eventually senseless by the terrific rushing of the air about her. There was a dazed consciousness of dizzy height and numbing speed, a confused impression of natural sensations gone mad, and then vertigo and oblivion.

A vestige of these sensations clung to her as she recovered consciousness; so she cried out and clutched wildly as though to stay a headlong and involuntary flight. Her fingers closed on soft fabric, and a relieving sense of stability pervaded her. She took cognizance of her surroundings.

She was lying on a dais covered with black velvet. This dais stood in a great, dim room whose walls were hung with dusky tapestries across which crawled dragons reproduced with repellent realism. Floating shadows merely hinted at the lofty ceiling, and gloom that lent itself to illusion lurked in the corners. There seemed to be neither windows nor doors in the walls, or else they were concealed by the nighted tapestries. Where the dim light came from, Yasmina could not determine. The great room was a realm of mysteries, or shadows, and shadowy shapes in which she could not have sworn to observe movement, yet which invaded her mind with a dim and formless terror.

But her gaze fixed itself on a tangible object. On another, smaller dais of jet, a few feet away, a man sat cross-legged, gazing contemplatively at her. His long black velvet robe, embroidered with gold thread, fell loosely about him, masking his figure. His hands were folded in his sleeves. There was a velvet cap upon his head. His face was calm, placid, not unhandsome, his eyes lambent and slightly oblique. He did not move a muscle as he sat regarding her, nor did his expression alter when he saw she was conscious.

Yasmina felt fear crawl like a trickle of ice-water down her supple spine. She lifted herself on her elbows and stared apprehensively at the stranger.

'Who are you?' she demanded. Her voice sounded brittle and inadequate.

'I am the Master of Yimsha.' The tone was rich and resonant, like the mellow tones of a temple bell.

'Why did you bring me here?' she demanded.

'Were you not seeking me?'

'If you are one of the Black Seers – yes!' she answered recklessly, believing that he could read her thoughts anyway.

He laughed softly, and chills crawled up and down her spine again.

'You would turn the wild children of the hills against the Seers of Yimsha!' He smiled. 'I have read it in your mind, princess. Your weak, human mind, filled with petty dreams of hate and revenge.'

'You slew my brother!' A rising tide of anger was vying with her fear; her hands were clenched, her lithe body rigid. 'Why did you persecute him? He never harmed you. The priests say the Seers are above meddling in human affairs. Why did you destroy the king of Vendhya?'

'How can an ordinary human understand the motives of a Seer?' returned the Master calmly. 'My acolytes in the temples of Turan, who are the priests behind the priests of Tarim, urged me to bestir myself in behalf of Yezdigerd. For reasons of my own, I complied. How can I explain my mystic reasons to your puny intellect? You could not understand.'

'I understand this: that my brother died!' Tears of grief and rage shook in her voice. She rose upon her knees and stared at him with wide blazing eyes, as supple and dangerous in that moment as a she-panther.

'As Yezdigerd desired,' agreed the Master calmly. 'For a while it was my whim to further his ambitions.'

'Is Yezdigerd your vassal?' Yasmina tried to keep the timbre of her voice unaltered. She had felt her knee pressing something hard and symmetrical under a fold of velvet. Subtly she shifted her position, moving her hand under the fold.

'Is the dog that licks up the offal in the temple yard the vassal of the god?' returned the Master.

He did not seem to notice the actions she sought to dissemble. Concealed by the velvet, her fingers closed on what she knew was the golden hilt of a dagger. She bent her head to hide the light of triumph in her eyes.

'I am weary of Yezdigerd,' said the Master. 'I have turned to other amusements – ha!'

With a fierce cry Yasmina sprang like a jungle cat, stabbing murderously. Then she stumbled and slid to the floor, where she cowered, staring up at the man on the dais. He had not moved; his cryptic smile was unchanged. Tremblingly she lifted her hand and stared at it with dilated eyes. There was no dagger in her fingers; they grasped a stalk of golden lotus, the crushed blossoms drooping on the bruised stem.

She dropped it as if it had been a viper, and scrambled away from the proximity of her tormenter. She returned to her own dais, because that was at least more dignified for a queen than groveling on the floor at the feet of a sorcerer, and eyed him apprehensively, expecting reprisals.

But the Master made no move.

'All substance is one to him who holds the key of the cosmos,' he said cryptically. 'To an adept nothing is immutable. At will, steel blossoms bloom in unnamed gardens, or flower-swords flash in the moonlight.'

'You are a devil,' she sobbed.

'Not I!' he laughed. 'I was born on this planet, long ago. Once I was a common man, nor have I lost all human attributes in the numberless eons of my adeptship. A human steeped in the dark arts is greater than a devil. I am of human origin, but I rule demons. You have seen the Lords of the Black Circle – it would blast your soul to hear from what far realm I summoned them and from what doom I guard them with ensorcelled crystal and golden serpents.

'But only I can rule them. My foolish Khemsa thought to make himself great – poor fool, bursting material doors and hurtling himself and his mistress through the air from hill to hill! Yet if he had not been destroyed his power might have grown to rival mine.'

He laughed again. 'And you, poor, silly thing! Plotting to send a hairy hill chief to storm Yimsha! It was such a jest that I myself could have designed, had it occurred to me, that you should fall in his hands. And I read in your childish mind an intention to seduce by your feminine wiles to attempt your purpose, anyway.

'But for all your stupidity, you are a woman fair to look upon. It is my whim to keep you for my slave.'

The daughter of a thousand proud emperors gasped with shame and fury at the word.

'You dare not!'

His mocking laughter cut her like a whip across her naked shoulders.

'The king dares not trample a worm in the road? Little fool, do you not realize that your royal pride is no more than a straw blown on the wind? I, who have known the kisses of the queens of Hell! You have seen how I deal with a rebel!'

Cowed and awed, the girl crouched on the velvet-covered dais. The light grew dimmer and more phantom-like. The features of the Master became shadowy. His voice took on a newer tone of command.

'I will never yield to you!' Her voice trembled with fear but it carried a ring of resolution.

'You will yield,' he answered with horrible conviction. 'Fear and pain shall teach you. I will lash you with horror and agony to the last quivering ounce of your endurance, until you become as melted wax to be bent and molded in my hands as I desire. You shall know such discipline as no mortal woman ever knew, until my slightest command is to you as the unalterable will of the gods. And first, to humble your pride, you shall travel back through the lost ages, and view all the shapes that have been you. *Aie, yil la khosa!'*

At these words the shadowy room swam before Yasmina's affrighted gaze. The roots of her hair prickled her scalp, and her tongue clove to her palate. Somewhere a gong sounded a deep, ominous note. The dragons on the tapestries glowed like blue fire, and then faded out. The Master on his dais was but a shapeless shadow. The dim light gave way to soft, thick darkness, almost tangible, that pulsed with strange radiations. She could no longer see the Master. She could see nothing. She had a strange sensation that the walls and ceiling had withdrawn immensely from her.

Then somewhere in the darkness a glow began, like a firefly that rhythmically dimmed and quickened. It grew to a golden ball, and as it expanded its light grew more intense, flaming whitely. It burst suddenly, showering the darkness with white sparks that did not illumine the shadows. But like an impression left in the gloom, a faint luminance remained, and revealed a slender dusky shaft shooting up from the shadowy floor. Under the girl's dilated gaze it spread, took shape; stems and broad leaves appeared, and great black poisonous blossoms that towered above her as she cringed against the velvet. A subtle perfume pervaded the atmosphere. It was the dread figure of the black lotus that had grown up as she watched, as it grows in the haunted, forbidden jungles of Khitai.

The broad leaves were murmurous with evil life. The blossoms bent toward her like sentient things, nodding serpent-like on pliant stems. Etched against soft, impenetrable darkness it loomed over her, gigantic, blackly visible in some mad way. Her brain reeled with the drugging scent and she sought to crawl from the dais. Then she clung to it as it seemed to be pitching at an impossible slant. She cried out with terror and clung to the velvet, but she felt her fingers ruthlessly torn away. There was a sensation as of all sanity and stability crumbling and vanishing. She was a quivering atom of sentiency driven through a black, roaring, icy void by a thundering wind that threatened to extinguish her feeble flicker of animate life like a candle blown out in a storm.

Then there came a period of blind impulse and movement, when the atom that was she mingled and merged with myriad other atoms of spawning life in the yeasty morass of existence, molded by formative forces until she emerged again a conscious individual, whirling down an endless spiral of lives.

In a mist of terror she relived all her former existences, recognized and *was* again all the bodies that had carried her ego throughout the changing ages. She bruised her feet again over the long, weary road of life that stretched out behind her into the immemorial past. Back beyond the dimmest dawns of Time she crouched shuddering in primordial jungles, hunted by slavering beasts of prey. Skin-clad, she waded thigh-deep in rice swamps, battling with squawking water-fowl for the precious grains. She labored with the oxen to drag the pointed stick through the stubborn soil, and she crouched endlessly over looms in peasant huts.

She saw walled cities burst into flame, and fled screaming before the slayers. She reeled naked and bleeding over burning sands, dragged at the slaver's stirrup, and she knew the grip of hot, fierce hands on her writhing flesh, the shame and agony of brutal lust. She screamed under the bite of the lash, and moaned on the rack; mad with terror she fought against the hands that forced her head inexorably down on the bloody block.

She knew the agonies of childbirth, and the bitterness of love betrayed. She suffered all the woes and wrongs and brutalities that man has inflicted on woman throughout the eons; and she endured all the spite and malice of women for woman. And like the flick of a fiery whip throughout was the consciousness she retained of her Devi-ship. She was all the women she had ever been, yet in her knowing she was Yasmina. This consciousness was not lost in the throes of reincarnation. At one and the same time she was a naked slave-wench groveling under the whip, and the proud Devi of Vendhya. And she suffered not only as the slave-girl suffered, but as Yasmina, to whose pride the whip was like a white-hot brand.

Life merged into life in flying chaos, each with its burden of woe and shame and agony, until she dimly heard her own voice screaming unbearably, like one long-drawn cry of suffering echoing down the ages.

Then she awakened on the velvet-covered dais in the mystic room.

In a ghostly gray light she saw again the dais and the cryptic robed figure seated upon it. The hooded head was bent, the high shoulders faintly etched against the uncertain dimness. She could make out no details clearly, but the hood, where the velvet cap had been, stirred a formless uneasiness in her. As she stared, there stole over her a nameless fear that froze her tongue to her palate – a feeling that it was not the Master who sat so silently on that black dais.

Then the figure moved and rose upright, towering above her. It stooped over her and the long arms in their wide black sleeves bent about her. She fought against them in speechless fright, surprised by their lean hardness. The hooded head bent down toward her averted face. And she screamed, and screamed again in poignant fear and loathing. Bony arms gripped her lithe body, and from that hood looked forth a countenance of death and decay – features like rotting parchment on a moldering skull.

She screamed again, and then, as those champing, grinning jaws bent toward her lips, she lost consciousness . . .

9

The Castle of the Wizards

The sun had risen over the white Himelian peaks. At the foot of a long slope a group of horsemen halted and stared upward. High above them a stone tower poised on the pitch of the mountainside. Beyond and above that gleamed the walls of a greater keep, near the line where the snow began that capped Yimsha's pinnacle. There was a touch of unreality about the whole – purple slopes pitching up to that fantastic castle, toy-like with distance, and above it the white glistening peak shouldering the cold blue.

'We'll leave the horses here,' grunted Conan. 'That treacherous slope is safer for a man on foot. Besides, they're done.'

He swung down from the black stallion which stood with wide-braced legs and drooping head. They had pushed hard throughout the night, gnawing at scraps from saddle-bags, and pausing only to give the horses the rests they had to have.

'That first tower is held by the acolytes of the Black Seers,' said Conan. 'Or so men say; watch-dogs for their masters – lesser sorcerers. They won't sit sucking their thumbs as we climb this slope.'

Kerim Shah glanced up the mountain, then back the way they had come; they were already far up Yimsha's side, and a vast expanse of lesser peaks and crags spread out beneath them. Among these labyrinths the Turanian sought in vain for a movement of color that would betray men. Evidently the pursuing Afghulis had lost their chief's trail in the night.

'Let us go, then.' They tied the weary horses in a clump of tamarisk and without further comment turned up the slope. There was no cover. It was a naked incline, strewn with boulders not big enough to conceal a man. But they did conceal something else.

The party had not gone fifty steps when a snarling shape burst from behind a rock. It was one of the gaunt savage dogs that infested the hill villages, and its eyes glared redly, its jaws dripped foam. Conan was leading, but it did not attack him. It dashed past him and leaped at Kerim Shah. The Turanian leaped aside, and the great dog flung itself upon the Irakzai behind him. The man yelled and threw up his arm, which was torn by the brute's fangs as it bore him backward, and the next instant half a dozen tulwars were hacking at the beast. Yet not until it was literally dismembered did the hideous creature cease its efforts to seize and rend its attackers.

Kerim Shah bound up the wounded warrior's gashed arm, looked at him narrowly, and then turned away without a word. He rejoined Conan, and they renewed the climb in silence.

Presently Kerim Shah said: 'Strange to find a village dog in this place.'

'There's no offal here,' grunted Conan.

Both turned their heads to glance back at the wounded warrior toiling after them among his companions. Sweat glistened on his dark face and his lips were drawn back from his teeth in a grimace of pain. Then both looked again at the stone tower squatting above them.

A slumberous quiet lay over the uplands. The tower showed no sign of life, nor did the strange pyramidal structure beyond it. But the men who toiled upward went with the tenseness of men walking on the edge of a crater. Kerim Shah had unslung the powerful Turanian bow that killed at five hundred paces, and the Irakzai looked to their own lighter and less lethal bows.

But they were not within bow-shot of the tower when something shot down out of the sky without warning. It passed so close to Conan that he felt the wind of rushing wings, but it was an Irakzai who staggered and fell, blood jetting from a severed jugular. A hawk with wings like burnished steel shot up again, blood dripping from the scimitar-beak, to reel against the sky as Kerim Shah's bowstring twanged. It dropped like a plummet, but no man saw where it struck the earth.

Conan bent over the victim of the attack, but the man was already dead. No one spoke; useless to comment on the fact that never before had a hawk been known to swoop on a man. Red rage began to vie with fatalistic lethargy in the wild souls of the Irakzai. Hairy fingers nocked arrows and men glared vengefully at the tower whose very silence mocked them.

But the next attack came swiftly. They all saw it – a white puff-ball of smoke that tumbled over the tower-rim and came drifting and rolling down the slope toward them. Others followed it. They seemed harmless, mere woolly globes of cloudy foam, but Conan stepped aside to avoid contact with the first. Behind him one of the Irakzai reached out and thrust his sword into the unstable mass. Instantly a sharp report shook the mountainside. There was a burst of blinding flame, and then the puffball had vanished, and the too-curious warrior remained only a heap of charred and blackened bones. The crisped hand still gripped the ivory sword-hilt, but the blade was gone – melted and destroyed by that awful heat. Yet men standing almost within reach of the victim had not suffered except to be dazzled and half blinded by the sudden flare.

'Steel touches it off,' grunted Conan. 'Look out – here they come!'

The slope above them was almost covered by the billowing spheres. Kerim Shah bent his bow and sent a shaft into the mass, and those touched by the arrow burst like bubbles in spurting flame. His men followed his example and for the next few minutes it was as if a thunderstorm raged on the mountain slope, with bolts of lightning striking and bursting in showers of flame. When the barrage ceased, only a few arrows were left in the quivers of the archers.

They pushed on grimly, over soil charred and blackened, where the naked rock had in places been turned to lava by the explosion of those diabolical bombs.

Now they were almost within arrow-flight of the silent tower, and they spread their line, nerves taut, ready for any horror that might descend upon them.

On the tower appeared a single figure, lifting a ten-foot bronze horn. Its strident bellow roared out across the echoing slopes, like the blare of trumpets on Judgment Day. And it began to be fearfully answered. The ground trembled under the feet of the invaders, and rumblings and grindings welled up from the subterranean depths.

The Irakzai screamed, reeling like drunken men on the shuddering slope, and Conan, eyes glaring, charged recklessly up the incline, knife in hand, straight at the door that showed in the tower-wall. Above him the great horn roared and bellowed in brutish mockery. And then Kerim Shah drew a shaft to his ear and loosed.

Only a Turanian could have made that shot. The bellowing of the horn ceased suddenly, and a high, thin scream shrilled in its place. The green-robed figure on the tower staggered, clutching at the long shaft which quivered in its bosom, and then pitched across the parapet. The great horn tumbled upon the battlement and hung precariously, and another robed figure rushed to seize it, shrieking in horror. Again the Turanian bow twanged, and again it was answered by a death-howl. The second acolyte, in falling, struck the horn with his elbow and knocked it clattering over the parapet to shatter on the rocks far below.

At such headlong speed had Conan covered the ground that before the clattering echoes of that fall had died away, he was hacking at the door. Warned by his savage instinct, he gave back suddenly as a tide of molten lead splashed down from above. But the next instant he was back again, attacking the panels with redoubled fury. He was galvanized by the fact that his enemies had resorted to earthly weapons. The sorcery of the acolytes was limited. Their necromantic resources might well be exhausted.

Kerim Shah was hurrying up the slope, his hill-men behind him in a straggling crescent. They loosed as they ran, their arrows splintering against the walls or arching over the parapet.

The heavy teak portal gave way beneath the Cimmerian's assault, and he peered inside warily, expecting anything. He was looking into a circular chamber from which a stair wound upward. On the opposite side of the chamber a door gaped open, revealing the outer slope – and the backs of half a dozen green-robed figures in full retreat.

Conan yelled, took a step into the tower, and then native caution jerked him back, just as a great block of stone fell crashing to the floor where his foot had been an instant before. Shouting to his followers, he raced around the tower.

The acolytes had evacuated their first line of defence. As Conan rounded the tower he saw their green robes twinkling up the mountain ahead of him. He gave chase, panting with earnest blood-lust, and behind him Kerim Shah and the Irakzai came pelting, the latter yelling like wolves at the flight of their enemies, their fatalism momentarily submerged by temporary triumph.

The tower stood on the lower edge of a narrow plateau whose upward slant was barely perceptible. A few hundred yards away this plateau ended abruptly in a chasm which had been invisible farther down the mountain. Into this chasm the acolytes apparently leaped without checking their speed. Their pursuers saw the green robes flutter and disappear over the edge.

A few moments later they themselves were standing on the brink of the mighty moat that cut them off from the castle of the Black Seers. It was a sheer-walled ravine that extended in either direction as far as they could see, apparently girdling the mountain, some four hundred yards in width and five hundred feet deep. And in it, from rim to rim, a strange, translucent mist sparkled and shimmered.

Looking down, Conan grunted. Far below him, moving across the glimmering floor, which shone like burnished silver, he saw the forms of the green-robed acolytes. Their outline was wavering and indistinct, like figures seen under deep water. They walked in single file, moving toward the opposite wall.

Kerim Shah nocked an arrow and sent it singing downward. But when it struck the mist that filled the chasm it seemed to lose momentum and direction, wandering widely from its course.

'If they went down, so can we!' grunted Conan, while Kerim Shah stared after his shaft in amazement. 'I saw them last at this spot—'

Squinting down he saw something shining like a golden thread across the canyon floor far below. The acolytes seemed to be following this thread, and there suddenly came to him Khemsa's cryptic words – 'Follow the golden vein!' On the brink, under his very hand as he crouched, he found it, a thin vein of sparkling gold running from an outcropping of ore to the edge and down across the silvery floor. And he found something else, which had before been invisible to him because of the peculiar refraction of the light. The gold vein followed a narrow ramp which slanted down into the ravine, fitted with niches for hand and foot hold.

'Here's where they went down,' he grunted to Kerim Shah. 'They're no adepts, to waft themselves through the air! We'll follow them—'

It was at that instant that the man who had been bitten by the mad dog cried out horribly and leaped at Kerim Shah, foaming and gnashing his teeth. The Turanian, quick as a cat on his feet, sprang aside and the madman pitched head-first over the brink. The others rushed to the edge and glared after him in amazement. The maniac did not fall plummet-like. He floated slowly down through the rosy haze like a man sinking in deep water. His limbs moved like a man trying to swim, and his features were purple and convulsed beyond the contortions of his madness. Far down at last on the shining floor his body settled and lay still.

'There's death in that chasm,' muttered Kerim Shah, drawing back from the rosy mist that shimmered almost at his feet. 'What now, Conan?'

'On!' answered the Cimmerian grimly. 'Those acolytes are human; if the mist doesn't kill them, it won't kill me.'

He hitched his belt, and his hands touched the girdle Khemsa had given him; he scowled, then smiled bleakly. He had forgotten that girdle; yet thrice had death passed him by to strike another victim.

The acolytes had reached the farther wall and were moving up it like great green flies. Letting himself upon the ramp, he descended warily. The rosy cloud lapped about his ankles, ascending as he lowered himself. It reached his knees, his thighs, his waist, his arm-pits. He felt as one feels a thick heavy fog on a damp night. With it lapping about his chin he hesitated, and then ducked under. Instantly his breath ceased; all air was shut off from him and he felt his ribs caving in on his vitals. With a frantic effort he heaved himself up, fighting for life. His head rose above the surface and he drank air in great gulps.

Kerim Shah leaned down toward him, spoke to him, but Conan neither heard nor heeded. Stubbornly, his mind fixed on what the dying Khemsa had told him, the Cimmerian groped for the gold vein, and found that he had moved off it in his descent. Several series of hand-holds were niched in the ramp. Placing himself directly over the thread, he began climbing down once more. The rosy mist rose about him, engulfed him. Now his head was under, but he was still drinking pure air. Above him he saw his companions staring down at him, their features blurred by the haze that shimmered over his head. He gestured for them to

65

follow, and went down swiftly, without waiting to see whether they complied or not.

Kerim Shah sheathed his sword without comment and followed, and the Irakzai, more fearful of being left alone than of the terrors that might lurk below, scrambled after him. Each man clung to the golden thread as they saw the Cimmerian do.

Down the slanting ramp they went to the ravine floor and moved out across the shining level, treading the gold vein like rope-walkers. It was as if they walked along an invisible tunnel through which air circulated freely. They felt death pressing in on them above and on either hand, but it did not touch them.

The vein crawled up a similar ramp on the other wall up which the acolytes had disappeared, and up it they went with taut nerves, not knowing what might be waiting for them among the jutting spurs of rock that fanged the lip of the precipice.

It was the green-robed acolytes who awaited them, with knives in their hands. Perhaps they had reached the limits to which they could retreat. Perhaps the Stygian girdle about Conan's waist could have told why their necromantic spells had proven so weak and so quickly exhausted. Perhaps it was knowledge of death decreed for failure that sent them leaping from among the rocks, eyes glaring and knives glittering, resorting in their desperation to material weapons.

There among the rocky fangs on the precipice lip was no war of wizard craft. It was a whirl of blades, where real steel bit and real blood spurted, where sinewy arms dealt forthright blows that severed quivering flesh, and men went down to be trodden under foot as the fight raged over them.

One of the Irakzai bled to death among the rocks, but the acolytes were down – slashed and hacked asunder or hurled over the edge to float sluggishly down to the silver floor that shone so far below.

Then the conquerors shook blood and sweat from their eyes, and looked at one another. Conan and Kerim Shah still stood upright, and four of the Irakzai.

They stood among the rocky teeth that serrated the precipice brink, and from that spot a path wound up a gentle slope to a broad stair, consisting of half a dozen steps, a hundred feet across, cut out of a green jade-like substance. They led up to a broad stage or roofless gallery of the same polished stone, and above it rose, tier upon tier, the castle of the Black Seers. It seemed to have been carved out of the sheer stone of the mountain. The architecture was faultless, but unadorned. The many casements were barred and masked with curtains within. There was no sign of life, friendly or hostile.

They went up the path in silence, and warily as men treading the lair of a serpent. The Irakzai were dumb, like men marching to a certain doom. Even Kerim Shah was silent. Only Conan seemed unaware what a monstrous dislocating and uprooting of accepted thought and action their invasion constituted, what an unprecedented violation of tradition. He was not of the East; and he came of a breed who fought devils and wizards as promptly and matter-of-factly as they battled human foes.

He strode up the shining stairs and across the wide green gallery straight toward the great golden-bound teak door that opened upon it. He cast but a single glance upward at the higher tiers of the great pyramidal structure towering above him. He reached a hand for the bronze prong that jutted like a handle from the door – then checked himself, grinning hardly. The handle was made in the shape of a serpent, head lifted on arched neck; and Conan had a suspicion that that metal head would come to grisly life under his hand.

He struck it from the door with one blow, and its bronze clink on the glassy floor did not lessen his caution. He flipped it aside with his knife-point, and again turned to the door. Utter silence reigned over the towers. Far below them the mountain slopes fell away into a purple haze of distance. The sun glittered on snow-clad peaks on either hand. High above, a vulture hung like a black dot in the cold blue of the sky. But for it, the men before the gold-bound door were the only evidence of life, tiny figures on a green jade gallery poised on the dizzy height, with that fantastic pile of stone towering above them.

A sharp wind off the snow slashed them, whipping their tatters about. Conan's long knife splintering through the teak panels roused the startled echoes. Again and again he struck, hewing through polished wood and metal bands alike. Through the sundered ruins he glared into the interior, alert and suspicious as a wolf. He saw a broad chamber, the polished stone walls untapestried, the mosaic floor uncarpeted. Square, polished ebon stools and a stone dais formed the only furnishings. The room was empty of human life. Another door showed in the opposite wall.

'Leave a man on guard outside,' grunted Conan. 'I'm going in.'

Kerim Shah designated a warrior for that duty, and the man fell back toward the middle of the gallery, bow in hand. Conan strode into the castle, followed by the Turanian and the three remaining Irakzai. The one outside spat, grumbled in his beard, and started suddenly as a low mocking laugh reached his ears.

He lifted his head and saw, on the tier above him, a tall, black-robed figure, naked head nodding slightly as he stared down. His whole attitude suggested mockery and malignity. Quick as a flash the Irakzai bent his bow and loosed, and the arrow streaked upward to strike full in the black-robed breast. The mocking smile did not alter. The Seer plucked out the missile and threw it back at the bowman, not as a weapon is hurled, but with a contemptuous gesture. The Irakzai dodged, instinctively throwing up his arm. His fingers closed on the revolving shaft.

Then he shrieked. In his hand the wooden shaft suddenly *writhed*. Its rigid outline became pliant, melting in his grasp. He tried to throw it from him, but it was too late. He held a living serpent in his naked hand, and already it had coiled about his wrist and its wicked wedge-shaped head darted at his muscular arm. He screamed again and his eyes became distended, his features purple. He went to his knees shaken by an awful convulsion, and then lay still.

The men inside had wheeled at his first cry. Conan took a swift stride toward the open doorway, and then halted short, baffled. To the men behind him it seemed that he strained against empty air. But though he could see nothing, there was a slick, smooth, hard surface under his hands, and he knew that a sheet of crystal had been let down in the doorway. Through it he saw the Irakzai lying motionless on the glassy gallery, an ordinary arrow sticking in his arm.

Conan lifted his knife and smote, and the watchers were dumbfounded to see his blow checked apparently in midair, with the loud clang of steel that meets an unyielding substance. He wasted no more effort. He knew that not even the legendary tulwar of Amir Khurum could shatter that invisible curtain.

In a few words he explained the matter to Kerim Shah, and the Turanian shrugged his shoulders. 'Well, if our exit is barred, we must find another. In the meanwhile our way lies forward, does it not?'

With a grunt the Cimmerian turned and strode across the chamber to the opposite door, with a feeling of treading on the threshold of doom. As he lifted his knife to shatter the door, it swung silently open as if of its own accord. He strode into the great hall, flanked with tall glassy columns. A hundred feet from the door began the broad jade-green steps of a stair that tapered toward the top like the side of a pyramid. What lay beyond that stair he could not tell. But between him and its shimmering foot stood a curious altar of gleaming black jade. Four great golden serpents twined their tails about this altar and reared their wedge-shaped heads in the air, facing the four quarters of the compass like the enchanted guardians of a fabled treasure. But on the altar, between the arching necks, stood only a crystal globe filled with a cloudy smoke-like substance, in which floated four golden pomegranates.

The sight stirred some dim recollection in his mind; then Conan heeded the altar no longer, for on the lower steps of the stair stood four black-robed figures. He had not seen them come. They were simply there, tall, gaunt, their vulture-heads nodding in unison, their feet and hands hidden by their flowing garments.

One lifted his arm and the sleeve fell away revealing his hand – and it was not a hand at all. Conan halted in mid-stride, compelled against his will. He had encountered a force differing subtly from

Khemsa's mesmerism, and he could not advance, though he felt it in his power to retreat if he wished. His companions had likewise halted, and they seemed even more helpless than he, unable to move in either direction.

The seer whose arm was lifted beckoned to one of the Irakzai, and the man moved toward him like one in a trance, eyes staring and fixed, blade hanging in limp fingers. As he pushed past Conan, the Cimmerian threw an arm across his breast to arrest him. Conan was so much stronger than the Irakzai that in ordinary circumstances he could have broken his spine between his hands. But now the muscular arm was brushed aside like straw and the Irakzai moved toward the stair, treading jerkily and mechanically. He reached the steps and knelt stiffly, proffering his blade and bending his head. The Seer took the sword. It flashed as he swung it up and down. The Irakzai's head tumbled from his shoulders and thudded heavily on the black marble floor. An arch of blood jetted from the severed arteries and the body slumped over and lay with arms spread wide.

Again a malformed hand lifted and beckoned, and another Irakzai stumbled stiffly to his doom. The ghastly drama was re-enacted and another headless form lay beside the first.

As the third tribesman clumped his way past Conan to his death, the Cimmerian, his veins bulging in his temples with his efforts to break past the unseen barrier that held him, was suddenly aware of allied forces, unseen, but waking into life about him. This realization came without warning, but so powerfully that he could not doubt his instinct. His left hand slid involuntarily under his Bakhariot belt and closed on the Stygian girdle. And as he gripped it he felt new strength flood his numbed limbs; the will to live was a pulsing white-hot fire, matched by the intensity of his burning rage.

The third Irakzai was a decapitated corpse, and the hideous finger was lifting again when Conan felt the bursting of the invisible barrier. A fierce, involuntary cry burst from his lips as he leaped with the explosive suddenness of pent-up ferocity. His left hand gripped the sorcerer's girdle as a drowning man grips a floating

70

log, and the long knife was a sheen of light in his right. The men on the steps did not move. They watched calmly, cynically; if they felt surprise they did not show it. Conan did not allow himself to think what might chance when he came within knife-reach of them. His blood was pounding in his temples, a mist of crimson swam before his sight. He was afire with the urge to kill – to drive his knife deep into flesh and bone, and twist the blade in blood and entrails.

Another dozen strides would carry him to the steps where the sneering demons stood. He drew his breath deep, his fury rising redly as his charge gathered momentum. He was hurtling past the altar with its golden serpents when like a levin-flash there shot across his mind again as vividly as if spoken in his external ear, the cryptic words of Khemsa: 'Break the crystal ball!'

His reaction was almost without his own volition. Execution followed impulse so spontaneously that the greatest sorcerer of the age would not have had time to read his mind and prevent his action. Wheeling like a cat from his headlong charge, he brought his knife crashing down upon the crystal. Instantly the air vibrated with a peal of terror, whether from the stairs, the altar, or the crystal itself he could not tell. Hisses filled his ears as the golden serpents, suddenly vibrant with hideous life, writhed and smote at him. But he was fired to the speed of a maddened tiger. A whirl of steel sheared through the hideous trunks that waved toward him, and he smote the crystal sphere again and yet again. And the globe burst with a noise like a thunderclap, raining fiery shards on the black marble, and the gold pomegranates, as if released from captivity, shot upward toward the lofty roof and were gone.

A mad screaming, bestial and ghastly, was echoing through the great hall. On the steps writhed four black-robed figures, twisting in convulsions, froth dripping from their livid mouths. Then with one frenzied crescendo of inhuman ululation they stiffened and lay still, and Conan knew that they were dead. He stared down at the altar and the crystal shards. Four headless golden serpents still coiled about the altar, but no alien life now animated the dully gleaming metal.

Kerim Shah was rising slowly from his knees, whither he had been dashed by some unseen force. He shook his head to clear the ringing from his ears.

'Did you hear that crash when you struck? It was as if a thousand crystal panels shattered all over the castle as that globe burst. Were the souls of the wizards imprisoned in those golden balls? – Ha!'

Conan wheeled as Kerim Shah drew his sword and pointed.

Another figure stood at the head of the stair. His robe, too, was black, but of richly embroidered velvet, and there was a velvet cap on his head. His face was calm, and not unhandsome.

'Who the devil are you?' demanded Conan, staring up at him, knife in hand.

'I am the Master of Yimsha!' His voice was like the chime of a temple bell, but a note of cruel mirth ran through it.

'Where is Yasmina?' demanded Kerim Shah.

The Master laughed down at him.

'What is that to you, dead man? Have you so quickly forgotten my strength, once lent to you, that you come armed against me, you poor fool? I think I will take your heart, Kerim Shah!'

He held out his hand as if to receive something, and the Turanian cried out sharply like a man in mortal agony. He reeled drunkenly, and then, with a splintering of bones, a rending of flesh and muscle and a snapping of mail-links, his breast burst outward with a shower of blood, and through the ghastly aperture something red and dripping shot through the air into the Master's outstretched hand, as a bit of steel leaps to the magnet. The Turanian slumped to the floor and lay motionless, and the Master laughed and hurled the object to fall before Conan's feet – a still-quivering human heart.

With a roar and a curse Conan charged the stair. From Khemsa's girdle he felt strength and deathless hate flow into him to combat the terrible emanation of power that met him on the steps. The air filled with a shimmering steely haze through which he plunged like a swimmer, head lowered, left arm bent about his face, knife gripped low in his right hand. His half-blinded eyes, glaring over the crook of his elbow, made out the hated shape of the Seer before and above him, the outline wavering as a reflection wavers in disturbed water.

He was racked and torn by forces beyond his comprehension, but he felt a driving power outside and beyond his own lifting him inexorably upward and onward, despite the wizard's strength and his own agony.

Now he had reached the head of the stairs, and the Master's face floated in the steely haze before him, and a strange fear shadowed the inscrutable eyes. Conan waded through the mist as through a surf, and his knife lunged upward like a live thing. The keen point ripped the Master's robe as he sprang back with a low cry. Then before Conan's gaze, the wizard vanished – simply disappeared like a burst bubble, and something long and undulating darted up one of the smaller stairs that led up to left and right from the landing.

Conan charged after it, up the left-hand stair, uncertain as to just what he had seen whip up those steps, but in a berserk mood that drowned the nausea and horror whispering at the back of his consciousness.

He plunged out into a broad corridor whose uncarpeted floor and untapestried walls were of polished jade, and something long and swift whisked down the corridor ahead of him, and into a curtained door. From within the chamber rose a scream of urgent terror. The sound lent wings to Conan's flying feet and he hurtled through the curtains and headlong into the chamber within.

A frightful scene met his glare. Yasmina cowered on the farther edge of a velvet-covered dais, screaming her loathing and horror, an arm lifted as if to ward off attack, while before her swayed the hideous head of a giant serpent, shining neck arching up from dark-gleaming coils. With a choked cry Conan threw his knife.

Instantly the monster whirled and was upon him like the rush of wind through tall grass. The long knife quivered in its neck, point and a foot of blade showing on one side, and the hilt and a hand's-breadth of steel on the other, but it only seemed to madden the giant reptile. The great head towered above the man who faced it, and then darted down, the venom-dripping jaws gaping wide. But Conan had plucked a dagger from his girdle and he stabbed upward as the head dipped down. The point tore through the lower jaw and transfixed the upper, pinning them together. The next instant the great trunk had looped itself about the Cimmerian as the snake, unable to use its fangs, employed its remaining form of attack.

Conan's left arm was pinioned among the bone-crushing folds, but his right was free. Bracing his feet to keep upright, he stretched forth his hand, gripped the hilt of the long knife jutting from the serpent's neck, and tore it free in a shower of blood. As if divining his purpose with more than bestial intelligence, the snake writhed and knotted, seeking to cast its loops about his right arm. But with the speed of light the long knife rose and fell, shearing halfway through the reptile's giant trunk.

Before he could strike again, the great pliant loops fell from him and the monster dragged itself across the floor, gushing blood from its ghastly wounds. Conan sprang after it, knife lifted, but his vicious swipe cut empty air as the serpent writhed away from him and struck its blunt nose against a paneled screen of sandalwood. One of the panels gave inward and the long, bleeding barrel whipped through it and was gone.

Conan instantly attacked the screen. A few blows rent it apart and he glared into the dim alcove beyond. No horrific shape coiled there; there was blood on the marble floor, and bloody tracks led to a cryptic arched door. Those tracks were of a man's bare feet . . .

'Conan!' He wheeled back into the chamber just in time to catch the Devi of Vendhya in his arms as she rushed across the room and threw herself upon him, catching him about the neck with a frantic clasp, half hysterical with terror and gratitude and relief.

His wild blood had been stirred to its uttermost by all that had passed. He caught her to him in a grasp that would have made her wince at another time, and crushed her lips with his. She made no resistance; the Devi was drowned in the elemental woman. She closed her eyes and drank in his fierce, hot, lawless kisses with all the abandon of passionate thirst. She was panting with his violence when he ceased for breath, and glared down at her lying limp in his mighty arms.

'I knew you'd come for me,' she murmured. 'You would not leave me in this den of devils.'

At her words recollection of their environment came to him suddenly. He lifted his head and listened intently. Silence reigned over the castle of Yimsha, but it was a silence impregnated with menace. Peril crouched in every corner, leered invisibly from every hanging.

'We'd better go while we can,' he muttered. 'Those cuts were enough to kill any common beast – or *man* – but a wizard has a dozen lives. Wound one, and he writhes away like a crippled snake to soak up fresh venom from some source of sorcery.'

He picked up the girl and carrying her in his arms like a child, he strode out into the gleaming jade corridor and down the stairs, nerves tautly alert for any sign or sound.

'I met the Master,' she whispered, clinging to him and shuddering. 'He worked his spells on me to break my will. The most awful thing was a moldering corpse which seized me in its arms – I fainted then and lay as one dead, I do not know how long. Shortly after I regained consciousness I heard sounds of strife below, and cries, and then that snake came slithering through the curtains – ah!' She shook at the memory of that horror. 'I knew somehow that it was not an illusion, but a real serpent that sought my life.'

'It was not a shadow, at least,' answered Conan cryptically. 'He knew he was beaten, and chose to slay you rather than let you be rescued.'

'What do you mean, *he?*' she asked uneasily, and then shrank against him, crying out, and forgetting her question. She had seen the corpses at the foot of the stairs. Those of the Seers were not good to look at; as they lay twisted and contorted, their hands and feet were exposed to view, and at the sight Yasmina went livid and hid her face against Conan's powerful shoulder.

10

Yasmina and Conan

Conan passed through the hall quickly enough, traversed the outer chamber and approached the door that led upon the gallery. Then he saw the floor sprinkled with tiny, glittering shards. The crystal sheet that had covered the doorway had been shivered to bits, and he remembered the crash that had accompanied the shattering of the crystal globe. He believed that every piece of crystal in the castle had broken at that instant, and some dim instinct or memory of esoteric lore vaguely suggested the truth of the monstrous connection between the Lords of the Black Circle and the golden pomegranates. He felt the short hair bristle chilly at the back of his neck and put the matter hastily out of his mind.

He breathed a deep sigh of relief as he stepped out upon the green jade gallery. There was still the gorge to cross, but at least he could see the white peaks glistening in the sun, and the long slopes falling away into the distant blue hazes.

The Irakzai lay where he had fallen, an ugly blotch on the glassy smoothness. As Conan strode down the winding path, he was surprised to note the position of the sun. It had not yet passed its zenith; and yet it seemed to him that hours had passed since he plunged into the castle of the Black Seers.

He felt an urge to hasten, not a mere blind panic, but an instinct of peril growing behind his back. He said nothing to Yasmina, and she seemed content to nestle her dark head against his arching breast and find security in the clasp of his iron arms. He paused an instant on the brink of the chasm, frowning down. The haze which danced in the gorge was no longer rose-hued and sparkling. It was smoky, dim, ghostly, like the life-tide that flickered thinly in a wounded man. The thought came vaguely to Conan that the spells of magicians were more closely bound to their personal beings than were the actions of common men to the actors.

But far below, the floor shone like tarnished silver, and the gold thread sparkled undimmed. Conan shifted Yasmina across his shoulder, where she lay docilely, and began the descent. Hurriedly he descended the ramp, and hurriedly he fled across the echoing floor. He had a conviction that they were racing with time, that their chances of survival depended upon crossing that gorge of horrors before the wounded Master of the castle should regain enough power to loose some other doom upon them.

When he toiled up the farther ramp and came out upon the crest, he breathed a gusty sigh of relief and stood Yasmina upon her feet.

'You walk from here,' he told her; 'it's downhill all the way.'

She stole a glance at the gleaming pyramid across the chasm; it reared up against the snowy slope like the citadel of silence and immemorial evil.

'Are you a magician, that you have conquered the Black Seers of Yimsha, Conan of Ghor?' she asked, as they went down the path, with his heavy arm about her supple waist.

'It was a girdle Khemsa gave me before he died,' Conan answered. 'Yes, I found him on the trail. It is a curious one, which I'll show you when I have time. Against some spells it was weak, but against others it was strong, and a good knife is always a hearty incantation.'

'But if the girdle aided you in conquering the Master,' she argued, 'why did it not aid Khemsa?'

He shook his head. 'Who knows? But Khemsa had been the Master's slave; perhaps that weakened its magic. He had no hold on me as he had on Khemsa. Yet I can't say that I conquered him. He retreated, but I have a feeling that we haven't seen the last of him. I want to put as many miles between us and his lair as we can.'

He was further relieved to find horses tethered among the tamarisks as he had left them. He loosed them swiftly and mounted the black stallion, swinging the girl up before him. The others followed, freshened by their rest.

'And what now?' she asked. 'To Afghulistan?'

'Not just now!' He grinned hardly. 'Somebody – maybe the

governor – killed my seven headmen. My idiotic followers think I had something to do with it, and unless I am able to convince them otherwise, they'll hunt me like a wounded jackal.'

'Then what of me? If the headmen are dead, I am useless to you as a hostage. Will you slay me, to avenge them?'

He looked down at her, with eyes fiercely aglow, and laughed at the suggestion.

'Then let us ride to the border,' she said. 'You'll be safe from the Afghulis there—'

'Yes, on a Vendhyan gibbet.'

'I am Queen of Vendhya,' she reminded him with a touch of her old imperiousness. 'You have saved my life. You shall be rewarded.'

She did not intend it as it sounded, but he growled in his throat, ill pleased.

'Keep your bounty for your city-bred dogs, princess! If you're a queen of the plains, I'm a chief of the hills, and not one foot toward the border will I take you!'

'But you would be safe—' she began bewilderedly.

'And you'd be the Devi again,' he broke in. 'No, girl; I prefer you as you are now – a woman of flesh and blood, riding on my saddle-bow.'

'But you can't *keep* me!' she cried. 'You can't—'

'Watch and see!' he advised grimly.

'But I will pay you a vast ransom—'

'Devil take your ransom!' he answered roughly, his arms hardening about her supple figure. 'The kingdom of Vendhya could give me nothing I desire half so much as I desire you. I took you at the risk of my neck; if your courtiers want you back, let them come up the Zhaibar and fight for you.'

'But you have no followers now!' she protested. 'You are hunted! How can you preserve your own life, much less mine?'

'I still have friends in the hills,' he answered. 'There is a chief of the Khurakzai who will keep you safely while I bicker with the Afghulis. If they will have none of me, by Crom! I will ride northward with you to the steppes of the *kozaki*. I was a hetman

78

among the Free Companions before I rode southward. I'll make you a queen on the Zaporoska River!'

'But I can not!' she objected. 'You must not hold me—'

'If the idea's so repulsive,' he demanded, 'why did you yield your lips to me so willingly?'

'Even a queen is human,' she answered, coloring. 'But because I am a queen, I must consider my kingdom. Do not carry me away into some foreign country. Come back to Vendhya with me!'

'Would you make me your king?' he asked sardonically.

'Well, there are customs—' she stammered, and he interrupted her with a hard laugh.

'Yes, civilized customs that won't let you do as you wish. You'll marry some withered old king of the plains, and I can go my way with only the memory of a few kisses snatched from your lips. Ha!'

'But I must return to my kingdom!' she repeated helplessly.

'Why?' he demanded angrily. 'To chafe your rump on gold thrones, and listen to the plaudits of smirking, velvet-skirted fools? Where is the gain? Listen: I was born in the Cimmerian hills where the people are all barbarians. I have been a mercenary soldier, a corsair, a *kozak*, and a hundred other things. What king has roamed the countries, fought the battles, loved the women, and won the plunder that I have?

'I came into Ghulistan to raise a horde and plunder the kingdoms to the south – your own among them. Being chief of the Afghulis was only a start. If I can conciliate them, I'll have a dozen tribes following me within a year. But if I can't I'll ride back to the steppes and loot the Turanian borders with the *kozaki*. And you'll go with me. To the devil with your kingdom; they fended for themselves before you were born.'

She lay in his arms looking up at him, and she felt a tug at her spirit, a lawless, reckless urge that matched his own and was by it called into being. But a thousand generations of sovereignship rode heavy upon her.

'I can't! I can't!' she repeated helplessly.

'You haven't any choice,' he assured her. 'You – what the devil!'

They had left Yimsha some miles behind them, and were riding along a high ridge that separated two deep valleys. They had just topped a steep crest where they could gaze down into the valley on their right hand. And there was a running fight in progress. A strong wind was blowing away from them, carrying the sound from their ears, but even so the clashing of steel and thunder of hoofs welled up from far below.

They saw the glint of the sun on lance-tip and spired helmet. Three thousand mailed horsemen were driving before them a ragged band of turbaned riders, who fled snarling and striking like fleeing wolves.

'Turanians,' muttered Conan. 'Squadrons from Secunderam. What the devil are they doing here?'

'Who are the men they pursue?' asked Yasmina. 'And why do they fall back so stubbornly? They can not stand against such odds.'

'Five hundred of my mad Afghulis,' he growled, scowling down into the vale. 'They're in a trap, and they know it.'

The valley was indeed a cul-de-sac at that end. It narrowed to a high-walled gorge, opening out further into a round bowl, completely rimmed with lofty, unscalable walls.

The turbaned riders were being forced into this gorge, because there was nowhere else for them to go, and they went reluctantly, in a shower of arrows and a whirl of swords. The helmeted riders harried them, but did not press in too rashly. They knew the desperate fury of the hill tribes, and they knew too that they had their prey in a trap from which there was no escape. They had recognized the hill-men as Afghulis, and they wished to hem them in and force a surrender. They needed hostages for the purpose they had in mind.

Their emir was a man of decision and initiative. When he reached the Gurashah valley, and found neither guides nor emissary waiting for him, he pushed on, trusting to his own knowledge of the country. All the way from Secunderam there had been fighting, and tribesmen were licking their wounds in many a crag-perched village. He knew there was a good chance that neither he nor any of his helmeted spearmen would ever ride through the gates of Secunderam again, for the tribes would all be up behind him now, but he was determined to carry out his orders – which were to take Yasmina Devi from the Afghulis at all costs, and to bring her captive to Secunderam, or if confronted by impossibility, to strike off her head before he himself died.

Of all this, of course, the watchers on the ridge were not aware. But Conan fidgeted with nervousness.

'Why the devil did they get themselves trapped?' he demanded of the universe at large. 'I know what they're doing in these parts – they were hunting me, the dogs! Poking into every valley – and found themselves penned in before they knew it. The poor fools! They're making a stand in the gorge, but they can't hold out for long. When the Turanians have pushed them back into the bowl, they'll slaughter them at their leisure.'

The din welling up from below increased in volume and intensity. In the strait of the narrow gut, the Afghulis, fighting desperately, were for the time holding their own against the mailed riders, who could not throw their whole weight against them.

Conan scowled darkly, moved restlessly, fingering his hilt, and finally spoke bluntly: 'Devi, I must go down to them. I'll find a place for you to hide until I come back to you. You spoke of your kingdom – well, I don't pretend to look on those hairy devils as my children, but after all, such as they are, they're my henchmen. A chief should never desert his followers, even if they desert him first. They think they were right in kicking me out – hell, I won't be cast off! I'm still chief of the Afghulis, and I'll prove it! I can climb down on foot into the gorge.'

'But what of me?' she queried. 'You carried me away forcibly from *my* people; now will you leave me to die in the hills alone while you go down and sacrifice yourself uselessly?'

His veins swelled with the conflict of his emotions.

'That's right,' he muttered helplessly. 'Crom knows what I *can* do.'

She turned her head slightly, a curious expression dawning on her beautiful face. Then:

'Listen!' she cried. 'Listen!'

A distant fanfare of trumpets was borne faintly to their ears. They stared into the deep valley on the left, and caught a glint of steel on the farther side. A long line of lances and polished helmets moved along the vale, gleaming in the sunlight.

'The riders of Vendhya!' she cried exultingly.

'There are thousands of them!' muttered Conan. 'It has been long since a Kshatriya host has ridden this far into the hills.'

'They are searching for me!' she exclaimed. 'Give me your horse! I will ride to my warriors! The ridge is not so precipitous on the left, and I can reach the valley floor. I will lead my horsemen into the valley at the upper end and fall upon the Turanians! We will crush them in the vise! Quick, Conan! Will you sacrifice your men to your own desire?'

The burning hunger of the steppes and the wintry forests glared out of his eyes, but he shook his head and swung off the stallion, placing the reins in her hands.

'You win!' he grunted. 'Ride like the devil!'

She wheeled away down the left-hand slope and he ran swiftly along the ridge until he reached the long ragged cleft that was the defile in which the fight raged. Down the rugged wall he scrambled like an ape, clinging to projections and crevices, to fall at last, feet first, into the mêlée that raged in the mouth of the gorge. Blades were whickering and clanging about him, horses rearing and stamping, helmet plumes nodding among turbans that were stained crimson.

As he hit, he yelled like a wolf, caught a gold-worked rein, and dodging the sweep of a scimitar, drove his long knife upward through the rider's vitals. In another instant he was in the saddle, yelling ferocious orders to the Afghulis. They stared at him stupidly for an instant; then as they saw the havoc his steel was wreaking among their enemies, they fell to their work again, accepting him without comment. In that inferno of licking blades and spurting blood there was no time to ask or answer questions.

The riders in their spired helmets and gold-worked hauberks swarmed about the gorge mouth, thrusting and slashing, and the narrow defile was packed and jammed with horses and men, the warriors crushed breast to breast, stabbing with shortened blades, slashing murderously when there was an instant's room to swing a sword. When a man went down he did not get up from beneath the stamping, swirling hoofs. Weight and sheer strength counted heavily there, and the chief of the Afghulis did the work of ten. At such times accustomed habits sway men strongly, and the warriors, who were used to seeing Conan in their vanguard, were heartened mightily, despite their distrust of him.

But superior numbers counted too. The pressure of the men behind forced the horsemen of Turan deeper and deeper into the gorge, in the teeth of the flickering tulwars. Foot by foot the Afghulis were shoved back, leaving the defile-floor carpeted with dead, on which the riders trampled. As he hacked and smote like a man possessed, Conan had time for some chilling doubts – would Yasmina keep her word? She had but to join her warriors, turn southward and leave him and his band to perish.

But at last, after what seemed centuries of desperate battling, in the valley outside there rose another sound above the clash of steel and yells of slaughter. And then with a burst of trumpets that shook the walls, and rushing thunder of hoofs, five thousand riders of Vendhya smote the hosts of Secunderam.

That stroke split the Turanian squadrons asunder, shattered, tore and rent them and scattered their fragments all over the valley. In an instant the surge had ebbed back out of the gorge; there was a chaotic, confused swirl of fighting, horsemen wheeling and smiting singly and in clusters, and then the emir went down with a Kshatriya lance through his breast, and the riders in their spired helmets turned their horses down the valley, spurring like mad and seeking to slash a way through the swarms which had come upon them from the rear. As they scattered in flight, the conquerors scattered in pursuit, and all across the valley floor, and up on the slopes near the mouth and over the crests streamed the fugitives and the pursuers. The Afghulis, those left to ride, rushed out of the gorge and joined in the harrying of their foes, accepting the unexpected alliance as unquestioningly as they had accepted the return of their repudiated chief.

The sun was sinking toward the distant crags when Conan, his garments hacked to tatters and the mail under them reeking and clotted with blood, his knife dripping and crusted to the hilt, strode over the corpses to where Yasmina Devi sat her horse among her nobles on the crest of the ridge, near a lofty precipice.

'You kept your word, Devi!' he roared. 'By Crom, though, I had some bad seconds down in that gorge – *look out!*'

Down from the sky swooped a vulture of tremendous size with a thunder of wings that knocked men sprawling from their horses.

The scimitar-like beak was slashing for the Devi's soft neck, but Conan was quicker – a short run, a tigerish leap, the savage thrust of a dripping knife, and the vulture voiced a horribly human cry, pitched sideways and went tumbling down the cliffs to the rocks and river a thousand feet below. As it dropped, its black wings thrashing the air, it took on the semblance, not of a bird, but of a black-robed human body that fell, arms in wide black sleeves thrown abroad.

Conan turned to Yasmina, his red knife still in his hand, his blue eyes smoldering, blood oozing from wounds on his thickly muscled arms and thighs.

'You are the Devi again,' he said, grinning fiercely at the gold-clasped gossamer robe she had donned over her hill-girl attire, and awed not at all by the imposing array of chivalry about him. 'I have you to thank for the lives of some three hundred and fifty of my rogues, who are at least convinced that I didn't betray them. You have put my hands on the reins of conquest again.'

'I still owe you my ransom,' she said, her dark eyes glowing as they swept over him. 'Ten thousand pieces of gold I will pay you—'

He made a savage, impatient gesture, shook the blood from his knife and thrust it back in its scabbard, wiping his hands on his mail.

'I will collect your ransom in my own way, at my own time,' he said. 'I will collect it in your palace at Ayodhya, and I will come with fifty thousand men to see that the scales are fair.'

She laughed, gathering her reins into her hands. 'And I will meet you on the shores of the Jhumda with a hundred thousand!'

His eyes shone with fierce appreciation and admiration, and stepping back, he lifted his hand with a gesture that was like the assumption of kingship, indicating that her road was clear before her.

THE SLITHERING SHADOW

1

The desert shimmered in the heat waves. Conan the Cimmerian stared out over the aching desolation and involuntarily drew the back of his powerful hand over his blackened lips. He stood like a bronze image in the sand, apparently impervious to the murderous sun, though his only garment was a silk loin-cloth, girdled by a wide gold-buckled belt from which hung a saber and a broad-bladed poniard. On his clean-cut limbs were evidences of scarcely healed wounds.

At his feet rested a girl, one white arm clasping his knee, against which her blond head drooped. Her white skin contrasted with his hard bronzed limbs; her short silken tunic, low-necked and sleeveless, girdled at the waist, emphasized rather than concealed her lithe figure.

Conan shook his head, blinking. The sun's glare half blinded him. He lifted a small canteen from his belt and shook it, scowling at the faint splashing within.

The girl moved wearily, whimpering.

'Oh, Conan, we shall die here! I am so thirsty!'

The Cimmerian growled wordlessly, glaring truculently at the surrounding waste, with outthrust jaw, and blue eyes smoldering savagely from under his black tousled mane, as if the desert were a tangible enemy.

He stooped and put the canteen to the girl's lips.

'Drink till I tell you to stop, Natala,' he commanded.

She drank with little panting gasps, and he did not check her. Only when the canteen was empty did she realize that he had deliberately allowed her to drink all their water supply, little enough that it was.

Tears sprang to her eyes. 'Oh, Conan,' she wailed, wringing her hands, 'why did you let me drink it all? I did not know – now there is none for you!'

'Hush,' he growled. 'Don't waste your strength in weeping.'

Straightening, he threw the canteen from him.

'Why did you do that?' she whispered.

He did not reply, standing motionless and immobile, his fingers closing slowly about the hilt of his saber. He was not looking at the girl; his fierce eyes seemed to plumb the mysterious purple hazes of the distance.

Endowed with all the barbarian's ferocious love of life and instinct to live, Conan the Cimmerian yet knew that he had reached the end of his trail. He had not come to the limits of his endurance, but he knew another day under the merciless sun in those waterless wastes would bring him down. As for the girl, she had suffered enough. Better a quick painless sword-stroke than the lingering agony that faced him. Her thirst was temporarily quenched; it was a false mercy to let her suffer until delirium and death brought relief. Slowly he slid the saber from its sheath.

He halted suddenly, stiffening. Far out on the desert to the south, something glimmered through the heat waves.

At first he thought it was a phantom, one of the mirages which had mocked and maddened him in that accursed desert. Shading his sun-dazzled eyes, he made out spires and minarets, and gleaming walls. He watched it grimly, waiting for it to fade and vanish. Natala had ceased to sob; she struggled to her knees and followed his gaze.

'Is it a city, Conan?' she whispered, too fearful to hope. 'Or is it but a shadow?'

The Cimmerian did not reply for a space. He closed and opened his eyes several times; he looked away, then back. The city remained where he had first seen it.

'The devil knows,' he grunted. 'It's worth a try, though.'

He thrust the saber back in its sheath. Stooping, he lifted Natala in his mighty arms as though she had been an infant. She resisted weakly.

'Don't waste your strength carrying me, Conan,' she pleaded. 'I can walk.'

'The ground gets rockier here,' he answered. 'You would soon wear your sandals to shreds,' glancing at her soft green foot-wear. 'Besides, if we are to reach that city at all, we must do it quickly, and I can make better time this way.'

The chance for life had lent fresh vigor and resilience to the Cimmerian's steely thews. He strode out across the sandy waste as if he had just begun the journey. A barbarian of barbarians, the vitality and endurance of the wild were his, granting him survival where civilized men would have perished.

He and the girl were, so far as he knew, the sole survivors of Prince Almuric's army, that mad motley horde which, following the defeated rebel prince of Koth, swept through the Lands of Shem like a devastating sandstorm and drenched the outlands of Stygia with blood. With a Stygian host on its heels, it had cut its way through the black kingdom of Kush, only to be annihilated on the edge of the southern desert. Conan likened it in his mind to a great torrent, dwindling gradually as it rushed southward, to run dry at last in the sands of the naked desert. The bones of its members – mercenaries, outcasts, broken men, outlaws – lay strewn from the Kothic uplands to the dunes of the wilderness.

From that final slaughter, when the Stygians and the Kushites closed in on the trapped remnants, Conan had cut his way clear and fled on a camel with the girl. Behind them the land swarmed with enemies; the only way open to them was the desert to the south. Into those menacing depths they had plunged.

The girl was a Brythunian, whom Conan had found in the slave-market of a stormed Shemite city, and appropriated. She had had nothing to say in the matter, but her new position was so far superior to the lot of any Hyborian woman in a Shemitish seraglio, that she accepted it thankfully. So she had shared in the adventures of Almuric's damned horde.

For days they had fled into the desert, pursued so far by Stygian horsemen that when they shook off the pursuit, they dared not turn back. They pushed on, seeking water, until the camel died. Then they went on foot. For the past few days their suffering had been intense. Conan had shielded Natala all he could, and the rough life of the camp had given her more stamina and strength than the average woman possesses; but even so, she was not far from collapse.

The sun beat fiercely on Conan's tangled black mane. Waves of dizziness and nausea rose in his brain, but he set his teeth and strode on unwaveringly. He was convinced that the city was a reality and not a mirage. What they would find there he had no idea. The inhabitants might be hostile. Nevertheless it was a fighting chance, and that was as much as he had ever asked.

The sun was nigh to setting when they halted in front of the massive gate, grateful for the shade. Conan stood Natala on her feet, and stretched his aching arms. Above them the walls towered some thirty feet in height, composed of a smooth greenish substance that shone almost like glass. Conan scanned the parapets, expecting to be challenged, but saw no one. Impatiently he shouted, and banged on the gate with his saber-hilt, but only the hollow echoes mocked him. Natala cringed close to him, frightened by the silence. Conan tried the portal, and stepped back, drawing his saber, as it swung silently inward. Natala stifled a cry.

'Oh, look, Conan!'

Just inside the gate lay a human body. Conan glared at it narrowly, then looked beyond it. He saw a wide open expanse, like a court, bordered by the arched doorways of houses composed of the same greenish material as the outer walls. These edifices were lofty and imposing, pinnacled with shining domes and minarets. There was no sign of life among them. In the center of the court rose the square curb of a well, and the sight stung Conan, whose mouth felt caked with dry dust. Taking Natala's wrist he drew her through the gate, and closed it behind them.

'Is he dead?' she whispered, shrinkingly indicating the man who lay limply before the gate. The body was that of a tall powerful individual, apparently in his prime; the skin was yellow, the eyes slightly slanted; otherwise the man differed little from the Hyborian type. He was clad in high-strapped sandals and a tunic of purple silk, and a short sword in a cloth-of-gold scabbard hung from his girdle. Conan felt his flesh. It was cold. There was no sign of life in the body.

'Not a wound on him,' grunted the Cimmerian, 'but he's dead as Almuric with forty Stygian arrows in him. In Crom's name, let's see to the well! If there's water in it, we'll drink, dead men or no.'

There was water in the well, but they did not drink of it. Its level was a good fifty feet below the curb, and there was nothing to draw it up with. Conan cursed blackly, maddened by the sight of the stuff just out of his reach, and turned to look for some means of obtaining it. Then a scream from Natala brought him about.

The supposedly dead man was rushing upon him, eyes blazing with indisputable life, his short sword gleaming in his hand. Conan cursed amazedly, but wasted no time in conjecture. He met the hurtling attacker with a slashing cut of his saber that sheared through flesh and bone. The fellow's head thudded on the flags; the body staggered drunkenly, an arch of blood jetting from the severed jugular; then it fell heavily.

Conan glared down, swearing softly.

'This fellow is no deader now than he was a few minutes agone. Into what madhouse have we strayed?'

Natala, who had covered her eyes with her hands at the sight, peeked between her fingers and shook with fear.

'Oh, Conan, will the people of the city not kill us, because of this?'

'Well,' he growled, 'this creature would have killed us if I hadn't lopped off his head.'

He glanced at the archways that gaped blankly from the green walls above them. He saw no hint of movement, heard no sound.

'I don't think any one saw us,' he muttered. 'I'll hide the evidence—'

He lifted the limp carcass by its swordbelt with one hand, and grasping the head by its long hair in the other, he half carried, half dragged the ghastly remains over to the well.

'Since we can't drink this water,' he gritted vindictively, 'I'll see that nobody else enjoys drinking it. Curse such a well, anyway!' He heaved the body over the curb and let it drop, tossing the head after it. A dull splash sounded far beneath.

'There's blood on the stones,' whispered Natala.

'There'll be more unless I find water soon,' growled the Cimmerian, his short store of patience about exhausted. The girl had almost forgotten her thirst and hunger in her fear, but not Conan.

'We'll go into one of these doors,' he said. 'Surely we'll find people after awhile.'

'Oh, Conan!' she wailed, snuggling up as close to him as she could. 'I'm afraid! This is a city of ghosts and dead men! Let us go back into the desert! Better to die there, than to face these terrors!'

'We'll go into the desert when they throw us off the walls,' he snarled. 'There's water somewhere in this city, and I'll find it, if I have to kill every man in it.'

'But what if they come to life again?' she whispered.

'Then I'll keep killing them until they stay dead!' he snapped. 'Come on! That doorway is as good as another! Stay behind me, but don't run unless I tell you to.'

She murmured a faint assent and followed him so closely that she stepped on his heels, to his irritation. Dusk had fallen, filling the strange city with purple shadows. They entered the open doorway, and found themselves in a wide chamber, the walls of which were hung with velvet tapestries, worked in curious designs. Floor, walls and ceiling were of the green glassy stone, the walls decorated with gold frieze-work. Furs and satin cushions littered the floor. Several doorways let into other rooms. They passed through, and traversed several chambers, counterparts of the first. They saw no one, but the Cimmerian grunted suspiciously.

'Some one was here not long ago. This couch is still warm from contact with a human body. That silk cushion bears the imprint of some one's hips. Then there's a faint scent of perfume lingering in the air.'

A weird unreal atmosphere hung over all. Traversing this dim silent palace was like an opium dream. Some of the chambers were unlighted, and these they avoided. Others were bathed in a soft weird light that seemed to emanate from jewels set in the walls in fantastic designs. Suddenly, as they passed into one of these illumined chambers, Natala cried out and clutched her companion's arm. With a curse he wheeled, glaring for an enemy, bewildered because he saw none.

'What's the matter?' he snarled. 'If you ever grab my sword-arm again, I'll skin you. Do you want me to get my throat cut? What were you yelling about?'

'Look there,' she quavered, pointing.

Conan grunted. On a table of polished ebony stood golden vessels, apparently containing food and drink. The room was unoccupied.

'Well, whoever this feast is prepared for,' he growled, 'he'll have to look elsewhere tonight.'

'Dare we eat it, Conan?' ventured the girl nervously. 'The people might come upon us, and—'

'*Lir an mannanan mac lir!*' he swore, grabbing her by the nape of her neck and thrusting her into a gilded chair at the end of the table with no great ceremony. 'We starve and you make objections! Eat!'

He took the chair at the other end, and seizing a jade goblet, emptied it at a gulp. It contained a crimson wine-like liquor of a peculiar tang, unfamiliar to him, but it was like nectar to his parched gullet. His thirst allayed, he attacked the food before him with rare gusto. It too was strange to him: exotic fruits and unknown meats. The vessels were of exquisite workmanship, and there were golden knives and forks as well. These Conan ignored, grasping the meat-joints in his fingers and tearing them with his strong teeth. The Cimmerian's table manners were rather wolfish at any time. His civilized companion ate more daintily, but just as ravenously. It occurred to Conan that the food might be poisoned, but the thought did not lessen his appetite; he preferred to die of poisoning rather than starvation.

His hunger satisfied, he leaned back with a deep sigh of relief. That there were humans in that silent city was evidenced by the fresh food, and perhaps every dark corner concealed a lurking enemy. But he felt no apprehension on that score, having a large confidence in his own fighting ability. He began to feel sleepy, and considered the idea of stretching himself on a near-by couch for a nap.

Not so Natala. She was no longer hungry and thirsty, but she felt no desire to sleep. Her lovely eyes were very wide indeed as she timidly glanced at the doorways, boundaries of the unknown. The silence and mystery of the strange place preyed on her. The chamber seemed larger, the table longer than she had first noticed, and she realized that she was farther from her grim protector than she wished to be. Rising quickly, she went around the table and seated herself on his knee, glancing nervously at the arched doorways. Some were lighted and some were not, and it was at the unlighted ones she gazed longest.

'We have eaten, drunk and rested,' she urged. 'Let us leave this place, Conan. It's evil. I can feel it.'

'Well, we haven't been harmed so far,' he began, when a soft but sinister rustling brought him about. Thrusting the girl off his knee he rose with the quick ease of a panther, drawing his saber, facing the doorway from which the sound had seemed to come. It was not repeated, and he stole forward noiselessly, Natala following with her heart in her mouth. She knew he suspected peril. His outthrust head was sunk between his giant shoulders, he glided forward in a half crouch, like a stalking tiger. He made no more noise than a tiger would have made.

At the doorway he halted, Natala peering fearfully from behind him. There was no light in the room, but it was partially illuminated by the radiance behind them, which streamed across it into yet another chamber. And in this chamber a man lay on a raised dais. The soft light bathed him, and they saw he was a counterpart of the man Conan had killed before the outer gate, except that his garments were richer, and ornamented with jewels which twinkled in the uncanny light. Was he dead, or merely sleeping? Again came that faint sinister sound, as if some one had thrust aside a hanging. Conan drew back, drawing the clinging Natala with him. He clapped his hand over her mouth just in time to check her shriek.

From where they now stood, they could no longer see the dais, but they could see the shadow it cast on the wall behind it. And now another shadow moved across the wall: a huge shapeless black blot. Conan felt his hair prickle curiously as he watched. Distorted though it might be, he felt that he had never seen a man or beast which cast such a shadow. He was consumed with curiosity, but some instinct held him frozen in his tracks. He heard Natala's quick panting gasps as she stared with dilated eyes. No other sound disturbed the tense stillness. The great shadow engulfed that of the dais. For a long instant only its black bulk was thrown on the smooth wall. Then slowly it receded, and once more the dais was etched darkly against the wall. But the sleeper was no longer upon it.

An hysterical gurgle rose in Natala's throat, and Conan gave her an admonitory shake. He was aware of an iciness in his own veins. Human foes he did not fear; anything understandable, however grisly, caused no tremors in his broad breast. But this was beyond his ken.

After a while, however, his curiosity conquered his uneasiness, and he moved out into the unlighted chamber again, ready for anything. Looking into the other room, he saw it was empty. The dais stood as he had first seen it, except that no bejeweled human lay thereon. Only on its silken covering shone a single drop of blood, like a great crimson gem. Natala saw it and gave a low choking cry, for which Conan did not punish her. Again he felt the icy hand of fear. On that dais a man had lain; *something* had crept into the chamber and carried him away. What that something was, Conan had no idea, but an aura of unnatural horror hung over those dim-lit chambers.

He was ready to depart. Taking Natala's hand, he turned back, then hesitated. Somewhere back among the chambers they had traversed, he heard the sound of a footfall. A human foot, bare or softly shod, had made that sound, and Conan, with the wariness of a wolf, turned quickly aside. He believed he could come again into the outer court, and yet avoid the room from which the sound had appeared to come.

But they had not crossed the first chamber on their new route, when the rustle of a silken hanging brought them about suddenly. Before a curtained alcove stood a man eyeing them intently.

He was exactly like the others they had encountered: tall, well made, clad in purple garments, with a jeweled girdle. There was neither surprise nor hostility in his amber eyes. They were dreamy as a lotus-eater's. He did not draw the short sword at his side. After a tense moment he spoke, in a far-away detached tone, and a language his hearers did not understand.

On a venture Conan replied in Stygian, and the stranger answered in the same tongue: 'Who are you?'

. 'I am Conan, a Cimmerian,' answered the barbarian. 'This is Natala, of Brythunia. What city is this?'

The man did not at once reply. His dreamy sensuous gaze rested on Natala, and he drawled, 'Of all my rich visions, this is the strangest! Oh, girl of the golden locks, from what far dreamland do you come? From Andarra, or Tothra, or Kuth of the star-girdle?'

'What madness is this?' growled the Cimmerian harshly, not relishing the man's words or manner.

The other did not heed him.

'I have dreamed more gorgeous beauties,' he murmured; 'lithe women with hair dusky as night, and dark eyes of unfathomed mystery. But your skin is white as milk, your eyes as clear as dawn, and there is about you a freshness and daintiness alluring as honey. Come to my couch, little dream-girl!'

He advanced and reached for her, and Conan struck aside his hand with a force that might have broken his arm. The man reeled back, clutching the numbed member, his eyes clouding.

'What rebellion of ghosts is this?' he muttered. 'Barbarian,

I command ye – begone! Fade! Dissipate! Fade! Vanish!'

'I'll vanish your head from your shoulders!' snarled the infuriated Cimmerian, his saber gleaming in his hand. 'Is this the welcome you give strangers? By Crom, I'll drench these hangings in blood!'

The dreaminess had faded from the other's eyes, to be replaced by a look of bewilderment.

'Thog!' he ejaculated. 'You are real! Whence come you? Who are you? What do you in Xuthal?'

'We came from the desert,' Conan growled. 'We wandered into the city at dusk, famishing. We found a feast set for some one, and we ate it. I have no money to pay for it. In my country, no starving man is denied food, but you civilized people must have your recompense – if you are like all I ever met. We have done no harm and we were just leaving. By Crom, I do not like this place, where dead men rise, and sleeping men vanish into the bellies of shadows!'

The man started violently at the last comment, his yellow face turning ashy.

'What do you say? Shadows? Into the bellies of shadows?'

'Well,' answered the Cimmerian cautiously, 'whatever it is that takes a man from a sleeping-dais and leaves only a spot of blood.'

'You have seen? You have *seen*?' The man was shaking like a leaf; his voice cracked on the high-pitched note.

'Only a man sleeping on a dais, and a shadow that engulfed him,' answered Conan.

The effect of his words on the other was horrifying. With an awful scream the man turned and rushed from the chamber. In his blind haste he caromed from the side of the door, righted himself, and fled through the adjoining chambers, still screaming at the top of his voice. Amazed, Conan stared after him, the girl trembling as she clutched the giant's arm. They could no longer see the flying figure, but they still heard his frightful screams, dwindling in the distance, and echoing as from vaulted roofs. Suddenly one cry, louder than the others, rose and broke short, followed by blank silence.

'Crom!'

Conan wiped the perspiration from his forehead with a hand that was not entirely steady.

'Surely this is a city of the mad! Let's get out of here, before we meet other madmen!'

'It is all a nightmare!' whimpered Natala. 'We are dead and damned! We died out on the desert and are in hell! We are disembodied spirits – *ow!*' Her yelp was induced by a resounding spank from Conan's open hand.

'You're no spirit when a pat makes you yell like that,' he commented, with the grim humor which frequently manifested itself at inopportune times. 'We are alive, though we may not be if we loiter in this devil-haunted pile. Come!'

They had traversed but a single chamber when again they stopped short. Some one or something was approaching. They faced the doorway whence the sounds came, waiting for they knew not what. Conan's nostrils widened, and his eyes narrowed. He caught the faint scent of the perfume he had noticed earlier in the night. A figure framed itself in the doorway. Conan swore under his breath; Natala's red lips opened wide.

It was a woman who stood there staring at them in wonder. She was tall, lithe, shaped like a goddess; clad in a narrow girdle crusted with jewels. A burnished mass of night-black hair set off the whiteness of her ivory body. Her dark eyes, shaded by long dusky lashes, were deep with sensuous mystery. Conan caught his breath at her beauty, and Natala stared with dilated eyes. The Cimmerian had never seen such a woman; her facial outline was Stygian, but she was not dusky-skinned like the Stygian women he had known; her limbs were like alabaster.

But when she spoke, in a deep rich musical voice, it was in the Stygian tongue.

'Who are you? What do you in Xuthal? Who is that girl?'

'Who are you?' bluntly countered Conan, who quickly wearied of answering questions.

'I am Thalis the Stygian,' she replied. 'Are you mad, to come here?'

'I've been thinking I must be,' he growled. 'By Crom, if I am sane, I'm out of place here, because these people are all maniacs. We stagger in from the desert, dying of thirst and hunger, and we come upon a dead man who tries to stab me in the back. We enter a palace rich and luxuriant, yet apparently empty. We find a meal set, but with no feasters. Then we see a shadow devour a sleeping man—' He watched her narrowly and saw her change color slightly. 'Well?'

'Well what?' she demanded, apparently regaining control of herself.

'I was just waiting for you to run through the rooms howling like a wild woman,' he answered. 'The man I told about the shadow did.'

She shrugged her slim ivory shoulders. 'That was the screams I heard, then. Well, to every man his fate, and it's foolish to squeal like a rat in a trap. When Thog wants me, he will come for me.'

'Who is Thog?' demanded Conan suspiciously.

She gave him a long appraising stare that brought color to Natala's face and made her bite her small red lip.

'Sit down on that divan and I will tell you,' she said. 'But first tell me your names.'

'I am Conan, a Cimmerian, and this is Natala, a daughter of Brythunia,' he answered. 'We are refugees of an army destroyed on the borders of Kush. But I am not desirous of sitting down, where black shadows might steal up on my back.'

With a light musical laugh, she seated herself, stretching out her supple limbs with studied abandon.

'Be at ease,' she advised. 'If Thog wishes you, he will take you, wherever you are. That man you mentioned, who screamed and ran – did you not hear him give one great cry, and then fall silent? In his frenzy, he must have run full into that which he sought to escape. No man can avoid his fate.'

Conan grunted non-committally, but he sat down on the edge of a couch, his saber across his knees, his eyes wandering suspiciously about the chamber. Natala nestled against him, clutching him jealously, her legs tucked up under her. She eyed the stranger woman with suspicion and resentment. She felt small and dust-stained and insignificant before this glamorous beauty, and she could not mistake the look in the dark eyes which feasted on every detail of the bronzed giant's physique.

'What is this place, and who are these people?' demanded Conan.

'This city is called Xuthal; it is very ancient. It is built over an oasis, which the founders of Xuthal found in their wanderings. They came from the east, so long ago that not even their descendants remember the age.'

'Surely there are not many of them; these palaces seem empty.'

'No; and yet more than you might think. The city is really one great palace, with every building inside the walls closely connected with the others. You might walk among these chambers for hours and see no one. At other times, you would meet hundreds of the inhabitants.'

'How is that?' Conan inquired uneasily; this savored too strongly of sorcery for comfort.

'Much of the time these people lie in sleep. Their dream-life is as important – and to them as real – as their waking life. You have heard of the black lotus? In certain pits of the city it grows. Through the ages they have cultivated it, until, instead of death, its juice induces dreams, gorgeous and fantastic. In these dreams they spend most of their time. Their lives are vague, erratic, and without plan. They dream, they wake, drink, love, eat and dream again. They seldom finish anything they begin, but leave it half completed and sink back again into the slumber of the black lotus. That meal you found – doubtless one awoke, felt the urge of hunger, prepared the meal for himself, then forgot about it and wandered away to dream again.'

'Where do they get their food?' interrupted Conan. 'I saw no fields or vineyards outside the city. Have they orchards and cattle-pens within the walls?'

She shook her head. 'They manufacture their own food out of the primal elements. They are wonderful scientists, when they are not drugged with their dream-flower. Their ancestors were mental giants, who built this marvelous city in the desert, and though the race became slaves to their curious passions, some of their wonderful knowledge still remains. Have you wondered about these lights? They are jewels, fused with radium. You rub them with your thumb to make them glow, and rub them again, the opposite way, to extinguish them. That is but a single example of their science. But much they have forgotten. They take little interest in waking life, choosing to lie most of the time in death-like sleep.'

'Then the dead man at the gate—' began Conan.

'Was doubtless slumbering. Sleepers of the lotus are like the dead. Animation is apparently suspended. It is impossible to detect the slightest sign of life. The spirit has left the body and is roaming at will through other, exotic worlds. The man at the gate was a good example of the irresponsibility of these people's lives. He was guarding the gate, where custom decrees a watch be kept, though no enemy has ever advanced across the desert. In other parts of the city you would find other guards, generally sleeping as soundly as the man at the gate.'

Conan mulled over this for a space.

'Where are the people now?'

'Scattered in different parts of the city; lying on couches, on silken divans, in cushion-littered alcoves, on fur-covered daises; all wrapt in the shining veil of dreams.'

Conan felt the skin twitch between his massive shoulders. It was not soothing to think of hundreds of people lying cold and still throughout the tapestried palaces, their glassy eyes turned unseeingly upward. He remembered something else.

'What of the thing that stole through the chambers and carried away the man on the dais?'

A shudder twitched her ivory limbs.

'That was Thog, the Ancient, the god of Xuthal, who dwells in the sunken dome in the center of the city. He has always dwelt in Xuthal. Whether he came here with the ancient founders, or was here when they built the city, none knows. But the people of Xuthal worship him. Mostly he sleeps below the city, but sometimes at irregular intervals he grows hungry, and then he steals through the secret corridors and the dim-lit chambers, seeking prey. Then none is safe.'

Natala moaned with terror and clasped Conan's mighty neck as if to resist an effort to drag her from her protector's side.

'Crom!' he ejaculated aghast. 'You mean to tell me these people lie down calmly and sleep, with this demon crawling among them?'

'It is only occasionally that he is hungry,' she repeated. 'A god must have his sacrifices. When I was a child in Stygia the people lived under the shadow of the priests. None ever knew when he or she would be seized and dragged to the altar. What difference whether the priests give a victim to the gods, or the god comes for his own victim?'

'Such is not the custom of my people,' Conan growled, 'nor of Natala's either. The Hyborians do not sacrifice humans to their god, Mitra, and as for my people – by Crom, I'd like to see a priest try to drag a Cimmerian to the altar! There'd be blood spilt, but not as the priest intended.'

'You are a barbarian,' laughed Thalis, but with a glow in her luminous eyes. 'Thog is very ancient and very terrible.'

'These folk must be either fools or heroes,' grunted Conan, 'to lie down and dream their idiotic dreams, knowing they might awaken in his belly.'

She laughed. 'They know nothing else. For untold generations Thog has preyed on them. He has been one of the factors which have reduced their numbers from thousands to hundreds. A few more generations and they will be extinct, and Thog must either fare forth into the world for new prey, or retire to the underworld whence he came so long ago.

'They realize their ultimate doom, but they are fatalists, incapable of resistance or escape. Not one of the present generation has been out of sight of these walls. There is an oasis a day's march to the south – I have seen it on the old maps their ancestors drew on parchment – but no man of Xuthal has visited it for three generations, much less made any attempt to explore the fertile grasslands which the maps show lying another day's march beyond it. They are a fast-fading race, drowned in lotus-dreams, stimulating their waking hours by means of the golden wine which heals wounds, prolongs life, and invigorates the most sated debauchee.

'Yet they cling to life, and fear the deity they worship. You saw how one went mad at the knowledge that Thog was roving the palaces. I have seen the whole city screaming and tearing its hair, and running frenziedly out of the gates, to cower outside the walls and draw lots to see which would be bound and flung back through the arched doorways to satisfy Thog's lust and hunger. Were they not all slumbering now, the word of his coming would send them raving and shrieking again through the outer gates.'

'Oh, Conan!' begged Natala hysterically. 'Let us flee!'

'In good time,' muttered Conan, his eyes burning on Thalis' ivory limbs. 'What are you, a Stygian woman, doing here?'

'I came here when a young girl,' she answered, leaning lithely back against the velvet divan, and intertwining her slender fingers behind her dusky head. 'I am the daughter of a king, no common woman, as you can see by my skin, which is as white as that of your little blond there. I was abducted by a rebel prince, who, with an army of Kushite bowmen, pushed southward into the wilderness, searching for a land he could make his own. He and all his warriors perished in the desert, but one, before he died, placed me on a camel and walked beside it until he dropped and died in his tracks. The beast wandered on, and I finally passed into delirium from thirst and hunger, and awakened in this city. They told me I had been seen from the walls, early in the dawn, lying senseless beside a dead camel. They went forth and brought me in and revived me with their wonderful golden wine. And only the sight of a woman would have led them to have ventured that far from their walls.

'They were naturally much interested in me, especially the men. As I could not speak their language, they learned to speak mine. They are very quick and able of intellect; they learned my language long before I learned theirs. But they were more interested in me than in my language. I have been, and am, the only thing for which a man of them will forgo his lotus-dreams for a space.'

She laughed wickedly, flashing her audacious eyes meaningly at Conan.

'Of course the women are jealous of me,' she continued tranquilly. 'They are handsome enough in their yellow-skinned way, but they are dreamy and uncertain as the men, and these latter like me not only for my beauty, but for my reality. I am no dream! Though I have dreamed the dreams of the lotus, I am a normal woman, with earthly emotions and desires. With such these moon-eyed yellow women can not compare.

'That is why it would be better for you to cut that girl's throat with your saber, before the men of Xuthal waken and catch her. They will put her through paces she never dreamed of! She is too soft to endure what I have thrived on. I am a daughter of Luxur, and before I had known fifteen summers I had been led through the temples of Derketo, the dusky goddess, and had been initiated into the mysteries. Not that my first years in Xuthal were years of unmodified pleasure! The people of Xuthal have forgotten more than the priestesses of Derketo ever dreamed. They live only for sensual joys. Dreaming or waking, their lives are filled with exotic ecstasies, beyond the ken of ordinary men.'

'Damned degenerates!' growled Conan.

'It is all in the point of view,' smiled Thalis lazily.

'Well,' he decided, 'we're merely wasting time. I can see this is no place for ordinary mortals. We'll be gone before your morons awake, or Thog comes to devour us. I think the desert would be kinder.'

Natala, whose blood had curdled in her veins at Thalis's words, fervently agreed. She could speak Stygian only brokenly, but she understood it well enough. Conan stood up, drawing her up beside him.

'If you'll show us the nearest way out of this city,' he grunted, 'we'll take ourselves off.' But his gaze lingered on the Stygian's sleek limbs and ivory breasts.

She did not miss his look, and she smiled enigmatically as she rose with the lithe ease of a great lazy cat.

'Follow me,' she directed and led the way, conscious of Conan's eyes fixed on her supple figure and perfectly poised carriage. She did not go the way they had come, but before Conan's suspicions could be roused, she halted in a wide ivory-cased chamber, and pointed to a tiny fountain which gurgled in the center of the ivory floor.

'Don't you want to wash your face, child?' she asked Natala. 'It is stained with dust, and there is dust in your hair.'

Natala colored resentfully at the suggestion of malice in the Stygian's faintly mocking tone, but she complied, wondering miserably just how much havoc the desert sun and wind had wrought on her complexion – a feature for which women of her race were justly noted. She knelt beside the fountain, shook back her hair, slipped her tunic down to her waist, and began to lave not only her face, but her white arms and shoulders as well.

'By Crom!' grumbled Conan. 'A woman will stop to consider her beauty, if the devil himself were on her heels. Haste, girl; you'll be dusty again before we've got out of sight of this city. And Thalis, I'd take it kindly if you'd furnish us with a bit of food and drink.'

For answer Thalis leaned herself against him, slipping one white arm about his bronzed shoulders. Her sleek naked flank pressed against his thigh and the perfume of her foamy hair was in his nostrils.

'Why dare the desert?' she whispered urgently. 'Stay here! I will teach you the ways of Xuthal. I will protect you. I will love you! You are a real man: I am sick of these moon-calves who sigh and dream and wake, and dream again. I am hungry for the hard, clean passion of a man from the earth. The blaze of your dynamic eyes makes my heart pound in my bosom, and the touch of your iron-thewed arm maddens me.

'Stay here! I will make you king of Xuthal! I will show you all the ancient mysteries, and the exotic ways of pleasure! I—' She had thrown both arms about his neck and was standing on tiptoe, her vibrant body shivering against his. Over her ivory shoulder he saw Natala, throwing back her damp tousled hair, stop short, her lovely eyes dilating, her red lips parting in a shocked O. With an embarrassed grunt, Conan disengaged Thalis's clinging arms and put her aside with one massive arm. She threw a swift glance at the Brythunian girl and smiled enigmatically, seeming to nod her splendid head in mysterious cogitation.

Natala rose and jerked up her tunic, her eyes blazing, her lips pouting sulkily. Conan swore under his breath. He was no more monogamous in his nature than the average soldier of fortune, but there was an innate decency about him that was Natala's best protection.

Thalis did not press her suit. Beckoning them with her slender hand to follow, she turned and walked across the chamber. There, close to the tapestried wall, she halted suddenly. Conan, watching her, wondered if she had heard the sounds that might be made by a nameless monster stealing through the midnight chambers, and his skin crawled at the thought.

'What do you hear?' he demanded.

'Watch that doorway,' she replied, pointing.

He wheeled, sword ready. Only the empty arch of the entrance met his gaze. Then behind him sounded a quick faint scuffling noise, a half-choked gasp. He whirled. Thalis and Natala had vanished. The tapestry was settling back in place, as if it had been lifted away from the wall. As he gaped bewilderedly, from behind that tapestried wall rang a muffled scream in the voice of the Brythunian girl.

2

When Conan turned, in compliance with Thalis's request, to glare at the doorway opposite, Natala had been standing just behind him, close to the side of the Stygian. The instant the Cimmerian's back was turned, Thalis, with a pantherish quickness almost incredible, clapped her hand over Natala's mouth, stifling the cry she tried to give. Simultaneously the Stygian's other arm was passed about the blond girl's supple waist, and she was jerked back against the wall, which seemed to give way as Thalis' shoulder pressed against it. A section of the wall swung inward, and through a slit that opened in the tapestry Thalis slid with her captive, just as Conan wheeled back.

Inside was utter blackness as the secret door swung to again. Thalis paused to fumble at it for an instant, apparently sliding home a bolt, and as she took her hand from Natala's mouth to perform this act, the Brythunian girl began to scream at the top of her voice. Thalis's laugh was like poisoned honey in the darkness.

'Scream if you will, little fool. It will only shorten your life.'

At that Natala ceased suddenly, and cowered shaking in every limb.

'Why did you do this?' she begged. 'What are you going to do?'

'I am going to take you down this corridor for a short distance,' answered Thalis, 'and leave you for one who will sooner or later come for you.'

'Ohhhhhh!' Natala's voice broke in a sob of terror. 'Why should you harm me? I have never injured you!'

'I want your warrior. You stand in my way. He desires me – I could read the look in his eyes. But for you, he would be willing to stay here and be my king. When you are out of the way, he will follow me.'

'He will cut your throat,' answered Natala with conviction, knowing Conan better than Thalis did.

'We shall see,' answered the Stygian coolly from the confidence of her power over men. 'At any rate, you will not know whether he stabs or kisses me, because you will be the bride of him who dwells in darkness. Come!'

Half mad with terror, Natala fought like a wild thing, but it availed her nothing. With a lithe strength she would not have believed possible in a woman, Thalis picked her up and carried her down the black corridor as if she had been a child. Natala did not scream again, remembering the Stygian's sinister words; the only sounds were her desperate quick panting and Thalis' soft taunting lascivious laughter. Then the Brythunian's fluttering hand closed on something in the dark – a jeweled dagger-hilt jutting from Thalis's gem-crusted girdle. Natala jerked it forth and struck blindly and with all her girlish power.

A scream burst from Thalis's lips, feline in its pain and fury. She reeled, and Natala slipped from her relaxing grasp, to bruise her tender limbs on the smooth stone floor. Rising, she scurried to the nearest wall and stood there panting and trembling, flattening herself against the stones. She could not see Thalis, but she could hear her. The Stygian was quite certainly not dead. She was cursing in a steady stream, and her fury was so concentrated and deadly that Natala felt her bones turn to wax, her blood to ice.

'Where are you, you little she-devil?' gasped Thalis. 'Let me get my fingers on you again, and I'll—' Natala grew physically sick as Thalis described the bodily injuries she intended to inflict on her rival. The Stygian's choice of language would have shamed the toughest courtesan in Aquilonia.

Natala heard her groping in the dark, and then a light sprang up. Evidently whatever fear Thalis felt of the black corridor was submerged in her anger. The light came from one of the radium gems which adorned the walls of Xuthal. This Thalis had rubbed, and now she stood bathed in its reddish glow: a light different from that which the others had emitted. One hand was pressed to her side and blood trickled between the fingers. But she did not seem weakened or badly hurt, and her eyes blazed fiendishly. What little courage remained to Natala ebbed away at sight of the Stygian standing limned in that weird glow, her beautiful face contorted with a passion that was no less than hellish. She now advanced with a pantherish tread, drawing her hand away from her wounded side, and shaking the blood drops impatiently from her fingers. Natala saw that she had not badly harmed her rival. The blade had glanced from the jewels of Thalis's girdle and inflicted only a very superficial flesh-wound, only enough to rouse the Stygian's unbridled fury.

'Give me that dagger, you fool!' she gritted, striding up to the cowering girl.

Natala knew she ought to fight while she had the chance, but she simply could not summon up the courage. Never much of a fighter, the darkness, violence and horror of her adventure had left her limp, mentally and physically. Thalis snatched the dagger from her lax fingers and threw it contemptuously aside.

'You little slut!' she ground between her teeth, slapping the girl viciously with either hand. 'Before I drag you down the corridor and throw you into Thog's jaws I'll have a little of your blood myself! You would dare to knife me – well, for that audacity you shall pay!'

Seizing her by the hair, Thalis dragged her down the corridor a short distance, to the edge of the circle of light. A metal ring showed in the wall, above the level of a man's head. From it depended a silken cord. As in a nightmare Natala felt her tunic being stripped from her, and the next instant Thalis had jerked up her wrists and bound them to the ring, where she hung, naked as the day she was born, her feet barely touching the floor. Twisting her head, Natala saw Thalis unhook a jewel-handled whip from where it hung on the wall, near the ring. The lashes consisted of seven round silk cords, harder yet more pliant than leather thongs.

With a hiss of vindictive gratification, Thalis drew back her arm, and Natala shrieked as the cords curled across her loins. The tortured girl writhed, twisted and tore agonizedly at the thongs which imprisoned her wrists. She had forgotten the lurking menace her cries might summon, and so apparently had Thalis. Every stroke evoked screams of anguish. The whippings Natala had received in the Shemite slave-markets paled to insignificance before this. She had never guessed the punishing power of hard-woven silk cords. Their caress was more exquisitely painful than any birch twigs or leather thongs. They whistled venomously as they cut the air.

Then, as Natala twisted her tear-stained face over her shoulder to shriek for mercy, something froze her cries. Agony gave place to paralyzing horror in her beautiful eyes.

Struck by her expression, Thalis checked her lifted hand and whirled quick as a cat. Too late! An awful cry rang from her lips as she swayed back, her arms upflung. Natala saw her for an instant, a white figure of fear etched against a great black shapeless mass that towered over her; then the white figure was whipped off its feet, the shadow receded with it, and in the circle of dim light Natala hung alone, half fainting with terror.

From the black shadows came sounds, incomprehensible and blood-freezing. She heard Thalis's voice pleading frenziedly, but no voice answered. There was no sound except the Stygian's panting voice, which suddenly rose to screams of agony, and then broke in hysterical laughter, mingled with sobs. This dwindled to a convulsive panting, and presently this too ceased, and a silence more terrible hovered over the secret corridor.

Nauseated with horror, Natala twisted about and dared to look fearfully in the direction the black shape had carried Thalis. She saw nothing, but she sensed an unseen peril, more grisly than she could understand. She fought against a rising tide of hysteria. Her bruised wrists, her smarting body were forgotten in the teeth of this menace which she dimly felt threatened not only her body, but her soul as well.

She strained her eyes into the blackness beyond the rim of the dim light, tense with fear of what she might see. A whimpering gasp escaped her lips. The darkness was taking form. Something huge and bulky grew up out of the void. She saw a great mis-shapen head emerging into the light. At least she took it for a head, though it was not the member of any sane or normal creature. She saw a great toad-like face, the features of which were as dim and unstable as those of a specter seen in a mirror of nightmare. Great pools of light that might have been eyes blinked at her, and she shook at the cosmic lust reflected there. She could tell nothing about the creature's body. Its outline seemed to waver and alter subtly even as she looked at it; yet its substance was apparently solid enough. There was nothing misty or ghostly about it.

As it came toward her, she could not tell whether it walked, wriggled, flew or crept. Its method of locomotion was absolutely beyond her comprehension. When it had emerged from the shadows she was still uncertain as to its nature. The light from the radium gem did not illumine it as it would have illumined an ordinary creature. Impossible as it seemed, the being seemed almost impervious to the light. Its details were still obscure and indistinct, even when it halted so near that it almost touched her shrinking flesh. Only the blinking toad-like face stood out with any distinctness. The thing was a blur in the sight, a black blot of shadow that normal radiance would neither dissipate nor illuminate.

She decided she was mad, because she could not tell whether the being looked up at her or towered above her. She was unable to say whether the dim repulsive face blinked up at her from the shadows at her feet, or looked down at her from an immense height. But if her sight convinced her that whatever its mutable qualities, it was yet composed of solid substance, her sense of feel further assured her of that fact. A dark tentacle-like member slid about her body, and she screamed at the touch of it on her naked flesh. It was neither warm nor cold, rough nor smooth; it was like nothing that had ever touched her before, and at its caress she knew such fear and shame as she had never dreamed of. All the obscenity and salacious infamy spawned in the muck of the abysmal pits of Life seemed to drown her in seas of cosmic filth. And in that instant she knew that whatever form of life this thing represented it was not a beast.

She began to scream uncontrollably, the monster tugged at her as if to tear her from the ring by sheer brutality; then something crashed above their heads, and a form hurtled down through the air to strike the stone floor.

3

When Conan wheeled to see the tapestry settling back in place and to hear Natala's muffled cry, he hurled himself against the wall with a maddened roar. Rebounding from the impact that would have splintered the bones of a lesser man, he ripped away the tapestry revealing what appeared to be a blank wall. Beside himself with fury he lifted his saber as though to hew through the marble, when a sudden sound brought him about, eyes blazing.

A score of figures faced him, yellow men in purple tunics, with shortswords in their hands. As he turned they surged in on him with hostile cries. He made no attempt to conciliate them. Maddened at the disappearance of his sweetheart, the barbarian reverted to type.

A snarl of bloodthirsty gratification hummed in his bull-throat as he leaped, and the first attacker, his short sword overreached by the whistling saber, went down with his brains gushing from his split skull. Wheeling like a cat, Conan caught a descending wrist on his edge, and the hand gripping the short sword flew into the air scattering a shower of red drops. But Conan had not paused or hesitated. A pantherish twist and shift of his body avoided the blundering rush of two yellow swordsmen, and the blade of one missing its objective, was sheathed in the breast of the other.

A yell of dismay went up at this mischance, and Conan allowed himself a short bark of laughter as he bounded aside from a whistling cut and slashed under the guard of yet another man of Xuthal. A long spurt of crimson followed his singing edge and the man crumpled screaming, his belly-muscles cut through.

The warriors of Xuthal howled like mad wolves. Unaccustomed to battle, they were ridiculously slow and clumsy compared to the tigerish barbarian whose motions were blurs of quickness possible only to steel thews knit to a perfect fighting-brain. They floundered and stumbled, hindered by their own numbers; they struck too quick or too soon, and cut only empty air. He was never motionless or in the same place an instant; springing, side-stepping, whirling, twisting, he offered a constantly shifting target for their swords, while his own curved blade sang death about their ears.

But whatever their faults, the men of Xuthal did not lack courage. They swarmed about him yelling and hacking, and through the arched doorways rushed others, awakened from their slumbers by the unwonted clamor.

III

Conan, bleeding from a cut on the temple, cleared a space for an instant with a devastating sweep of his dripping saber, and cast a quick glance about for an avenue of escape. At that instant he saw the tapestry on one of the walls drawn aside, disclosing a narrow stairway. On this stood a man in rich robes, vague-eyed and blinking, as if he had just awakened and had not yet shaken the dusts of slumber from his brain. Conan's sight and action were simultaneous.

A tigerish leap carried him untouched through the hemming ring of swords, and he bounded toward the stair with the pack giving tongue behind him. Three men confronted him at the foot of the marble steps, and he struck them with a deafening crash of steel. There was a frenzied instant when the blades flamed like summer lightning; then the group fell apart and Conan sprang up the stair. The oncoming horde tripped over three writhing forms at its foot: one lay face-down in a sickening welter of blood and brains; another propped himself on his hands, blood spurting blackly from his severed throat veins; the other howled like a dying dog as he clawed at the crimson stump that had been an arm.

As Conan rushed up the marble stair, the man above shook himself from his stupor and drew a sword that sparkled frostily in the radium light. He thrust downward as the barbarian surged upon him. But as the point sang toward his throat, Conan ducked deeply. The blade slit the skin of his back, and Conan straightened, driving his saber upward as a man might wield a butcher-knife, with all the power of his mighty shoulders.

So terrific was his headlong drive that the sinking of the saber to the hilt into the belly of his enemy did not check him. He caromed against the wretch's body, knocking it sideways. The impact sent Conan crashing against the wall; the other, the saber torn through his body, fell headlong down the stair, ripped open to the spine from groin to broken breastbone. In a ghastly mess of streaming entrails the body tumbled against the men rushing up the stairs, bearing them back with it.

*

Half stunned, Conan leaned against the wall an instant, glaring down upon them; then with a defiant shake of his dripping saber, he bounded up the steps.

Coming into an upper chamber, he halted only long enough to see that it was empty. Behind him the horde was yelling with such intensified horror and rage, that he knew he had killed some notable man there on the stair, probably the king of that fantastic city.

He ran at random, without plan. He desperately wished to find and succor Natala, who he was sure needed aid badly; but harried as he was by all the warriors in Xuthal, he could only run on, trusting to luck to elude them and find her. Among those dark or dimly lighted upper chambers he quickly lost all sense of direction, and it was not strange that he eventually blundered into a chamber into which his foes were just pouring.

They yelled vengefully and rushed for him, and with a snarl of disgust he turned and fled back the way he had come. At least he thought it was the way he had come. But presently, racing into a particularly ornate chamber, he was aware of his mistake. All the chambers he had traversed since mounting the stair had been empty. This chamber had an occupant, who rose up with a cry as he charged in.

Conan saw a yellow-skinned woman, loaded with jeweled ornaments but otherwise nude, staring at him with wide eyes. So much he glimpsed as she raised her hand and jerked a silken rope hanging from the wall. Then the floor dropped from under him, and all his steel-trap coordination could not save him from the plunge into the black depths that opened beneath him.

He did not fall any great distance, though it was far enough to have snapped the leg bones of a man not built of steel springs and whalebone.

He hit cat-like on his feet and one hand, instinctively retaining his grasp on his saber hilt. A familiar cry rang in his ears as he rebounded on his feet as a lynx rebounds with snarling bared fangs. So Conan, glaring from under his tousled mane, saw the white naked figure of Natala writhing in the lustful grasp of a black nightmare shape that could have only been bred in the lost pits of hell.

The sight of that awful shape alone might have frozen the Cimmerian with fear. In juxtaposition to his girl, the sight sent a red wave of murderous fury through Conan's brain. In a crimson mist he smote the monster.

It dropped the girl, wheeling toward its attacker, and the maddened Cimmerian's saber, shrilling through the air, sheared clear through the black viscous bulk and rang on the stone floor, showering blue sparks. Conan went to his knees from the fury of the blow; the edge had not encountered the resistance he had expected. As he bounded up, the thing was upon him.

It towered above him like a clinging black cloud. It seemed to flow about him in almost liquid waves, to envelop and engulf him. His madly slashing saber sheared through it again and again, his ripping poniard tore and rent it; he was deluged with a slimy liquid that must have been its sluggish blood. Yet its fury was nowise abated.

He could not tell whether he was slashing off its members or whether he was cleaving its bulk, which knit behind the slicing blade. He was tossed to and fro in the violence of that awful battle, and had a dazed feeling that he was fighting not one, but an aggregation of lethal creatures. The thing seemed to be biting, clawing, crushing and clubbing him all at the same time. He felt fangs and talons rend his flesh; flabby cables that were yet hard as iron encircled his limbs and body, and worse than all, something like a whip of scorpions fell again and again across his shoulders, back and breast, tearing the skin and filling his veins with a poison that was like liquid fire.

They had rolled beyond the circle of light, and it was in utter blackness that the Cimmerian battled. Once he sank his teeth, beast-like, into the flabby substance of his foe, revolting as the stuff writhed and squirmed like living rubber from between his iron jaws.

In that hurricane of battle they were rolling over and over, farther and farther down the tunnel. Conan's brain reeled with the punishment he was taking. His breath came in whistling gasps between his teeth. High above him he saw a great toad-like face, dimly limned in an eery glow that seemed to emanate from it. And with a panting cry that was half curse, half gasp of straining agony, he lunged toward it, thrusting with all his waning power. Hilt-deep the saber sank, somewhere below the grisly face, and a convulsive shudder heaved the vast bulk that half enveloped the Cimmerian. With a volcanic burst of contraction and expansion, it tumbled backward, rolling now with frantic haste down the corridor. Conan went with it, bruised, battered, invincible, hanging on like a bulldog to the hilt of his saber which he could not withdraw, tearing and ripping at the shuddering bulk with the poniard in his left hand, goring it to ribbons.

The thing glowed all over now with a weird phosphorous radiance, and this glow was in Conan's eyes, blinding him, as suddenly the heaving billowing mass fell away from beneath him, the saber tearing loose and remaining in his locked hand. This hand and arm hung down into space, and far below him the glowing body of the monster was rushing downward like a meteor. Conan dazedly realized that he lay on the brink of a great round well, the edge of which was slimy stone. He lay there watching the hurtling glow dwindling and dwindling until it vanished into a dark shining surface that seemed to surge upward to meet it. For an instant a dimming witchfire glimmered in those dusky depths; then it disappeared and Conan lay staring down into the blackness of the ultimate abyss from which no sound came.

4

Straining vainly at the silk cords which cut into her wrists, Natala sought to pierce the darkness beyond the radiant circle. Her tongue seemed frozen to the roof of her mouth. Into that blackness she had seen Conan vanish, locked in mortal combat with the unknown demon, and the only sounds that had come to her straining ears had been the panting gasps of the barbarian, the impact of struggling bodies, and the thud and rip of savage blows. These ceased, and Natala swayed dizzily on her cords, half fainting.

A footstep roused her out of her apathy of horror, to see Conan emerging from the darkness. At the sight she found her voice in a shriek which echoed down the vaulted tunnel. The manhandling the Cimmerian had received was appalling to behold. At every step he dripped blood. His face was skinned and bruised as if he had been beaten with a bludgeon. His lips were pulped, and blood oozed down his face from a wound in his scalp. There were deep gashes in his thighs, calves and forearms, and great bruises showed on his limbs and body from impacts against the stone floor. But his shoulders, back and upper-breast muscles had suffered most. The flesh was bruised, swollen and lacerated, the skin hanging in loose strips, as if he had been lashed with wire whips.

'Oh, Conan!' she sobbed. 'What has happened to you?'

He had no breath for conversation, but his smashed lips writhed in what might have been grim humor as he approached her. His hairy breast, glistening with sweat and blood, heaved with his panting. Slowly and laboriously he reached up and cut her cords, then fell back against the wall and leaned there, his trembling legs braced wide. She scrambled up from where she had fallen and caught him in a frenzied embrace, sobbing hysterically.

'Oh, Conan, you are wounded unto death! Oh, what shall we do?'

'Well,' he panted, 'you can't fight a devil out of hell and come off with a whole skin!'

'Where is it?' she whispered. 'Did you kill it?'

'I don't know. It fell into a pit. It was hanging in bloody shreds, but whether it can be killed by steel I know not.'

'Oh, your poor back!' she wailed, wringing her hands.

'It lashed me with a tentacle,' he grimaced, swearing as he moved. 'It cut like wire and burned like poison. But it was its damnable squeezing that got my wind. It was worse than a python. If half my guts are not mashed out of place, I'm much mistaken.'

'What shall we do?' she whimpered.

He glanced up. The trap was closed. No sound came from above.

'We can't go back through the secret door,' he muttered. 'That room is full of dead men, and doubtless warriors keep watch there. They must have thought my doom sealed when I plunged through the floor above, or else they dare not follow me into this tunnel. – Twist that radium gem off the wall. – As I groped my way back up the corridor I felt arches opening into other tunnels. We'll follow the first we come to. It may lead to another pit, or to the open air. We must chance it. We can't stay here and rot.'

Natala obeyed, and holding the tiny point of light in his left hand and his bloody saber in his right, Conan started down the corridor. He went slowly, stiffly, only his animal vitality keeping him on his feet. There was a blank glare in his bloodshot eyes, and Natala saw him involuntarily lick his battered lips from time to time. She knew his suffering was ghastly, but with the stoicism of the wilds he made no complaint.

Presently the dim light shone on a black arch, and into this Conan turned. Natala cringed at what she might see, but the light revealed only a tunnel similar to that they had just left.

How far they went she had no idea, before they mounted a long stair and came upon a stone door, fastened with a golden bolt.

She hesitated, glancing at Conan. The barbarian was swaying on his feet, the light in his unsteady hand flinging fantastic shadows back and forth along the wall.

'Open the door, girl,' he muttered thickly. 'The men of Xuthal will be waiting for us, and I would not disappoint them. By Crom, the city has not seen such a sacrifice as I will make!'

She knew he was half delirious. No sound came from beyond the door. Taking the radium gem from his blood-stained hand, she threw the bolt and drew the panel inward. The inner side of a cloth-of-gold tapestry met her gaze and she drew it aside and peeked through, her heart in her mouth. She was looking into an empty chamber in the center of which a silvery fountain tinkled.

Conan's hand fell heavily on her naked shoulder.

'Stand aside, girl,' he mumbled. 'Now is the feasting of swords.'

'There is no one in the chamber,' she answered. 'But there is water—'

'I hear it,' he licked his blackened lips. 'We will drink before we die.'

He seemed blinded. She took his darkly stained hand and led him through the stone door. She went on tiptoe, expecting a rush of yellow figures through the arches at any instant.

'Drink while I keep watch,' he muttered.

'No, I am not thirsty. Lie down beside the fountain and I will bathe your wounds.'

'What of the swords of Xuthal?' He continually raked his arm across his eyes as if to clear his blurred sight.

'I hear no one. All is silent.'

He sank down gropingly and plunged his face into the crystal jet, drinking as if he could not get enough. When he raised his head there was sanity in his bloodshot eyes and he stretched his massive limbs out on the marble floor as she requested, though he kept his saber in his hand, and his eyes continually roved toward the archways. She bathed his torn flesh and bandaged the deeper wounds with strips torn from a silk hanging. She shuddered at the appearance of his back; the flesh was discolored, mottled and spotted black and blue and a sickly yellow, where it was not raw. As she worked she sought frantically for a solution to their problem. If they stayed where they were, they would eventually be discovered. Whether the men of Xuthal were searching the palaces for them, or had returned to their dreams, she could not know.

As she finished her task, she froze. Under the hanging that partly concealed an alcove, she saw a hand's breadth of yellow flesh.

Saying nothing to Conan, she rose and crossed the chamber softly, grasping his poniard. Her heart pounded suffocatingly as she cautiously drew aside the hanging. On the dais lay a young yellow woman, naked and apparently lifeless. At her hand stood a jade jar nearly full of peculiar golden-colored liquid. Natala believed it to be the elixir described by Thalis, which lent vigor and vitality to the degenerate Xuthal. She leaned across the supine form and grasped the vessel, her poniard poised over the girl's bosom. The latter did not wake.

With the jar in her possession, Natala hesitated, realizing it would be the safer course to put the sleeping girl beyond the power of waking and raising an alarm. But she could not bring herself to plunge the Cimmerian poniard into that still bosom, and at last she drew back the hanging and returned to Conan, who lay where she had left him, seemingly only partly conscious.

She bent and placed the jar to his lips. He drank, mechanically at first, then with a suddenly roused interest. To her amazement he sat up and took the vessel from her hands. When he lifted his face, his eyes were clear and normal. Much of the drawn haggard look had gone from his features, and his voice was not the mumble of delirium.

'Crom! Where did you get this?'

She pointed. 'From that alcove, where a yellow hussy is sleeping.'

He thrust his muzzle again into the golden liquid.

'By Crom,' he said with a deep sigh, 'I feel new life and power rush like wildfire through my veins. Surely this is the very elixir of Life!'

'We had best go back into the corridor,' Natala ventured nervously. 'We shall be discovered if we stay here long. We can hide there until your wounds heal—'

'Not I,' he grunted. 'We are not rats, to hide in dark burrows. We leave this devil-city now, and let none seek to stop us.'

'But your wounds!' she wailed.

'I do not feel them,' he answered. 'It may be a false strength this liquor has given me, but I swear I am aware of neither pain nor weakness.'

With sudden purpose he crossed the chamber to a window she had not noticed. Over his shoulder she looked out. A cool breeze tossed her tousled locks. Above was the dark velvet sky, clustered with stars. Below them stretched a vague expanse of sand.

'Thalis said the city was one great palace,' said Conan. 'Evidently some of the chambers are built like towers on the wall. This one is. Chance has led us well.'

'What do you mean?' she asked, glancing apprehensively over her shoulder.

'There is a crystal jar on that ivory table,' he answered. 'Fill it with water and tie a strip of that torn hanging about its neck for a handle while I rip up this tapestry.'

She obeyed without question, and when she turned from her task she saw Conan rapidly tying together the long tough strips of silk to make a rope, one end of which he fastened to the leg of the massive ivory table.

'We'll take our chance with the desert,' said he. 'Thalis spoke of an oasis a day's march to the south, and grasslands beyond that. If we reach the oasis we can rest until my wounds heal. This wine is like sorcery. A little while ago I was little more than a dead man; now I am ready for anything. Here is enough silk left for you to make a garment of.'

Natala had forgotten her nudity. The mere fact caused her no qualms, but her delicate skin would need protection from the desert sun. As she knotted the silk length about her supple body, Conan turned to the window and with a contemptuous wrench tore away the soft gold bars that guarded it. Then, looping the loose end of his silk rope about Natala's hips, and cautioning her to hold on with both hands, he lifted her through the window and lowered her the thirty-odd feet to the earth. She stepped out of the loop, and drawing it back up, he made fast the vessels of water and wine, and lowered them to her. He followed them, sliding down swiftly, hand over hand.

As he reached her side, Natala gave a sigh of relief. They stood alone at the foot of the great wall, the paling stars overhead and the naked desert about them. What perils yet confronted them she could not know, but her heart sang with joy because they were out of that ghostly, unreal city.

'They may find the rope,' grunted Conan, slinging the precious jars across his shoulders, wincing at the contact with his mangled flesh. 'They may even pursue us, but from what Thalis said, I doubt it. That way is south,' a bronze muscular arm indicated their course; 'so somewhere in that direction lies the oasis. Come!'

Taking her hand with a thoughtfulness unusual for him, Conan strode out across the sands, suiting his stride to the shorter legs of his companion. He did not glance back at the silent city, brooding dreamily and ghostlily behind them.

'Conan,' Natala ventured finally, 'when you fought the monster, and later, as you came up the corridor, did you see anything of – of Thalis?'

He shook his head. 'It was dark in the corridor; but it was empty.'

She shuddered. 'She tortured me – yet I pity her.'

'It was a hot welcome we got in that accursed city,' he snarled. Then his grim humor returned. 'Well, they'll remember our visit long enough, I'll wager. There are brains and guts and blood to be cleaned off the marble tiles, and if their god still lives, he carries more wounds than I. We got off light, after all: we have wine and water and a good chance of reaching a habitable country, though I look as if I've gone through a meat-grinder, and you have a sore—'

'It's all your fault,' she interrupted. 'If you had not looked so long and admiringly at that Stygian cat—'

'Crom and his devils!' he swore. 'When the oceans drown the world, women will take time for jealousy. Devil take their conceit! Did I tell the Stygian to fall in love with me? After all, she was only human!'

DRUMS OF TOMBALKU

(Draft)

I

Three men squatted beside the water hole, beneath the sunset sky that painted the desert umber and red. Two were Ghanatas, desert warriors, their tatters scarcely concealing their wiry dark frames. Men called them Gobir and Saidu; they looked like vultures as they crouched beside the water hole. The third was yellow-haired and gray-eyed; he was called Amalric.

Nearby a camel ground its cud noisily, and a pair of weary horses vainly nuzzled the bare sand. The men munched dried dates cheerlessly, the desert men intent only on the working of their jaws, Amalric occasionally glancing at the dull red sky, or out across the level monotony where the shadows were gathering and deepening. He was first to see the horseman who rode up and drew rein with a jerk that set the steed rearing.

The rider was a dark-skinned giant. His wide silk pantaloons were gathered in about his bare ankles. They were supported by a broad girdle wrapped repeatedly about his huge belly; that girdle also supported a flaring-tipped scimitar few men could wield with one hand. With that scimitar the man was famed wherever the sons of the desert rode. He was Tilutan, the pride of the Ghanata.

Across his saddle bow a limp shape lay, or rather hung. Breath hissed through the teeth of the Ghanatas as they caught the gleam of smooth, white limbs. A girl hung across Tilutan's saddle bow, face down, her loose hair flowing over his stirrup in a rippling black wave. The giant grinned with a glint of white teeth, and cast her casually onto the sand, where she lay laxly, unconscious. Instinctively Gobir and Saidu turned toward Amalric, and Tilutan watched him from his saddle. Three Ghanatas and an outlander. The entrance of a woman into the scene wrought a subtle change in the atmosphere.

Almaric was the only one who was apparently oblivious to the tenseness. He raked back his rebellious yellow locks absently, and glanced indifferently at the girl's limp figure. If there was a momentary gleam in his grey eyes, the others did not catch it.

Tilutan swung down from his saddle, contemptuously tossing the rein to Amalric.

'Tend my horse,' he said. 'By Jhil, I did not find a desert antelope, but I found this little filly. She was reeling through the sands, and she fell just as I approached. I think she fainted from weariness and thirst. Get away from there, you jackals, and let me give her a drink.'

The big man stretched her out beside the water hole and began laving her face and wrists, trickling a few drops between her parched lips. She moaned presently and stirred vaguely. Gobir and Saidu crouched with their hands on their knees, staring at her over Tilutan's burly shoulder. Amalric stood a little apart from them, his interest seeming only casual.

'She is coming to,' announced Gobir.

Saidu said nothing, but he licked his lips involuntarily, animal-like.

Amalric's gaze travelled impersonally over the prostrate form, from the torn sandals to the loose crown of glossy black hair. Her only garment was a silk kirtle, girdled at the waist. It left her arms, neck and part of her bosom bare, and the skirt ended several inches above her knees. On the parts revealed rested the gaze of the Ghanatas with devouring intensity, taking in the soft contours, childish in their white tenderness, yet rounded with budding womanhood.

Amalric shrugged his shoulders.

'After Tilutan, who?' he asked carelessly.

A pair of lean heads turned toward him, bloodshot eyes rolled at the question, then the Ghanatas turned and mutually stared at one another. Sudden rivalry crackled electrically between them.

'Cast the dice,' urged Amalric. 'No need to fight.' His hand came from under his worn tunic, and he threw down a pair of dice before them. A claw-like hand seized them.

'Aye!' agreed Gobir. 'We cast – after Tilutan, the winner!'

Amalric cast a glance toward the giant who still bent above his captive, bringing life back into her exhausted body. As he looked, her long-lashed lids parted. Deep violet eyes stared up into the leering face bewilderedly. An explosive exclamation of gratification escaped the thick lips of Tilutan. Wrenching a flask from his girdle, he put it to her mouth. She drank the wine mechanically. Amalric avoided her wandering gaze. He was one man and the three Ghanatas were all his match.

Gobir and Saidu bent above the dice; Saidu cupped them in his palm, breathed on them for luck, shook and threw. Two vulture-like heads bent over the spinning cubes in the dim light. And Amalric drew and struck with the same motion. The edge sliced through a thick neck, severing the windpipe, and Gobir fell across the dice, spurting blood, his head hanging by a shred.

Simultaneously, Saidu, with the desperate quickness of a desert man, shot to his feet and hacked ferociously at the slayer's head. Amalric barely had time to catch the stroke on his lifted sword. The whistling scimitar beat the straight blade down on Amalric's head, staggering him. He released his sword and threw both arms about Saidu, dragging him into close quarters where his scimitar was useless. Under the desert man's rags, the wiry frame was like steel cords.

Tilutan, comprehending the matter instantly, had cast the girl down and risen with a roar. He rushed toward the struggling pair like a charging bull, his great scimitar flaming in his hand. Amalric saw him coming, and his flesh turned cold. Saidu was jerking and wrenching, handicapped by the scimitar he was still seeking futilely to turn against his antagonist. Their feet twisted and stamped in the sand, their bodies ground against one another. Amalric smashed his sandal heel down on the Ghanata's bare instep, feeling bones give way. Saidu howled and plunged convulsively, and Amalric gave a desperate heave. The pair lurched drunkenly about, just as Tilutan struck with a rolling drive of his broad shoulders. Amalric felt the steel rasp the under part of his arm, and chug deep into Saidu's body. The Ghanata gave an agonized scream, and his convulsive start tore himself free of Amalric's grasp. Tilutan roared a ferocious oath and, wrenching his steel free, hurled the dying man aside. Before he could srike again, Amalric, his skin crawling with the fear of that great curved blade, had grappled with him.

Despair swept over him as he felt the strength of the warrior. Tilutan was wiser than Saidu. He dropped the scimitar and with a bellow, caught Amalric's throat with both hands. The great fingers locked like iron, and Amalric, striving vainly to break their grip, was borne down, with the Ghanata's great weight pinning him to the earth. The smaller man was shaken like a rat in the jaws of a dog. His head was smashed savagely against the sandy earth. As in a red mist he saw the furious face of his opponent, lips writhed back in a bestial grin of hate, teeth glistening. An inhuman snarling slavered from his thick throat.

'You want her, you dog!' the Ghanata mouthed, insane with rage and lust. 'Arrrrghhh! I break your back! I tear out your throat! I – my scimitar! I cut off your head and make her kiss it!'

A final ferocious smash of Amalric's head against the hardpacked sand, and Tilutan half-lifted him and hurled him down in an excess of bestial passion. Rising, the man ran, stooping like an ape, and caught up his scimitar where it lay like a broad crescent of steel in the sand. Yelling in ferocious exultation, he turned and charged back, brandishing the blade on high. Amalric rose slowly to meet him, dazed, shaken, sick from the manhandling he had received.

Tilutan's girdle had become unwound in the fight, and now the end dangled about his feet. He tripped, stumbled, fell headlong, throwing out his arms to save himself. The scimitar flew from his hand.

Amalric, galvanized, caught up the scimitar and took a reeling step forward. The desert swam darkly to his gaze. In the dusk before him he saw Tilutan's face suddenly ashy. The wide mouth gaped, the whites of the eyeballs rolled up. The giant froze on one knee and a hand, as if incapable of further motion. Then the scimitar fell, cleaving the round, shaven head to the chin, where its downward course was checked with a sickening jerk. Amalric had a dim impression of a face divided by a widening red line, fading in the thickening shadows. Then darkness caught him with a rush.

Something soft and cool was touching Amalric's face with gentle persistence. He groped blindly and his hand closed on something warm, firm and resilient. Then his sight cleared and he looked into a soft oval face, framed in lustrous black hair. As in a trance he gazed unspeaking, hungrily dwelling on each detail of the full red lips, dark violet eyes, and alabaster throat. With a start he realized the vision was speaking in a soft musical voice. The words were strange, yet possessed an illusive familiarity. A small white hand holding a dripping bunch of silk was passed gently over his throbbing head and face. He sat up dizzily.

It was night, under the star-splashed skies. The camel still munched its cud; a horse whinnied restlessly. Not far away lay a hulking dark figure with its cleft head in a horrible puddle of blood and brains. Amalric looked up at the girl who knelt beside him, talking in her gentle, unknown tongue. As the mists cleared from his brain, he began to understand her. Harking back into half-forgotten tongues he had learned and spoken in the past, he remembered a language used by a scholarly class in a southern province of Koth.

'Who are you, girl?' he demanded, prisoning a small hand in his own hardened fingers.

'I am Lissa.' The name was spoken with almost the suggestion of a lisp. It was like the rippling of a slender stream.

'I am glad you are conscious. I feared you were not alive.'

'A little more and I wouldn't have been,' he muttered, glancing at the grisly sprawl that had been Tilutan. She paled, refusing to follow his gaze. Her hand trembled, and in their nearness, Amalric thought he could feel the quick throb of her heart.

'It was horrible,' she faltered. 'Like an awful dream. Anger – and blows – and blood—'

'It might have been worse,' he growled.

She seemed sensitive to every changing inflection of his voice or mood. Her free hand stole timidly to his arm.

'I did not mean to offend you. It was very brave for you to risk your life for a stranger. You are noble as the knights about which I have read.'

He cast a quick glance at her. Her wide clear eyes met his, reflecting only the thought she had spoken. He started to speak, then changed his mind and said another thing.

'What are you doing in the desert?'

'I came from Gazal,' she answered. 'I – I was running away. I could not stand it any longer. But it was hot and lonely and weary, and I saw only sand, sand – and the blazing blue sky. The sands burned my feet, and my sandals were worn out quickly. I was so thirsty, my canteen was soon empty. And then I wished to return to Gazal, but one direction looked like another. I did not know which way to go. I was terribly afraid, and started running in the direction in which I thought Gazal to be. I do not remember much after that. I ran until I could run no further, and I must have lain in the burning sand for a while. I remember rising and staggering on, and toward the last I thought I heard someone shouting, and saw a huge man on a black horse riding toward me, and then I knew no more until I awoke and found myself lying with my head in that man's lap, while he gave me wine to drink. Then there was shouting and fighting—' She shuddered. 'When it was all over, I crept to where you lay like a dead man, and I tried to bring you to—'

'Why?' he demanded.

She seemed at a loss. 'Why,' she floundered, 'why, you were hurt – and – why, it is what anyone would do. Besides, I realized that you were fighting to protect me from these men. The people of Gazal have always said that the desert people were wicked and would harm the helpless.'

'That's no exclusive characteristic,' muttered Amalric. 'Where is this Gazal?'

'It can not be far,' she answered. 'I walked a whole day – and then I do not know how far the warrior carried me after he found me. But he must have discovered me about sunset, so he could not have come far.'

'In what direction?' he demanded.

'I do not know. I travelled eastward when I left the city.'

'City?' he muttered. 'A day's travel from this spot? I had thought there was only desert for a thousand miles.'

'Gazal is in the desert,' she answered. 'It is built amidst the palms of an oasis.'

Putting her aside, he got to his feet, swearing softly as he fingered his throat, the skin of which was bruised and lacerated. He examined the three Ghanatas in turn, finding no sign of life in them. Then, one by one, he dragged them a short distance out into the desert. Somewhere the jackals were yelping. Returning to the water hole where the girl squatted patiently, he cursed to find only the black stallion of Tilutan with the camel. The other horses had broken their tethers and bolted during the fight.

Amalric went to the girl and proffered her a handful of dried dates. She nibbled at them eagerly, while the other sat and watched her, his chin on his fists, an increasing impatience throbbing in his veins.

'Why did you run away?' he asked abruptly. 'Are you a slave?'

'We have no slaves in Gazal,' she answered. 'Oh, I was weary – so weary of the eternal monotony. I wished to see something of the outer world. Tell me, from what land do you come?'

'I was born in the western hills of Aquilonia,' he answered.

She clapped her hands like a delighted child.

'I know where it is! I have seen it on the maps. It is the western-most country of the Hyborians, and its king is Epeus the Sword-wielder!'

Amalric experienced a distinct shock. His head jerked up and he stared at his fair companion.

'Epeus? Why, Epeus has been dead for nine hundred years. The king's name is Vilerus.'

'Oh, of course,' she said, rather embarrassedly. 'I am foolish. Of course, Epeus was king nine centuries ago, as you say. But tell me – tell me all about the world!'

'Why, that is a big order,' he answered nonplussed. 'You have not travelled?'

'This is the very first time that I have ever been out of sight of the walls of Gazal,' she admitted to him.

His gaze was fixed on the curve of her white bosom. He was not interested in her adventures at the moment, and Gazal might have been Hell for all he cared.

He started to speak, then changing his mind caught her roughly in his arms, his muscles tensing for the struggle he expected. But he encountered no resistance. Her soft, yielding body lay across his knees, and she looked up at him somewhat in surprise, but without fear or embarrassment. She might have been a child submitting to a new kind of play. Something about her direct gaze confused him. If she had screamed, wept, fought, or smiled knowingly, he would have known how to deal with her.

'Who in Mitra's name are you, girl?' he asked roughly. 'You are neither touched with the sun, nor playing a game with me. Your speech shows you to be no ignorant country lass, innocent in ignorance. Yet you seem to know nothing of the world and its ways.'

'I am a daughter of Gazal,' she answered helplessly. 'If you saw Gazal, perhaps you would understand.'

He lifted her and placed her on the sand. Rising, he brought a saddle blanket and set it out for her.

'Sleep, Lissa,' he said, his voice harsh with conflicting emotions. 'Tomorrow I mean to see Gazal.'

At dawn they started westward. Amalric had lifted Lissa onto the camel, showing her how to maintain her balance. She clung to the seat with both hands, showing no knowledge whatever of camels, which again surprized the young Aquilonian. A girl raised in the desert, she had never before been on a camel, nor, until the preceding night, had she ever ridden or been carried on a horse. Amalric had manufactured a sort of cloak for her, and she wore it without question, not asking whence it came, accepting it as she accepted all things he did for her, gratefully but blindly, without asking the reason. Amalric did not tell her that the silk that shielded her from the sun had once covered the skin of her abductor.

As they rode she again begged him to tell her something of the world, like a child asking for a story.

'I know Aquilonia is far from this desert,' she said. 'Stygia lies between, and the Lands of Shem, and other countries. How is it that you are here, so far from your homeland?'

He rode for a space in silence, his hand on the camel's guide-rope.

'Argos and Stygia were at war,' he said abruptly. 'Koth became embroiled. The Kothians urged a simultaneous invasion of Stygia. Argos raised an army of mercenaries, which went into ships and sailed southward along the coast. At the same time, a Kothic army was to invade Stygia by land. I was one of that mercenary army. We met the Stygian fleet and defeated it, driving it back into Khemi. We should have landed, looted the city, and advanced along the course of the Styx – but our admiral was cautious. Our leader was Prince Zapayo da Kova, a Zingaran. We cruised southward until we reached the jungle-clad coasts of Kush. There we landed, and the ships anchored, while the army pushed eastward along the Stygian frontier, burning and pillaging as we went. It was our intention to turn northward at a certain point and strike into the heart of Stygia to form a juncture with the Kothic host which was supposed to be pushing down from the north. Then word came that we were betrayed. Koth had concluded a separate peace with the Stygians. A Stygian army was pushing southward to intercept us, while another already had cut us off from the coast.

'Prince Zapayo, in desperation, conceived the mad idea of marching eastward, hoping to skirt the Stygian border and eventually reach the eastern lands of Shem. But the army from the north overtook us. We turned and fought. All day we fought, and finally they gave before us, their retreat turning into rout. But the next day the pursuing army came up from the west, and crushed between the hosts, our army ceased to be. We were broken, annihilated, destroyed. There were few left to flee. But when night fell, I broke away with my companion, a Cimmerian named Conan, a brute of a man with the strength of a bull.

'We rode southward into the desert, because there was no

other direction in which we might go. Conan had been in this part of the world before, and he believed we had a chance to survive. Far to the south we found an oasis, but Stygian riders harried us, and we fled again, from oasis to oasis, fleeing, starving, thirsting, until we found ourselves in a barren, unknown land of blazing and empty sand. We rode until our horses were reeling, and we were half delirious. Then one night we saw fires and rode up to them, taking a desperate chance that we might make friends. As soon as we came within range, a shower of arrows greeted us. Conan's horse was hit and it reared, throwing its rider. His neck must have broken like a twig, for he never moved. I got away in the darkness, somehow, though my horse died under me. I had only a glance at the attackers. They were tall, lean brown men, wearing strange, barbaric garments. I wandered on foot through the desert, and fell in with those three vultures you saw yesterday. They were jackals – Ghanatas – members of a robber tribe of mixed blood. The only reason they didn't murder me was because I had nothing they wished. For a month I have been wandering and thieving with them because there was nothing else I could do.'

'I did not know it was like that,' Lissa murmured faintly. 'They said there were wars and cruelty out in the world, but it seemed like a dream and far away. Listening to you speak of treachery and battle seems almost like seeing it.'

'Do no enemies ever come against Gazal?' he demanded.

She shook her head. 'Men ride wide of Gazal. Sometimes I have seen black dots moving in lines along the horizon, and the old men said they were armies moving to war. But they never come near to Gazal.'

Amalric felt a dim stirring of uneasiness. This desert, seemingly empty of life, nevertheless contained some of the fiercest tribes on earth – the Ghanatas, who ranged far to the east; the masked Tibu, whom he believed dwelt further to the south; and somewhere off to the southwest lay the semi-mythical empire of Tombalku, ruled by a wild and barbaric race. It was strange that a city in the midst of this savage land should be left so completely alone that one of its inhabitants did not even know the meaning of war.

When he turned his gaze elsewhere, strange thoughts assailed him. Was the girl touched by the sun? Was she a demon in womanly form come out of the desert to lure him to some cryptic doom? A glance at her clinging childishly to the high peak of the camel saddle was sufficient to dispel these broodings. Then again doubt assailed him. Was he bewitched? Had she cast a spell on him?

Westward they forged steadily, halting only to nibble dates and drink water at midday. Amalric fashioned a frail shelter out of his sword and sheath and the saddle blankets to shield her from the burning sun. Weary and stiff from the tossing, bucking gait of the camel, she had to be lifted down in his arms. As he felt again the voluptuous sweetness of her soft body, he felt a hot throb of passion sear through him, and he stood momentarily motionless, intoxicated with the nearness of her, before he laid her down in the shade of the makeshift tent.

He felt a touch of almost anger at the clear gaze with which she met his, at the docility with which she yielded her young body to his hands. It was as if she were unaware of things which might harm her; her innocent trust shamed him and pent a helpless wrath within him.

As they ate, he did not taste the dates he munched; his eyes burned on her, avidly drinking in every detail of her lithe young figure. She seemed as unaware of his intentness as a child. When he lifted her to place her again on the camel, and her arms went instinctively about his neck, he shuddered. But he lifted her up on her mount, and they took up the journey once more.

It was just before sundown when Lissa pointed and cried out: 'Look! The towers of Gazal!'

On the desert rim he saw them – spires and minarets, rising in a jade-green cluster against the blue sky. But for the girl, he would have thought it the phantom city of a mirage. He glanced at Lissa curiously. She showed no signs of eager joy at her homecoming. Instead, she sighed, and her slim shoulders seemed to droop.

As they approached, the details swam more plainly into view. Sheer from the desert sands rose the wall which enclosed the towers. And Amalric saw that the wall was crumbling in many places. The towers, too, he saw, were much in disrepair. Roofs sagged, broken battlements gaped, spires leaned drunkenly. Panic assailed him; was it a city of the dead to which he rode, guided by a vampire? A quick glance at the girl reassured him. No demon could lurk in that divinely molded exterior. She glanced at him with a strange and wistful questioning in her deep eyes, turned resolutely toward the desert, then, with a deep sigh, set her face toward the city, as if gripped by a subtle and fatalistic despair.

Now through the gaps of the jade-green wall, Amalric saw figures moving within the city. No one hailed them as they rode through a broad breach in the wall, and came out into a broad street. Close at hand, limned in the sinking sun, the decay was more apparent. Grass grew rank in the streets, pushing through shattered paving; grass grew rank in the small plazas. Streets and courts likewise were littered with rubbish of masonry and fallen stones.

Domes rose, cracked and discolored. Portals gaped, vacant of doors. Everywhere ruin had laid his hand. Then Amalric saw one spire untouched; a shining red cylindrical tower which rose in the extreme southeastern corner of the city.

It shone among the ruins, and Amalric pointed to it.

'Why is that tower less in ruins than the others?' he asked. Lissa turned pale; she trembled and caught his hand convulsively.

'Do not speak of it!' she whispered. 'Do not look toward it – do not even *think* of it!'

Amalric scowled; the nameless implication of her words somehow changed the aspect of the mysterious tower. Now it seemed like a serpent's head rearing among ruin and desolation.

The young Aquilonian looked warily about him. After all, he had no assurance that the people of Gazal would receive him in a friendly manner. He saw people moving leisurely about the streets. They halted and stared at him, and for some reason his flesh crawled. They were men and women with kindly features, and their looks were mild. But their interest seemed so slight – so vague and impersonal. They made no movement to approach him or to speak to him. It might have been the most common thing in the world for an armed horseman to ride into their city from the desert; yet Amalric knew that was not the case, and the casual manner in which the people of Gazal received him caused a faint uneasiness in his bosom.

Lissa spoke to them, indicating Amalric, whose hand she lifted like an affectionate child. 'This is Amalric of Aquilonia, who rescued me from the desert people and has brought me home.'

A polite murmur of welcome rose from the people, and several of them approached to extend their hands. Amalric thought he had never seen such vague, kindly faces. Their eyes were soft and mild, without fear and without wonder. Yet they were not the eyes of stupid oxen; rather, they were the eyes of people wrapped in dreams.

Their stare gave him a feeling of unreality; he hardly knew what was said to him. His mind was occupied by the strangeness of it all; these quiet, dreamy people in their silken tunics and soft sandals, moving with aimless vagueness among the discolored ruins. A lotus paradise of illusion? Somehow, the thought of that sinister red tower struck a discordant note.

One of the men, his face smooth and unlined, but his hair silver, was saying: 'Aquilonia? There was an invasion – we heard – King Bragorus of Nemedia – how went the war?'

'He was driven back,' answered Amalric briefly, resisting a shudder. Nine hundred years had passed since Bragorus led his spearmen across the marches of Aquilonia.

His questioner did not press him further; the people drifted away, and Lissa tugged at his hand. He turned, feasted his eyes upon her; in a realm of illusion and dream, her soft firm body anchored his wandering conjectures. She was no dream; she was real; her body was sweet and tangible as cream and honey.

'Come, let us go to rest and eat.'

'What of the people?' he demurred. 'Will you not tell them of your experiences?'

'They would not heed, except for a few minutes,' she answered. 'They would listen a little, and then drift away. They hardly know I have been gone. Come!'

Amalric led the horse and camel into an enclosed court where the grass grew high, and water seeped from a broken fountain into a marble trough. There he tethered them, and then turned to Lissa. Taking his hand, she led him across the court into an arched doorway. Night had fallen. In the open space above the court, the stars were clustering, etching the jagged pinnacles. Through a series of dark chambers Lissa went, moving with the sureness of long practice. Amalric groped after her, guided by her little hand in his. He found it no pleasant adventure. The scent of dust and decay hung in the thick darkness. At times, what felt like broken tiles underfoot caused him to move carefully. At other times there was the softness of worn carpets. His free hand touched the fretted arches of doorways. Then the stars gleamed through a broken roof, showing him a dim, winding hallway hung with rotting tapestries. They rustled in a faint wind, and their noise was like the whispering of witches, causing the hair to stir next his scalp.

Then they came into a chamber dimly lighted by the starshine streaming through open windows. Lissa released his hand, fumbled an instant, and produced a faint light of some sort. It was a glassy knob which glowed with a golden radiance. She set it on a marble table and indicated that Amalric should recline on a couch thickly littered with silks. Groping into some mysterious recess, she produced a gold vessel of wine and others containing food unfamiliar to Amalric. There were dates, but the other food, which he did not recognize, was pallid and insipid to his taste. The wine was pleasant to the palate, but no more heady than dish water.

Seated on a marble seat opposite him, Lissa nibbled daintily.

'What sort of place is this?' he demanded. 'You are like these people – yet strangely unlike.'

'They say I am like our ancestors,' answered Lissa. 'Long ago they came into the desert and built this city over a great oasis which was in reality only a series of springs. The stone they took from the ruins of a much older city – only the red tower—' her voice dropped and she glanced nervously at the star-framed windows – 'only the red tower stood there. It was empty – then.

'Our ancestors, who were called Gazali, once dwelt in the southern part of Koth. They were noted for their scholarly wisdom. But they sought to revive the worship of Mitra which the Kothians had long ago abandoned, and the king drove them from his kingdom. They came southward, many of them, priests, scholars, teachers, scientists, along with their Shemitish slaves.

'They reared Gazal in the desert; but the slaves revolted almost as soon as the city was built and, fleeing, mixed with the wild tribes of the desert. They were not treated badly, but word came to them in the night – a word which sent them fleeing madly from the city into the desert.

'My people dwelt here, learning to manufacture their food and drink from such material as was at hand. Their learning was a marvel. When the slaves fled, they took with them every camel, horse and donkey in the city. There was no communication with the outer world. There are whole chambers in Gazal that are filled with maps and books and chronicles. But they are all nine hundred years old, at the least, for it was nine hundred years ago that my people fled from Koth. Since then, no man of the outside world has set forth in Gazal. And the people are slowly vanishing. They have become so dreamy and introspective that they have neither human passions nor ambitions. The city falls into ruins and none moves hand to repair it. Horror—' she choked, and shuddered, 'when horror came upon them, they could neither flee nor fight.'

'What do you mean?' he whispered, a cold wind blowing on his spine. The rustling of rotten hangings down nameless black corridors stirred dim fear in his soul.

She shook her head, rose, and came around the marble table. She laid hands on his shoulders. Her eyes were wet and shone with horror and a desperate yearning that caught at his throat. Instinctively, his arm went around her lithe form, and he felt her tremble.

'Hold me!' she begged. 'I am afraid! Oh, I have dreamed of such a man as you. I am not like my people; they are dead men walking forgotten streets; but I am alive. I am warm and sentient. I hunger and thirst and yearn for life. I cannot abide the silent streets and ruined halls and dim people of Gazal, though I have never known anything else. That is why I ran away – I yearned for life—'

She was sobbing uncontrollably in his arms. Her hair streamed over his face; her fragrance made him dizzy. Her firm body strained against him. She was lying across his knees, her arms locked about his neck. Straining her to his breast, he crushed her lips with his. Eyes, lips, cheeks, hair, throat, breasts, he showered with hot kisses, until her sobs changed to panting gasps. The passion that slumbered in her woke in one overpowering wave. The glowing gold ball, struck by his groping fingers, tumbled to the floor and was extinguished. Only the starshine gleamed through the windows.

Lying in Amalric's arms on the silk-heaped couch, Lissa opened her heart and whispered her dreams and hopes and aspirations, childish, pathetic, terrible.

'I'll take you away,' he muttered. 'Tomorrow. You are right. Gazal is a city of the dead; we will seek life and the outer world. It is violent, rough, and cruel, but it is better than this living death—'

The night was broken by a shuddering cry of agony, horror and despair. Its timbre brought out cold sweat on Amalric's skin. He started upright from the couch, but Lissa clung to him desperately.

'No, no!' she begged in a frantic whisper. 'Do not go! Stay!'

'But murder is being done!' he exclaimed, fumbling for his sword. The cries seemed to come from across an outer court. Mingled with them there was an indescribable tearing, rending sound. They rose higher and thinner, unbearable in their hopeless agony, then sank away in a long, shuddering sob.

'I have heard men dying on the rack cry out like that!' muttered Amalric, shaking with horror. 'What devil's work is this?'

Lissa was trembling violently in a frenzy of terror. He felt the wild pounding of her heart.

'It is the Horror of which I spoke!' she whispered. 'The Horror which dwells in the red tower. Long ago it came – and some say it dwelt there in the lost years and returned after the building of

Gazal. It devours human beings. What it is, no one knows, since none have seen it and lived to tell. It is a god or a devil. That is why the slaves fled; why the desert people shun Gazal. Many of us have gone into its awful belly. Eventually, all will have gone, and it will rule over an empty city, as men say it ruled over the ruins from which Gazal was reared.'

'Why have the people stayed to be devoured?' he demanded.

'I do not know,' she whimpered; 'they dream—'

'Hypnosis,' muttered Amalric; 'hypnosis coupled with decay. I saw it in their eyes. This devil has them mesmerized. Mitra, what a foul secret!'

Lissa pressed her face against his bosom and clung to him.

'But what are we to do?' he asked uneasily.

'There is nothing to do,' she whispered. 'Your sword would be helpless. Perhaps it will not harm us. It has taken a victim tonight. We must wait like sheep for the butcher.'

'I'll be damned if I will!' Amalric exclaimed, galvanized. 'We will not wait for morning. We'll go tonight. Make a bundle of food and drink. I'll get the horse and camel and bring them to the court outside. Meet me there!'

Since the unknown monster had already struck, Amalric felt that he was safe in leaving the girl alone for a few minutes. But his flesh crawled as he groped his way down the winding corridor and through the black chambers where the swinging tapestries whispered. He found the beasts huddled nervously together in the court where he had left them. The stallion whinnied anxiously and nuzzled him, as if sensing peril in the breathless night.

He saddled and bridled and hurriedly led them through the narrow opening onto the street. A few minutes later he was standing in the starlit court. And even as he reached it; he was electrified by an awful scream which rang shudderingly upon the air. It came from the chamber where he had left Lissa.

He answered that piteous cry with a wild yell; drawing his sword, he rushed across the court and hurled himself through the window. The golden ball was glowing again, carving out black shadows in the shrinking corners. Silks lay scattered on the floor. The marble seat was upset. But the chamber was empty.

A sick weakness overcame Amalric and he staggered against the marble table, the dim light waving dizzily to his sight. Then he was swept by a mad rage. The red tower! There the fiend would bear his victim!

He darted across the court, found the streets and raced toward the tower which glowed with an unholy light under the stars. The streets did not run straight. He cut through silent black buildings and crossed courts whose rank grass waved in the night wind.

Ahead of him, clustered about the crimson tower, rose a heap of ruins where decay had eaten more savagely than at the rest of the city. Apparently none dwelt among them. They reeled and tumbled, a crumbling mass of quaking masonry, with the red tower rearing up among them like a poisonous red flower from charnel-house ruin.

To reach the tower he would be forced to traverse the ruins. Recklessly, he plunged into the black mass, groping for a door. He found one and entered, thrusting his sword ahead of him. Then he saw such a vista as men sometimes see in fantastic dreams. Far ahead of him stretched a long corridor, visible in a faint, unhallowed glow, its black walls hung with strange shuddersome tapestries. Far down it he saw a receding figure – a white, naked, stooped figure, lurching along, dragging something the sight of which filled him with sweating horror. Then the apparition vanished from his sight, and with it vanished the eery glow. Amalric stood in the soundless dark, seeing nothing, hearing nothing; thinking only of that stooped white figure that dragged a limp human being down a long, black corridor.

As he groped onward, a vague memory stirred in his brain – the memory of a grisly tale mumbled to him over a dying fire in the skull-heaped, devil-devil hut of a black witchman – a tale of a god which dwelt in a crimson house in a ruined city and which was worshipped by darksome cults in dank jungles and along sullen dusky rivers. And there stirred, too, in his mind an incantation whispered in his ear in awed and shuddering tones, while the night had held its breath, the lions had ceased to roar along the river, and the very fronds had ceased their scraping one against the other.

Ollam-onga, whispered a dark wind down the sightless corridor. *Ollam-onga* whispered the dust that ground beneath his stealthy feet. Sweat stood on his skin and the sword shook in his hand. He stole through the house of a god, and fear held him by its bony hand. *The house of the god* – the full horror of the phrase filled his mind. All the ancestral fears and the fears that reached beyond ancestry and primordial race-memory crowded upon him; horror cosmic and unhuman sickened him. His weak humanity crushed him in its realization as he went through the house of darkness that was the house of a god.

About him shimmered a glow so faint that it was scarcely discernible; he knew that he was approaching the tower itself. Another instant and he groped his way through an arched door and stumbled upon strangely spaced steps. Up them he went and, as he climbed, that blind fury which is mankind's last defence against diabolism and all the hostile forces of the universe, surged in him, and he forgot his fear. Burning with terrible eagerness, he climbed up and up through the thick, evil darkness until he came into a chamber lit by a weird glow.

And before him stood a white, naked figure. Amalric halted, his tongue cleaving to his palate. It was a naked white man, to all appearance, who stood there, gazing at him with mighty arms folded on an alabaster breast. The features were classic, cleanly carven, with more than human beauty. But the eyes were balls of luminous fire, such as never looked from any human head. In those eyes, Amalric glimpsed the frozen fires of the ultimate hells, touched by awful shadows.

Then before him the form began to grow dim in outline – to waver. With a terrible effort, the Aquilonian burst the bonds of silence and spoke a cryptic and awful incantation. And as the frightful words cut the silence, the white giant halted – froze – again his outlines stood out clear and bold against the golden background.

'Now fall on, damn you!' cried Amalric hysterically. 'I have bound you into your human shape! The black wizard spoke truly! It was the master word he gave me! Fall on, *Ollam-onga* – till you break the spell by feasting on my heart, you are no more than a man like me!'

With a roar that was like the gust of a whirlwind, the creature charged. Amalric sprang aside from the clutch of those hands whose strength was more than that of a giant. A single taloned finger, spread wide and catching in his tunic, ripped the garment from him like a rotten rag as the monster plunged by. But Amalric, nerved to more than human quickness by the horror of the fight, wheeled and drove his sword through the thing's back, so that the point stood out a foot from the broad breast.

A fiendish howl of agony shook the tower; the monster whirled and rushed at Amalric, but the youth sprang aside and raced up the stairs to the dais. There he wheeled and, catching up a marble seat, hurled it down upon the horror that was lumbering up the stairs. Full in the face the massive missile struck, carrying the fiend back down the steps. He rose, an awful sight, streaming blood and again essayed the stairs. In desperation, Amalric lifted a jade bench whose weight wrenched a groan of effort from him, and hurled it.

Beneath the impact of the hurtling bulk, Ollam-onga pitched back down the stair and lay among the marble shards, which were flooded with his blood. With a last, desperate effort, he heaved himself up on his hands, eyes glazing, and throwing back his bloody head, voiced an awful cry. Amalric shuddered and recoiled from the abysmal horror of that scream. *And it was answered*. From somewhere in the air above the tower a faint medley of fiendish cries came back like an echo. Then the mangled white figure went limp among the blood-stained shards. And Amalric knew that one of the gods of Kush was no more. With the thought came blind, unreasoning horror.

In a fog of terror he rushed down the stair, shrinking from the thing that lay staring on the floor. The night seemed to cry out against him, aghast at the sacrilege. Reason, exultant over his triumph, was submerged in a flood of cosmic fear.

As he put foot on the head of the steps, he halted short. Up from the darkness Lissa came to him, her white arms outstretched, her eyes pools of horror and revulsion.

'Amalric!' It was a haunting cry. He crushed her in his arms.

'I saw *It*,' she whimpered – 'dragging a dead man through the corridor. I screamed and fled; then when I returned, I heard you cry out and knew you had gone to search for me in the red tower—'

'And you came to share my fate,' his voice was almost inarticulate. Then, as she tried to peer in trembling fascination past him, he covered her eyes with his hands and turned her about. Better that she should not see what lay on the crimson floor. As he half led, half carried her down the shadowed stairs, a glance over his shoulder showed him that a naked white figure lay no longer among the broken marble. The incantation had bound Ollam-onga into his human form in life, but not in death. Blindness momentarily assailed Amalric; then, galvanized into frantic haste, he hurried Lissa down the stairs and through the dark ruins.

He did not slacken pace until they reached the street where the camel and stallion huddled against one another. Quickly he placed the girl on the camel and swung up on the stallion. Taking the lead-line, he headed straight for the broken wall. A few minutes later he breathed gustily. The open air of the desert cooled his blood; it was free of the scent of decay and hideous antiquity.

There was a small water-pouch hanging from his saddle bow. They had no food, and his sword was in the chamber of the red tower. He had not dared touch it. Without food and unarmed, they faced the desert, but its peril seemed less grim than the horror of the city behind them.

Without speaking they rode. Amalric headed south; somewhere in that direction there was a water hole. Just at dawn, as they mounted a crest of sand, he looked back toward Gazal, unreal in the pink light. And he stiffened as Lissa, sharing his vision, cried out. From a breach in the wall rode seven horsemen; their steeds were black, and the riders were cloaked in black from head to foot. Horror swept over Amalric as he realized there had been no horses in Gazal. Turning, he urged their mounts on.

The sun rose, red, and then gold, and then a ball of white-beaten flame. On and on the fugitives pressed, reeling with heat and fatigue, blinded by the glare. They moistened their lips with water from time to time, and behind them, at an even pace, rode seven black dots. Evening began to fall, and the sun reddened and lurched toward the desert rim. And a cold hand clutched at Amalric's heart. The riders were closing in. As darkness came on, so came the black riders. Amalric glanced at Lissa, and a groan burst from him. His stallion stumbled and fell. The sun had gone down, the moon was blotted out suddenly by a bat-shaped shadow. In the utter darkness the stars glowed red, and behind him Amalric heard a rising rush as of an approaching wind. A black, speeding clump bulked against the night, in which glinted sparks of awful light.

'Ride girl!' he cried despairingly. 'Go on – save yourself; it is me they want!'

For answer she slid down from the camel and threw her arms about him.

'I will die with you!'

Seven black shapes loomed against the stars, racing like the wind. Under the hoods shone balls of evil fire. Jaw bones seemed to clack together. Suddenly, a horse swept past Amalric, a vague bulk in the unnatural darkness. There was the sound of an impact as the unknown steed caromed among the oncoming shapes. A horse screamed in frenzy, and a bull-like voice bellowed in a strange tongue. From somewhere in the night a clamor of yells answered.

Some sort of violent action was taking place. Horse's hoofs stamped and clattered. There was the impact of savage blows, and the same stentorian voice was cursing lustily. Then the moon abruptly came out and lit a fantastic scene.

A man on a giant horse whirled, slashed and smote apparently at thin air, and from another direction swept a wild horde of riders, their curved swords flashing in the moonlight. Away over the crest of a rise, seven black figures were vanishing, their cloaks floating out like the wings of bats.

Amalric was swamped by wild men who leaped from their horses and swarmed around him. Sinewy, naked arms pinioned him; fierce brown, hawk-like faces snarled at him. Lissa screamed. Then the attackers were thrust right and left as the man on the great horse reined through the crowd. He bent from his saddle and glared closely at Amalric.

'The devil!' he roared. 'Amalric the Aquilonian!'

'Conan!' Amalric exclaimed bewilderedly. 'Conan! Alive!'

'More alive than you seem to be,' answered the other. 'By Crom, man, you look as if all the devils in this desert had been hunting you through the night. What things were those pursuing you? I was riding around the camp my men had pitched to make sure no enemies were in hiding, when the moon went out like a candle, and then I heard sounds of flight. I rode towards the sounds and, by Crom, I was among those devils before I knew what was happening. I had my sword in my hand and I laid about me – by Crom, their eyes blazed like fire in the dark! I know my edge bit them, but when the moon came out, they were gone like a puff of wind. Were they men or fiends?'

'Ghouls sent up from Hell,' shuddered Amalric. 'Ask me no more; there are some things that cannot be discussed.'

Conan did not press the matter, nor did he look incredulous. His beliefs included night fiends, ghosts, hobgoblins and dwarfs.

'Trust you to find a woman, even in a desert,' he said, glancing at Lissa, who had crept to Amalric and was clinging close to him, glancing fearfully at the wild figures which hemmed them in.

'Wine!' roared Conan. 'Bring flasks! Here!' He seized a leather flask from those who thrust it out to him, and placed it in Amalric's hand. 'Give the girl a swig and drink some yourself,' he advised. 'Then we'll put you on horses and take you to the camp. You need food, rest and sleep. I can see that.'

A richly caparisoned horse was brought, rearing and prancing, and willing hands helped Amalric into the saddle. Then the girl was handed up to him, and they moved off southward, surrounded by the wiry brown riders in their picturesque semi-nakedness. Conan rode ahead, humming a riding song of the mercenaries.

'Who is he?' whispered Lissa, her arms about her lover's neck; he was holding her on the saddle in front of him.

'Conan, the Cimmerian,' muttered Amalric. 'The man I wandered with in the desert after the defeat of the mercenaries. These are the men who struck him down. I left him lying under their spears, apparently dead. Now we meet him obviously in command of, and respected by them.'

'He is a terrible man,' she whispered.

He smiled. 'You never saw a white-skinned barbarian before. He is a wanderer and a plunderer and a slayer, but he has his own code of morals. I don't think we have anything to fear from him.'

In his heart he was not sure. In a way, it might be said that he had forfeited Conan's comradeship when he had ridden away into the desert, leaving the Cimmerian senseless on the ground. But he had not known that Conan was alive. Doubt haunted Amalric. Savagely loyal to his companions, the Cimmerian's wild nature saw no reason why the rest of the world should not be plundered. He lived by the sword. And Amalric suppressed a shudder as he thought of what might chance did Conan desire Lissa.

Later on, having eaten and drunk in the camp of the riders, Amalric sat by a small fire in front of Conan's tent; Lissa, covered with a silken cloak, slumbered with her curly head on his knees. And across from him the firelight played on Conan's face, interchanging lights and shadows.

'Who are these men?' asked the young Aquilonian.

'The riders of Tombalku,' answered the Cimmerian.

'Tombalku!' exclaimed Amalric. 'Then it is no myth.'

'Far from it!' agreed Conan. 'When my accursed steed fell with me, I was knocked senseless, and when I recovered consciousness the devils had me bound hand and foot. This angered me, so I snapped several of the cords they had tied me with, but they rebound them as fast as I could break them – never did I get a hand entirely free. But to them my strength seemed remarkable—'

Amalric gazed at Conan unspeaking. The man was tall and broad as Tilutan had been, without the dead man's surplus flesh. He could have broken the Ghanata's neck with his naked hands.

'They decided to carry me to their city instead of killing me out of hand,' Conan went on. 'They thought a man like me should be a long time in dying by torture, and so give them sport. Well, they bound me on a horse without a saddle, and we went to Tombalku.

'There were two kings of Tombalku. They took me before them – one a lean, brown-skinned devil named Zehbeh, the other a big, hulking black who dozed on his ivory-tusk throne. They spoke a dialect I could understand a little, it being much like that of the western Mandingo who dwell on the coast. Zehbeh asked one of his priests what should be done with me, and the priest cast dice made of sheep bone, and said I should be flayed alive before the altar of Jhil. Everyone cheered and that woke the other king.

'I spat at the priest and cursed him roundly, and the kings as well, telling them that if I were to be skinned, by Crom, I wanted a good belly-full of wine before they began. Then I damned them for thieves and cowards and sons of harlots.

'At this the black king roused and sat up to stare at me. Then he rose and shouted: "Amra!" and I knew him – Sakumbe, a Suba from the Black Coast, a fat adventurer I had known well in the days when I was a corsair along the coast. He trafficked in ivory, gold dust and slaves, and would cheat the devil out of his eye-teeth. Well, he knew me and descended from his throne and embraced me for joy – the fat, smelly devil – and took my cords off with his own hands. Then he announced that I was Amra, the Lion, his friend, and that no harm should come to me. Then followed much discussion because Zehbeh and his priest, Daura, wanted my life. But Sakumbe yelled for his witch-finder, Askia, and he came, all feathers and bells and snake-skins – a wizard of the Black Coast, and a son of the devil if there ever was one.

'Askia pranced and made incantations, and announced that Sakumbe was the chosen of Ajujo, the Dark One, and all the black people of Tombalku shouted, and Zehbeh backed down.

'The blacks in Tombalku are the real power. Several centuries ago, the Aphaki, a Shemitish race, pushed into the southern desert and established the kingdom of Tombalku. They mixed with the desert blacks and the result was a brown, straight-haired race. They are the dominant caste in Tombalku, but they are in the minority, and Sakumbe is the real ruler of Tombalku. The Aphaki worship Jhil, but the blacks worship Ajujo the Dark One, and his kin. Askia came to Tombalku with Sakumbe and revived the worship of Ajujo, which was crumbling because of the Aphaki priests. Askia made black magic which defeated the wizardry of the Aphaki, and the blacks hailed him as a prophet sent by the dark gods. Sakumbe and Askia wax as Zehbeh and Daura wane.

'Well, as I am Sakumbe's friend, and Askia spoke for me, the blacks received me with great applause. Sakumbe had Kordofo, the general of the horsemen, poisoned, and gave me his place, which delighted the blacks and exasperated the Aphaki.

'You will like Tombalku! It was made for men like us to loot! There are half a dozen powerful factions plotting and intriguing against each other – there are continual brawls in the taverns and streets, secret murders, mutilations and executions. And there are women, gold, wine – all that a mercenary wants! By Crom, Amalric, you could not have come at a better time! I am high in favor and power! Why, what's the matter? You do not seem as enthusiastic as I remember you having once been in such matters.'

'I crave your pardon, Conan,' apologized Amalric. 'I do not lack interest, but weariness and want of sleep overcomes me.'

But it was not of gold, women and intrigue that the Aquilonian was thinking, but of the girl who slumbered on his lap. There was no joy in the thought of taking her into such a welter of intrigue and blood as Conan had described. A subtle change had come over Amalric, almost without his knowledge.

THE POOL OF THE BLACK ONE

Into the west, unknown of man,
Ships have sailed since the world began.
Read, if you dare, what Skelos wrote,
With dead hands fumbling his silken coat;
And follow the ships through the wind-blown wrack—
Follow the ships that come not back.

1

Sancha, once of Kordava, yawned daintily, stretched her supple limbs luxuriously, and composed herself more comfortably on the ermine-fringed silk spread on the carack's poop-deck. That the crew watched her with burning interest from waist and forecastle she was lazily aware, just as she was also aware that her short silk kirtle veiled little of her voluptuous contours from their eager eyes. Wherefore she smiled insolently and prepared to snatch a few more winks before the sun, which was just thrusting his golden disk above the ocean, should dazzle her eyes.

But at that instant a sound reached her ears unlike the creaking of timbers, thrum of cordage and lap of waves. She sat up, her gaze fixed on the rail, over which, to her amazement, a dripping figure clambered. Her dark eyes opened wide, her red lips parted in an O of surprise. The intruder was a stranger to her. Water ran in rivulets from his great shoulders and down his heavy arms. His single garment – a pair of bright crimson silk breeks – was soaking wet, as was his broad gold-buckled girdle and the sheathed sword it supported. As he stood at the rail, the rising sun etched him like a great bronze statue. He ran his fingers through his streaming black mane, and his blue eyes lit as they rested on the girl.

'Who are you?' she demanded. 'Whence did you come?'

He made a gesture toward the sea that took in a whole quarter of the compass, while his eyes did not leave her supple figure.

'Are you a merman, that you rise up out of the sea?' she asked, confused by the candor of his gaze, though she was accustomed to admiration.

Before he could reply, a quick step sounded on the boards, and the master of the carack was glaring at the stranger, fingers twitching at sword-hilt.

'Who the devil are you, sirrah?' this one demanded in no friendly tone.

'I am Conan,' the other answered imperturbably. Sancha pricked up her ears anew; she had never heard Zingaran spoken with such an accent as the stranger spoke it.

'And how did you get aboard my ship?' The voice grated with suspicion.

'I swam.'

'Swam!' exclaimed the master angrily. 'Dog, would you jest with me? We are far beyond sight of land. Whence do you come?'

Conan pointed with a muscular brown arm toward the east, banded in dazzling gold by the lifting sun.

'I came from the Islands.'

'Oh!' The other regarded him with increased interest. Black brows drew down over scowling eyes, and the thin lip lifted unpleasantly.

'So you are one of those dogs of the Barachans.'

A faint smile touched Conan's lips.

'And do you know who I am?' his questioner demanded.

'This ship is the *Wastrel*; so you must be Zaporavo.'

'Aye!' It touched the captain's grim vanity that the man should know him. He was a tall man, tall as Conan, though of leaner build. Framed in his steel morion his face was dark, saturnine and hawk-like, wherefore men called him the Hawk. His armor and garments were rich and ornate, after the fashion of a Zingaran grandee. His hand was never far from his sword-hilt.

There was little favor in the gaze he bent on Conan. Little love was lost between Zingaran renegades and the outlaws who infested the Baracha Islands off the southern coast of Zingara. These men were mostly sailors from Argos, with a sprinkling of other nationalities. They raided the shipping, and harried the Zingaran coast towns, just as the Zingaran buccaneers did, but these dignified their profession by calling themselves Freebooters, while they dubbed the Barachans pirates. They were neither the first nor the last to gild the name of thief.

Some of these thoughts passed through Zaporavo's mind as he toyed with his sword-hilt and scowled at his uninvited guest. Conan gave no hint of what his own thoughts might be. He stood with folded arms as placidly as if upon his own deck; his lips smiled and his eyes were untroubled.

'What are you doing here?' the Freebooter demanded abruptly.

'I found it necessary to leave the rendezvous at Tortage before moonrise last night,' answered Conan. 'I departed in a leaky boat, and rowed and bailed all night. Just at dawn I saw your topsails, and left the miserable tub to sink, while I made better speed in the water.'

'There are sharks in these waters,' growled Zaporavo, and was vaguely irritated by the answering shrug of the mighty shoulders. A glance toward the waist showed a screen of eager faces staring upward. A word would send them leaping up on the poop in a storm of swords that would overwhelm even such a fighting-man as the stranger looked to be.

'Why should I burden myself with every nameless vagabond that the sea casts up?' snarled Zaporavo, his look and manner more insulting than his words.

'A ship can always use another good sailor,' answered the other without resentment. Zaporavo scowled, knowing the truth of that assertion. He hesitated, and doing so, lost his ship, his command, his girl, and his life. But of course he could not see into the future, and to him Conan was only another wastrel, cast up, as he put it, by the sea. He did not like the man; yet the fellow had given him no provocation. His manner was not insolent, though rather more confident than Zaporavo liked to see.

'You'll work for your keep,' snarled the Hawk. 'Get off the poop. And remember, the only law here is my will.'

The smile seemed to broaden on Conan's thin lips. Without hesitation but without haste he turned and descended into the waist. He did not look again at Sancha, who, during the brief conversation, had watched eagerly, all eyes and ears.

As he came into the waist the crew thronged about him – Zingarans, all of them, half naked, their gaudy silk garments splashed with tar, jewels glinting in ear-rings and dagger-hilts. They were eager for the time-honored sport of baiting the stranger. Here he would be tested, and his future status in the crew decided. Up on the poop Zaporavo had apparently already forgotten the stranger's existence, but Sancha watched, tense with interest. She had become familiar with such scenes, and knew the baiting would be brutal and probably bloody.

But her familiarity with such matters was scanty compared to that of Conan. He smiled faintly as he came into the waist and saw the menacing figures pressing truculently about him. He paused and eyed the ring inscrutably, his composure unshaken. There was a certain code about these things. If he had attacked the captain, the whole crew would have been at his throat, but they would give him a fair chance against the one selected to push the brawl.

The man chosen for this duty thrust himself forward – a wiry brute, with a crimson sash knotted about his head like a turban. His lean chin jutted out, his scarred face was evil beyond belief. Every glance, each swaggering movement was an affront. His way of beginning the baiting was as primitive, raw and crude as himself.

'Baracha, eh?' he sneered. 'That's where they raise dogs for men. We of the Fellowship spit on 'em – like this!'

He spat in Conan's face and snatched at his own sword.

The Barachan's movement was too quick for the eye to follow. His sledge-like fist crunched with a terrible impact against his tormentor's jaw, and the Zingaran catapulted through the air and fell in a crumpled heap by the rail.

Conan turned towards the others. But for a slumbering glitter in his eyes, his bearing was unchanged. But the baiting was over as suddenly as it had begun. The seamen lifted their companion; his broken jaw hung slack, his head lolled unnaturally.

'By Mitra, his neck's broken!' swore a black-bearded sea-rogue.

'You Freebooters are a weak-boned race,' laughed the pirate. 'On the Barachas we take no account of such taps as that. Will you play at sword-strokes, now, any of you? No? Then all's well, and we're friends, eh?'

There were plenty of tongues to assure him that he spoke truth. Brawny arms swung the dead man over the rail, and a dozen fins cut the water as he sank. Conan laughed and spread his mighty arms as a great cat might stretch itself, and his gaze sought the deck above. Sancha leaned over the rail, red lips parted, dark eyes aglow with interest. The sun behind her outlined her lithe figure through the light kirtle which its glow made transparent. Then across her fell Zaporavo's scowling shadow and a heavy hand fell possessively on her slim shoulder. There were menace and meaning in the glare he bent on the man in the waist; Conan grinned back, as if at a jest none knew but himself.

Zaporavo made the mistake so many autocrats make; alone in somber grandeur on the poop, he underestimated the man below him. He had his opportunity to kill Conan, and he let it pass, engrossed in his own gloomy ruminations. He did not find it easy to think any of the dogs beneath his feet constituted a menace to him. He had stood in the high places so long, and had ground so many foes underfoot, that he unconsciously assumed himself to be above the machinations of inferior rivals.

Conan, indeed, gave him no provocation. He mixed with the crew, lived and made merry as they did. He proved himself a skilled sailor, and by far the strongest man any of them had seen. He did the work of three men, and was always first to spring to any heavy or dangerous task. His mates began to rely upon him. He did not quarrel with them, and they were careful not to quarrel with him. He gambled with them, putting up his girdle and sheath for a stake, won their money and weapons, and gave them back with a laugh. The crew instinctively looked toward him as the leader of the forecastle. He vouchsafed no information as to what had caused him to flee the Barachas, but the knowledge that he was capable of a deed bloody enough to have exiled him from that wild band increased the respect felt toward him by the fierce Freebooters. Toward Zaporavo and the mates he was imperturbably courteous, never insolent or servile.

The dullest was struck by the contrast between the harsh, taciturn, gloomy commander, and the pirate whose laugh was gusty and ready, who roared ribald songs in a dozen languages, guzzled ale like a toper, and – apparently – had no thought for the morrow.

Had Zaporavo known he was being compared, even though unconsciously, with a man before the mast, he would have been speechless with amazed anger. But he was engrossed with his broodings, which had become blacker and grimmer as the years crawled by, and with his vague grandiose dreams; and with the girl whose possession was a bitter pleasure, just as all his pleasures were.

And she looked more and more at the black-maned giant who towered among his mates at work or play. He never spoke to her, but there was no mistaking the candor of his gaze. She did not mistake it, and she wondered if she dared the perilous game of leading him on.

No great length of time lay between her and the palaces of Kordava, but it was as if a world of change separated her from the life she had lived before Zaporavo tore her screaming from the flaming caravel his wolves had plundered. She, who had been the spoiled and petted daughter of the Duke of Kordava, learned what it was to be a buccaneer's plaything, and because she was supple enough to bend without breaking, she lived where other women had died, and because she was young and vibrant with life, she came to find pleasure in the existence.

The life was uncertain, dream-like, with sharp contrasts of battle, pillage, murder, and flight. Zaporavo's red visions made it even more uncertain than that of the average Freebooter. No one knew what he planned next. Now they had left all charted coasts behind and were plunging further and further into that unknown billowy waste ordinarily shunned by seafarers, and into which, since the beginnings of Time, ships had ventured, only to vanish from the sight of man for ever. All known lands lay behind them, and day upon day the blue surging immensity lay empty to their sight. Here there was no loot – no towns to sack nor ships to burn. The men murmured, though they did not let their murmurings reach the ears of their implacable master, who tramped the poop day and night in gloomy majesty, or pored over ancient charts and time-yellowed maps, reading in tomes that were crumbling masses of worm-eaten parchment. At times he talked to Sancha, wildly it seemed to her, of lost continents, and fabulous isles dreaming unguessed amidst the blue foam of nameless gulfs, where horned dragons guarded treasures gathered by pre-human kings, long, long ago.

Sancha listened, uncomprehending, hugging her slim knees, her thoughts constantly roving away from the words of her grim companion back to a clean-limbed bronze giant whose laughter was gusty and elemental as the sea wind.

So, after many weary weeks, they raised land to westward, and at dawn dropped anchor in a shallow bay, and saw a beach which was like a white band bordering an expanse of gently grassy slopes, masked by green trees. The wind brought scents of fresh vegetation and spices, and Sancha clapped her hands with glee at the prospect of adventuring ashore. But her eagerness turned to sulkiness when Zaporavo ordered her to remain aboard until he sent for her. He never gave any explanation for his commands; so she never knew his reason, unless it was the lurking devil in him that frequently made him hurt her without cause.

So she lounged sulkily on the poop and watched the men row ashore through the calm water that sparkled like liquid jade in the morning sunlight. She saw them bunch together on the sands, suspicious, weapons ready, while several scattered out through the trees that fringed the beach. Among these, she noted, was Conan. There was no mistaking that tall brown figure with its springy step.

Men said he was no civilized man at all, but a Cimmerian, one of those barbaric tribesmen who dwelt in the gray hills of the far North, and whose raids struck terror in their southern neighbors. At least, she knew that there was something about him, some super-vitality or barbarism that set him apart from his wild mates.

Voices echoed along the shore, as the silence reassured the buccaneers. The clusters broke up, as men scattered along the beach in search of fruit. She saw them climbing and plucking among the trees, and her pretty mouth watered. She stamped a little foot and swore with a proficiency acquired by association with her blasphemous companions.

The men on shore had indeed found fruit, and were gorging on it, finding one unknown golden-skinned variety especially luscious. But Zaporavo did not seek or eat fruit. His scouts having found nothing indicating men or beasts in the neighborhood, he stood staring inland, at the long reaches of grassy slopes melting into one another. Then, with a brief word, he shifted his sword-belt and strode in under the trees. His mate expostulated with him against going alone, and was rewarded by a savage blow in the mouth. Zaporavo had his reasons for wishing to go alone. He desired to learn if this island were indeed that mentioned in the mysterious *Book of Skelos*, whereon, nameless sages aver, strange monsters guard crypts filled with hieroglyph-carven gold. Nor, for murky reasons of his own, did he wish to share his knowledge, if it were true, with any one, much less his own crew.

Sancha, watching eagerly from the poop, saw him vanish into the leafy fastness. Presently she saw Conan, the Barachan, turn, glance briefly at the men scattered up and down the beach; then the pirate went quickly in the direction taken by Zaporavo, and likewise vanished among the trees.

Sancha's curiosity was piqued. She waited for them to reappear, but they did not. The seamen still moved aimlessly up and down the beach, and some had wandered inland. Many had lain down in the shade to sleep. Time passed and she fidgeted about restlessly. The sun began to beat down hotly, in spite of the canopy above the poop-deck. Here it was warm, silent, draggingly monotonous;

a few yards away across a band of blue shallow water, the cool shady mystery of tree-fringed beach and woodland-dotted meadow beckoned her. Moreover, the mystery concerning Zaporavo and Conan tempted her.

She well knew the penalty for disobeying her merciless master, and she sat for some time, squirming with indecision. At last she decided that it was worth even one of Zaporavo's whippings to play truant, and with no more ado she kicked off her soft leather sandals, slipped out of her kirtle and stood up on the deck naked as Eve. Clambering over the rail and down the chains, she slid into the water and swam ashore. She stood on the beach a few moments, squirming as the sands tickled her small toes, while she looked for the crew. She saw only a few, at some distance up or down the beach. Many were fast asleep under the trees, bits of golden fruit still clutched in their fingers. She wondered why they should sleep so soundly, so early in the day.

None hailed her as she crossed the white girdle of sand and entered the shade of the woodland. The trees, she found, grew in irregular clusters, and between these groves stretched rolling expanses of meadow-like slopes. As she progressed inland, in the direction taken by Zaporavo, she was entranced by the green vistas that unfolded gently before her, soft slope beyond slope, carpeted with green sward and dotted with groves. Between the slopes lay gentle declivities, likewise swarded. The scenery seemed to melt into itself, or each scene into the other; the view was singular, at once broad and restricted. Over all a dreamy silence lay like an enchantment.

Then she came suddenly onto the level summit of a slope, circled with tall trees, and the dreamily faery-like sensation vanished abruptly at the sight of what lay on the reddened and trampled grass. Sancha involuntarily cried out and recoiled, then stole forward, wide-eyed, trembling in every limb.

It was Zaporavo who lay there on the sward, staring sightlessly upward, a gaping wound in his breast. His sword lay near his nerveless hand. The Hawk had made his last swoop.

It is not to be said that Sancha gazed on the corpse of her lord without emotion. She had no cause to love him, yet she felt at least the sensation any girl might feel when looking on the body of the man who was first to possess her. She did not weep or feel any need of weeping, but she was seized by a strong trembling, her blood seemed to congeal briefly, and she resisted a wave of hysteria.

She looked about her for the man she expected to see. Nothing met her eyes but the ring of tall, thickly leafed forest giants, and the blue slopes beyond them. Had the Freebooter's slayer dragged himself away, mortally wounded? No bloody tracks led away from the body.

Puzzled, she swept the surrounding trees, stiffening as she caught a rustle in the emerald leaves that seemed not to be of the wind. She went toward the trees, staring into the leafy depths.

'Conan?' Her call was inquiring; her voice sounded strange and small in the vastness of silence that had grown suddenly tense.

Her knees began to tremble as a nameless panic swept over her.

'Conan!' she cried desperately. 'It is I – Sancha! Where are you? Please, Conan—' Her voice faltered away. Unbelieving horror dilated her brown eyes. Her red lips parted to an inarticulate scream. Paralysis gripped her limbs; where she had such desperate need of swift flight, she could not move. She could only shriek wordlessly.

2

When Conan saw Zaporavo stalk alone into the woodland, he felt that the chance he had watched for had come. He had eaten no fruit, nor joined in the horse-play of his mates; all his faculties were occupied with watching the buccaneer chief. Accustomed to Zaporavo's moods, his men were not particularly surprised that their captain should choose to explore an unknown and probably hostile isle alone. They turned to their own amusement, and did not notice Conan when he glided like a stalking panther after the chieftain.

Conan did not underrate his dominance of the crew. But he had not gained the right, through battle and foray, to challenge the captain to a duel to the death. In these empty seas there had been no opportunity for him to prove himself according to Freebooter law. The crew would stand solidly against him if he attacked the chieftain openly. But he knew that if he killed Zaporavo without their knowledge, the leaderless crew would not be likely to be swayed by loyalty to a dead man. In such wolf-packs only the living counted.

So he followed Zaporavo with sword in hand and eagerness in his heart, until he came out onto a level summit, circled with tall trees, between whose trunks he saw the green vistas of the slopes melting into the blue distance. In the midst of the glade Zaporavo, sensing pursuit, turned, hand on hilt.

The buccaneer swore.

'Dog, why do you follow me?'

'Are you mad, to ask?' laughed Conan, coming swiftly toward his erstwhile chief. His lips smiled, and in his blue eyes danced a wild gleam.

Zaporavo ripped out his sword with a black curse, and steel clashed against steel as the Barachan came in recklessly and wide open, his blade singing a wheel of blue flame about his head.

Zaporavo was the veteran of a thousand fights by sea and by land. There was no man in the world more deeply and thoroughly versed than he in the lore of swordcraft. But he had never been pitted against a blade wielded by thews bred in the wild lands beyond the borders of civilization. Against his fighting-craft was matched blinding speed and strength impossible to a civilized man. Conan's manner of fighting was unorthodox, but instinctive and natural as that of a timber wolf. The intricacies of the sword were as useless against his primitive fury as a human boxer's skill against the onslaughts of a panther.

Fighting as he had never fought before, straining every last ounce of effort to parry the blade that flickered like lightning about his head, Zaporavo in desperation caught a full stroke near his hilt, and felt his whole arm go numb beneath the terrific impact. That stroke was instantly followed by a thrust with such terrible drive behind it that the sharp point ripped through chain-mail and ribs like paper, to transfix the heart beneath. Zaporavo's lips writhed in brief agony, but, grim to the last, he made no sound. He was dead before his body relaxed on the trampled grass, where blood drops glittered like spilt rubies in the sun.

Conan shook the red drops from his sword, grinned with unaffected pleasure, stretched like a huge cat – and abruptly stiffened, the expression of satisfaction on his face being replaced by a stare of bewilderment. He stood like a statue, his sword trailing in his hand.

As he lifted his eyes from his vanquished foe, they had absently rested on the surrounding trees, and the vistas beyond. And he had seen a fantastic thing – a thing incredible and inexplicable. Over the soft rounded green shoulder of a distant slope had loped a tall black naked figure, bearing on its shoulder an equally naked white form. The apparition vanished as suddenly as it had appeared, leaving the watcher gasping in surprise.

The pirate stared about him, glanced uncertainly back the way he had come, and swore. He was nonplussed – a bit upset, if the term might be applied to one of such steely nerves as his. In the midst of realistic, if exotic surroundings, a vagrant image of fantasy and nightmare had been introduced. Conan doubted neither his eyesight nor his sanity. He had seen something alien and uncanny, he knew; the mere fact of a black figure racing across the landscape carrying a white captive was bizarre enough, but this black figure had been unnaturally tall.

Shaking his head doubtfully, Conan started off in the direction in which he had seen the thing. He did not argue the wisdom of his move; with his curiosity so piqued, he had no choice but to follow its promptings.

Slope after slope he traversed, each with its even sward and clustered groves. The general trend was always upward, though he ascended and descended the gentle inclines with monotonous regularity. The array of rounded shoulders and shallow declivities was bewildering and apparently endless. But at last he advanced up what he believed was the highest summit on the island, and halted at the sight of green shining walls and towers, which, until he had reached the spot on which he then stood, had merged so perfectly with the green landscape as to be invisible, even to his keen sight.

He hesitated, fingered his sword, then went forward, bitten by the worm of curiosity. He saw no one as he approached a tall archway in the curving wall. There was no door. Peering warily through, he saw what seemed to be a broad open court, grass-carpeted, surrounded by a circular wall of the green semi-translucent substance. Various arches opened from it. Advancing on the balls of his bare feet, sword ready, he chose one of these arches at random, and passed into another similar court. Over an inner wall he saw the pinnacles of strangely shaped tower-like structures. One of these towers was built in, or projected into the court in which he found himself, and a broad stair led up to it, along the side of the wall. Up this he went, wondering if it were all real, or if he were not in the midst of a black lotus dream.

At the head of the stair he found himself on a walled ledge, or balcony, he was not sure which. He could now make out more details of the towers, but they were meaningless to him. He realized uneasily that no ordinary human beings could have built them. There was symmetry about their architecture, and system, but it was a mad symmetry, a system alien to human sanity. As for the plan of the whole town, castle, or whatever it was intended for, he could see just enough to get the impression of a great number of courts, mostly circular, each surrounded by its own wall, and connected with the others by open arches, and all, apparently, grouped about the cluster of fantastic towers in the center.

Turning in the other direction from these towers, he got a fearful shock, and crouched down suddenly behind the parapet of the balcony, glaring amazedly.

The balcony or ledge was higher than the opposite wall, and he was looking over that wall into another swarded court. The inner curve of the further wall of that court differed from the others he had seen, in that, instead of being smooth, it seemed to be banded with long lines or ledges, crowded with small objects the nature of which he could not determine.

However, he gave little heed to the wall at the time. His attention was centered on the band of beings that squatted about a dark green pool in the midst of the court. These creatures were black and naked, made like men, but the least of them, standing upright, would have towered head and shoulders above the tall pirate. They were rangy rather than massive, but were finely formed, with no suggestion of deformity or abnormality, save as their great height was abnormal. But even at that distance Conan sensed the basic diabolism of their features.

In their midst, cringing and naked, stood a youth that Conan recognized as the youngest sailor aboard the *Wastrel*. He, then, had been the captive the pirate had seen borne across the grass-covered slope. Conan had heard no sound of fighting – saw no blood-stains or wounds on the sleek ebon limbs of the giants. Evidently the lad had wandered inland away from his companions and been snatched up by a black man lurking in ambush. Conan mentally termed the creatures black men, for lack of a better term; instinctively he knew that these tall ebony beings were not men, as he understood the term.

No sound came to him. The blacks nodded and gestured to one another, but they did not seem to speak – vocally, at least. One, squatting on his haunches before the cringing boy, held a pipe-like thing in his hand. This he set to his lips, and apparently blew, though Conan heard no sound. But the Zingaran youth heard or felt, and cringed. He quivered and writhed as if in agony; a regularity became evident in the twitching of his limbs, which quickly became rhythmic. The twitching became a violent jerking, the jerking regular movements. The youth began to dance, as cobras dance by compulsion to the tune of the faquir's fife. There was naught of zest or joyful abandon in that dance. There was, indeed, abandon that was awful to see, but it was not joyful. It was as if the mute tune of the pipes grasped the boy's inmost soul with salacious fingers and with brutal torture wrung from it every involuntary expression of secret passion. It was a convulsion of obscenity, a spasm of lasciviousness – an exudation of secret hungers framed by compulsion: desire without pleasure, pain mated awfully to lust. It was like watching a soul stripped naked, and all its dark and unmentionable secrets laid bare.

Conan glared frozen with repulsion and shaken with nausea. Himself as cleanly elemental as a timber wolf, he was yet not ignorant of the perverse secrets of rotting civilizations. He had roamed the cities of Zamora, and known the women of Shadizar the Wicked. But he sensed here a cosmic vileness transcending mere human degeneracy – a perverse branch on the tree of Life, developed along lines outside human comprehension. It was not at the agonized contortions and posturing of the wretched boy that he was shocked, but at the cosmic obscenity of these beings which could drag to light the abysmal secrets that sleep in the unfathomed darkness of the human soul, and find pleasure in the brazen flaunting of such things as should not be hinted at, even in restless nightmares.

Suddenly the black torturer laid down the pipes and rose, towering over the writhing white figure. Brutally grasping the boy by neck and haunch, the giant up-ended him and thrust him head-first into the green pool. Conan saw the white glimmer of his naked body amid the green water, as the black giant held his captive deep under the surface. Then there was a restless movement among the other blacks, and Conan ducked quickly below the balcony wall, not daring to raise his head lest he be seen.

After a while his curiosity got the better of him, and he cautiously peered out again. The blacks were filing out of an archway into another court. One of them was just placing something on a ledge of the further wall, and Conan saw it was the one who had tortured the boy. He was taller than the others, and wore a jeweled head-band. Of the Zingaran boy there was no trace. The giant followed his fellows, and presently Conan saw them emerge from the archway by which he had gained access to that castle of horror, and file away across the green slopes, in the direction from which he had come. They bore no arms, yet he felt that they planned further aggression against the Freebooters.

But before he went to warn the unsuspecting buccaneers, he wished to investigate the fate of the boy. No sound disturbed the quiet. The pirate believed that the towers and courts were deserted save for himself.

He went swiftly down the stair, crossed the court and passed through an arch into the court the blacks had just quitted. Now he saw the nature of the striated wall. It was banded by narrow ledges, apparently cut out of the solid stone, and ranged along these ledges or shelves were thousands of tiny figures, mostly grayish in color. These figures, not much longer than a man's hand, represented men, and so cleverly were they made that Conan recognized various racial characteristics in the different idols, features typical of Zingarans, Argoseans, Ophireans and Kushite corsairs. These last were black in color, just as their models were black in reality. Conan was aware of a vague uneasiness as he stared at the dumb sightless figures. There was a mimicry of reality about them that was somehow disturbing. He felt of them gingerly and could not decide of what material they were made. It felt like petrified bone; but he could not imagine petrified substance being found in the locality in such abundance as to be used so lavishly.

He noticed that the images representing types with which he was familiar were all on the higher ledges. The lower ledges were occupied by figures the features of which were strange to him. They either embodied merely the artists' imagination, or typified racial types long vanished and forgotten.

Shaking his head impatiently, Conan turned toward the pool. The circular court offered no place of concealment; as the body of the boy was nowhere in sight, it must be lying at the bottom of the pool.

Approaching the placid green disk, he stared into the glimmering surface. It was like looking through a thick green glass, unclouded, yet strangely illusory. Of no great dimensions, the pool was round as a well, bordered by a rim of green jade. Looking down he could see the rounded bottom – how far below the surface he could not decide. But the pool seemed incredibly deep – he was aware of a dizziness as he looked down, much as if he were looking into an abyss. He was puzzled by his ability to see the bottom; but it lay beneath his gaze, impossibly remote, illusive, shadowy, yet visible. At times he thought a faint luminosity was apparent deep in the jade-colored depth, but he could not be sure. Yet he was sure that the pool was empty except for the shimmering water.

Then where in the name of Crom was the boy whom he had seen brutally drowned in that pool? Rising, Conan fingered his sword, and gazed around the court again. His gaze focussed on a spot on one of the higher ledges. There he had seen the tall black place something – cold sweat broke suddenly out on Conan's brown hide.

Hesitantly, yet as if drawn by a magnet, the pirate approached the shimmering wall. Dazed by a suspicion too monstrous to voice, he glared up at the last figure on that ledge. A horrible familiarity made itself evident. Stony, immobile, dwarfish, yet unmistakable, the features of the Zingaran boy stared unseeingly at him. Conan recoiled, shaken to his soul's foundations. His sword trailed in his paralyzed hand as he glared, open-mouthed, stunned by the realization which was too abysmal and awful for the mind to grasp.

Yet the fact was indisputable; the secret of the dwarfish figures was revealed, though behind that secret lay the darker and more cryptic secret of their being.

3

How long Conan stood drowned in dizzy cogitation, he never knew. A voice shook him out of his gaze, a feminine voice that shrieked more and more loudly, as if the owner of the voice were being borne nearer. Conan recognized that voice, and his paralysis vanished instantly.

A quick bound carried him high up on the narrow ledges, where he clung, kicking aside the clustering images to obtain room for his feet. Another spring and a scramble, and he was clinging to the rim of the wall, glaring over it. It was an outer wall; he was looking into the green meadow that surrounded the castle.

Across the grassy level a giant black was striding, carrying a squirming captive under one arm as a man might carry a rebellious child. It was Sancha, her black hair falling in disheveled rippling waves, her olive skin contrasting abruptly with the glossy ebony of her captor. He gave no heed to her wrigglings and cries as he made for the outer archway.

As he vanished within, Conan sprang recklessly down the wall and glided into the arch that opened into the further court. Crouching there, he saw the giant enter the court of the pool, carrying his writhing captive. Now he was able to make out the creature's details.

The superb symmetry of body and limbs was more impressive at close range. Under the ebon skin long, rounded muscles rippled, and Conan did not doubt that the monster could rend an ordinary man limb from limb. The nails of the fingers provided further weapons, for they were grown like the talons of a wild beast. The face was a carven ebony mask. The eyes were tawny, a vibrant gold that glowed and glittered. But the face was inhuman; each line, each feature was stamped with evil – evil transcending the mere evil of humanity. The thing was not a human – it could not be; it was a growth of Life from the pits of blasphemous creation – a perversion of evolutionary development.

The giant cast Sancha down on the sward, where she grovelled, crying with pain and terror. He cast a glance about as if uncertain, and his tawny eyes narrowed as they rested on the images over-turned and knocked from the wall. Then he stooped, grasped his captive by her neck and crotch, and strode purposefully toward the green pool. And Conan glided from his archway, and raced like a wind of death across the sward.

The giant wheeled, and his eyes flared as he saw the bronzed avenger rushing toward him. In the instant of surprise his cruel grip relaxed and Sancha wriggled from his hands and fell to the grass. The taloned hands spread and clutched, but Conan ducked beneath their swoop and drove his sword through the giant's groin. The black went down like a felled tree, gushing blood, and the next instant Conan was seized in a frantic grasp as Sancha sprang up and threw her arms around him in a frenzy of terror and hysterical relief.

He cursed as he disengaged himself, but his foe was already dead; the tawny eyes were glazed, the long ebony limbs had ceased to twitch.

'Oh, Conan,' Sancha was sobbing, clinging tenaciously to him, 'what will become of us? What are these monsters? Oh, surely this is hell and that was the devil—'

'Then hell needs a new devil.' The Barachan grinned fiercely. 'But how did he get hold of you? Have they taken the ship?'

'I don't know.' She tried to wipe away her tears, fumbled for her skirt, and then remembered that she wore none. 'I came ashore. I saw you follow Zaporavo, and I followed you both. I found Zaporavo – was – was it you who—'

'Who else?' he grunted. 'What then?'

'I saw a movement in the trees,' she shuddered. 'I thought it was you. I called – then I saw that – that black *thing* squatting like an ape among the branches, leering down at me. It was like a nightmare; I couldn't run. All I could do was squeal. Then it dropped from the tree and seized me – oh, oh, oh!' She hid her face in her hands, and was shaken anew at the memory of the horror.

'Well, we've got to get out of here,' he growled, catching her wrist. 'Come on; we've got to get to the crew—'

'Most of them were asleep on the beach as I entered the woods,' she said.

'Asleep?' he exclaimed profanely. 'What in the seven devils of hell's fire and damnation—'

'Listen!' She froze, a white quivering image of fright.

'I heard it!' he snapped. 'A moaning cry! Wait!'

He bounded up the ledges again and, glaring over the wall, swore with a concentrated fury that made even Sancha gasp. The black men were returning, but they came not alone or empty-handed. Each bore a limp human form; some bore two. Their captives were the Freebooters; they hung slackly in their captors' arms, and but for an occasional vague movement or twitching, Conan would have believed them dead. They had been disarmed but not stripped; one of the blacks bore their sheathed swords, a great armload of bristling steel. From time to time one of the seamen voiced a vague cry, like a drunkard calling out in sottish sleep.

Like a trapped wolf Conan glared about him. Three arches led out of the court of the pool. Through the eastern arch the blacks had left the court, and through it they would presumably return. He had entered by the southern arch. In the western arch he had hidden, and had not had time to notice what lay beyond it. Regardless of his ignorance of the plan of the castle, he was forced to make his decision promptly.

Springing down the wall, he replaced the images with frantic haste, dragged the corpse of his victim to the pool and cast it in. It sank instantly and, as he looked, he distinctly saw an appalling contraction – a shrinking, a hardening. He hastily turned away, shuddering. Then he seized his companion's arm and led her hastily toward the southern archway, while she begged to be told what was happening.

'They've bagged the crew,' he answered hastily. 'I haven't any plan, but we'll hide somewhere and watch. If they don't look in the pool, they may not suspect our presence.'

'But they'll see the blood on the grass!'

'Maybe they'll think one of their own devils spilled it,' he answered. 'Anyway, we'll have to take the chance.'

They were in the court from which he had watched the torture of the boy, and he led her hastily up the stair that mounted the southern wall, and forced her into a crouching position behind the balustrade of the balcony; it was poor concealment, but the best they could do.

Scarcely had they settled themselves, when the blacks filed into the court. There was a resounding clash at the foot of the stairs, and Conan stiffened, grasping his sword. But the blacks passed through an archway on the southwestern side, and they heard a series of thuds and groans. The giants were casting their victims down on the sward. An hysterical giggle rose to Sancha's lips, and Conan quickly clapped his hand over her mouth, stifling the sound before it could betray them.

After a while they heard the padding of many feet on the sward below, and then silence reigned. Conan peered over the wall. The court was empty. The blacks were once more gathered about the pool in the adjoining court, squatting on their haunches. They seemed to pay no heed to the great smears of blood on the sward and the jade rim of the pool. Evidently blood stains were nothing unusual. Nor were they looking into the pool. They were engrossed in some inexplicable conclave of their own; the tall black was playing again on his golden pipes, and his companions listened like ebony statues.

Taking Sancha's hand, Conan glided down the stair, stooping so that his head would not be visible above the wall. The cringing girl followed perforce, staring fearfully at the arch that let into the court of the pool, but through which, at that angle, neither the pool nor its grim throng were visible. At the foot of the stair lay the swords of the Zingarans. The clash they had heard had been the casting down of the captured weapons.

Conan drew Sancha toward the southwestern arch, and they silently crossed the sward and entered the court beyond. There the Freebooters lay in careless heaps, mustaches bristling, ear-rings glinting. Here and there one stirred or groaned restlessly. Conan bent down to them, and Sancha knelt beside him, leaning forward with her hands on her thighs.

'What is that sweet cloying smell?' she asked nervously. 'It's on all their breaths.'

'It's that damned fruit they were eating,' he answered softly. 'I remember the smell of it. It must have been like the black lotus, that makes men sleep. By Crom, they are beginning to awake – but they're unarmed, and I have an idea that those black devils won't wait long before they begin their magic on them. What chance will the lads have, unarmed and stupid with slumber?'

He brooded for an instant, scowling with the intentness of his thoughts; then seized Sancha's olive shoulder in a grip that made her wince.

'Listen! I'll draw those black swine into another part of the castle and keep them busy for a while. Meanwhile you shake these fools awake, and bring their swords to them – it's a fighting chance. Can you do it?'

'I – I – don't know!' she stammered, shaking with terror, and hardly knowing what she was saying.

With a curse, Conan caught her thick tresses near her head and shook her until the walls danced to her dizzy sight.

'You *must* do it!' he hissed at her. 'It's our only chance!'

'I'll do my best!' she gasped, and with a grunt of commendation and an encouraging slap on the back that nearly knocked her down, he glided away.

A few moments later he was crouching at the arch that opened into the court of the pool, glaring upon his enemies. They still sat about the pool, but were beginning to show evidences of an evil impatience. From the court where lay the rousing buccaneers he heard their groans growing louder, beginning to be mingled with incoherent curses. He tensed his muscles and sank into a pantherish crouch, breathing easily between his teeth.

The jeweled giant rose, taking his pipes from his lips – and at that instant Conan was among the startled blacks with a tigerish bound. And as a tiger leaps and strikes among his prey, Conan leaped and struck: thrice his blade flickered before any could lift a hand in defense; then he bounded from among them and raced across the sward. Behind him sprawled three black figures, their skulls split.

But though the unexpected fury of his surprise had caught the giants off guard, the survivors recovered quickly enough. They were at his heels as he ran through the western arch, their long legs sweeping them over the ground at headlong speed. However, he felt confident of his ability to outfoot them at will; but that was not his purpose. He intended leading them on a long chase, in order to give Sancha time to rouse and arm the Zingarans.

And as he raced into the court beyond the western arch, he

swore. This court differed from the others he had seen. Instead of being round, it was octagonal, and the arch by which he had entered was the only entrance or exit.

Wheeling, he saw that the entire band had followed him in; a group clustered in the arch, and the rest spread out in a wide line as they approached. He faced them, backing slowly toward the northern wall. The line bent into a semicircle, spreading out to hem him in. He continued to move backward, but more and more slowly, noting the spaces widening between the pursuers. They feared lest he should try to dart around a horn of the crescent, and lengthened their line to prevent it.

He watched with the calm alertness of a wolf, and when he struck it was with the devastating suddenness of a thunderbolt – full at the center of the crescent. The giant who barred his way went down cloven to the middle of the breast-bone, and the pirate was outside their closing ring before the blacks to right and left could come to their stricken comrade's aid. The group at the gate prepared to receive his onslaught, but Conan did not charge them. He had turned and was watching his hunters without apparent emotion, and certainly without fear.

This time they did not spread out in a thin line. They had learned that it was fatal to divide their forces against such an incarnation of clawing, rending fury. They bunched up in a compact mass, and advanced on him without undue haste, maintaining their formation.

Conan knew that if he fell foul of that mass of taloned muscle and bone, there could be but one culmination. Once let them drag him down among them where they could reach him with their talons and use their greater body-weight to advantage, even his primitive ferocity would not prevail. He glanced around the wall and saw a ledge-like projection above a corner on the western side. What it was he did not know, but it would serve his purpose. He began backing toward that corner, and the giants advanced more rapidly. They evidently thought that they were herding him into the corner themselves, and Conan found time to reflect that they probably looked on him as a member of a lower order, mentally inferior to themselves. So much the better. Nothing is more disastrous than underestimating one's antagonist.

Now he was only a few yards from the wall, and the blacks were closing in rapidly, evidently thinking to pin him in the corner before he realized his situation. The group at the gate had deserted their post and were hastening to join their fellows. The giants half-crouched, eyes blazing like golden hell-fire, teeth glistening whitely, taloned hands lifted as if to fend off attack. They expected an abrupt and violent move on the part of their prey, but when it came, it took them by surprise.

Conan lifted his sword, took a step toward them, then wheeled and raced to the wall. With a fleeting coil and release of steel muscles, he shot high in the air, and his straining arm hooked its fingers over the projection. Instantly there was a rending crash and the jutting ledge gave way, precipitating the pirate back into the court.

He hit on his back, which for all its springy sinews would have broken but for the cushioning of the sword, and rebounding like a great cat, he faced his foes. The dancing recklessness was gone from his eyes. They blazed like blue bale-fire; his mane bristled, his thin lips snarled. In an instant the affair had changed from a daring game to a battle of life and death, and Conan's savage nature responded with all the fury of the wild.

The blacks, halted an instant by the swiftness of the episode, now made to sweep on him and drag him down. But in that instant a shout broke the stillness. Wheeling, the giants saw a disreputable throng crowding the arch. The buccaneers weaved drunkenly, they swore incoherently; they were addled and bewildered, but they grasped their swords and advanced with a ferocity not dimmed in the slightest by the fact that they did not understand what it was all about.

As the blacks glared in amazement, Conan yelled stridently and struck them like a razor-edged thunderbolt. They fell like ripe grains beneath his blade, and the Zingarans, shouting with muddled fury, ran groggily across the court and fell on their gigantic foes with bloodthirsty zeal. They were still dazed; emerging hazily from drugged slumber, they had felt Sancha frantically shaking them and shoving swords into their fists, and had vaguely heard her urging them to some sort of action. They had not understood all she said, but the sight of strangers, and blood streaming, was enough for them.

In an instant the court was turned into a battle-ground which soon resembled a slaughter-house. The Zingarans weaved and rocked on their feet, but they wielded their swords with power and effect, swearing prodigiously, and quite oblivious to all wounds except those instantly fatal. They far outnumbered the blacks, but these proved themselves no mean antagonists. Towering above their assailants, the giants wrought havoc with talons and teeth, tearing out men's throats, and dealing blows with clenched fists that crushed in skulls. Mixed and mingled in that mêlée, the buccaneers could not use their superior agility to the best advantage, and many were too stupid from their drugged sleep to avoid blows aimed at them. They fought with a blind wild-beast ferocity, too intent on dealing death to evade it. The sound of the hacking swords was like that of butchers' cleavers, and the shrieks, yells and curses were appalling.

Sancha, shrinking in the archway, was stunned by the noise and fury; she got a dazed impression of a whirling chaos in which steel flashed and hacked, arms tossed, snarling faces appeared and vanished, and straining bodies collided, rebounded, locked and mingled in a devil's dance of madness.

Details stood out briefly, like black etchings on a background of blood. She saw a Zingaran sailor, blinded by a great flap of scalp torn loose and hanging over his eyes, brace his straddling legs and drive his sword to the hilt in a black belly. She distinctly heard the buccaneer grunt as he struck, and saw the victim's tawny eyes roll up in sudden agony; blood and entrails gushed out over the driven blade. The dying black caught the blade with his naked hands, and the sailor tugged blindly and stupidly; then a black arm hooked about the Zingaran's head, a black knee was planted with cruel force in the middle of his back. His head was jerked back at a terrible angle, and something cracked above the noise of the fray, like the breaking of a thick branch. The conqueror dashed his victim's body to the earth – and as he did, something like a beam of blue light flashed across his shoulders from behind, from right to left. He staggered, his head toppled forward on his breast, and thence, hideously, to the earth.

Sancha turned sick. She gagged and wished to vomit. She made abortive efforts to turn and flee from the spectacle, but her legs would not work. Nor could she close her eyes. In fact, she opened them wider. Revolted, repelled, nauseated, yet she felt the awful fascination she had always experienced at sight of blood. Yet this battle transcended anything she had ever seen fought out between human beings in port raids or sea battles. Then she saw Conan.

Separated from his mates by the whole mass of the enemy, Conan had been enveloped in a black wave of arms and bodies, and dragged down. Then they would quickly have stamped the life out of him, but he had pulled down one of them with him, and the black's body protected that of the pirate beneath him. They kicked and tore at the Barachan and dragged at their writhing comrade, but Conan's teeth were set desperately in his throat, and the pirate clung tenaciously to his dying shield.

An onslaught of Zingarans caused a slackening of the press, and Conan threw aside the corpse and rose, blood-smeared and terrible. The giants towered above him like great black shadows, clutching, buffeting the air with terrible blows. But he was as hard to hit or grapple as a blood-mad panther, and at every turn or flash of his blade, blood jetted. He had already taken punishment enough to kill three ordinary men, but his bull-like vitality was undiminished.

His war cry rose above the medley of the carnage, and the bewildered but furious Zingarans took fresh heart and redoubled their strokes, until the rending of flesh and the crunching of bone beneath the swords almost drowned the howls of pain and wrath.

The blacks wavered, and broke for the gate, and Sancha squealed at their coming and scurried out of the way. They jammed in the narrow archway, and the Zingarans stabbed and hacked at their straining backs with strident yelps of glee. The gate was a shambles before the survivors broke through and scattered, each for himself.

The battle became a chase. Across grassy courts, up shimmering stairs, over the slanting roofs of fantastic towers, even along the broad coping of the walls, the giants fled, dripping blood at each step, harried by their merciless pursuers as by wolves. Cornered, some of them turned at bay and men died. But the ultimate result was always the same – a mangled black body twitching on the sward, or hurled writhing and twisting from parapet or tower roof.

Sancha had taken refuge in the court of the pool, where she crouched, shaking with terror. Outside rose a fierce yelling, feet pounded the sward, and through the arch burst a black, red-stained figure. It was the giant who wore the gemmed headband. A squat pursuer was close behind, and the black turned, at the very brink of the pool. In his extremity he had picked up a sword dropped by a dying sailor, and as the Zingaran rushed recklessly at him, he struck with the unfamiliar weapon. The buccaneer dropped with his skull crushed, but so awkwardly the blow was dealt, the blade shivered in the giant's hand.

He hurled the hilt at the figures which thronged the arch, and bounded toward the pool, his face a convulsed mask of hate. Conan burst through the men at the gate, and his feet spurned the sword in his headlong charge.

But the giant threw his great arms wide and from his lips rang an inhuman cry – the only sound made by a black during the entire fight. It screamed to the sky its awful hate; it was like a voice howling from the pits. At the sound the Zingarans faltered and hesitated. But Conan did not pause. Silently and murderously he drove at the ebon figure poised on the brink of the pool.

But even as his dripping sword gleamed in the air, the black wheeled and bounded high. For a flash of an instant they saw him poised in midair above the pool; then with an earth-shaking roar, the green waters rose and rushed up to meet him, enveloping him in a green volcano.

Conan checked his headlong rush just in time to keep from

toppling into the pool, and he sprang back, thrusting his men behind him with mighty swings of his arms. The green pool was like a geyser now, the noise rising to deafening volume as the great column of water reared and reared, blossoming at the crest with a great crown of foam.

Conan was driving his men to the gate, herding them ahead of him, beating them with the flat of his sword; the roar of the water-spout seemed to have robbed them of their faculties. Seeing Sancha standing paralyzed, staring with wide-eyed terror at the seething pillar, he accosted her with a bellow that cut through the thunder of the water and made her jump out of her daze. She ran to him, arms outstretched, and he caught her up under one arm and raced out of the court.

In the court which opened on the outer world, the survivors had gathered, weary, tattered, wounded and blood-stained, and stood gaping dumbly at the great unstable pillar that towered momentarily nearer the blue vault of the sky. Its green trunk was laced with white; its foaming crown was thrice the circumference of its base. Momentarily it threatened to burst and fall in an engulfing torrent, yet it continued to jet skyward.

Conan's eyes swept the bloody, naked group, and he cursed to see only a score. In the stress of the moment he grasped a corsair by the neck and shook him so violently that blood from the man's wounds spattered all near them.

'Where are the rest?' he bellowed in his victim's ear.

'That's all!' the other yelled back, above the roar of the geyser. 'The others were all killed by those black—'

'Well, get out of here!' roared Conan, giving him a thrust that sent him staggering headlong toward the outer archway. 'That fountain is going to burst in a moment—'

'We'll all be drowned!' squawked a Freebooter, limping toward the arch.

'Drowned, hell!' yelled Conan. 'We'll be turned to pieces of petrified bone! Get out, blast you!'

He ran to the outer archway, one eye on the green roaring tower that loomed so awfully above him, the other on stragglers.

Dazed with blood-lust, fighting, and the thunderous noise, some of the Zingarans moved like men in a trance. Conan hurried them up; his method was simple. He grasped loiterers by the scruff of the neck, impelled them violently through the gate, added impetus with a lusty kick in the rear, spicing his urgings for haste with pungent comments on the victim's ancestry. Sancha showed an inclination to remain with him, but he jerked away her twining arms, blaspheming luridly, and accelerated her movements with a tremendous slap on the posterior that sent her scurrying across the plateau.

Conan did not leave the gate until he was sure all his men who yet lived were out of the castle and started across the level meadow. Then he glanced again at the roaring pillar looming against the sky, dwarfing the towers, and he too fled that castle of nameless horrors.

The Zingarans had already crossed the rim of the plateau and were fleeing down the slopes. Sancha waited for him at the crest of the first slope beyond the rim, and there he paused for an instant to look back at the castle. It was as if a gigantic green-stemmed and white-blossomed flower swayed above the towers; the roar filled the sky. Then the jade-green and snowy pillar broke with a noise like the rending of the skies, and walls and towers were blotted out in a thunderous torrent.

Conan caught the girl's hand, and fled. Slope after slope rose and fell before them, and behind sounded the rushing of a river. A glance over his straining shoulder showed a broad green ribbon rising and falling as it swept over the slopes. The torrent had not spread out and dissipated; like a giant serpent it flowed over the depressions and the rounded crests. It held a consistent course – *it was following them.*

The realization roused Conan to a greater pitch of endurance. Sancha stumbled and went to her knees with a moaning cry of despair and exhaustion. Catching her up, Conan tossed her over his giant shoulder and ran on. His breast heaved, his knees trembled; his breath tore in great gasps through his teeth. He reeled in his gait. Ahead of him he saw the sailors toiling, spurred on by the terror that gripped them.

The ocean burst suddenly on his view, and in his swimming gaze floated the *Wastrel*, unharmed. Men tumbled into the boats helter-skelter. Sancha fell into the bottom and lay there in a crumpled heap. Conan, though the blood thundered in his ears and the world swam red to his gaze, took an oar with the panting sailors.

With hearts ready to burst from exhaustion, they pulled for the ship. The green river burst through the fringe of trees. Those trees fell as if their stems had been cut away, and as they sank into the jade-colored flood, they vanished. The tide flowed out over the beach, lapped at the ocean, and the waves turned a deeper, more sinister green.

Unreasoning, instinctive fear held the buccaneers, making them urge their agonized bodies and reeling brains to greater effort; what they feared they knew not, but they did know that in that abominable smooth green ribbon was a menace to body and to soul. Conan knew, and as he saw the broad line slip into the waves and stream through the water toward them, without altering its shape or course, he called up his last ounce of reserve strength so fiercely that the oar snapped in his hands.

But their prows bumped against the timbers of the *Wastrel*, and the sailors staggered up the chains, leaving the boats to drift as they would. Sancha went up on Conan's broad shoulder, hanging limp as a corpse, to be dumped unceremoniously on to the deck as the Barachan took the wheel, gasping orders to his skeleton of a crew. Throughout the affair, he had taken the lead without question, and they had instinctively followed him. They reeled about like drunken men, fumbling mechanically at ropes and braces. The anchor chain, unshackled, splashed into the water, the sails unfurled and bellied in a rising wind. The *Wastrel* quivered and shook herself, and swung majestically seaward. Conan glared shoreward; like a tongue of emerald flame, a ribbon licked out on the water futilely, an oar's length from the *Wastrel*'s keel. It advanced no further. From that end of the tongue, his gaze followed an unbroken stream of lambent green, across the white beach, and over the slopes, until it faded in the blue distance.

The Barachan, regaining his wind, grinned at the panting crew. Sancha was standing near him, hysterical tears coursing down her cheeks. Conan's breeks hung in blood-stained tatters; his girdle and sheath were gone, his sword, driven upright into the deck beside him, was notched and crusted with red. Blood thickly clotted his black mane, and one ear had been half torn from his head. His arms, legs, breast and shoulders were bitten and clawed as if by panthers. But he grinned as he braced his powerful legs, and swung on the wheel in sheer exuberance of muscular might.

'What now?' faltered the girl.

'The plunder of the seas!' he laughed. 'A paltry crew, and that chewed and clawed to pieces, but they can work the ship, and crews can always be found. Come here, girl, and give me a kiss.'

'A kiss?' she cried hysterically. 'You think of kisses at a time like this?'

His laughter boomed above the snap and thunder of the sails, as he caught her up off her feet in the crook of one mighty arm, and smacked her red lips with resounding relish.

'I think of Life!' he roared. 'The dead are dead, and what has passed is done! I have a ship and a fighting crew and a girl with lips like wine, and that's all I ever asked. Lick your wounds, bullies, and break out a cask of ale. You're going to work ship as she never was worked before. Dance and sing while you buckle to it, damn you! To the devil with empty seas! We're bound for waters where the seaports are fat, and the merchant ships are crammed with plunder!'

RED NAILS

1

The Skull on the Crag

The woman on the horse reined in her weary steed. It stood with its legs wide-braced, its head drooping, as if it found even the weight of the gold-tassled, red-leather bridle too heavy. The woman drew a booted foot out of the silver stirrup and swung down from the gilt-worked saddle. She made the reins fast to the fork of a sapling, and turned about, hands on her hips, to survey her surroundings.

They were not inviting. Giant trees hemmed in the small pool where her horse had just drunk. Clumps of undergrowth limited the vision that quested under the somber twilight of the lofty arches formed by intertwining branches. The woman shivered with a twitch of her magnificent shoulders, and then cursed.

She was tall, full-bosomed and large-limbed, with compact shoulders. Her whole figure reflected an unusual strength, without detracting from the femininity of her appearance. She was all woman, in spite of her bearing and her garments. The latter were incongruous, in view of her present environs. Instead of a skirt she wore short, wide-legged silk breeches, which ceased a hand's breadth short of her knees, and were upheld by a wide silken sash worn as a girdle. Flaring-topped boots of soft leather came almost to her knees, and a low-necked, wide-collared, wide-sleeved silk shirt completed her costume. On one shapely hip she wore a straight double-edged sword, and on the other a long dirk. Her unruly golden hair, cut square at her shoulders, was confined by a band of crimson satin.

Against the background of somber, primitive forest she posed with an unconscious picturesqueness, bizarre and out of place. She should have been posed against a background of sea-clouds, painted masts and wheeling gulls. There was the color of the sea in her wide eyes. And that was as it should have been, because this was Valeria of the Red Brotherhood, whose deeds are celebrated in song and ballad wherever seafarers gather.

She strove to pierce the sullen green roof of the arched branches and see the sky which presumably lay about it, but presently gave it up with a muttered oath.

Leaving her horse tied she strode off toward the east, glancing back toward the pool from time to time in order to fix her route in her mind. The silence of the forest depressed her. No birds sang in the lofty boughs, nor did any rustling in the bushes indicate the presence of any small animals. For leagues she had traveled in a realm of brooding stillness, broken only by the sounds of her own flight.

She had slaked her thirst at the pool, but she felt the gnawings of hunger and began looking about for some of the fruit on which she had sustained herself since exhausting the food she had brought in her saddlebags.

Ahead of her, presently, she saw an outcropping of dark, flint-like rock that sloped upward into what looked like a rugged crag rising among the trees. Its summit was lost to view amidst a cloud of encircling leaves. Perhaps its peak rose above the tree-tops, and from it she could see what lay beyond – if, indeed, anything lay beyond but more of this apparently illimitable forest through which she had ridden for so many days.

A narrow ridge formed a natural ramp that led up the steep face of the crag. After she had ascended some fifty feet she came to the belt of leaves that surrounded the rock. The trunks of the trees did not crowd close to the crag, but the ends of their lower branches extended about it, veiling it with their foliage. She groped on in leafy obscurity, not able to see either above or below her; but presently she glimpsed blue sky, and a moment later came out in the clear, hot sunlight and saw the forest roof stretching away under her feet.

She was standing on a broad shelf which was about even with the tree-tops, and from it rose a spire-like jut that was the ultimate peak of the crag she had climbed. But something else caught her attention in the litter of blown dead leaves which carpeted the shelf. She kicked them aside and looked down on the skeleton of a man. She ran an experienced eye over the bleached frame, but saw no broken bones nor any sign of violence. The man must have died a natural death; though why he should have climbed a tall crag to die she could not imagine.

She scrambled up to the summit of the spire and looked toward the horizons. The forest roof – which looked like a floor from her vantage-point – was just as impenetrable as from below. She could not even see the pool by which she had left her horse. She glanced northward, in the direction from which she had come. She saw only the rolling green ocean stretching away and away, with only a vague blue line in the distance to hint of the hill-range she had crossed days before, to plunge into this leafy waste.

West and east the view was the same; though the blue hill-line was lacking in those directions. But when she turned her eyes southward she stiffened and caught her breath. A mile away in that direction the forest thinned out and ceased abruptly, giving way to a cactus-dotted plain. And in the midst of that plain rose the walls and towers of a city. Valeria swore in amazement. This passed belief. She would not have been surprised to sight human habitations of another sort – the beehive-shaped huts of the black people, or the cliff-dwellings of the mysterious brown race which legends declared inhabited some country of this unexplored region. But it was a startling experience to come upon a walled city here so many long weeks' march from the nearest outposts of any sort of civilization.

Her hands tiring from clinging to the spire-like pinnacle, she let herself down on the shelf, frowning in indecision. She had come far – from the camp of the mercenaries by the border town of Sukhmet amidst the level grasslands, where desperate adventurers of many races guard the Stygian frontier against the raids that come up like a red wave from Darfar. Her flight had been blind, into a country of which she was wholly ignorant. And now she wavered between an urge to ride directly to that city in the plain, and the instinct of caution which prompted her to skirt it widely and continue her solitary flight.

Her thoughts were scattered by the rustling of the leaves below her. She wheeled cat-like, snatched at her sword; and then she froze motionless, staring wide-eyed at the man before her.

He was almost a giant in stature, muscles rippling smoothly under his skin which the sun had burned brown. His garb was similar to hers, except that he wore a broad leather belt instead of a girdle. Broadsword and poniard hung from this belt.

'Conan, the Cimmerian!' ejaculated the woman. 'What are *you* doing on my trail?'

He grinned hardly, and his fierce blue eyes burned with a light any woman could understand as they ran over her magnificent figure, lingering on the swell of her splendid breasts beneath the light shirt, and the clear white flesh displayed between breeches and boot-tops.

'Don't you know?' he laughed. 'Haven't I made my admiration for you plain ever since I first saw you?'

'A stallion could have made it no plainer,' she answered disdainfully. 'But I never expected to encounter you so far from the ale-barrels and meat-pots of Sukhmet. Did you really follow me from Zarallo's camp, or were you whipped forth for a rogue?'

He laughed at her insolence and flexed his mighty biceps.

'You know Zarallo didn't have enough knaves to whip me out of camp,' he grinned. 'Of course I followed you. Lucky thing for you, too, wench! When you knifed that Stygian officer, you forfeited Zarallo's favor and protection, and you outlawed yourself with the Stygians.'

'I know it,' she replied sullenly. 'But what else could I do? You know what my provocation was.'

'Sure,' he agreed. 'If I'd been there, I'd have knifed him myself.

But if a woman must live in the war-camps of men, she can expect such things.'

Valeria stamped her booted foot and swore.

'Why won't men let me live a man's life?'

'That's obvious!' Again his eager eyes devoured her. 'But you were wise to run away. The Stygians would have had you skinned. That officer's brother followed you; faster than you thought, I don't doubt. He wasn't far behind you when I caught up with him. His horse was better than yours. He'd have caught you and cut your throat within a few more miles.'

'Well?' she demanded.

'Well what?' He seemed puzzled.

'What of the Stygian?'

'Why, what do you suppose?' he returned impatiently. 'I killed him, of course, and left his carcass for the vultures. That delayed me, though, and I almost lost your trail when you crossed the rocky spurs of the hills. Otherwise I'd have caught up with you long ago.'

'And now you think you'll drag me back to Zarallo's camp?' she sneered.

'Don't talk like a fool,' he grunted. 'Come, girl, don't be such a spitfire. I'm not like that Stygian you knifed, and you know it.'

'A penniless vagabond,' she taunted.

He laughed at her.

'What do you call yourself? You haven't enough money to buy a new seat for your breeches. Your disdain doesn't deceive me. You know I've commanded bigger ships and more men than you ever did in your life. As for being penniless – what rover isn't, most of the time? I've squandered enough gold in the sea-ports of the world to fill a galleon. You know that, too.'

'Where are the fine ships and the bold lads you commanded, now?' she sneered.

'At the bottom of the sea, mostly,' he replied cheerfully. 'The Zingarans sank my last ship off the Shemite shore – that's why I joined Zarallo's Free Companions. But I saw I'd been stung when we marched to the Darfar border. The pay was poor and the wine was sour, and I don't like black women. And that's the only kind that came to our camp at Sukhmet – rings in their noses and their teeth filed – bah! Why did you join Zarallo's? Sukhmet's a long way from salt water.'

'Red Ortho wanted to make me his mistress,' she answered sullenly. 'I jumped overboard one night and swam ashore when we were anchored off the Kushite coast. Off Zabhela, it was. There a Shemite trader told me that Zarallo had brought his Free Companies south to guard the Darfar border. No better employment offered. I joined an eastbound caravan and eventually came to Sukhmet.'

'It was madness to plunge southward as you did,' commented Conan, 'but it was wise, too, for Zarallo's patrols never thought to look for you in this direction. Only the brother of the man you killed happened to strike your trail.'

'And now what do you intend doing?' she demanded.

'Turn west,' he answered. 'I've been this far south, but not this far east. Many days' traveling to the west will bring us to the open savannas, where the black tribes graze their cattle. I have friends among them. We'll get to the coast and find a ship. I'm sick of the jungle.'

'Then be on your way,' she advised. 'I have other plans.'

'Don't be a fool!' He showed irritation for the first time. 'You can't keep on wandering through this forest.'

'I can if I choose.'

'But what do you intend doing?'

'That's none of your affair,' she snapped.

'Yes, it is,' he answered calmly. 'Do you think I've followed you this far, to turn around and ride off empty-handed? Be sensible, wench. I'm not going to harm you.'

He stepped toward her, and she sprang back, whipping out her sword.

'Keep back, you barbarian dog! I'll spit you like a roast pig!'

He halted, reluctantly, and demanded: 'Do you want me to take that toy away from you and spank you with it?'

'Words! Nothing but words!' she mocked, lights like the gleam of the sun on blue water dancing in her reckless eyes.

He knew it was the truth. No living man could disarm Valeria of the Brotherhood with his bare hands. He scowled, his sensations a tangle of conflicting emotions. He was angry, yet he was amused and filled with admiration for her spirit. He burned with eagerness to seize that splendid figure and crush it in his iron arms, yet he greatly desired not to hurt the girl. He was torn between a desire to shake her soundly, and a desire to caress her. He knew if he came any nearer her sword would be sheathed in his heart. He had seen Valeria kill too many men in border forays and tavern brawls to have any illusions about her. He knew she was as quick and ferocious as a tigress. He could draw his broadsword and disarm her, beat the blade out of her hand, but the thought of drawing a sword on a woman, even without intent of injury, was extremely repugnant to him.

'Blast your soul, you hussy!' he exclaimed in exasperation. 'I'm going to take off your—'

He started toward her, his angry passion making him reckless, and she poised herself for a deadly thrust. Then came a startling interruption to a scene at once ludicrous and perilous.

'What's that?'

It was Valeria who exclaimed, but they both started violently, and Conan wheeled like a cat, his great sword flashing into his hand. Back in the forest had burst forth an appalling medley of screams – the screams of horses in terror and agony. Mingled with their screams there came the snap of splintering bones.

'Lions are slaying the horses!' cried Valeria.

'Lions, nothing!' snorted Conan, his eyes blazing. 'Did you hear a lion roar? Neither did I! Listen at those bones snap – not even a lion could make that much noise killing a horse.'

He hurried down the natural ramp and she followed, their personal feud forgotten in the adventurers' instinct to unite against common peril. The screams had ceased when they worked their way downward through the green veil of leaves that brushed the rock.

'I found your horse tied by the pool back there,' he muttered, treading so noiselessly that she no longer wondered how he had surprised her on the crag. 'I tied mine beside it and followed the tracks of your boots. Watch, now!'

They had emerged from the belt of leaves, and stared down into the lower reaches of the forest. Above them the green roof spread its dusky canopy. Below them the sunlight filtered in just enough to make a jade-tinted twilight. The giant trunks of trees less than a hundred yards away looked dim and ghostly.

'The horses should be beyond that thicket, over there,' whispered Conan, and his voice might have been a breeze moving through the branches. 'Listen!'

Valeria had already heard, and a chill crept through her veins; so she unconsciously laid her white hand on her companion's muscular brown arm. From beyond the thicket came the noisy crunching of bones and the loud rending of flesh, together with the grinding, slobbering sounds of a horrible feast.

'Lions wouldn't make that noise,' whispered Conan. 'Something's eating our horses, but it's not a lion – Crom!'

The noise stopped suddenly, and Conan swore softly. A suddenly risen breeze was blowing from them directly toward the spot where the unseen slayer was hidden.

'Here it comes!' muttered Conan, half lifting his sword.

The thicket was violently agitated, and Valeria clutched Conan's arm hard. Ignorant of jungle-lore she yet knew that no animal she had ever seen could have shaken the tall brush like that.

'It must be as big as an elephant,' muttered Conan, echoing her thought. 'What the devil—' His voice trailed away in stunned silence.

Through the thicket was thrust a head of nightmare and lunacy. Grinning jaws bared rows of dripping yellow tusks; above the yawning mouth wrinkled a saurian-like snout. Huge eyes, like those of a python a thousand times magnified, stared unwinkingly at the petrified humans clinging to the rock above it. Blood smeared the scaly, flabby lips and dripped from the huge mouth.

The head, bigger than that of a crocodile, was further extended on a long scaled neck on which stood up rows of serrated spikes, and after it, crushing down the briars and saplings, waddled the body of a titan, a gigantic, barrel-bellied torso on absurdly short legs. The whitish belly almost raked the ground, while the serrated back-bone rose higher than Conan could have reached on tiptoe. A long spiked tail, like that of a gargantuan scorpion, trailed out behind.

'Back up the crag, quick!' snapped Conan, thrusting the girl behind him. 'I don't think he can climb, but he can stand on his hind-legs and reach us—'

With a snapping and rending of bushes and saplings the monster came hurtling through the thickets, and they fled up the rock before him like leaves blown before a wind. As Valeria plunged into the leafy screen a backward glance showed her the Titan rearing up fearsomely on his massive hinder legs, even as Conan had predicted. The sight sent panic racing through her. As he reared, the beast seemed more gigantic than ever; his snouted head towered among the trees. Then Conan's iron hand closed on her wrist and she was jerked headlong into the blinding welter of the leaves, and out again into the hot sunshine above, just as the monster fell forward with his front feet on the crag with an impact that made the rock vibrate.

Behind the fugitives the huge head crashed through the twigs, and they looked down for a horrifying instant at the nightmare visage framed among the green leaves, eyes flaming, jaws gaping. Then the giant tusks clashed together futilely, and after that the head was withdrawn, vanishing from their sight as if it had sunk in a pool.

Peering down through broken branches that scraped the rock, they saw it squatting on its haunches at the foot of the crag, staring unblinkingly up at them.

Valeria shuddered.

'How long do you suppose he'll crouch there?'

Conan kicked the skull on the leaf-strewn shelf.

'That fellow must have climbed up here to escape him, or one like him. He must have died of starvation. There are no bones broken. That thing must be a dragon, such as the black people speak of in their legends. If so, it won't leave here until we're both dead.'

Valeria looked at him blankly, her resentment forgotten. She fought down a surging of panic. She had proved her reckless courage a thousand times in wild battles on sea and land, on the blood-slippery decks of burning war-ships, in the storming of walled cities, and on the trampled sandy beaches where the desperate men of the Red Brotherhood bathed their knives in one another's blood in their fights for leadership. But the prospect now confronting her congealed her blood. A cutlass stroke in the heat of battle was nothing; but to sit idle and helpless on a bare rock until she perished of starvation, besieged by a monstrous survival of an elder age – the thought sent panic throbbing through her brain.

'He must leave to eat and drink,' she said helplessly.

'He won't have to go far to do either,' Conan pointed out. 'He's just gorged on horsemeat, and like a real snake, he can go for a long time without eating or drinking again. But he doesn't sleep after eating, like a real snake, it seems. Anyway, he can't climb this crag.'

Conan spoke imperturbably. He was a barbarian, and the terrible patience of the wilderness and its children was as much a part of him as his lusts and rages. He could endure a situation like this with a coolness impossible to a civilized person.

'Can't we get into the trees and get away, traveling like apes through the branches?' she asked desperately.

He shook his head. 'I thought of that. The branches that touch the crag down there are too light. They'd break with our weight. Besides, I have an idea that devil could tear up any tree around here by its roots.'

'Well, are we going to sit here on our rumps until we starve, like that?' she cried furiously, kicking the skull clattering across the ledge. 'I won't do it! I'll go down there and cut his damned head off—'

Conan had seated himself on a rocky projection at the foot of

188

the spire. He looked up with a glint of admiration at her blazing eyes and tense, quivering figure, but, realizing that she was in just the mood for any madness, he let none of his admiration sound in his voice.

'Sit down,' he grunted, catching her by her wrist and pulling her down on his knee. She was too surprised to resist as he took her sword from her hand and shoved it back in its sheath. 'Sit still and calm down. You'd only break your steel on his scales. He'd gobble you up in one gulp, or smash you like an egg with that spiked tail of his. We'll get out of this jam some way, but we shan't do it by getting chewed up and swallowed.'

She made no reply, nor did she seek to repulse his arm from about her waist. She was frightened, and the sensation was new to Valeria of the Red Brotherhood. So she sat on her companion's – or captor's – knee with a docility that would have amazed Zarallo, who had anathematized her as a she-devil out of hell's seraglio.

Conan played idly with her curly yellow locks, seemingly intent only upon his conquest. Neither the skeleton at his feet nor the monster crouching below disturbed his mind or dulled the edge of his interest.

The girl's restless eyes, roving the leaves below them, discovered splashes of color among the green. It was fruit, large, darkly crimson globes suspended from the boughs of a tree whose broad leaves were a peculiarly rich and vivid green. She became aware of both thirst and hunger, though thirst had not assailed her until she knew she could not descend from the crag to find food and water.

'We need not starve,' she said. 'There is fruit we can reach.'

Conan glanced where she pointed.

'If we ate that we wouldn't need the bite of a dragon,' he grunted. 'That's what the black people of Kush call the Apples of Derketa. Derketa is the Queen of the Dead. Drink a little of the juice, or spill it on your flesh, and you'd be dead before you could tumble to the foot of this crag.'

'Oh!'

She lapsed into dismayed silence. There seemed no way out

of their predicament, she reflected gloomily. She saw no way of escape, and Conan seemed to be concerned only with her supple waist and curly tresses. If he was trying to formulate a plan of escape he did not show it.

'If you'll take your hands off me long enough to climb up on that peak,' she said presently, 'you'll see something that will surprise you.'

He cast her a questioning glance, then obeyed with a shrug of his massive shoulders. Clinging to the spire-like pinnacle, he stared out over the forest roof.

He stood a long moment in silence, posed like a bronze statue on the rock.

'It's a walled city, right enough,' he muttered presently. 'Was that where you were going, when you tried to send me off alone to the coast?'

'I saw it before you came. I knew nothing of it when I left Sukhmet.'

'Who'd have thought to find a city here? I don't believe the Stygians ever penetrated this far. Could black people build a city like that? I see no herds on the plain, no signs of cultivation, or people moving about.'

'How could you hope to see all that, at this distance?' she demanded.

He shrugged his shoulders and dropped down on the shelf.

'Well, the folk of the city can't help us just now. And they might not, if they could. The people of the Black Countries are generally hostile to strangers. Probably stick us full of spears—'

He stopped short and stood silent, as if he had forgotten what he was saying, frowning down at the crimson spheres gleaming among the leaves.

'Spears!' he muttered. 'What a blasted fool I am not to have thought of that before! That shows what a pretty woman does to a man's mind.'

'What are you talking about?' she inquired.

Without answering her question, he descended to the belt of leaves and looked down through them. The great brute squatted below, watching the crag with the frightful patience of the reptile folk. So might one of his breed have glared up at their troglodyte ancestors, treed on a high-flung rock, in the dim dawn ages. Conan cursed him without heat, and began cutting branches, reaching out and severing them as far from the end as he could reach. The agitation of the leaves made the monster restless. He rose from his haunches and lashed his hideous tail, snapping off saplings as if they had been toothpicks. Conan watched him warily from the corner of his eye, and just as Valeria believed the dragon was about to hurl himself up the crag again, the Cimmerian drew back and climbed up to the ledge with the branches he had cut. There were three of these, slender shafts about seven feet long, but not larger than his thumb. He had also cut several strands of tough, thin vine.

'Branches too light for spear-hafts, and creepers no thicker than cords,' he remarked, indicating the foliage about the crag. 'It won't hold our weight – but there's strength in union. That's what the Aquilonian renegades used to tell us Cimmerians when they came into the hills to raise an army to invade their own country. But we always fight by clans and tribes.'

'What the devil has that got to do with those sticks?' she demanded.

'You wait and see.'

Gathering the sticks in a compact bundle, he wedged his poniard hilt between them at one end. Then with the vines he bound them together, and when he had completed his task, he had a spear of no small strength, with a sturdy shaft seven feet in length.

'What good will that do?' she demanded. 'You told me that a blade couldn't pierce his scales—'

'He hasn't got scales all over him,' answered Conan. 'There's more than one way of skinning a panther.'

Moving down to the edge of the leaves, he reached the spear up and carefully thrust the blade through one of the Apples of Derketa, drawing aside to avoid the darkly purple drops that dripped from the pierced fruit. Presently he withdrew the blade and showed her the blue steel stained with a dull purplish crimson.

'I don't know whether it will do the job or not,' quoth he. 'There's enough poison there to kill an elephant, but – well, we'll see.'

Valeria was close behind him as he let himself down among the leaves. Cautiously holding the poisoned pike away from him, he thrust his head through the branches and addressed the monster.

'What are you waiting down there for, you misbegotten off-spring of questionable parents?' was one of his more printable queries. 'Stick your ugly head up here again, you long-necked brute – or do you want me to come down there and kick you loose from your illegitimate spine?'

There was more of it – some of it couched in eloquence that made Valeria stare, in spite of her profane education among the seafarers. And it had its effect on the monster. Just as the incessant yapping of a dog worries and enrages more constitutionally silent animals, so the clamorous voice of a man rouses fear in some bestial bosoms and insane rage in others. Suddenly and with appalling quickness, the mastodonic brute reared up on its mighty hind legs and elongated its neck and body in a furious effort to reach this vociferous pigmy whose clamor was disturbing the primeval silence of its ancient realm.

But Conan had judged his distance with precision. Some five feet below him the mighty head crashed terribly but futilely through the leaves. And as the monstrous mouth gaped like that of a great snake, Conan drove his spear into the red angle of the jawbone hinge. He struck downward with all the strength of both arms, driving the long poniard blade to the hilt in flesh, sinew and bone.

Instantly the jaws clashed convulsively together, severing the triple-pieced shaft and almost precipitating Conan from his perch. He would have fallen but for the girl behind him, who caught his sword-belt in a desperate grasp. He clutched at a rocky projection, and grinned his thanks back to her.

Down on the ground the monster was wallowing like a dog with pepper in its eyes. He shook his head from side to side, pawed at it, and opened his mouth repeatedly to its widest extent. Presently he got a huge front foot on the stump of the shaft and managed to tear the blade out. Then he threw up his head, jaws wide and spouting blood, and glared up at the crag with such concentrated and intelligent fury that Valeria trembled and drew her sword. The scales along his back and flanks turned from rusty brown to a dull lurid red. Most horribly the monster's silence was broken. The sounds that issued from his blood-streaming jaws did not sound like anything that could have been produced by an earthly creation.

With harsh, grating roars, the dragon hurled himself at the crag that was the citadel of his enemies. Again and again his mighty head crashed upward through the branches, snapping vainly on empty air. He hurled his full ponderous weight against the rock until it vibrated from base to crest. And rearing upright he gripped it with his front legs like a man and tried to tear it up by the roots, as if it had been a tree.

This exhibition of primordial fury chilled the blood in Valeria's veins, but Conan was too close to the primitive himself to feel anything but a comprehending interest. To the barbarian, no such gulf existed between himself and other men, and the animals, as existed in the conception of Valeria. The monster below them, to Conan, was merely a form of life differing from himself mainly in physical shape. He attributed to it characteristics similar to his own, and saw in its wrath a counterpart of his rages, in its roars and bellowings merely reptilian equivalents to the curses he had bestowed upon it. Feeling a kinship with all wild things, even dragons, it was impossible for him to experience the sick horror which assailed Valeria at the sight of the brute's ferocity.

He sat watching it tranquilly, and pointed out the various changes that were taking place in its voice and actions.

'The poison's taking hold,' he said with conviction.

'I don't believe it.' To Valeria it seemed preposterous to suppose that anything, however lethal, could have any effect on that mountain of muscle and fury.

'There's pain in his voice,' declared Conan. 'First he was merely angry because of the stinging in his jaw. Now he feels the bite of the poison. Look! He's staggering. He'll be blind in a few more minutes. What did I tell you?'

For suddenly the dragon had lurched about and went crashing off through the bushes.

'Is he running away?' inquired Valeria uneasily.

'He's making for the pool!' Conan sprang up, galvanized into swift activity. 'The poison makes him thirsty. Come on! He'll be blind in a few moments, but he can smell his way back to the foot of the crag, and if our scent's here still, he'll sit there until he dies. And others of his kind may come at his cries. Let's go!'

'Down there?' Valeria was aghast.

'Sure! We'll make for the city! They may cut our heads off there, but it's our only chance. We may run into a thousand more dragons on the way, but it's sure death to stay here. If we wait until he dies, we may have a dozen more to deal with. After me, in a hurry!'

He went down the ramp as swiftly as an ape, pausing only to aid his less agile companion, who, until she saw the Cimmerian climb, had fancied herself the equal of any man in the rigging of a ship or on the sheer face of a cliff.

They descended into the gloom below the branches and slid to the ground silently, though Valeria felt as if the pounding of her heart must surely be heard from far away. A noisy gurgling and lapping beyond the dense thicket indicated that the dragon was drinking at the pool.

'As soon as his belly is full he'll be back,' muttered Conan. 'It may take hours for the poison to kill him – if it does at all.'

Somewhere beyond the forest the sun was sinking to the horizon. The forest was a misty twilight place of black shadows and dim vistas. Conan gripped Valeria's wrist and glided away from the foot of the crag. He made less noise than a breeze blowing among the tree-trunks, but Valeria felt as if her soft boots were betraying their flight to all the forest.

'I don't think he can follow a trail,' muttered Conan. 'But if a wind blew our body-scent to him, he could smell us out.'

'Mitra grant that the wind blow not!' Valeria breathed.

Her face was a pallid oval in the gloom. She gripped her sword in her free hand, but the feel of the shagreen-bound hilt inspired only a feeling of helplessness in her.

They were still some distance from the edge of the forest when they heard a snapping and crashing behind them. Valeria bit her lip to check a cry.

'He's on our trail!' she whispered fiercely.

Conan shook his head.

'He didn't smell us at the rock, and he's blundering about through the forest trying to pick up our scent. Come on! It's the city or nothing now! He could tear down any tree we'd climb. If only the wind stays down—'

They stole on until the trees began to thin out ahead of them. Behind them the forest was a black impenetrable ocean of shadows. The ominous crackling still sounded behind them, as the dragon blundered in his erratic course.

'There's the plain ahead,' breathed Valeria. 'A little more and we'll—'

'Crom!' swore Conan.

'Mitra!' whispered Valeria.

Out of the south a wind had sprung up.

It blew over them directly into the black forest behind them. Instantly a horrible roar shook the woods. The aimless snapping and crackling of the bushes changed to a sustained crashing as the dragon came like a hurricane straight toward the spot from which the scent of his enemies was wafted.

'Run!' snarled Conan, his eyes blazing like those of a trapped wolf. 'It's all we can do!'

Sailors' boots are not made for sprinting, and the life of a pirate does not train one for a runner. Within a hundred yards Valeria was panting and reeling in her gait, and behind them the crashing gave way to a rolling thunder as the monster broke out of the thickets and into the more open ground.

Conan's iron arm about the woman's waist half lifted her; her feet scarcely touched the earth as she was borne along at a speed she could never have attained herself. If he could keep out of the

195

beast's way for a bit, perhaps that betraying wind would shift – but the wind held, and a quick glance over his shoulder showed Conan that the monster was almost upon them, coming like a war-galley in front of a hurricane. He thrust Valeria from him with a force that sent her reeling a dozen feet to fall in a crumpled heap at the foot of the nearest tree, and the Cimmerian wheeled in the path of the thundering titan.

Convinced that his death was upon him, the Cimmerian acted according to his instinct, and hurled himself full at the awful face that was bearing down on him. He leaped, slashing like a wildcat, felt his sword cut deep into the scales that sheathed the mighty snout – and then a terrific impact knocked him rolling and tumbling for fifty feet with all the wind and half the life battered out of him.

How the stunned Cimmerian regained his feet, not even he could have ever told. But the only thought that filled his brain was of the woman lying dazed and helpless almost in the path of the hurtling fiend, and before the breath came whistling back into his gullet he was standing over her with his sword in his hand.

She lay where he had thrown her, but she was struggling to a sitting posture. Neither tearing tusks nor trampling feet had touched her. It had been a shoulder or front leg that struck Conan, and the blind monster rushed on, forgetting the victims whose scent it had been following, in the sudden agony of its death throes. Headlong on its course it thundered until its low-hung head crashed into a gigantic tree in its path. The impact tore the tree up by the roots and must have dashed the brains from the misshapen skull. Tree and monster fell together, and the dazed humans saw the branches and leaves shaken by the convulsions of the creature they covered – and then grow quiet.

Conan lifted Valeria to her feet and together they started away at a reeling run. A few moments later they emerged into the still twilight of the treeless plain.

Conan paused an instant and glanced back at the ebon fastness behind them. Not a leaf stirred, nor a bird chirped. It stood as silent as it must have stood before Man was created.

'Come on,' muttered Conan, taking his companion's hand. 'It's touch and go now. If more dragons come out of the woods after us—'

He did not have to finish the sentence.

The city looked very far away across the plain, farther than it had looked from the crag. Valeria's heart hammered until she felt as if it would strangle her. At every step she expected to hear the crashing of the bushes and see another colossal nightmare bearing down upon them. But nothing disturbed the silence of the thickets.

With the first mile between them and the woods, Valeria breathed more easily. Her buoyant self-confidence began to thaw out again. The sun had set and darkness was gathering over the plain, lightened a little by the stars that made stunted ghosts out of the cactus growths.

'No cattle, no plowed fields,' muttered Conan. 'How do these people live?'

'Perhaps the cattle are in pens for the night,' suggested Valeria, 'and the fields and grazing pastures are on the other side of the city.'

'Maybe,' he grunted. 'I didn't see any from the crag, though.'

The moon came up behind the city, etching walls and towers blackly in the yellow glow. Valeria shivered. Black against the moon the strange city had a somber, sinister look.

Perhaps something of the same feeling occurred to Conan, for he stopped, glanced about him, and grunted: 'We stop here, No use coming to their gates in the night. They probably wouldn't let us in. Besides, we need rest, and we don't know how they'll receive us. A few hours' sleep will put us in better shape to fight or run.'

He led the way to a bed of cactus which grew in a circle – a phenomenon common to the southern desert. With his sword he chopped an opening, and motioned Valeria to enter.

'We'll be safe from snakes here, anyhow.'

She glanced fearfully back toward the black line that indicated the forest some six miles away.

'Suppose a dragon comes out of the woods?'

'We'll keep watch,' he answered, though he made no suggestion as to what they would do in such an event. He was staring at the city, a few miles away. Not a light shone from spire or tower. A great black mass of mystery, it reared cryptically against the moonlit sky.

'Lie down and sleep. I'll keep the first watch.'

She hesitated, glancing at him uncertainly, but he sat down cross-legged in the opening, facing toward the plain, his sword across his knees, his back to her. Without further comment she lay down on the sand inside the spiky circle.

'Wake me when the moon is at its zenith,' she directed.

He did not reply nor look toward her. Her last impression, as she sank into slumber, was of his muscular figure, immobile as a statue hewn out of bronze, outlined against the low-hanging stars.

2

By the Blaze of the Fire Jewels

Valeria awoke with a start, to the realization that a gray dawn was stealing over the plain.

She sat up, rubbing her eyes. Conan squatted beside the cactus, cutting off the thick pears and dexterously twitching out the spikes.

'You didn't awake me,' she accused. 'You let me sleep all night!'

'You were tired,' he answered. 'Your posterior must have been sore, too, after that long ride. You pirates aren't used to horseback.'

'What about yourself?' she retorted.

'I was a *kozak* before I was a pirate,' he answered. 'They live in the saddle. I snatch naps like a panther watching beside the trail for a deer to come by. My ears keep watch while my eyes sleep.'

And indeed the giant barbarian seemed as much refreshed as if he had slept the whole night on a golden bed. Having removed the thorns, and peeled off the tough skin, he handed the girl a thick, juicy cactus leaf.

'Skin your teeth in that pear. It's food and drink to a desert man. I was a chief of the Zuagirs once – desert men who live by plundering the caravans.'

'Is there anything you haven't been?' inquired the girl, half in derision and half in fascination.

'I've never been king of an Hyborian kingdom,' he grinned, taking an enormous mouthful of cactus. 'But I've dreamed of being even that. I may be too, some day. Why shouldn't I?'

She shook her head in wonder at his calm audacity, and fell to devouring her pear. She found it not unpleasing to the palate, and full of cool and thirst-satisfying juice. Finishing his meal, Conan wiped his hands in the sand, rose, ran his fingers through his thick black mane, hitched at his sword-belt and said:

'Well, let's go. If the people in that city are going to cut our throats they may as well do it now, before the heat of the day begins.'

His grim humor was unconscious, but Valeria reflected that it might be prophetic. She too hitched her sword belt as she rose. Her terrors of the night were past. The roaring dragons of the distant forest were like a dim dream. There was a swagger in her stride as she moved off beside the Cimmerian. Whatever perils lay ahead of them, their foes would be men. And Valeria of the Red Brotherhood had never seen the face of the man she feared.

Conan glanced down at her as she strode along beside him with her swinging stride that matched his own.

'You walk more like a hillman than a sailor,' he said. 'You must be an Aquilonian. The suns of Darfar never burnt your white skin brown. Many a princess would envy you.'

'I am from Aquilonia,' she replied. His compliments no longer irritated her. His evident admiration pleased her. For another man to have kept her watch while she slept would have angered her; she had always fiercely resented any man's attempting to shield or protect her because of her sex. But she found a secret pleasure in the fact that this man had done so. And he had not taken advantage of her fright and the weakness resulting from it. After all, she reflected, her companion was no common man.

The sun rose behind the city, turning the towers to a sinister crimson.

'Black last night against the moon,' grunted Conan, his eyes clouding with the abysmal superstition of the barbarian. 'Blood-red as a threat of blood against the sun this dawn. I do not like this city.'

But they went on, and as they went Conan pointed out the fact that no road ran to the city from the north.

'No cattle have trampled the plain on this side of the city,' said he. 'No plowshare has touched the earth for years, maybe centuries. But look: once this plain was cultivated.'

Valeria saw the ancient irrigation ditches he indicated, half filled in places, and overgrown with cactus. She frowned with perplexity as her eyes swept over the plain that stretched on all sides of the city to the forest edge, which marched in a vast, dim ring. Vision did not extend beyond that ring.

She looked uneasily at the city. No helmets or spear-heads gleamed on battlements, no trumpets sounded, no challenge rang from the towers. A silence as absolute as that of the forest brooded over the walls and minarets.

The sun was high above the eastern horizon when they stood before the great gate in the northern wall, in the shadow of the lofty rampart. Rust flecked the iron bracings of the mighty bronze portal. Spiderwebs glistened thickly on hinge and sill and bolted panel.

'It hasn't been opened for years!' exclaimed Valeria.

'A dead city,' grunted Conan. 'That's why the ditches were broken and the plain untouched.'

'But who built it? Who dwelt here? Where did they go? Why did they abandon it?'

'Who can say? Maybe an exiled clan of Stygians built it. Maybe not. It doesn't look like Stygian architecture. Maybe the people were wiped out by enemies, or a plague exterminated them.'

'In that case their treasures may still be gathering dust and cobwebs in there,' suggested Valeria, the acquisitive instincts of her profession waking in her; prodded, too, by feminine curiosity. 'Can we open the gate? Let's go in and explore a bit.'

Conan eyed the heavy portal dubiously, but placed his massive shoulder against it and thrust with all the power of his muscular calves and thighs. With a rasping screech of rusty hinges the gate moved ponderously inward, and Conan straightened and drew his sword. Valeria stared over his shoulder, and made a sound indicative of surprise.

They were not looking into an open street or court as one would have expected. The opened gate, or door, gave directly into a long, broad hall which ran away and away until its vista grew indistinct in the distance. It was of heroic proportions, and the floor of a curious red stone, cut in square tiles, that seemed to smolder as if with reflection of flames. The walls were of a shiny green material.

'Jade, or I'm a Shemite!' swore Conan.

'Not in such quantity!' protested Valeria.

'I've looted enough from the Khitan caravans to know what I'm talking about,' he asserted. 'That's jade!'

The vaulted ceiling was of lapis lazuli, adorned with clusters of great green stones that gleamed with a poisonous radiance.

'Green fire-stones,' growled Conan. 'That's what the people of Punt call them. They're supposed to be the petrified eyes of those prehistoric snakes the ancients called Golden Serpents. They glow like a cat's eyes in the dark. At night this hall would be lighted by them, but it would be a hellishly weird illumination. Let's look around. We might find a cache of jewels.'

'Shut the door,' advised Valeria. 'I'd hate to have to outrun a dragon down this hall.'

Conan grinned, and replied: 'I don't believe the dragons ever leave the forest.'

But he complied, and pointed out the broken bolt on the inner side.

'I thought I heard something snap when I shoved against it. That bolt's freshly broken. Rust has eaten nearly through it. If the people ran away, why should it have been bolted on the inside?'

'They undoubtedly left by another door,' suggested Valeria.

She wondered how many centuries had passed since the light of outer day had filtered into that great hall through the open door. Sunlight was finding its way somehow into the hall, and they quickly saw the source. High up in the vaulted ceiling skylights were set in slot-like openings – translucent sheets of some crystal-line substance. In the splotches of shadow between them, the green jewels winked like the eyes of angry cats. Beneath their feet the dully lurid floor smoldered with changing hues and colors of flame. It was like treading the floors of hell with evil stars blinking overhead.

Three balustraded galleries ran along on each side of the hall, one above the other.

'A four-storied house,' grunted Conan, 'and this hall extends to the roof. It's long as a street. I seem to see a door at the other end.'

Valeria shrugged her white shoulders.

'Your eyes are better than mine, then, though I'm accounted sharp-eyed among the sea-rovers.'

They turned into an open door at random, and traversed a series of empty chambers, floored like the hall, and with walls of the same green jade, or of marble or ivory or chalcedony, adorned with friezes of bronze, gold or silver. In the ceilings the green fire-gems were set, and their light was as ghostly and illusive as Conan had predicted. Under the witch-fire glow the intruders moved like specters.

Some of the chambers lacked this illumination, and their door-ways showed black as the mouth of the Pit. These Conan and Valeria avoided, keeping always to the lighted chambers.

Cobwebs hung in the corners, but there was no perceptible accumulation of dust on the floor, or on the tables and seats of marble, jade or carnelian which occupied the chambers. Here and there were rugs of that silk known as Khitan which is practically indestructible. Nowhere did they find any windows, or doors open-ing into streets or courts. Each door merely opened into another chamber or hall.

'Why don't we come to a street?' grumbled Valeria. 'This place or whatever we're in must be as big as the king of Turan's seraglio.'

'They must not have perished of plague,' said Conan, meditat-ing upon the mystery of the empty city. 'Otherwise we'd find skeletons. Maybe it became haunted, and everybody got up and left. Maybe—'

'Maybe, hell!' broke in Valeria rudely. 'We'll never know. Look at these friezes. They portray men. What race do they belong to?'

Conan scanned them and shook his head.

'I never saw people exactly like them. But there's the smack of the East about them – Vendhya, maybe, or Kosala.'

'Were you a king in Kosala?' she asked, masking her keen curi-osity with derision.

'No. But I was a war-chief of the Afghulis who live in the Himelian mountains above the borders of Vendhya. These people favor the Kosalans. But why should Kosalans be building a city this far to west?'

The figures portrayed were those of slender, olive-skinned men and women, with finely chiseled, exotic features. They wore filmy robes and many delicate jeweled ornaments, and were depicted mostly in attitudes of feasting, dancing or love-making.

'Easterners, all right,' grunted Conan, 'but from where I don't know. They must have lived a disgustingly peaceful life, though, or they'd have scenes of wars and fights. Let's go up that stair.'

It was an ivory spiral that wound up from the chamber in which they were standing. They mounted three flights and came into a broad chamber on the fourth floor, which seemed to be the highest tier in the building. Skylights in the ceiling illuminated the room, in which light the fire-gems winked pallidly. Glancing through the doors they saw, except on one side, a series of similarly lighted chambers. This other door opened upon a balustraded gallery that overhung a hall much smaller than the one they had recently explored on the lower floor.

'Hell!' Valeria sat down disgustedly on a jade bench. 'The people who deserted this city must have taken all their treasures with them. I'm tired of wandering through these bare rooms at random.'

'All these upper chambers seem to be lighted,' said Conan. 'I wish we could find a window that overlooked the city. Let's have a look through that door over there.'

'You have a look,' advised Valeria. 'I'm going to sit here and rest my feet.'

Conan disappeared through the door opposite that one opening upon the gallery, and Valeria leaned back with her hands clasped behind her head, and thrust her booted legs out in front of her. These silent rooms and halls with their gleaming green clusters of ornaments and burning crimson floors were beginning to depress her. She wished they could find their way out of the maze into which they had wandered and emerge into a street. She wondered idly what furtive, dark feet had glided over those flaming floors in past centuries, how many deeds of cruelty and mystery those winking ceiling-gems had blazed down upon.

It was a faint noise that brought her out of her reflections. She was on her feet with her sword in her hand before she realized what had disturbed her. Conan had not returned, and she knew it was not he that she had heard.

The sound had come from somewhere beyond the door that opened on to the gallery. Soundlessly in her soft leather boots she glided through it, crept across the balcony and peered down between the heavy balustrades.

A man was stealing along the hall.

The sight of a human being in this supposedly deserted city was a startling shock. Crouching down behind the stone balusters, with every nerve tingling, Valeria glared down at the stealthy figure.

The man in no way resembled the figures depicted on the friezes. He was slightly above middle height, very dark, though not negroid. He was naked but for a scanty silk clout that only partly covered his muscular hips, and a leather girdle, a hand's breadth broad, about his lean waist. His long black hair hung in lank strands about his shoulders, giving him a wild appearance. He was gaunt, but knots and cords of muscles stood out on his arms and legs, without that fleshy padding that presents a pleasing symmetry of contour. He was built with an economy that was almost repellent.

Yet it was not so much his physical appearance as his attitude that impressed the woman who watched him. He slunk along, stooped in a semi-crouch, his head turning from side to side. He grasped a wide-tipped blade in his right hand, and she saw it shake with the intensity of the emotion that gripped him. He was afraid, trembling in the grip of some dire terror. When he turned his head she caught the blaze of wild eyes among the lank strands of black hair.

He did not see her. On tiptoe he glided across the hall and vanished through an open door. A moment later she heard a choking cry, and then silence fell again.

Consumed with curiosity, Valeria glided along the gallery until she came to a door above the one through which the man had passed. It opened into another, smaller gallery that encircled a large chamber.

This chamber was on the third floor, and its ceiling was not so high as that of the hall. It was lighted only by the fire-stones, and their weird green glow left the spaces under the balcony in shadows.

Valeria's eyes widened. The man she had seen was still in the chamber.

He lay face down on a dark crimson carpet in the middle of the room. His body was limp, his arms spread wide. His curved sword lay near him.

She wondered why he should lie there so motionless. Then her eyes narrowed as she stared down at the rug on which he lay. Beneath and about him the fabric showed a slightly different color, a deeper, brighter crimson.

Shivering slightly, she crouched down closer behind the balustrade, intently scanning the shadows under the overhanging gallery. They gave up no secret.

Suddenly another figure entered the grim drama. He was a man similar to the first, and he came in by a door opposite that which gave upon the hall.

His eyes glared at the sight of the man on the floor, and he spoke something in a staccato voice that sounded like 'Chicmec!' The other did not move.

The man stepped quickly across the floor, bent, gripped the fallen man's shoulder and turned him over. A choking cry escaped him as the head fell back limply, disclosing a throat that had been severed from ear to ear.

The man let the corpse fall back upon the blood-stained carpet, and sprang to his feet, shaking like a wind-blown leaf. His face was an ashy mask of fear. But with one knee flexed for flight, he froze suddenly, became as immobile as an image, staring across the chamber with dilated eyes.

In the shadows beneath the balcony a ghostly light began to glow and grow, a light that was not part of the fire-stone gleam. Valeria felt her hair stir as she watched it; for, dimly visible in the throbbing radiance, there floated a human skull, and it was from this skull – human yet appallingly misshapen – that the spectral light seemed to emanate. It hung there like a disembodied head, conjured out of night and the shadows, growing more and more distinct; human, and yet not human as she knew humanity.

The man stood motionless, an embodiment of paralysed horror, staring fixedly at the apparition. The thing moved out from the wall and a grotesque shadow moved with it. Slowly the shadow became visible as a man-like figure whose naked torso and limbs shone whitely, with the hue of bleached bones. The bare skull on its shoulders grinned eyelessly, in the midst of its unholy nimbus, and the man confronting it seemed unable to take his eyes from it. He stood still, his sword dangling from nerveless fingers, on his face the expression of a man bound by the spells of a mesmerist.

Valeria realized that it was not fear alone that paralysed him.

Some hellish quality of that throbbing glow had robbed him of his power to think and act. She herself, safely above the scene, felt the subtle impact of a nameless emanation that was a threat to sanity.

The horror swept toward its victim and he moved at last, but only to drop his sword and sink to his knees, covering his eyes with his hands. Dumbly he awaited the stroke of the blade that now gleamed in the apparition's hand as it reared above him like Death triumphant over mankind.

Valeria acted according to the first impulse of her wayward nature. With one tigerish movement she was over the balustrade and dropping to the floor behind the awful shape. It wheeled at the thud of her soft boots on the floor, but even as it turned, her keen blade lashed down, and a fierce exultation swept her as she felt the edge cleave solid flesh and mortal bone.

The apparition cried out gurglingly and went down, severed through shoulder, breast-bone and spine, and as it fell the burning skull rolled clear, revealing a lank mop of black hair and a dark face twisted in the convulsions of death. Beneath the horrific masquerade there was a human being, a man similar to the one kneeling supinely on the floor.

The latter looked up at the sound of the blow and the cry, and now he glared in wild-eyed amazement at the white-skinned woman who stood over the corpse with a dripping sword in her hand.

He staggered up, yammering as if the sight had almost unseated his reason. She was amazed to realize that she understood him. He was gibbering in the Stygian tongue, though in a dialect unfamiliar to her.

'Who are you? Whence come you? What do you in Xuchotl?' Then rushing on, without waiting for her to reply: 'But you are a friend – goddess or devil, it makes no difference! You have slain the Burning Skull! It was but a man beneath it, after all! We deemed it a demon *they* conjured up out of the catacombs! *Listen!*'

He stopped short in his ravings and stiffened, straining his ears with painful intensity. The girl heard nothing.

'We must hasten!' he whispered. '*They* are west of the Great

Hall! They may be all around us here! They may be creeping upon us even now!'

He seized her wrist in a convulsive grasp she found hard to break.

'Whom do you mean by "they"?' she demanded.

He stared at her uncomprehendingly for an instant, as if he found her ignorance hard to understand.

'They?' he stammered vaguely. 'Why – why, the people of Xotalanc! The clan of the man you slew. They who dwell by the eastern gate.'

'You mean to say this city is inhabited?' she exclaimed.

'Aye! Aye!' He was writhing in the impatience of apprehension. 'Come away! Come quick! We must return to Tecuhltli!'

'Where is that?' she demanded.

'The quarter by the western gate!' He had her wrist again and was pulling her toward the door through which he had first come. Great beads of perspiration dripped from his dark forehead, and his eyes blazed with terror.

'Wait a minute!' she growled, flinging off his hand. 'Keep your hands off me, or I'll split your skull. What's all this about? Who are you? Where would you take me?'

He took a firm grip on himself, casting glances to all sides, and began speaking so fast his words tripped over each other.

'My name is Techotl. I am of Tecuhltli. I and this man who lies with his throat cut came into the Halls of Silence to try and ambush some of the Xotalancas. But we became separated and I returned here to find him with his gullet slit. The Burning Skull did it, I know, just as he would have slain me had you not killed him. But perhaps he was not alone. Others may be stealing from Xotalanc! The gods themselves blench at the fate of those they take alive!'

At the thought he shook as with an ague and his dark skin grew ashy. Valeria frowned puzzledly at him. She sensed intelligence behind this rigmarole, but it was meaningless to her.

. She turned toward the skull, which still glowed and pulsed on the floor, and was reaching a booted toe tentatively toward it, when the man who called himself Techotl sprang forward with a cry.

'Do not touch it! Do not even look at it! Madness and death lurk in it. The wizards of Xotalanc understand its secret – they found it in the catacombs, where lie the bones of terrible kings who ruled in Xuchotl in the black centuries of the past. To gaze upon it freezes the blood and withers the brain of a man who understands not its mystery. To touch it causes madness and destruction.'

She scowled at him uncertainly. He was not a reassuring figure, with his lean, muscle-knotted frame, and snaky locks. In his eyes, behind the glow of terror, lurked a weird light she had never seen in the eyes of a man wholly sane. Yet he seemed sincere in his protestations.

'Come!' he begged, reaching for her hand, and then recoiling as he remembered her warning. 'You are a stranger. How you came here I do not know, but if you were a goddess or a demon, come to aid Tecuhltli, you would know all the things you have asked me. You must be from beyond the great forest, whence our ancestors came. But you are our friend, or you would not have slain my enemy. Come quickly, before the Xotalancas find us and slay us!'

From his repellent, impassioned face she glanced to the sinister skull, smoldering and glowing on the floor near the dead man. It was like a skull seen in a dream, undeniably human, yet with disturbing distortions and malformations of contour and outline. In life the wearer of that skull must have presented an alien and monstrous aspect. Life? It seemed to possess some sort of life of its own. Its jaws yawned at her and snapped together. Its radiance grew brighter, more vivid, yet the impression of nightmare grew too; it was a dream; all life was a dream – it was Techotl's urgent voice which snapped Valeria back from the dim gulfs whither she was drifting.

'Do not look at the skull! Do not look at the skull!' It was a far cry across unreckoned voids.

Valeria shook herself like a lion shaking his mane. Her vision cleared. Techotl was chattering: 'In life it housed the awful brain

209

of a king of magicians! It holds still the life and fire of magic drawn from outer spaces!'

With a curse Valeria leaped, lithe as a panther, and the skull crashed to flaming bits under her swinging sword. Somewhere in the room, or in the void, or in the dim reaches of her consciousness, an inhuman voice cried out in pain and rage.

Techotl's hand was plucking at her arm and he was gibbering: 'You have broken it! You have destroyed it! Not all the black arts of Xotalanc can rebuild it! Come away! Come away quickly, now!'

'But I can't go,' she protested. 'I have a friend somewhere near by—'

The flare of his eyes cut her short as he stared past her with an expression grown ghastly. She wheeled just as four men rushed through as many doors, converging on the pair in the center of the chamber.

They were like the others she had seen, the same knotted muscles bulging on otherwise gaunt limbs, the same lank blue-black hair, the same mad glare in their wide eyes. They were armed and clad like Techotl, but on the breast of each was painted a white skull.

There were no challenges or war-cries. Like blood-mad tigers the men of Xotalanc sprang at the throats of their enemies. Techotl met them with the fury of desperation, ducked the swipe of a wide-headed blade, and grappled with the wielder, and bore him to the floor where they rolled and wrestled in murderous silence.

The other three swarmed on Valeria, their weird eyes red as the eyes of mad dogs.

She killed the first who came within reach before he could strike a blow, her long straight blade splitting his skull even as his own sword lifted for a stroke. She side-stepped a thrust, even as she parried a slash. Her eyes danced and her lips smiled without mercy. Again she was Valeria of the Red Brotherhood, and the hum of her steel was like a bridal song in her ears.

Her sword darted past a blade that sought to parry, and sheathed six inches of its point in a leather-guarded midriff. The man gasped agonizedly and went to his knees, but his tall mate lunged in, in ferocious silence, raining blow on blow so furiously that Valeria had no opportunity to counter. She stepped back coolly, parrying the strokes and watching for her chance to thrust home. He could not long keep up that flailing whirlwind. His arm would tire, his wind would fail; he would weaken, falter, and then her blade would slide smoothly into his heart. A sidelong glance showed her Techotl kneeling on the breast of his antagonist and striving to break the other's hold on his wrist and to drive home a dagger.

Sweat beaded the forehead of the man facing her, and his eyes were like burning coals. Smite as he would, he could not break past nor beat down her guard. His breath came in gusty gulps, his blows began to fall erratically. She stepped back to draw him out – and felt her thighs locked in an iron grip. She had forgotten the wounded man on the floor.

Crouching on his knees, he held her with both arms locked about her legs, and his mate croaked in triumph and began working his way around to come at her from the left side. Valeria wrenched and tore savagely, but in vain. She could free herself of this clinging menace with a downward flick of her sword, but in that instant the curved blade of the tall warrior would crash through her skull. The wounded man began to worry at her bare thigh with his teeth like a wild beast.

She reached down with her left hand and gripped his long hair, forcing his head back so that his white teeth and rolling eyes gleamed up at her. The tall Xotalanc cried out fiercely and leaped in, smiting with all the fury of his arm. Awkwardly she parried the stroke, and it beat the flat of her blade down on her head so that she saw sparks flash before her eyes, and staggered. Up went the sword again, with a low, beast-like cry of triumph – and then a giant form loomed behind the Xotalanc and steel flashed like a jet of blue lightning. The cry of the warrior broke short and he went down like an ox beneath the pole-ax, his brains gushing from his skull that had been split to the throat.

'Conan!' gasped Valeria. In a gust of passion she turned on the Xotalanc whose long hair she still gripped in her left hand. 'Dog of hell!' Her blade swished as it cut the air in an upswinging arc with a blur in the middle, and the headless body slumped down, spurting blood. She hurled the severed head across the room.

'What the devil's going on here?' Conan bestrode the corpse of the man he had killed, broadsword in hand, glaring about him in amazement.

Techotl was rising from the twitching figure of the last Xotalanc, shaking red drops from his dagger. He was bleeding from the stab deep in the thigh. He stared at Conan with dilated eyes.

'What is all this?' Conan demanded again, not yet recovered from the stunning surprise of finding Valeria engaged in a savage battle with these fantastic figures in a city he had thought empty and uninhabited. Returning from an aimless exploration of the upper chambers to find Valeria missing from the room where he had left her, he had followed the sounds of strife that burst on his dumfounded ears.

'Five dead dogs!' exclaimed Techotl, his flaming eyes reflecting a ghastly exultation. 'Five slain! Five crimson nails for the black pillar! The gods of blood be thanked!'

He lifted quivering hands on high, and then, with the face of a fiend, he spat on the corpses and stamped on their faces, dancing in his ghoulish glee. His recent allies eyed him in amazement, and Conan asked, in the Aquilonian tongue: 'Who is this madman?'

Valeria shrugged her shoulders.

'He says his name's Techotl. From his babblings I gather that his people live at one end of this crazy city, and these others at the other end. Maybe we'd better go with him. He seems friendly, and it's easy to see that the other clan isn't.'

Techotl had ceased his dancing and was listening again, his head tilted sidewise, dog-like, triumph struggling with fear in his repellent countenance.

'Come away, now!' he whispered. 'We have done enough! Five dead dogs! My people will welcome you! They will honor you! But come! It is far to Tecuhltli. At any moment the Xotalancs may come on us in numbers too great even for your swords.'

'Lead the way,' grunted Conan.

Techotl instantly mounted a stair leading up to the gallery, beckoning them to follow him, which they did, moving rapidly to keep on his heels. Having reached the gallery, he plunged into a door that opened toward the west, and hurried through chamber after chamber, each lighted by skylights or green fire-jewels.

'What sort of a place can this be?' muttered Valeria under her breath.

'Crom knows!' answered Conan. 'I've seen *his* kind before, though. They live on the shores of Lake Zuad, near the border of Kush. They're a sort of mongrel Stygians, mixed with another race that wandered into Stygia from the east some centuries ago and were absorbed by them. They're called Tlazitlans. I'm willing to bet it wasn't they who built this city, though.'

Techotl's fear did not seem to diminish as they drew away from the chamber where the dead men lay. He kept twisting his head on his shoulder to listen for sounds of pursuit, and stared with burning intensity into every doorway they passed.

Valeria shivered in spite of herself. She feared no man. But the weird floor beneath her feet, the uncanny jewels over her head, dividing the lurking shadows among them, the stealth and terror of their guide, impressed her with a nameless apprehension, a sensation of lurking, inhuman peril.

'They may be between us and Tecuhltli!' he whispered once. 'We must beware lest they be lying in wait!'

'Why don't we get out of this infernal palace, and take to the streets?' demanded Valeria.

'There are no streets in Xuchotl,' he answered. 'No squares nor open courts. The whole city is built like one giant palace under one great roof. The nearest approach to a street is the Great Hall which traverses the city from the north gate to the south gate. The only doors opening into the outer world are the city gates, through which no living man has passed for fifty years.'

'How long have you dwelt here?' asked Conan.

'I was born in the castle of Tecuhltli thirty-five years ago. I have never set foot outside the city. For the love of the gods, let us go silently! These halls may be full of lurking devils. Olmec shall tell you all when we reach Tecuhltli.'

So in silence they glided on with the green fire-stones blinking overhead and the flaming floors smoldering under their feet, and it seemed to Valeria as if they fled through hell, guided by a dark-faced lank-haired goblin.

Yet it was Conan who halted them as they were crossing an unusually wide chamber. His wilderness-bred ears were keener even than the ears of Techotl whetted though these were by a lifetime of warfare in those silent corridors.

'You think some of your enemies may be ahead of us, lying in ambush?'

'They prowl through these rooms at all hours,' answered Techotl, 'as do we. The halls and chambers between Tecuhltli and Xotalanc are a disputed region, owned by no man. We call it the Halls of Silence. Why do you ask?'

'Because men are in the chambers ahead of us,' answered Conan. 'I heard steel clink against stone.'

Again a shaking seized Techotl, and he clenched his teeth to keep them from chattering.

'Perhaps they are your friends,' suggested Valeria.

'We dare not chance it,' he panted, and moved with frenzied activity. He turned aside and glided through a doorway on the left which led into a chamber from which an ivory staircase wound down into darkness.

'This leads to an unlighted corridor below us!' he hissed, great beads of perspiration standing out on his brow. 'They may be lurking there, too. It may all be a trick to draw us into it. But we must take the chance that they have laid their ambush in the rooms above. Come swiftly, now!'

Softly as phantoms they descended the stair and came to the mouth of a corridor black as night. They crouched there for a moment, listening, and then melted into it. As they moved along, Valeria's flesh crawled between her shoulders in momentary expectation of a sword-thrust in the dark. But for Conan's iron fingers gripping her arm she had no physical cognizance of her companions. Neither made as much noise as a cat would have made. The darkness was absolute. One hand, outstretched, touched a wall, and occasionally she felt a door under her fingers. The hallway seemed interminable.

Suddenly they were galvanized by a sound behind them. Valeria's flesh crawled anew, for she recognized it as the soft opening of a door. Men had come into the corridor behind them. Even with the thought she stumbled over something that felt like a human skull. It rolled across the floor with an appalling clatter.

'Run!' yelped Techotl, a note of hysteria in his voice, and was away down the corridor like a flying ghost.

Again Valeria felt Conan's hand bearing her up and sweeping her along as they raced after their guide. Conan could see in the dark no better than she, but he possessed a sort of instinct that made his course unerring. Without his support and guidance she would have fallen or stumbled against the wall. Down the corridor they sped, while the swift patter of flying feet drew closer and closer, and then suddenly Techotl panted: 'Here is the stair! After me, quick! Oh, quick!'

His hand came out of the dark and caught Valeria's wrist as she stumbled blindly on the steps. She felt herself half dragged, half lifted up the winding stair, while Conan released her and turned on the steps, his ears and instincts telling him their foes were hard at their backs. *And the sounds were not all those of human feet.*

Something came writhing up the steps, something that slithered and rustled and brought a chill in the air with it. Conan lashed down with his great sword and felt the blade shear through something that might have been flesh and bone, and cut deep into the stair beneath. Something touched his foot that chilled like the touch of frost, and then the darkness beneath him was disturbed by a frightful thrashing and lashing, and a man cried out in agony.

The next moment Conan was racing up the winding staircase, and through a door that stood open at the head.

Valeria and Techotl were already through, and Techotl slammed the door and shot a bolt across it – the first Conan had seen since they left the outer gate.

Then he turned and ran across the well-lighted chamber into which they had come, and as they passed through the farther door, Conan glanced back and saw the door groaning and straining under heavy pressure violently applied from the other side.

Though Techotl did not abate either his speed or his caution, he seemed more confident now. He had the air of a man who has come into familiar territory, within call of friends.

But Conan renewed his terror by asking: 'What was that thing that I fought on the stair?'

'The men of Xotalanc,' answered Techotl, without looking back. 'I told you the halls were full of them.'

'This wasn't a man,' grunted Conan. 'It was something that crawled, and it was as cold as ice to the touch. I think I cut it asunder. It fell back on the men who were following us, and must have killed one of them in its death throes.'

Techotl's head jerked back, his face ashy again. Convulsively he quickened his pace.

'It was the Crawler! A monster *they* have brought out of the catacombs to aid them! What it is, we do not know, but we have found our people hideously slain by it. In Set's name, hasten! If they put it on our trail, it will follow us to the very doors of Tecuhltli!'

'I doubt it,' grunted Conan. 'That was a shrewd cut I dealt it on the stair.'

'Hasten! Hasten!' groaned Techotl.

They ran through a series of green-lit chambers, traversed a broad hall, and halted before a giant bronze door.

Techotl said: 'This is Tecuhltli!'

3

The People of the Feud

Techotl smote on the bronze door with his clenched hand, and then turned sidewise, so that he could watch back along the hall.

'Men have been smitten down before this door, when they thought they were safe,' he said.

'Why don't they open the door?' asked Conan.

'They are looking at us through the Eye,' answered Techotl. 'They are puzzled at the sight of you.' He lifted his voice and called: 'Open the door, Xecelan! It is I, Techotl, with friends from the great world beyond the forest! – They will open,' he assured his allies.

'They'd better do it in a hurry, then,' said Conan grimly. 'I hear something crawling along the floor beyond the wall.'

Techotl went ashy again and attacked the door with his fists, screaming: 'Open, you fools, open! The Crawler is at our heels!'

Even as he beat and shouted, the great bronze door swung noiselessly back, revealing a heavy chain across the entrance, over which spearheads bristled and fierce countenances regarded them intently for an instant. Then the chain was dropped and Techotl grasped the arms of his friends in a nervous frenzy and fairly dragged them over the threshold. A glance over his shoulder just as the door was closing showed Conan the long dim vista of the hall, and dimly framed at the other end an ophidian shape that writhed slowly and painfully into view, flowing in a dull-hued length from a chamber door, its hideous blood-stained head wagging drunkenly. Then the closing door shut off the view.

Inside the square chamber into which they had come heavy bolts were drawn across the door, and the chain locked into place. The door was made to stand the battering of a siege. Four men stood on guard, of the same lank-haired, dark-skinned breed as Techotl, with spears in their hands and swords at their hips. In the wall near the door there was a complicated contrivance of mirrors which Conan guessed was the Eye Techotl had mentioned, so arranged that a narrow, crystal-paned slot in the wall could be looked through from within without being discernible from without. The four guardsmen stared at the strangers with wonder, but asked no question, nor did Techotl vouchsafe any information. He moved with easy confidence now, as if he had shed his cloak of indecision and fear the instant he crossed the threshold.

'Come!' he urged his new-found friends, but Conan glanced toward the door.

'What about those fellows who were following us? Won't they try to storm that door?'

Techotl shook his head.

'They know they cannot break down the Door of the Eagle. They will flee back to Xotalanc, with their crawling fiend. Come! I will take you to the rulers of Tecuhltli.'

One of the four guards opened the door opposite the one by which they had entered, and they passed through into a hallway which, like most of the rooms on that level, was lighted by both the slot-like skylights and the clusters of winking fire-gems. But unlike the other rooms they had traversed, this hall showed evidences of occupation. Velvet tapestries adorned the glossy jade walls, rich rugs were on the crimson floors and the ivory seats, benches and divans were littered with satin cushions.

The hall ended in an ornate door, before which stood no guard. Without ceremony Techotl thrust the door open and ushered his friends into a broad chamber, where some thirty dark-skinned men and women lounging on satin-covered couches sprang up with exclamations of amazement.

The men, all except one, were of the same type as Techotl, and the women were equally dark and strange-eyed, though not unbeautiful in a weird dark way. They wore sandals, golden breast-plates, and scanty silk skirts supported by gem-crusted girdles, and their black manes, cut square at their naked shoulders, were bound with silver circlets.

On a wide ivory seat on a jade dais sat a man and a woman who differed subtly from the others. He was a giant, with an enormous sweep of breast and the shoulders of a bull. Unlike the others, he was bearded, with a thick, blue-black beard which fell almost to his broad girdle. He wore a robe of purple silk which reflected changing sheens of color with his every movement, and one wide sleeve, drawn back to his elbow, revealed a forearm massive with corded muscles. The band which confined his blue-black locks was set with glittering jewels.

The woman beside him sprang to her feet with a startled exclamation as the strangers entered, and her eyes, passing over Conan, fixed themselves with burning intensity on Valeria. She was tall and lithe, by far the most beautiful woman in the room. She was clad more scantily even than the others; for instead of a skirt she wore merely a broad strip of gilt-worked purple cloth fastened to the middle of her girdle which fell below her knees. Another strip at the back of her girdle completed that part of her costume, which she wore with a cynical indifference. Her breast-plates and the circlet about her temples were adorned with gems. In her eyes alone of all the dark-skinned people there lurked no brooding gleam of madness. She spoke no word after her first exclamation; she stood tensely, her hands clenched, staring at Valeria.

The man on the ivory seat had not risen.

'Prince Olmec,' spoke Techotl, bowing low, with arms outspread and the palms of his hands turned upward, 'I bring allies from the world beyond the forest. In the Chamber of Tezcoti the Burning Skull slew Chicmec, my companion—'

'The Burning Skull!' It was a shuddering whisper of fear from the people of Tecuhltli.

'Aye! Then came I, and found Chicmec lying with his throat cut. Before I could flee, the Burning Skull came upon me, and when I looked upon it my blood became as ice and the marrow of my bones melted. I could neither fight nor run. I could only await the stroke. Then came this white-skinned woman and struck him down with her sword; and lo, it was only a dog of Xotalanc with white paint upon his skin and the living skull of an ancient wizard upon his head! Now that skull lies in many pieces, and the dog who wore it is a dead man!'

An indescribably fierce exultation edged the last sentence, and was echoed in the low, savage exclamations from the crowding listeners.

'But wait!' exclaimed Techotl. 'There is more! While I talked with the woman, four Xotalancs came upon us! One I slew – there is the stab in my thigh to prove how desperate was the fight. Two the woman killed. But we were hard pressed when this man came into the fray and split the skull of the fourth! Aye! Five crimson nails there are to be driven into the pillar of vengeance!'

He pointed at a black column of ebony which stood behind the dais. Hundreds of red dots scarred its polished surface – the bright scarlet heads of heavy copper nails driven into the black wood.

'Five red nails for five Xotalanca lives!' exulted Techotl, and the horrible exultation in the faces of the listeners made them inhuman.

'Who are these people?' asked Olmec, and his voice was like the low, deep rumble of a distant bull. None of the people of Xuchotl spoke loudly. It was as if they had absorbed into their souls the silence of the empty halls and deserted chambers.

'I am Conan, a Cimmerian,' answered the barbarian briefly. 'This woman is Valeria of the Red Brotherhood, an Aquilonian pirate. We are deserters from an army on the Darfar border, far to the north, and are trying to reach the coast.'

The woman on the dais spoke loudly, her words tripping in her haste.

'You can never reach the coast! There is no escape from Xuchotl! You will spend the rest of your lives in this city!'

'What do you mean?' growled Conan, clapping his hand to his hilt and stepping about so as to face both the dais and the rest of the room. 'Are you telling us we're prisoners?'

'She did not mean that,' interposed Olmec. 'We are your friends. We would not restrain you against your will. But I fear other circumstances will make it impossible for you to leave Xuchotl.'

His eyes flickered to Valeria, and he lowered them quickly.

'This woman is Tascela,' he said. 'She is a princess of Tecuhltli. But let food and drink be brought our guests. Doubtless they are hungry, and weary from their long travels.'

He indicated an ivory table, and after an exchange of glances, the adventurers seated themselves. The Cimmerian was suspicious. His fierce blue eyes roved about the chamber, and he kept his sword close to his hand. But an invitation to eat and drink never found him backward. His eyes kept wandering to Tascela, but the princess had eyes only for his white-skinned companion.

Techotl, who had bound a strip of silk about his wounded thigh, placed himself at the table to attend to the wants of his friends, seeming to consider it a privilege and honor to see after their needs. He inspected the food and drink the others brought in gold vessels and dishes, and tasted each before he placed it before his guests. While they ate, Olmec sat in silence on his ivory seat, watching them from under his broad black brows. Tascela sat beside him, chin cupped in her hands and her elbows resting on her knees. Her dark, enigmatic eyes, burning with a mysterious light, never left Valeria's supple figure. Behind her seat a sullen handsome girl waved an ostrich-plume fan with a slow rhythm.

The food was fruit of an exotic kind unfamiliar to the wanderers, but very palatable, and the drink was a light crimson wine that carried a heady tang.

'You have come from afar,' said Olmec at last. 'I have read the books of our fathers. Aquilonia lies beyond the lands of the Stygians and the Shemites, beyond Argos and Zingara; and Cimmeria lies beyond Aquilonia.'

'We have each a roving foot,' answered Conan carelessly.

'How you won through the forest is a wonder to me,' quoth Olmec. 'In bygone days a thousand fighting-men scarcely were able to carve a road through it perils.'

'We encountered a bench-legged monstrosity about the size of a mastodon,' said Conan casually, holding out his wine goblet which Techotl filled with evident pleasure. 'But when we'd killed it we had no further trouble.'

The wine vessel slipped from Techotl's hand to crash on the floor. His dusky skin went ashy. Olmec started to his feet, an image of stunned amazement, and a low gasp of awe or terror breathed up from the others. Some slipped to their knees as if their legs would not support them. Only Tascela seemed not to have heard. Conan glared about him bewilderedly.

'What's the matter? What are you gaping about?'

'You – you slew the dragon-god?'

'God? I killed a dragon. Why not? It was trying to gobble us up.'

'But dragons are immortal!' exclaimed Olmec. 'They slay each other, but no man ever killed a dragon! The thousand fighting-men of our ancestors who fought their way to Xuchotl could not prevail against them! Their swords broke like twigs against their scales!'

'If your ancestors had thought to dip their spears in the poisonous juice of Derketa's Apples,' quoth Conan, with his mouth full, 'and jab them in the eyes or mouth or somewhere like that, they'd have seen that dragons are not more immortal than any other chunk of beef. The carcass lies at the edge of the trees, just within the forest. If you don't believe me, go and look for yourself.'

Olmec shook his head, not in disbelief but in wonder.

'It was because of the dragons that our ancestors took refuge in Xuchotl,' said he. 'They dared not pass through the plain and plunge into the forest beyond. Scores of them were seized and devoured by the monsters before they could reach the city.'

'Then your ancestors didn't build Xuchotl?' asked Valeria.

'It was ancient when they first came into the land. How long it had stood here, not even its degenerate inhabitants knew.'

'Your people came from Lake Zuad?' questioned Conan.

'Aye. More than half a century ago a tribe of the Tlazitlans rebelled against the Stygian king, and, being defeated in battle, fled southward. For many weeks they wandered over grasslands, desert hills, and at last they came into the great forest, a thousand fighting-men with their women and children.

'It was in the forest that the dragons fell upon them, and tore many to pieces; so the people fled in a frenzy of fear before them, and at last came into the plain and saw the city of Xuchotl in the midst of it.

'They camped before the city, not daring to leave the plain, for the night was made hideous with the noise of the battling monsters throughout the forest. They made war incessantly upon one another. Yet they came not into the plain.

'The people of the city shut their gates and shot arrows at our people from the walls. The Tlazitlans were imprisoned on the plain, as if the ring of the forest had been a great wall; for to venture into the woods would have been madness.

'That night there came secretly to their camp a slave from

the city, one of their own blood, who with a band of exploring soldiers had wandered into the forest long before, when he was a young man. The dragons had devoured all his companions, but he had been taken into the city to dwell in servitude. His name was Tolkemec.' A flame lighted the dark eyes at a mention of the name, and some of the people muttered obscenely and spat. 'He promised to open the gates to the warriors. He asked only that all captives taken be delivered into his hands.

'At dawn he opened the gates. The warriors swarmed in and the halls of Xuchotl ran red. Only a few hundred folk dwelt there, decaying remnants of a once great race. Tolkemec said they came from the east, long ago, from Old Kosala, when the ancestors of those who now dwell in Kosala came up from the south and drove forth the original inhabitants of the land. They wandered far westward and finally found this forest-girdled plain, inhabited then by a tribe of black people.

'These they enslaved and set to building a city. From the hills to the east they brought jade and marble and lapis lazuli, and gold, silver and copper. Herds of elephants provided them with ivory. When their city was completed, they slew all the black slaves. And their magicians made a terrible magic to guard the city; for by their necromantic arts they re-created the dragons which had once dwelt in this lost land, and whose monstrous bones they found in the forest. Those bones they clothed in flesh and life, and the living beasts walked the earth as they walked it when Time was young. But the wizards wove a spell that kept them in the forest and they came not into the plain.

'So for many centuries the people of Xuchotl dwelt in their city, cultivating the fertile plain, until their wise men learned how to grow fruit within the city – fruit which is not planted in soil, but obtains its nourishment out of the air – and then they let the irrigation ditches run dry, and dwelt more and more in luxurious sloth, until decay seized them. They were a dying race when our ancestors broke through the forest and came into the plain. Their wizards had died, and the people had forgot their ancient necromancy. They could fight neither by sorcery nor the sword.

223

'Well, our fathers slew the people of Xuchotl, all except a hundred which were given living into the hands of Tolkemec, who had been their slave; and for many days and nights the halls re-echoed to their screams under the agony of his tortures.

'So the Tlazitlans dwelt here, for a while in peace, ruled by the brothers Tecuhltli and Xotalanc, and by Tolkemec. Tolkemec took a girl of the tribe to wife, and because he had opened the gates, and because he knew many of the arts of the Xuchotlans, he shared the rule of the tribe with the brothers who had led the rebellion and the flight.

'For a few years, then, they dwelt at peace within the city, doing little but eating, drinking and making love, and raising children. There was no necessity to till the plain, for Tolkemec taught them how to cultivate the air-devouring fruits. Besides, the slaying of the Xuchotlans broke the spell that held the dragons in the forest, and they came nightly and bellowed about the gates of the city. The plain ran red with the blood of their eternal warfare, and it was then that—' He bit his tongue in the midst of the sentence, then presently continued, but Valeria and Conan felt that he had checked an admission he had considered unwise.

'Five years they dwelt in peace. Then' – Olmec's eyes rested briefly on the silent woman at his side – 'Xotalanc took a woman to wife, a woman whom both Tecuhltli and old Tolkemec desired. In his madness, Tecuhltli stole her from her husband. Aye, she went willingly enough. Tolkemec, to spite Xotalanc, aided Tecuhltli. Xotalanc demanded that she be given back to him, and the council of the tribe decided that the matter should be left to the woman. She chose to remain with Tecuhltli. In wrath Xotalanc sought to take her back by force, and the retainers of the brothers came to blows in the Great Hall.

'There was much bitterness. Blood was shed on both sides. The quarrel became a feud, the feud an open war. From the welter three factions emerged – Tecuhltli, Xotalanc, and Tolkemec. Already, in the days of peace, they had divided the city between them. Tecuhltli dwelt in the western quarter of the city, Xotalanc in the eastern, and Tolkemec with his family by the southern gate.

'Anger and resentment and jealousy blossomed into bloodshed and rape and murder. Once the sword was drawn there was no turning back; for blood called for blood, and vengeance followed swift on the heels of atrocity. Tecuhltli fought with Xotalanc, and Tolkemec aided first one and then the other, betraying each faction as it fitted his purpose. Tecuhltli and his people withdrew into the quarter of the western gate, where we now sit. Xuchotl is built in the shape of an oval. Tecuhltli, which took its name from its prince, occupies the western end of the oval. The people blocked up all doors connecting the quarter with the rest of the city, except one on each floor, which could be defended easily. They went into the pits below the city and built a wall cutting off the western end of the catacombs, where lie the bodies of the ancient Xuchotlans, and of those Tlazitlans slain in the feud. They dwelt as in a besieged castle, making sorties and forays on their enemies.

'The people of Xotalanc likewise fortified the eastern quarter of the city, and Tolkemec did likewise with the quarter by the southern gate. The central part of the city was left bare and uninhabited. Those empty halls and chambers became a battleground, and a region of brooding terror.

'Tolkemec warred on both clans. He was a fiend in the form of a human, worse than Xotalanc. He knew many secrets of the city he never told the others. From the crypts of the catacombs he plundered the dead of their grisly secrets – secrets of ancient kings and wizards, long forgotten by the degenerate Xuchotlans our ancestors slew. But all his magic did not aid him the night we of Tecuhltli stormed his castle and butchered all his people. Tolkemec we tortured for many days.'

His voice sank to a caressing slur, and a faraway look grew in his eyes, as if he looked back over the years to a scene which caused him intense pleasure.

'Aye, we kept the life in him until he screamed for death as for a bride. At last we took him living from the torture chamber and cast him into a dungeon for the rats to gnaw as he died. From that dungeon, somehow, he managed to escape, and dragged himself into the catacombs. There without doubt he died, for the only way out of the catacombs beneath Tecuhltli is through Tecuhltli, and he never emerged by that way. His bones were never found, and the superstitious among our people swear that his ghost haunts the crypts to this day, wailing among the bones of the dead. Twelve years ago we butchered the people of Tolkemec, but the feud raged on between Tecuhltli and Xotalanc, as it will rage until the last man, the last woman is dead.

'It was fifty years ago that Tecuhltli stole the wife of Xotalanc. Half a century the feud has endured. I was born in it. All in this chamber, except Tascela, were born in it. We expect to die in it.

'We are a dying race, even as those Xuchotlans our ancestors slew. When the feud began there were hundreds in each faction. Now we of Tecuhltli number only these you see before you, and the men who guard the four doors: forty in all. How many Xotalancas there are we do not know, but I doubt if they are much more numerous than we. For fifteen years no children have been born to us, and we have seen none among the Xotalancas.

'We are dying, but before we die we will slay as many of the men of Xotalanc as the gods permit.'

And with his weird eyes blazing, Olmec spoke long of that grisly feud, fought out in silent chambers and dim halls under the blaze of the green fire-jewels, on floors smoldering with the flames of hell and splashed with deeper crimson from severed veins. In that long butchery a whole generation had perished. Xotalanc was dead, long ago, slain in a grim battle on an ivory stair. Tecuhltli was dead, flayed alive by the maddened Xotalancas who had captured him.

Without emotion Olmec told of hideous battles fought in black corridors, of ambushes on twisting stairs, and red butcheries. With a redder, more abysmal gleam in his deep dark eyes he told of men and women flayed alive, mutilated and dismembered, of captives howling under tortures so ghastly that even the barbarous Cimmerian grunted. No wonder Techotl had trembled with the terror of capture. Yet he had gone forth to slay if he could, driven by hate that was stronger than his fear. Olmec spoke further, of dark and mysterious matters, of black magic and wizardry conjured out of the black night of the catacombs, of weird creatures invoked

226

out of darkness for horrible allies. In these things the Xotalancas had the advantage, for it was in the eastern catacombs where lay the bones of the greatest wizards of the ancient Xuchotlans, with their immemorial secrets.

Valeria listened with morbid fascination. The feud had become a terrible elemental power driving the people of Xuchotl inexorably on to doom and extinction. It filled their whole lives. They were born in it, and they expected to die in it. They never left their barricaded castle except to steal forth into the Halls of Silence that lay between the opposing fortresses, to slay and be slain. Sometimes the raiders returned with frantic captives, or with grim tokens of victory in fight. Sometimes they did not return at all, or returned only as severed limbs cast down before the bolted bronze doors. It was a ghastly, unreal nightmare existence these people lived, shut off from the rest of the world, caught together like rabid rats in the same trap, butchering one another through the years, crouching and creeping through the sunless corridors to maim and torture and murder.

While Olmec talked, Valeria felt the blazing eyes of Tascela fixed upon her. The princess seemed not to hear what Olmec was saying. Her expression, as he narrated victories or defeats, did not mirror the wild rage or fiendish exultation that alternated on the faces of the other Tecuhltli. The feud that was an obsession to her clansmen seemed meaningless to her. Valeria found her indifferent callousness more repugnant than Olmec's naked ferocity.

'And we can never leave the city,' said Olmec. 'For fifty years no one has left it except those—' Again he checked himself.

'Even without the peril of the dragons,' he continued, 'we who were born and raised in the city would not dare leave it. We have never set foot outside the walls. We are not accustomed to the open sky and the naked sun. No; we were born in Xuchotl, and in Xuchotl we shall die.'

'Well,' said Conan, 'with your leave we'll take our chances with the dragons. This feud is none of our business. If you'll show us to the west gate we'll be on our way.'

Tascela's hands clenched, and she started to speak, but Olmec interrupted her: 'It is nearly nightfall. If you wander forth into the plain by night, you will certainly fall prey to the dragons.'

'We crossed it last night, and slept in the open without seeing any,' returned Conan.

Tascela smiled mirthlessly. 'You dare not leave Xuchotl!'

Conan glared at her with instinctive antagonism; she was not looking at him, but at the woman opposite him.

'I think they dare,' retorted Olmec. 'But look you, Conan and Valeria, the gods must have sent you to us, to cast victory into the laps of the Tecuhltli! You are professional fighters – why not fight for us? We have wealth in abundance – precious jewels are as common in Xuchotl as cobblestones are in the cities of the world. Some the Xuchotlans brought with them from Kosala. Some, like the firestones, they found in the hills to the east. Aid us to wipe out the Xotalancas, and we will give you all the jewels you can carry.'

'And will you help us destroy the dragons?' asked Valeria. 'With bows and poisoned arrows thirty men could slay all the dragons in the forest.'

'Aye!' replied Olmec promptly. 'We have forgotten the use of the bow, in years of hand-to-hand fighting, but we can learn again.'

'What do you say?' Valeria inquired of Conan.

'We're both penniless vagabonds,' he grinned hardily. 'I'd as soon kill Xotalancas as anybody.'

'Then you agree?' exclaimed Olmec, while Techotl fairly hugged himself with delight.

'Aye. And now suppose you show us chambers where we can sleep, so we can be fresh tomorrow for the beginning of the slaying.'

Olmec nodded, and waved a hand, and Techotl and a woman led the adventurers into a corridor which led through a door off to the left of the jade dais. A glance back showed Valeria Olmec sitting on his throne, chin on knotted fist, staring after them. His eyes burned with a weird flame. Tascela leaned back in her seat, whispering to the sullen-faced maid, Yasala, who leaned over her shoulder, her ear to the princess' moving lips.

The hallway was not so broad as most they had traversed, but it was long. Presently the woman halted, opened a door, and drew aside for Valeria to enter.

'Wait a minute,' growled Conan. 'Where do I sleep?'

Techotl pointed to a chamber across the hallway, but one door farther down. Conan hesitated, and seemed inclined to raise an objection, but Valeria smiled spitefully at him and shut the door in his face. He muttered something uncomplimentary about women in general, and strode off down the corridor after Techotl.

In the ornate chamber where he was to sleep, he glanced up at the slot-like skylights. Some were wide enough to admit the body of a slender man, supposing the glass were broken.

'Why don't the Xotalancas come over the roofs and shatter those skylights?' he asked.

'They cannot be broken,' answered Techotl. 'Besides, the roofs would be hard to clamber over. They are mostly spires and domes and steep ridges.'

He volunteered more information about the 'castle' of Tecuhltli. Like the rest of the city it contained four stories, or tiers of chambers, with towers jutting up from the roof. Each tier was named; indeed, the people of Xuchotl had a name for each chamber, hall and stair in the city, as people of more normal cities designate streets and quarters. In Tecuhltli the floors were named The Eagle's Tier, the Ape's Tier, The Tiger's Tier and The Serpent's Tier, in the order as enumerated, The Eagle's Tier being the highest, or fourth, floor.

'Who is Tascela?' asked Conan. 'Olmec's wife?'

Techotl shuddered and glanced furtively about him before answering.

'No. She is – Tascela! She was the wife of Xotalanc – the woman Tecuhltli stole, to start the feud.'

'What are you talking about?' demanded Conan. 'That woman is beautiful and young. Are you trying to tell me that she was a wife fifty years ago?'

'Aye! I swear it! She was a full-grown woman when the Tlazitlans journeyed from Lake Zuad. It was because the king of

Stygia desired her for a concubine that Xotalanc and his brother rebelled and fled into the wilderness. She is a witch, who possesses the secret of perpetual youth.'

'What's that?' asked Conan.

Techotl shuddered again.

'Ask me not! I dare not speak. It is too grisly, even for Xuchotl!'

And touching his finger to his lips, he glided from the chamber.

4

Scent of Black Lotus

Valeria unbuckled her sword-belt and laid it with the sheathed weapon on the couch where she meant to sleep. She noted that the doors were supplied with bolts, and asked where they led.

'Those lead into adjoining chambers,' answered the woman, indicating the doors on right and left. 'That one' – pointing to a copper-bound door opposite that which opened into the corridor – 'leads to a corridor which runs to a stair that descends into the catacombs. Do not fear; naught can harm you here.'

'Who spoke of fear?' snapped Valeria. 'I just like to know what sort of harbor I'm dropping anchor in. No, I don't want you to sleep at the foot of my couch. I'm not accustomed to being waited on – not by women, anyway. You have my leave to go.'

Alone in the room, the pirate shot the bolts on all the doors, kicked off her boots and stretched luxuriously out on the couch. She imagined Conan similarly situated across the corridor, but her feminine vanity prompted her to visualize him as scowling and muttering with chagrin as he cast himself on his solitary couch, and she grinned with gleeful malice as she prepared herself for slumber.

Outside, night had fallen. In the halls of Xuchotl the green fire-jewels blazed like the eyes of prehistoric cats. Somewhere among the dark towers a night wind moaned like a restless spirit. Through the dim passages stealthy figures began stealing, like disembodied shadows.

Valeria awoke suddenly on her couch. In the dusky emerald glow of the fire-gems she saw a shadowy figure bending over her. For a bemused instant the apparition seemed part of the dream she had been dreaming. She had seemed to lie on the couch in the chamber as she was actually lying, while over her pulsed and throbbed a gigantic black blossom so enormous that it hid the ceiling. Its exotic perfume pervaded her being, inducing a delicious, sensuous langour that was something more and less than sleep. She was sinking into scented billows of insensible bliss, when something touched her face. So supersensitive were her drugged senses, that the light touch was like a dislocating impact, jolting her rudely into full wakefulness. Then it was that she saw, not a gargantuan blossom, but a dark-skinned woman standing above her.

With the realization came anger and instant action. The woman turned lithely, but before she could run Valeria was on her feet and had caught her arm. She fought like a wildcat for an instant, and then subsided as she felt herself crushed by the superior strength of her captor. The pirate wrenched the woman around to face her, caught her chin with her free hand and forced her captive to meet her gaze. It was the sullen Yasala, Tascela's maid.

'What the devil were you doing bending over me? What's that in your hand?'

The woman made no reply, but sought to cast away the object. Valeria twisted her arm around in front of her, and the thing fell to the floor – a great black exotic blossom on a jade-green stem, large as a woman's head, to be sure, but tiny beside the exaggerated vision she had seen.

'The black lotus!' said Valeria between her teeth. 'The blossom whose scent brings deep sleep. You were trying to drug me! If you hadn't accidentally touched my face with the petals, you'd have – why did you do it? What's your game?'

Yasala maintained a sulky silence, and with an oath Valeria whirled her around, forced her to her knees and twisted her arm up behind her back.

'Tell me, or I'll tear your arm out of its socket!'

Yasala squirmed in anguish as her arm was forced excruciatingly up between her shoulder-blades, but a violent shaking of her head was the only answer she made.

'Slut!' Valeria cast her from her to sprawl on the floor. The pirate glared at the prostrate figure with blazing eyes. Fear and the memory of Tascela's burning eyes stirred in her, rousing all her tigerish instincts of self-preservation. These people were decadent; any sort of perversity might be expected to be encountered among them. But Valeria sensed here something that moved behind the scenes, some secret terror fouler than common degeneracy. Fear and revulsion of this weird city swept her. These people were neither sane nor normal; she began to doubt if they were even human. Madness smoldered in the eyes of them all – all except the cruel, cryptic eyes of Tascela, which held secrets and mysteries more abysmal than madness.

She lifted her head and listened intently. The halls of Xuchotl were as silent as if it were in reality a dead city. The green jewels bathed the chamber in a nightmare glow, in which the eyes of the woman on the floor glittered eerily up at her. A thrill of panic throbbed through Valeria, driving the last vestige of mercy from her fierce soul.

'Why did you try to drug me?' she muttered, grasping the woman's black hair, and forcing her head back to glare into her sullen, long-lashed eyes. 'Did Tascela send you?'

No answer. Valeria cursed venomously and slapped the woman first on one cheek and then the other. The blows resounded through the room, but Yasala made no outcry.

'Why don't you scream?' demanded Valeria savagely. 'Do you fear someone will hear you? Whom do you fear? Tascela? Olmec? Conan?'

Yasala made no reply. She crouched, watching her captor with eyes baleful as those of a basilisk. Stubborn silence always fans anger. Valeria turned and tore a handful of cords from a nearby hanging.

'You sulky slut!' she said between her teeth. 'I'm going to strip you stark naked and tie you across that couch and whip you until you tell me what you were doing here, and who sent you!'

Yasala made no verbal protest, nor did she offer any resistance, as Valeria carried out the first part of her threat with a fury that her captive's obstinacy only sharpened. Then for a space there was no sound in the chamber except the whistle and crackle of hard-woven silken cords on naked flesh. Yasala could not move her fast-bound hands or feet. Her body writhed and quivered under the chastisement, her head swayed from side to side in rhythm with the blows. Her teeth were sunk into her lower lip and a trickle of blood began as the punishment continued. But she did not cry out.

The pliant cords made no great sound as they encountered the quivering body of the captive; only a sharp crackling snap, but each cord left a red streak across Yasala's dark flesh. Valeria inflicted the punishment with all the strength of her war-hardened arm, with all the mercilessness acquired during a life where pain and torment were daily happenings, and with all the cynical ingenuity which only a woman displays towards a woman. Yasala suffered more, physically and mentally, than she would have suffered under a lash wielded by a man, however strong.

It was the application of this feminine cynicism which at last tamed Yasala.

A low whimper escaped from her lips, and Valeria paused, arm lifted, and raked back a damp yellow lock. 'Well, are you going to talk?' she demanded. 'I can keep this up all night, if necessary!'

'Mercy!' whispered the woman. 'I will tell.'

Valeria cut the cords from her wrists and ankles, and pulled to her feet. Yasala sank down on the couch, half reclining on one bare hip, supporting herself on her arm, and writhing at the contact of her smarting flesh with the couch. She was trembling in every limb.

'Wine!' she begged, dry-lipped, indicating with a quivering hand a gold vessel on an ivory table. 'Let me drink. I am weak with pain. Then I will tell you all.'

Valeria picked up the vessel, and Yasala rose unsteadily to receive it. She took it, raised it toward her lips – then dashed the contents full into the Aquilonian's face. Valeria reeled backward, shaking and clawing the stinging liquid out of her eyes. Through a smarting mist she saw Yasala dart across the room, fling back a bolt, throw open the copper-bound door and run down the hall. The pirate was after her instantly, sword out and murder in her heart.

But Yasala had the start, and she ran with the nervous agility of a woman who has just been whipped to the point of hysterical frenzy. She rounded a corner in the corridor, yards ahead of Valeria, and when the pirate turned it, she saw only an empty hall, and at the other end a door that gaped blackly. A damp moldy scent reeked up from it, and Valeria shivered. That must be the door that led to the catacombs. Yasala had taken refuge among the dead.

Valeria advanced to the door and looked down a flight of stone steps that vanished quickly into utter blackness. Evidently it was a shaft that led straight to the pits below the city, without opening upon any of the lower floors. She shivered slightly at the thought of the thousands of corpses lying in their stone crypts down there, wrapped in their moldering cloths. She had no intention of groping her way down those stone steps. Yasala doubtless knew every turn and twist of the subterranean tunnels.

She was turning back, baffled and furious, when a sobbing cry welled up from the blackness. It seemed to come from a great depth, but human words were faintly distinguishable, and the voice was that of a woman. 'Oh, help! Help, in Set's name! Ahhh!' It trailed away, and Valeria thought she caught the echo of a ghostly tittering.

Valeria felt her skin crawl. What had happened to Yasala down there in the thick blackness? There was no doubt that it had been she who had cried out. But what peril could have befallen her? Was a Xotalanca lurking down there? Olmec had assured them that the catacombs below Tecuhltli were walled off from the rest, too securely for their enemies to break through. Besides, that tittering had not sounded like a human being at all.

Valeria hurried back down the corridor, not stopping to close the door that opened on the stair. Regaining her chamber, she closed the door and shot the bolt behind her. She pulled on her boots and buckled her sword-belt about her. She was determined to make her way to Conan's room and urge him, if he still lived, to join her in an attempt to fight their way out of that city of devils.

But even as she reached the door that opened into the corridor, a long-drawn scream of agony rang through the halls, followed by the stamp of running feet and the loud clangor of swords.

5

Twenty Red Nails

Two warriors lounged in the guardroom on the floor known as the Tier of the Eagle. Their attitude was casual, though habitually alert. An attack on the great bronze door from without was always a possibility, but for many years no such assault had been attempted on either side.

'The strangers are strong allies,' said one. 'Olmec will move against the enemy tomorrow, I believe.'

He spoke as a soldier in a war might have spoken. In the miniature world of Xuchotl each handful of feudists was an army, and the empty halls between the castles was the country over which they campaigned.

The other meditated for a space.

'Suppose with their aid we destroy Xotalanc,' he said. 'What then, Xatmec?'

'Why,' returned Xatmec, 'we will drive red nails for them all. The captives we will burn and flay and quarter.'

'But afterward?' pursued the other. 'After we have slain them all? Will it not seem strange, to have no foes to fight? All my life I have fought and hated the Xotalancas. With the feud ended, what is left?'

Xatmec shrugged his shoulders. His thoughts had never gone beyond the destruction of their foes. They could not go beyond that.

Suddenly both men stiffened at a noise outside the door.

'To the door, Xatmec!' hissed the last speaker. 'I shall look through the Eye—'

Xatmec, sword in hand, leaned against the bronze door, straining his ear to hear through the metal. His mate looked into the mirror. He started convulsively. Men were clustered thickly outside the door; grim, dark-faced men with swords gripped in their teeth – *and their fingers thrust into their ears*. One who wore a feathered headdress had a set of pipes which he set to his lips, and even as the Tecuhltli started to shout a warning, the pipes began to skirl.

The cry died in the guard's throat as the thin, weird piping penetrated the metal door and smote on his ears. Xatmec leaned frozen against the door, as if paralysed in that position. His face was that of a wooden image, his expression one of horrified listening. The other guard, farther removed from the source of the sound, yet sensed the horror of what was taking place, the grisly threat that lay in that demoniac fifing. He felt the weird strains plucking like unseen fingers at the tissues of his brain, filling him with alien emotions and impulses of madness. But with a soul-tearing effort he broke the spell, and shrieked a warning in a voice he did not recognize as his own.

But even as he cried out, the music changed to an unbearable shrilling that was like a knife in the eardrums. Xatmec screamed in sudden agony, and all the sanity went out of his face like a flame blown out in a wind. Like a madman he ripped loose the chain, tore open the door and rushed out into the hall, sword lifted before his mate could stop him. A dozen blades struck him down, and over his mangled body the Xotalancas surged into the guardroom, with a long-drawn, blood-mad yell that sent the unwonted echoes reverberating.

His brain reeling from the shock of it all, the remaining guard leaped to meet them with goring spear. The horror of the sorcery he had just witnessed was submerged in the stunning realization that the enemy were in Tecuhltli. And as his spearhead ripped through a dark-skinned belly he knew no more, for a swinging sword crushed his skull, even as wild-eyed warriors came pouring in from the chambers behind the guardroom.

It was the yelling of men and the clanging of steel that brought Conan bounding from his couch, wide awake and broadsword in hand. In an instant he had reached the door and flung it open, and was glaring out into the corridor just as Techotl rushed up it, eyes blazing madly.

'The Xotalancas!' he screamed, in a voice hardly human. '*They are within the door.*'

Conan ran down the corridor, even as Valeria emerged from her chamber.

'What the devil is it?' she called.

'Techotl says the Xotalancas are in,' he answered hurriedly. 'That racket sounds like it.'

With the Tecuhltli on their heels they burst into the throneroom and were confronted by a scene beyond the most frantic dream of blood and fury. Twenty men and women, their black hair streaming, and the white skulls gleaming on their breasts, were locked in combat with the people of Tecuhltli. The women on both sides fought as madly as the men, and already the room and the hall beyond were strewn with corpses.

Olmec, naked but for a breech-clout, was fighting before his throne, and as the adventurers entered, Tascela ran from an inner chamber with a sword in her hand.

Xatmec and his mate were dead, so there was none to tell the Tecuhltli how their foes had found their way into their citadel. Nor was there any to say what had prompted that mad attempt. But the losses of the Xotalancas had been greater, their position more desperate, than the Tecuhltli had known. The maiming of their scaly ally, the destruction of the Burning Skull, and the news, gasped by a dying man, that mysterious white-skin allies had joined their enemies, had driven them to the frenzy of desperation and the wild determination to die dealing death to their ancient foes.

The Tecuhltli, recovering from the first stunning shock of the surprise that had swept them back into the throneroom and littered the floor with their corpses, fought back with an equally desperate fury, while the door-guards from the lower floors came racing to hurl themselves into the fray. It was the death-fight of rabid wolves, blind, panting, merciless. Back and forth it surged, from door to dais, blades whickering and striking into flesh, blood spurting, feet stamping the crimson floor where redder pools were forming. Ivory tables crashed over, seats were splintered, velvet hangings torn down were stained red. It was the bloody climax of a bloody half-century, and every man there sensed it.

But the conclusion was inevitable. The Tecuhltli outnumbered the invaders almost two to one, and they were heartened by that fact and by the entrance into the mêlée of their light-skinned allies.

These crashed into the fray with the devastating effect of a hurricane plowing through a grove of saplings. In sheer strength no three Tlazitlans were a match for Conan, and in spite of his weight he was quicker on his feet than any of them. He moved through the whirling, eddying mass with the surety and destructiveness of a gray wolf amidst a pack of alley curs, and he strode over a wake of crumpled figures.

Valeria fought beside him, her lips smiling and her eyes blazing. She was stronger than the average man, and far quicker and more ferocious. Her sword was like a living thing in her hand. Where Conan beat down opposition by the sheer weight and power of his blows, breaking spears, splitting skulls and cleaving bosoms to the breastbone, Valeria brought into action a finesse of swordplay that dazzled and bewildered her antagonists before it slew them. Again and again a warrior, heaving high his heavy blade, found her point in his jugular before he could strike. Conan, towering above the field, strode through the welter smiting right and left, but Valeria moved like an illusive phantom, constantly shifting, and thrusting and slashing as she shifted. Swords missed her again and again as the wielders flailed the empty air and died with her point in their hearts or throats, and her mocking laughter in their ears.

Neither sex nor condition was considered by the maddened combatants. The five women of the Xotalancas were down with their throats cut before Conan and Valeria entered the fray, and when a man or woman went down under the stamping feet, there was always a knife ready for the helpless throat, or a sandaled foot eager to crush the prostrate skull.

From wall to wall, from door to door rolled the waves of combat, spilling over into adjoining chambers. And presently only Tecuhltli and their white-skinned allies stood upright in the great throneroom. The survivors stared bleakly and blankly at each other, like survivors after Judgment Day or the destruction of the world. On legs wide-braced, hands gripping notched and dripping swords, blood trickling down their arms, they stared at one another across the mangled corpses of friends and foes. They had no breath left to shout, but a bestial mad howling rose from their lips. It was not a human cry of triumph. It was the howling of a rabid wolf-pack stalking among the bodies of its victims.

Conan caught Valeria's arm and turned her about.

'You've got a stab in the calf of your leg,' he growled.

She glanced down, for the first time aware of a stinging in the muscles of her leg. Some dying man on the floor had fleshed his dagger with his last effort.

'You look like a butcher yourself,' she laughed.

He shook a red shower from his hands.

'Not mine. Oh, a scratch here and there. Nothing to bother about. But that calf ought to be bandaged.'

Olmec came through the litter, looking like a ghoul with his naked massive shoulders splashed with blood, and his black beard dabbled in crimson. His eyes were red, like the reflection of flame on black water.

'We have won!' he croaked dazedly. 'The feud is ended! The dogs of Xotalanc lie dead! Oh, for a captive to flay alive! Yet it is good to look upon their dead faces. Twenty dead dogs! Twenty red nails for the black column!'

'You'd best see to your wounded,' grunted Conan, turning away from him. 'Here, girl, let me see that leg.'

'Wait a minute!' she shook him off impatiently. The fire of fighting still burned brightly in her soul. 'How do we know these are all of them? These might have come on a raid of their own.'

'They would not split the clan on a foray like this,' said Olmec, shaking his head, and regaining some of his ordinary intelligence. Without his purple robe the man seemed less like a prince than some repellent beast of prey. 'I will stake my head upon it that we have slain them all. There were less of them than I dreamed, and they must have been desperate. But how came they in Tecuhltli?'

Tascela came forward, wiping her sword on her naked thigh, and holding in her other hand an object she had taken from the body of the feathered leader of the Xotalancas.

'The pipes of madness,' she said. 'A warrior tells me that Xatmec opened the door to the Xotalancas and was cut down as they stormed into the guardroom. This warrior came to the guardroom from the inner hall just in time to see it happen and to hear the last of a weird strain of music which froze his very soul. Tolkemec used to talk of these pipes, which the Xuchotlans swore were hidden somewhere in the catacombs with the bones of the ancient wizard who used them in his lifetime. Somehow the dogs of Xotalanc found them and learned their secret.'

'Somebody ought to go to Xotalanc and see if any remain alive,' said Conan. 'I'll go if somebody will guide me.'

Olmec glanced at the remants of his people. There were only twenty left alive, and of these several lay groaning on the floor. Tascela was the only one of the Tecuhltli who had escaped without a wound. The princess was untouched, though she had fought as savagely as any.

'Who will go with Conan to Xotalanc?' asked Olmec.

Techotl limped forward. The wound in his thigh had started bleeding afresh, and he had another gash across his ribs.

'I will go!'

'No, you won't,' vetoed Conan. 'And you're not going either, Valeria. In a little while that leg will be getting stiff.'

'I will go,' volunteered a warrior, who was knotting a bandage about a slashed forearm.

'Very well, Yanath. Go with the Cimmerian. And you, too, Topal.' Olmec indicated another man whose injuries were slight.

'But first aid us to lift the badly wounded on these couches where we may bandage their hurts.'

This was done quickly. As they stooped to pick up a woman who had been stunned by a war-club, Olmec's beard brushed Topal's ear. Conan thought the prince muttered something to the warrior, but he could not be sure. A few moments later he was leading his companions down the hall.

Conan glanced back as he went out the door, at that shambles where the dead lay on the smoldering floor, blood-stained dark limbs knotted in attitudes of fierce muscular effort, dark faces frozen in masks of hate, glassy eyes glaring up at the green fire-jewels which bathed the ghastly scene in a dusky emerald witch-light. Among the dead the living moved aimlessly, like people moving in a trance. Conan heard Olmec call a woman and direct her to bandage Valeria's leg. The pirate followed the woman into an adjoining chamber, already beginning to limp slightly.

Warily the two Tecuhltli led Conan along the hall beyond the bronze door, and through chamber after chamber shimmering in the green fire. They saw no one, heard no sound. After they crossed the Great Hall which bisected the city from north to south, their caution was increased by the realization of their nearness to enemy territory. But chambers and halls lay empty to their wary gaze, and they came at last along a broad dim hallway and halted before a bronze door similar to the Eagle Door of Tecuhltli. Gingerly they tried it, and it opened silently under their fingers. Awed, they stared into the green-lit chambers beyond. For fifty years no Tecuhltli had entered those halls save as a prisoner going to a hideous doom. To go to Xotalanc had been the ultimate horror that could befall a man of the western castle. The terror of it had stalked through their dreams since earliest childhood. To Yanath and Topal that bronze door was like the portal of hell.

They cringed back, unreasoning horror in their eyes, and Conan pushed past them and strode into Xotalanc.

Timidly they followed him. As each man set foot over the

threshold he stared and glared wildly about him. But only their quick, hurried breathing disturbed the silence.

They had come into a square guardroom, like that behind the Eagle Door of Tecuhltli, and, similarly, a hall ran away from it to a broad chamber that was a counterpart of Olmec's throneroom.

Conan glanced down the hall with its rugs and divans and hangings, and stood listening intently. He heard no noise, and the rooms had an empty feel. He did not believe there were any Xotalancas left alive in Xuchotl.

'Come on,' he muttered, and started down the hall.

He had not gone far when he was aware that only Yanath was following him. He wheeled back to see Topal standing in an attitude of horror, one arm out as if to fend off some threatening peril, his distended eyes fixed with hypnotic intensity on something protruding from behind a divan.

'What the devil?' Then Conan saw what Topal was staring at, and he felt a faint twitching of the skin between his giant shoulders. A monstrous head protruded from behind the divan, a reptilian head, broad as the head of a crocodile, with down-curving fangs that projected over the lower jaw. But there was an unnatural limpness about the thing, and the hideous eyes were glazed.

Conan peered behind the couch. It was a great serpent which lay there limp in death, but such a serpent as he had never seen in his wanderings. The reek and chill of the deep black earth were about it, and its color was an indeterminable hue which changed with each new angle from which he surveyed it. A great wound in the neck showed what had caused its death.

'It is the Crawler!' whispered Yanath.

'It's the thing I slashed on the stair,' grunted Conan. 'After it trailed us to the Eagle Door, it dragged itself here to die. How could the Xotalancas control such a brute?'

The Tecuhltli shivered and shook their heads.

'They brought it up from the black tunnels below the catacombs. They discovered secrets unknown to Tecuhltli.'

'Well, it's dead, and if they'd had any more of them, they'd have brought them along when they came to Tecuhltli. Come on.'

They crowded close at his heels as he strode down the hall and thrust on the silver-worked door at the other end.

'If we don't find anybody on this floor,' he said, 'we'll descend into the lower floors. We'll explore Xotalanc from the roof to the catacombs. If Xotalanc is like Tecuhltli, all the rooms and halls in this tier will be lighted – what the devil!'

They had come into the broad throne-chamber, so similar to that one in Tecuhltli. There were the same jade dais and ivory seat, the same divans, rugs and hangings on the walls. No black, red-scarred column stood behind the throne-dais, but evidences of the grim feud were not lacking.

Ranged along the wall behind the dais were rows of glass-covered shelves. And on those shelves hundreds of human heads, perfectly preserved, stared at the startled watchers with emotion-less eyes, as they had stared for only the gods knew how many months and years.

Topal muttered a curse, but Yanath stood silent, the mad light growing in his wide eyes. Conan frowned, knowing that Tlazitlan sanity was hung on a hair-trigger.

Suddenly Yanath pointed to the ghastly relics with a twitching finger.

'There is my brother's head!' he murmured. 'And there is my father's younger brother! And there beyond them is my sister's eldest son!'

Suddenly he began to weep, dry-eyed, with harsh, loud sobs that shook his frame. He did not take his eyes from the heads. His sobs grew shriller, changed to frightful, high-pitched laughter, and that in turn became an unbearable screaming. Yanath was stark mad.

Conan laid a hand on his shoulder, and as if the touch had released all the frenzy in his soul, Yanath screamed and whirled, striking at the Cimmerian with his sword. Conan parried the blow, and Topal tried to catch Yanath's arm. But the madman avoided him and with froth flying from his lips, he drove his sword deep into Topal's body. Topal sank down with a groan, and Yanath whirled for an instant like a crazy dervish; then he ran at the shelves and began hacking at the glass with his sword, screeching blasphemously.

Conan sprang at him from behind, trying to catch him unaware and disarm him, but the madman wheeled and lunged at him, screaming like a lost soul. Realizing that the warrior was hopelessly insane, the Cimmerian side-stepped, and as the maniac went past, he swung a cut that severed the shoulder-bone and breast, and dropped the man dead beside his dying victim.

Conan bent over Topal, seeing that the man was at his last gasp. It was useless to seek to stanch the blood gushing from the horrible wound.

'You're done for, Topal,' grunted Conan. 'Any word you want to send to your people?'

'Bend closer,' gasped Topal, and Conan complied – and an instant later caught the man's wrist as Topal struck at his breast with a dagger.

'Crom!' swore Conan. 'Are you mad, too?'

'Olmec ordered it!' gasped the dying man. 'I know not why. As we lifted the wounded upon the couches he whispered to me, bidding me to slay you as we returned to Tecuhltli—' And with the name of his clan on his lips, Topal died.

Conan scowled down at him in puzzlement. This whole affair had an aspect of lunacy. Was Olmec mad, too? Were all the Tecuhltli madder than he had realized? With a shrug of his shoulders he strode down the hall and out of the bronze door, leaving the dead Tecuhltli lying before the staring dead eyes of their kinsmen's heads.

Conan needed no guide back through the labyrinth they had traversed. His primitive instinct of direction led him unerringly along the route they had come. He traversed it as warily as he had before, his sword in his hand, and his eyes fiercely searching each shadowed nook and corner; for it was his former allies he feared now, not the ghosts of the slain Xotalancas.

He had crossed the Great Hall and entered the chambers beyond when he heard something moving ahead of him – something which gasped and panted, and moved with a strange, floundering, scrambling noise. A moment later Conan saw a man crawling over the flaming floor toward him – a man whose progress left a broad bloody smear on the smoldering surface. It was Techotl and his eyes were already glazing; from a deep gash in his breast blood gushed steadily between the fingers of his clutching hand. With the other he clawed and hitched himself along.

'Conan,' he cried chokingly, 'Conan! Olmec has taken the yellow-haired woman!'

'So that's why he told Topal to kill me!' murmured Conan, dropping to his knee beside the man, who his experienced eye told him was dying. 'Olmec isn't so mad as I thought.'

Techotl's groping fingers plucked at Conan's arm. In the cold, loveless and altogether hideous life of the Tecuhltli his admiration and affection for the invaders from the outer world formed a warm, human oasis, constituted a tie that connected him with a more natural humanity that was totally lacking in his fellows, whose only emotions were hate, lust and the urge of sadistic cruelty.

'I sought to oppose him,' gurgled Techotl, blood bubbling frothily to his lips. 'But he struck me down. He thought he had slain me, but I crawled away. Ah, Set, how far I have crawled in my own blood! Beware, Conan! Olmec may have set an ambush for your return! Slay Olmec! He is a beast. Take Valeria and flee! Fear not to traverse the forest. Olmec and Tascela lied about the dragons. They slew each other years ago, all save the strongest. For a dozen years there has been only one dragon. If you have slain him, there is naught in the forest to harm you. He was the god Olmec worshipped; and Olmec fed human sacrifices to him, the very old and the very young, bound and hurled from the wall. Hasten! Olmec has taken Valeria to the Chamber of the—'

His head slumped down and he was dead before it came to rest on the floor.

Conan sprang up, his eyes like live coals. So that was Olmec's game, having first used the strangers to destroy his foes! He should have known that something of the sort would be going on in that black-bearded degenerate's mind.

The Cimmerian started toward Tecuhltli with reckless speed.

Rapidly he reckoned the numbers of his former allies. Only twenty-one, counting Olmec, had survived that fiendish battle in the throneroom. Three had died since, which left seventeen enemies with which to reckon. In his rage Conan felt capable of accounting for the whole clan single-handed.

But the innate craft of the wilderness rose to guide his berserk rage. He remembered Techotl's warning of an ambush. It was quite probable that the prince would make such provisions, on the chance that Topal might have failed to carry out his order. Olmec would be expecting him to return by the same route he had followed in going to Xotalanc.

Conan glanced up at the skylight under which he was passing and caught the blurred glimmer of stars. They had not yet begun to pale for dawn. The events of the night had been crowded into a comparatively short space of time.

He turned aside from his direct course and descended a winding staircase to the floor below. He did not know where the door was to be found that let into the castle on that level, but he knew he could find it. How he was to force the locks he did not know; he believed that the doors of Tecuhltli would all be locked and bolted, if for no other reason than the habits of half a century. But there was nothing else but to attempt it.

Sword in hand, he hurried noiselessly on through a maze of green-lit or shadowy rooms and halls. He knew he must be near Tecuhltli, when a sound brought him up short. He recognized it for what it was – a human being trying to cry out through a stifling gag. It came from somewhere ahead of him, and to the left. In those deathly-still chambers a small sound carried a long way.

Conan turned aside and went seeking after the sound, which continued to be repeated. Presently he was glaring through a doorway upon a weird scene. In the room into which he was looking a low rack-like frame of iron lay on the floor, and a giant figure was bound prostrate upon it. His head rested on a bed of iron spikes, which were already crimson-pointed with blood where they had pierced his scalp. A peculiar harness-like contrivance was fastened about his head, though in such a manner that the leather band did not protect his scalp from the spikes. This harness was connected by a slender chain to the mechanism that upheld a huge iron ball which was suspended above the captive's hairy breast. As long as the man could force himself to remain motionless the iron ball hung in its place. But when the pain of the iron points caused him to lift his head, the ball lurched downwards a few inches. Presently his aching neck muscles would no longer support his head in its unnatural position and it would fall back on the spikes again. It was obvious that eventually the ball would crush him to a pulp, slowly and inexorably. The victim was gagged, and above the gag his great black ox-eyes rolled wildly toward the man in the doorway, who stood in silent amazement. The man on the rack was Olmec, prince of Tecuhltli.

6

The Eyes of Tascela

'Why did you bring me into this chamber to bandage my leg?' demanded Valeria. 'Couldn't you have done it just as well in the throneroom?'

She sat on a couch with her wounded leg extended upon it, and the Tecuhltli woman had just bound it with silk bandages. Valeria's red-stained sword lay on the couch beside her.

She frowned as she spoke. The woman had done her task silently and efficiently, but Valeria liked neither the lingering, caressing touch of her slim fingers nor the expression in her eyes.

'They have taken the rest of the wounded into the other chambers,' answered the woman in the soft speech of the Tecuhltli women, which somehow did not suggest either softness or gentleness in the speakers. A little while before, Valeria had seen this same woman stab a Xotalanca woman through the breast and stamp the eyeballs out of a wounded Xotalanca man.

'They will be carrying the corpses of the dead down into the catacombs,' she added, 'lest the ghosts escape into the chambers and dwell there.'

'Do you believe in ghosts?' asked Valeria.

'I know the ghost of Tolkemec dwells in the catacombs,' she answered with a shiver. 'Once I saw it, as I crouched in a crypt among the bones of a dead queen. It passed by in the form of an ancient man with flowing white beard and locks, and luminous eyes that blazed in the darkness. It was Tolkemec; I saw him living when I was a child and he was being tortured.'

Her voice sank to a fearful whisper: 'Olmec laughs, but I know Tolkemec's ghost dwells in the catacombs! They say it is rats which gnaw the flesh from the bones of the newly dead – but ghosts eat flesh. Who knows but that—'

She glanced up quickly as a shadow fell across the couch. Valeria looked up to see Olmec gazing down at her. The prince had cleansed his hands, torso and beard of the blood that had splashed them; but he had not donned his robe, and his great dark-skinned hairless body and limbs renewed the impression of strength bestial in its nature. His deep black eyes burned with a more elemental light, and there was the suggestion of a twitching in the fingers that tugged at his thick blue-black beard.

He stared fixedly at the woman, and she rose and glided from the chamber. As she passed through the door she cast a look over her shoulder at Valeria, a glance full of cynical derision and obscene mockery.

'She has done a clumsy job,' criticized the prince, coming to the divan and bending over the bandage. 'Let me see—'

With a quickness amazing in one of his bulk he snatched her sword and threw it across the chamber. His next move was to catch her in his giant arms.

Quick and unexpected as the move was, she almost matched it; for even as he grabbed her, her dirk was in her hand and she stabbed murderously at his throat. More by luck than skill he caught her wrist, and then began a savage wrestling-match. She fought him with fists, feet, knees, teeth and nails, with all the strength of her magnificent body and all the knowledge of hand-to-hand fighting she had acquired in her years of roving and fighting on sea and land. It availed her nothing against his brute strength. She lost her dirk in the first moment of contact, and thereafter found herself powerless to inflict any appreciable pain on her giant attacker.

The blaze in his weird black eyes did not alter, and their expression filled her with fury, fanned by the sardonic smile that seemed carved upon his bearded lips. Those eyes and that smile contained all the cruel cynicism that seethes below the surface of a sophisticated and degenerate race, and for the first time in her life Valeria experienced fear of a man. It was like struggling against some huge elemental force; his iron arms thwarted her efforts with an ease that sent panic racing through her limbs. He seemed impervious to any pain she could inflict. Only once, when she sank her white teeth savagely into his wrist so that the blood started, did he react. And that was to buffet her brutally upon the side of the head with his open hand, so that stars flashed before her eyes and her head rolled on her shoulders.

Her shirt had been torn open in the struggle, and with cynical cruelty he rasped his thick beard across her bare breasts, bringing the blood to suffuse the fair skin, and fetching a cry of pain and outraged fury from her. Her convulsive resistance was useless; she was crushed down on a couch, disarmed and panting, her eyes blazing up at him like the eyes of a trapped tigress.

A moment later he was hurrying from the chamber, carrying her in his arms. She made no resistance, but the smoldering of her eyes showed that she was not unconquered in spirit, at least. She had not cried out. She knew that Conan was not within call, and it did not occur to her that any in Tecuhltli would oppose their prince. But she noticed that Olmec went stealthily, with his head on one side as if listening for sounds of pursuit, and he did not return to the throne-chamber. He carried her through a door that stood opposite that through which he had entered, crossed another room and began stealing down a hall. As she became convinced that he feared some opposition to the abduction, she threw back her head and screamed at the top of her lusty voice.

She was rewarded by a slap that half stunned her, and Olmec quickened his pace to a shambling run.

But her cry had been echoed, and twisting her head about,

Valeria, through the tears and stars that partly blinded her, saw Techotl limping after them.

Olmec turned with a snarl, shifting the woman to an uncomfortable and certainly undignified position under one huge arm, where he held her writhing and kicking vainly, like a child.

'Olmec!' protested Techotl. 'You cannot be such a dog as to do this thing! She is Conan's woman! She helped us slay the Xotalancas, and—'

Without a word Olmec balled his free hand into a huge fist and stretched the wounded warrior senseless at his feet. Stooping, and hindered not at all by the struggles and imprecations of his captive, he drew Techotl's sword from its sheath and stabbed the warrior in the breast. Then casting aside the weapon he fled on along the corridor. He did not see a woman's dark face peer cautiously after him from behind a hanging. It vanished, and presently Techotl groaned and stirred, rose dazedly and staggered drunkenly away, calling Conan's name.

Olmec hurried on down the corridor, and descended a winding ivory staircase. He crossed several corridors and halted at last in a broad chamber whose doors were veiled with heavy tapestries, with one exception – a heavy bronze door similar to the Door of the Eagle on the upper floor.

He was moved to rumble, pointing to it: 'That is one of the outer doors of Tecuhltli. For the first time in fifty years it is unguarded. We need not guard it now, for Xotalanc is no more.'

'Thanks to Conan and me, you bloody rogue!' sneered Valeria, trembling with fury and the shame of physical coercion. 'You treacherous dog! Conan will cut your throat for this!'

Olmec did not bother to voice his belief that Conan's own gullet had already been severed according to his whispered command. He was too utterly cynical to be at all interested in her thoughts or opinions. His flame-lit eyes devoured her, dwelling burningly on the generous expanse of clear white flesh exposed where her shirt and breeches had been torn in the struggle.

'Forget Conan,' he said thickly. 'Olmec is lord of Xuchotl.

Xotalanc is no more. There will be no more fighting. We shall spend our lives in drinking and lovemaking. First let us drink!'

He seated himself on an ivory table and pulled her down on his knees, like a dark-skinned satyr with a white nymph in his arms. Ignoring her unnymphlike profanity, he held her helpless with one great arm about her waist while the other reached across the table and secured a vessel of wine.

'Drink!' he commanded, forcing it to her lips, as she writhed her head away.

The liquor slopped over, stinging her lips, splashing down on her naked breasts.

'Your guest does not like your wine, Olmec,' spoke a cool, sardonic voice.

Olmec stiffened; fear grew in his flaming eyes. Slowly he swung his great head about and stared at Tascela who posed negligently in the curtained doorway, one hand on her smooth hip. Valeria twisted herself about in his iron grip, and when she met the burning eyes of Tascela, a chill tingled along her supple spine. New experiences were flooding Valeria's proud soul that night. Recently she had learned to fear a man; now she knew what it was to fear a woman.

Olmec sat motionless, a gray pallor growing under his swarthy skin. Tascela brought her other hand from behind her and displayed a small gold vessel.

'I feared she would not like your wine, Olmec,' purred the princess, 'so I brought some of mine, some I brought with me long ago from the shores of Lake Zuad – do you understand, Olmec?'

Beads of sweat stood out suddenly on Olmec's brow. His muscles relaxed, and Valeria broke away and put the table between them. But though reason told her to dart from the room, some fascination she could not understand held her rigid, watching the scene.

Tascela came toward the seated prince with a swaying, undulating walk that was mockery in itself. Her voice was soft, slurringly caressing, but her eyes gleamed. Her slim fingers stroked his beard lightly.

'You are selfish, Olmec,' she crooned, smiling. 'You would keep our handsome guest to yourself, though you knew I wished to entertain her. You are much at fault, Olmec!'

The mask dropped for an instant; her eyes flashed, her face was contorted and with an appalling show of strength her hand locked convulsively in his beard and tore out a great handful. This evidence of unnatural strength was no more terrifying than the momentary baring of the hellish fury that raged under her bland exterior.

Olmec lurched up with a roar, and stood swaying like a bear, his mighty hands clenching and unclenching.

'Slut!' His booming voice filled the room. 'Witch! She-devil! Tecuhltli should have slain you fifty years ago! Begone! I have endured too much from you! This white-skinned wench is mine! Get hence before I slay you!'

The princess laughed and dashed the blood-stained strands into his face. Her laughter was less merciful than the ring of flint on steel.

'Once you spoke otherwise, Olmec,' she taunted. 'Once, in your youth, you spoke words of love. Aye, you were my lover once, years ago, and because you loved me, you slept in my arms beneath the enchanted lotus – and thereby put into my hands the chains that enslaved you. You know you cannot withstand me. You know I have but to gaze into your eyes, with the mystic power a priest of Stygia taught me, long ago, and you are powerless. You remember the night beneath the black lotus that waved above us, stirred by no worldly breeze; you scent again the unearthly perfumes that stole and rose like a cloud about you to enslave you. You cannot fight against me. You are my slave as you were that night – as you shall be so long as you shall live, Olmec of Xuchotl!'

Her voice had sunk to a murmur like the rippling of a stream running through starlit darkness. She leaned close to the prince and spread her long tapering fingers upon his giant breast. His eyes glazed, his great hands fell limply to his sides.

With a smile of cruel malice, Tascela lifted the vessel and placed it to his lips.

'Drink!'

Mechanically the prince obeyed. And instantly the glaze passed from his eyes and they were flooded with fury, comprehension and an awful fear. His mouth gaped, but no sound issued. For an instant he reeled on buckling knees, and then fell in a sodden heap on the floor.

His fall jolted Valeria out of her paralysis. She turned and sprang toward the door, but with a movement that would have shamed a leaping panther, Tascela was before her. Valeria struck at her with her clenched fist, and all the power of her supple body behind the blow. It would have stretched a man senseless on the floor. But with a lithe twist of her torso, Tascela avoided the blow and caught the pirate's wrist. The next instant Valeria's left hand was imprisoned, and holding her wrists together with one hand, Tascela calmly bound them with a cord she drew from her girdle. Valeria thought she had tasted the ultimate in humiliation already that night, but her shame at being manhandled by Olmec was nothing to the sensations that now shook her supple frame. Valeria had always been inclined to despise the other members of her sex; and it was overwhelming to encounter another woman who could handle her like a child. She scarcely resisted at all when Tascela forced her into a chair and drawing her bound wrists down between her knees, fastened them to the chair.

Casually stepping over Olmec, Tascela walked to the bronze door and shot the bolt and threw it open, revealing a hallway without.

'Opening upon this hall,' she remarked, speaking to her feminine captive for the first time, 'there is a chamber which in old times was used as a torture room. When we retired into Tecuhltli, we brought most of the apparatus with us, but there was one piece too heavy to move. It is still in working order. I think it will be quite convenient now.'

An understanding flame of terror rose in Olmec's eyes. Tascela strode back to him, bent and gripped him by the hair.

'He is only paralysed temporarily,' she remarked conversationally. 'He can hear, think, and feel – aye, he can feel very well indeed!'

With which sinister observation she started toward the door, dragging the giant bulk with an ease that made the pirate's eyes dilate. She passed into the hall and moved down it without hesitation, presently disappearing with her captive into a chamber that opened into it, and whence shortly thereafter issued the clank of iron.

Valeria swore softly and tugged vainly, with her legs braced against the chair. The cords that confined her were apparently unbreakable.

Tascela presently returned alone; behind her a muffled groaning issued from the chamber. She closed the door but did not bolt it. Tascela was beyond the grip of habit, as she was beyond the touch of other human instincts and emotions.

Valeria sat dumbly, watching the woman in whose slim hands, the pirate realized, her destiny now rested.

Tascela grasped her yellow locks and forced back her head, looking impersonally down into her face. But the glitter in her dark eyes was not impersonal.

'I have chosen you for a great honor,' she said. 'You shall restore the youth of Tascela. Oh, you stare at that! My appearance is that of youth, but through my veins creeps the sluggish chill of approaching age, as I have felt it a thousand times before. I am old, so old I do not remember my childhood. But I was a girl once, and a priest of Stygia loved me, and gave me the secret of immortality and youth everlasting. He died, then – some said by poison. But I dwelt in my palace by the shores of Lake Zuad and the passing years touched me not. So at last a king of Stygia desired me, and my people rebelled and brought me to this land. Olmec called me a princess. I am not of royal blood. I am greater than a princess. I am Tascela, whose youth your own glorious youth shall restore.'

Valeria's tongue clove to the roof of her mouth. She sensed here a mystery darker than the degeneracy she had anticipated.

The taller woman unbound the Aquilonian's wrists and pulled her to her feet. It was not fear of the dominant strength that lurked in the princess' limbs that made Valeria a helpless, quivering captive in her hands. It was the burning, hypnotic, terrible eyes of Tascela.

7

He Comes from the Dark

'Well, I'm a Kushite!'

Conan glared down at the man on the iron rack.

'What the devil are you doing on that thing?'

Incoherent sounds issued from behind the gag and Conan bent and tore it away, evoking a bellow of fear from the captive; for his action caused the iron ball to lurch down until it nearly touched the broad breast.

'Be careful, for Set's sake!' begged Olmec.

'What for?' demanded Conan. 'Do you think I care what happens to you? I only wish I had time to stay here and watch that chunk of iron grind your guts out. But I'm in a hurry. Where's Valeria?'

'Loose me!' urged Olmec. 'I will tell you all!'

'Tell me first.'

'Never!' The prince's heavy jaws set stubbornly.

'All right.' Conan seated himself on a near-by bench. 'I'll find her myself, after you've been reduced to a jelly. I believe I can speed up that process by twisting my sword-point around in your ear,' he added, extending the weapon experimentally.

'Wait!' Words came in a rush from the captive's ashy lips. 'Tascela took her from me. I've never been anything but a puppet in Tascela's hands.'

'Tascela?' snorted Conan, and spat. 'Why, the filthy—'

'No, no!' panted Olmec. 'It's worse than you think. Tascela is old – centuries old. She renews her life and her youth by the sacrifice of beautiful young women. That's one thing that has reduced the clan to its present state. She will draw the essence of Valeria's life into her own body, and bloom with fresh vigor and beauty.'

'Are the doors locked?' asked Conan, thumbing his sword edge.

'Aye! But I know a way to get into Tecuhltli. Only Tascela and

I know, and she thinks me helpless and you slain. Free me and I swear I will help you rescue Valeria. Without my help you cannot win into Techultli; for even if you tortured me into revealing the secret, you couldn't work it. Let me go and we will steal on Tascela and kill her before she can work magic – before she can fix her eyes on us. A knife thrown from behind will do the work. I should have killed her thus long ago, but I feared that without her to aid us the Xotalancas would overcome us. She needed my help, too; that's the only reason she let me live this long. Now neither needs the other, and one must die. I swear that when we have slain the witch, you and Valeria shall go free without harm. My people will obey me when Tascela is dead.'

Conan stooped and cut the ropes that held the prince, and Olmec slid cautiously from under the great ball and rose, shaking his head like a bull and muttering imprecations as he fingered his lacerated scalp. Standing shoulder to shoulder the two men presented a formidable picture of primitive power. Olmec was as tall as Conan, and heavier; but there was something repellent about the Tlazitlan, something abysmal and monstrous that contrasted unfavorably with the clean-cut, compact hardness of the Cimmerian. Conan had discarded the remnants of his tattered, blood-soaked shirt, and stood with his remarkable muscular development impressively revealed. His great shoulders were as broad as those of Olmec, and more cleanly outlined, and his huge breast arched with a more impressive sweep to a hard waist that lacked the paunchy thickness of Olmec's midsection. He might have been an image of primal strength cut out of bronze. Olmec was darker, but not from the burning of the sun. If Conan was a figure out of the dawn of Time, Olmec was a shambling, somber shape from the darkness of Time's pre-dawn.

'Lead on,' demanded Conan. 'And keep ahead of me. I don't trust you any farther than I can throw a bull by the tail.'

Olmec turned and stalked on ahead of him, one hand twitching slightly as it plucked at his matted beard.

Olmec did not lead Conan back to the bronze door, which the

prince naturally supposed Tascela had locked, but to a certain chamber on the border of Tecuhltli.

'This secret has been guarded for half a century,' he said. 'Not even our own clan knew of it, and the Xotalancas never learned. Tecuhltli himself built this secret entrance, afterward slaying the slaves who did the work; for he feared that he might find himself locked out of his own kingdom some day because of the spite of Tascela, whose passion for him soon changed to hate. But she discovered the secret, and barred the hidden door against him one day as he fled back from an unsuccessful raid, and the Xotalancas took him and flayed him. But once, spying upon her, I saw her enter Tecuhltli by this route, and so learned the secret.'

He pressed upon a gold ornament in the wall, and a panel swung inward, disclosing an ivory stair leading upward.

'This stair is built within the wall,' said Olmec. 'It leads up to a tower upon the roof, and thence other stairs wind down to the various chambers. Hasten!'

'After you, comrade!' retorted Conan satirically, swaying his broadsword as he spoke, and Olmec shrugged his shoulders and stepped onto the staircase. Conan instantly followed him, and the door shut behind them. Far above a cluster of fire-jewels made the staircase a well of dusky dragon-light.

They mounted until Conan estimated that they were above the level of the fourth floor, and then came out into a cylindrical tower, in the domed roof of which was set the bunch of fire-jewels that lighted the stair. Through gold-barred windows, set with un-breakable crystal panes, the first windows he had seen in Xuchotl, Conan got a glimpse of high ridges, domes and more towers, looming darkly against the stars. He was looking across the roofs of Xuchotl.

Olmec did not look through the windows. He hurried down one of the several stairs that wound down from the tower, and when they had descended a few feet, this stair changed into a narrow corridor that wound tortuously on for some distance. It ceased at a steep flight of steps leading downward. There Olmec paused.

Up from below, muffled, but unmistakable, welled a woman's

scream, edged with fright, fury and shame. And Conan recognized Valeria's voice.

In the swift rage roused by that cry, and the amazement of wondering what peril could wring such a shriek from Valeria's reckless lips, Conan forgot Olmec. He pushed past the prince and started down the stair. Awakening instinct brought him about again, just as Olmec struck with his great mallet-like fist. The blow, fierce and silent, was aimed at the base of Conan's brain. But the Cimmerian wheeled in time to receive the buffet on the side of his neck instead. The impact would have snapped the vertebrae of a lesser man. As it was, Conan swayed backward, but even as he reeled he dropped his sword, useless at such close quarters, and grasped Olmec's extended arm, dragging the prince with him as he fell. Headlong they went down the steps together, in a revolving whirl of limbs and heads and bodies. And as they went Conan's iron fingers found and locked in Olmec's bull-throat.

The barbarian's neck and shoulder felt numb from the sledge-like impact of Olmec's huge fist, which had carried all the strength of the massive forearm, thick triceps and great shoulder. But this did not affect his ferocity to any appreciable extent. Like a bulldog he hung on grimly, shaken and battered and beaten against the steps as they rolled, until at last they struck an ivory panel-door at the bottom with such an impact that they splintered it its full length and crashed through its ruins. But Olmec was already dead, for those iron fingers had crushed out his life and broken his neck as they fell.

Conan rose, shaking the splinters from his great shoulder, blinking blood and dust out of his eyes.

He was in the great throneroom. There were fifteen people in that room besides himself. The first person he saw was Valeria. A curious black altar stood before the throne-dais. Ranged about it, seven black candles in golden candlesticks sent up oozing spirals of thick green smoke, disturbingly scented. These spirals united in a cloud near the ceiling, forming a smoky arch above the altar. On that altar lay Valeria, stark naked, her white flesh gleaming in shocking contrast to the glistening ebon stone. She was not bound.

She lay at full length, her arms stretched out above her head to their fullest extent. At the head of the altar knelt a young man, holding her wrists firmly. A young woman knelt at the other end of the altar, grasping her ankles. Between them she could neither rise nor move.

Eleven men and women of Tecuhltli knelt dumbly in a semi-circle, watching the scene with hot, lustful eyes.

On the ivory throne-seat Tascela lolled. Bronze bowls of incense rolled their spirals about her; the wisps of smoke curled about her naked limbs like caressing fingers. She could not sit still; she squirmed and shifted about with sensuous abandon, as if finding pleasure in the contact of the smooth ivory with her sleek flesh.

The crash of the door as it broke beneath the impact of the hurtling bodies caused no change in the scene. The kneeling men and women merely glanced incuriously at the corpse of their prince and at the man who rose from the ruins of the door, then swung their eyes greedily back to the writhing white shape on the black altar. Tascela looked insolently at him, and sprawled back on her seat, laughing mockingly.

'Slut!' Conan saw red. His hands clenched into iron hammers as he started for her. With his first step something clanged loudly and steel bit savagely into his leg. He stumbled and almost fell, checked in his headlong stride. The jaws of an iron trap had closed on his leg, with teeth that sank deep and held. Only the ridged muscles of his calf saved the bone from being splintered. The accursed thing had sprung out of the smoldering floor without warning. He saw the slots now, in the floor where the jaws had lain, perfectly camouflaged.

'Fool!' laughed Tascela. 'Did you think I would not guard against your possible return? Every door in this chamber is guarded by such traps. Stand there and watch now, while I fulfill the destiny of your handsome friend! Then I will decide your own.'

Conan's hand instinctively sought his belt, only to encounter an empty scabbard. His sword was on the stair behind him. His poniard was lying back in the forest, where the dragon had torn it from his jaw. The steel teeth in his leg were like burning coals, but the pain was not as savage as the fury that seethed in his soul. He was trapped, like a wolf. If he had had his sword he would have hewn off his leg and crawled across the floor to slay Tascela. Valeria's eyes rolled toward him with mute appeal, and his own helplessness sent red waves of madness surging through his brain.

Dropping on the knee of his free leg, he strove to get his fingers between the jaws of the trap, to tear them apart by sheer strength. Blood started from beneath his finger nails, but the jaws fitted close about his leg in a circle whose segments jointed perfectly, contracted until there was no space between his mangled flesh and the fanged iron. The sight of Valeria's naked body added flame to the fire of his rage.

Tascela ignored him. Rising languidly from her seat she swept the ranks of her subjects with a searching glance, and asked: 'Where are Xamec, Zlanath and Tachic?'

'They did not return from the catacombs, princess,' answered a man. 'Like the rest of us, they bore the bodies of the slain into the crypts, but they have not returned. Perhaps the ghost of Tolkemec took them.'

'Be silent, fool!' she ordered harshly. 'The ghost is a myth.'

She came down from her dais, playing with a thin gold-hilted dagger. Her eyes burned like nothing on the hither side of hell. She paused beside the altar and spoke in the tense stillness.

'Your life shall make me young, white woman!' she said. 'I shall lean upon your bosom and place my lips over yours, and slowly – ah, slowly! – sink this blade through your heart, so that your life, fleeing your stiffening body, shall enter mine, making me bloom again with youth and with life everlasting!'

Slowly, like a serpent arching toward its victim, she bent down through the writhing smoke, closer and closer over the now motionless woman who stared up into her glowing dark eyes – eyes that grew larger and deeper, blazing like black moons in the swirling smoke.

The kneeling people gripped their hands and held their breath, tense for the bloody climax, and the only sound was Conan's fierce panting as he strove to tear his leg from the trap.

All eyes were glued to the altar and the white figure there; the crash of a thunderbolt could hardly have broken the spell, yet it was only a low cry that shattered the fixity of the scene and brought all whirling about – a low cry, yet one to make the hair stand up stiffly on the scalp. They looked, and they saw.

Framed in the door to the left of the dais stood a nightmare figure. It was a man, with a tangle of white hair and a matted white beard that fell over his breast. Rags only partly covered his gaunt frame, revealing half-naked limbs strangely unnatural in appearance. The skin was not like that of a normal human. There was a suggestion of *scaliness* about it, as if the owner had dwelt long under conditions almost antithetical to those conditions under which human life ordinarily thrives. And there was nothing at all human about the eyes that blazed from the tangle of white hair. They were great gleaming disks that stared unwinkingly, luminous, whitish, and without a hint of normal emotion or sanity. The mouth gaped, but no coherent words issued – only a high-pitched tittering.

'Tolkemec!' whispered Tascela, livid, while the others crouched in speechless horror. 'No myth, then, no ghost! Set! You have dwelt for twelve years in darkness! Twelve years among the bones of the dead! What grisly food did you find? What mad travesty of life did you live, in the stark blackness of that eternal night? I see now why Xamec and Zlanath and Tachic did not return from the catacombs – and never will return. But why have you waited so long to strike? Were you seeking something, in the pits? Some secret weapon you knew was hidden there? And have you found it at last?'

That hideous tittering was Tolkemec's only reply, as he bounded into the room with a long leap that carried him over the secret trap before the door – by chance, or by some faint recollection of the ways of Xuchotl. He was not mad, as a man is mad. He had dwelt apart from humanity so long that he was no longer human. Only an unbroken thread of memory embodied in hate and the urge for vengeance had connected him with the humanity from which he had been cut off, and held him lurking near the people he hated. Only that thin string had kept him from racing and prancing off for ever into the black corridors and realms of the subterranean world he had discovered, long ago.

'You sought something hidden!' whispered Tascela, cringing back. 'And you have found it! You remember the feud! After all these years of blackness, you remember!'

For in the lean hand of Tolkemec now waved a curious jade-hued wand, on the end of which glowed a knob of crimson shaped like a pomegranate. She sprang aside as he thrust it out like a spear, and a beam of crimson fire lanced from the pomegranate. It missed Tascela, but the woman holding Valeria's ankles was in the way. It smote between her shoulders. There was a sharp crackling sound and the ray of fire flashed from her bosom and struck the black altar, with a snapping of blue sparks. The woman toppled sidewise, shriveling and withering like a mummy even as she fell.

Valeria rolled from the altar on the other side, and started for the opposite wall on all fours. For hell had burst loose in the throneroom of dead Olmec.

The man who had held Valeria's hands was the next to die. He turned to run, but before he had taken half a dozen steps, Tolkemec, with an agility appalling in such a frame, bounded around to a position that placed the man between him and the altar. Again the red fire-beam flashed and the Tecuhltli rolled life-less to the floor as the beam completed its course with a burst of blue sparks against the altar.

Then began slaughter. Screaming insanely the people rushed about the chamber, caroming from one another, stumbling and falling. And among them Tolkemec capered and pranced, deal-ing death. They could not escape by the doors; for apparently the metal of the portals served like the metal-veined stone altar to complete the circuit for whatever hellish power flashed like thunderbolts from the witch-wand the ancient waved in his hand. When he caught a man or a woman between him and a door or the altar, that one died instantly. He chose no special victim. He took them as they came, with his rags flapping about his wildly gyrating limbs, and the gusty echoes of his tittering sweeping the room above the screams. And bodies fell like falling leaves about the altar and at the doors. One warrior in desperation rushed at him, lifting a dagger, only to fall before he could strike. But the rest were like crazed cattle, with no thought for resistance, and no chance of escape.

The last Tecuhltli except Tascela had fallen when the princess reached the Cimmerian and the girl who had taken refuge beside him. Tascela bent and touched the floor, pressing a design upon it. Instantly the iron jaws released the bleeding limb and sank back into the floor.

'Slay him if you can!' she panted, and pressed a heavy knife into his hand. 'I have no magic to withstand him!'

With a grunt he sprang before the women, not heeding his lacerated leg in the heat of the fighting-lust. Tolkemec was coming toward him, his weird eyes ablaze, but he hesitated at the gleam of the knife in Conan's hand. Then began a grim game, as Tolkemec sought to circle about Conan and get the barbarian between him and the altar or a metal door, while Conan sought to avoid this and drive home his knife. The women watched tensely, holding their breath.

There was no sound except the rustle and scrape of quick-shifting feet. Tolkemec pranced and capered no more. He realized that grimmer game confronted him than the people who had died screaming and fleeing. In the elemental blaze of the barbarian's eyes he read an intent deadly as his own. Back and forth they weaved, and when one moved the other moved as if invisible threads bound them together. But all the time Conan was getting closer and closer to his enemy. Already the coiled muscles of his thighs were beginning to flex for a spring, when Valeria cried out. For a fleeting instant a bronze door was in line with Conan's moving body. The red line leaped, searing Conan's flank as he twisted aside, and even as he shifted he hurled the knife. Old Tolkemec went down, truly slain at last, the hilt vibrating on his breast.

Tascela sprang – not toward Conan, but toward the wand where it shimmered like a live thing on the floor. But as she leaped, so did Valeria, with a dagger snatched from a dead man, and the blade, driven with all the power of the pirate's muscles, impaled the princess of Tecuhltli so that the point stood out between her breasts. Tascela screamed once and fell dead, and Valeria spurned the body with her heel as it fell.

'I had to do that much, for my own self-respect!' panted Valeria, facing Conan across the limp corpse.

'Well, this cleans up the feud,' he grunted. 'It's been a hell of a night! Where did these people keep their food? I'm hungry.'

'You need a bandage on that leg,' Valeria ripped a length of silk from a hanging and knotted it about her waist, then tore off some smaller strips which she bound efficiently about the barbarian's lacerated limb.

'I can walk on it,' he assured her. 'Let's begone. It's dawn, outside this infernal city. I've had enough of Xuchotl. It's well the breed exterminated itself. I don't want any of their accursed jewels. They might be haunted.'

'There is enough clean loot in the world for you and me,' she said, straightening to stand tall and splendid before him.

The old blaze came back in his eyes, and this time she did not resist as he caught her fiercely in his arms.

'It's a long way to the coast,' she said presently, withdrawing her lips from his.

'What matter?' he laughed. 'There's nothing we can't conquer. We'll have our feet on a ship's deck before the Stygians open their ports for the trading season. And then we'll show the world what plundering means!'

JEWELS OF GWAHLUR

1

Paths of Intrigue

The cliffs rose sheer from the jungle, towering ramparts of stone that glinted jade-blue and dull crimson in the rising sun, and curved away and away to east and west above the waving emerald ocean of fronds and leaves. It looked insurmountable, that giant palisade with its sheer curtains of solid rock in which bits of quartz winked dazzlingly in the sunlight. But the man who was working his tedious way upward was already halfway to the top.

He came of a race of hillmen, accustomed to scaling forbidding crags, and he was a man of unusual strength and agility. His only garment was a pair of short red silk breeks, and his sandals were slung to his back, out of his way, as were his sword and dagger.

The man was powerfully built, supple as a panther. His skin was bronzed by the sun, his square-cut black mane confined by a silver band about his temples. His iron muscles, quick eyes and sure feet served him well here, for it was a climb to test these qualities to the utmost. A hundred and fifty feet below him waved the jungle. An equal distance above him the rim of the cliffs was etched against the morning sky.

He labored like one driven by the necessity of haste; yet he was forced to move at a snail's pace, clinging like a fly on a wall. His groping hands and feet found niches and knobs, precarious holds at best, and sometimes he virtually hung by his finger nails. Yet upward he went, clawing, squirming, fighting for every foot. At times he paused to rest his aching muscles, and, shaking the sweat out of his eyes, twisted his head to stare searchingly out over the jungle, combing the green expanse for any trace of human life or motion.

Now the summit was not far above him, and he observed, only a few feet above his head, a break in the sheer stone of the cliff. An instant later he had reached it – a small cavern, just below the edge of the rim. As his head rose above the lip of its floor, he grunted. He clung there, his elbows hooked over the lip. The cave was so tiny that it was little more than a niche cut in the stone, but held an occupant. A shriveled mummy, cross-legged, arms folded on the withered breast upon which the shrunken head was sunk, sat in the little cavern. The limbs were bound in place with rawhide thongs which had become mere rotted wisps. If the form had ever been clothed, the ravages of time had long ago reduced the garments to dust. But thrust between the crossed arms and the shrunken breast there was a roll of parchment, yellowed with age to the color of old ivory.

The climber stretched forth a long arm and wrenched away this cylinder. Without investigation he thrust it into his girdle and hauled himself up until he was standing in the opening of the niche. A spring upward and he caught the rim of the cliffs and pulled himself up and over almost with the same motion.

There he halted, panting, and stared downward.

It was like looking into the interior of a vast bowl, rimmed by a circular stone wall. The floor of the bowl was covered with trees and denser vegetation, though nowhere did the growth duplicate the jungle denseness of the outer forest. The cliffs marched around it without a break and of uniform height. It was a freak of nature, not to be paralleled, perhaps, in the whole world: a vast natural amphitheater, a circular bit of forested plain, three or four miles in diameter, cut off from the rest of the world, and confined within the ring of those palisaded cliffs.

But the man on the cliffs did not devote his thoughts to marveling at the topographical phenomenon. With tense eagerness he searched the tree-tops below him, and exhaled a gusty sigh when he caught the glint of marble domes amidst the twinkling green.

It was no myth, then; below him lay the fabulous and deserted palace of Alkmeenon.

Conan the Cimmerian, late of the Baracha Isles, of the Black Coast, and of many other climes where life ran wild, had come to the kingdom of Keshan following the lure of a fabled treasure that outshone the hoard of the Turanian kings.

Keshan was a barbaric kingdom lying in the eastern hinterlands of Kush where the broad grasslands merge with the forests that roll up from the south. The people were a mixed race, a dusky nobility ruling a population that was largely pure negro. The rulers – princes and high priests – claimed descent from a white race which, in a mythical age, had ruled a kingdom whose capital city was Alkmeenon. Conflicting legends sought to explain the reason for that race's eventual downfall, and the abandonment of the city by the survivors. Equally nebulous were the tales of the Teeth of Gwahlur, the treasure of Alkmeenon. But these misty legends had been enough to bring Conan to Keshan, over vast distances of plain, river-laced jungle, and mountains.

He had found Keshan, which in itself was considered mythical by many northern and western nations, and he had heard enough to confirm the rumors of the treasure that men called the Teeth of Gwahlur. But its hiding-place he could not learn, and he was confronted with the necessity of explaining his presence in Keshan. Unattached strangers were not welcome there.

But he was not nonplussed. With cool assurance he made his offer to the stately plumed, suspicious grandees of the barbarically magnificent court. He was a professional fighting-man. In search of employment (he said) he had come to Keshan. For a price he would train the armies of Keshan and lead them against Punt, their hereditary enemy, whose recent successes in the field had aroused the fury of Keshan's irascible king.

This proposition was not so audacious as it might seem. Conan's fame had preceded him, even into distant Keshan; his exploits as a chief of the black corsairs, those wolves of the southern coasts, had made his name known, admired and feared throughout the black kingdoms. He did not refuse tests devised by the dusky lords. Skirmishes along the borders were incessant, affording the Cimmerian plenty of opportunities to demonstrate his ability at hand-to-hand fighting. His reckless ferocity impressed the lords of Keshan, already aware of his reputation as a leader of men, and the prospects seemed favorable. All Conan secretly desired was employment to give him legitimate excuse for remaining in Keshan long enough to locate the hiding-place of the Teeth of Gwahlur. Then there came an interruption. Thutmekri came to Keshan at the head of an embassy from Zembabwei.

Thutmekri was a Stygian, an adventurer and a rogue whose wits had recommended him to the twin kings of the great hybrid trading kingdom which lay many days' march to the east. He and the Cimmerian knew each other of old, and without love. Thutmekri likewise had a proposition to make to the king of Keshan, and it also concerned the conquest of Punt – which kingdom, incidentally, lying east of Keshan, had recently expelled the Zembabwan traders and burned their fortresses.

His offer outweighed even the prestige of Conan. He pledged himself to invade Punt from the east with a host of black spearmen, Shemitish archers, and mercenary swordsmen, and to aid the king of Keshan to annex the hostile kingdom. The benevolent kings of Zembabwei desired only a monopoly of the trade of Keshan and her tributaries – and, as a pledge of good faith, some of the Teeth of Gwahlur. These would be put to no base usage. Thutmekri hastened to explain to the suspicious chieftains; they would be placed in the temple of Zembabwei beside the squat gold idols of Dagon and Derketo, sacred guests in the holy shrine of the kingdom, to seal the covenant between Keshan and Zembabwei. This statement brought a savage grin to Conan's hard lips.

The Cimmerian made no attempt to match wits and intrigue with Thutmekri and his Shemitish partner, Zargheba. He knew that if Thutmekri won his point, he would insist on the instant banishment of his rival. There was but one thing for Conan to do: find the jewels before the king of Keshan made up his mind and flee with them. But by this time he was certain that they were not hidden in Keshia, the royal city which was a swarm of thatched huts crowding about a mud wall that enclosed a palace of stone and mud and bamboo.

While he fumed with nervous impatience, the high priest Gorulga announced that before any decision could be reached, the will of the gods must be ascertained concerning the proposed alliance with Zembabwei and the pledge of objects long held holy and inviolate. The oracle of Alkmeenon must be consulted.

This was an awesome thing, and it caused tongues to wag excitedly in palace and bee-hive hut. Not for a century had the priests visited the silent city. The oracle, men said, was the Princess Yelaya, the last ruler of Alkmeenon, who had died in the full bloom of her youth and beauty, and whose body had miraculously remained unblemished throughout the ages. Of old, priests had made their way into the haunted city, and she had taught them wisdom. The last priest to seek the oracle had been a wicked man, who had sought to steal for himself the curiously cut jewels that men called the Teeth of Gwahlur. But some doom had come upon him in the deserted palace, from which his acolytes, fleeing, had told tales of horror that had for a hundred years frightened the priests from the city and the oracle.

But Gorulga, the present high priest, as one confident in his knowledge of his own integrity, announced that he would go with a handful of followers to revive the ancient custom. And in the excitement tongues buzzed indiscreetly, and Conan caught the clue for which he had sought for weeks – the overheard whisper of a lesser priest that sent the Cimmerian stealing out of Keshia the night before the dawn when the priests were to start.

Riding as hard as he dared for a night and a day and a night, he came in the early dawn to the cliffs of Alkmeenon, which stood in the southwestern corner of the kingdom, amidst uninhabited jungle which was taboo to common men. None but the priests dared approach the haunted vale within a distance of many miles. And not even a priest had entered Alkmeenon for a hundred years.

No man had ever climbed these cliffs, legends said, and none but the priests knew the secret entrance into the valley. Conan did not waste time looking for it. Steeps that balked these people, horsemen and dwellers of plain and level forest, were not impossible for a man born in the rugged hills of Cimmeria.

Now on the summit of the cliffs he looked down into the circular valley and wondered what plague, war or superstition had driven the members of that ancient race forth from their stronghold to mingle with and be absorbed by the tribes that hemmed them in.

This valley had been their citadel. There the palace stood, and there only the royal family and their court dwelt. The real city stood outside the cliffs. Those waving masses of green jungle vegetation hid its ruins. But the domes that glistened in the leaves below him were the unbroken pinnacles of the royal palace of Alkmeenon which had defied the corroding ages.

Swinging a leg over the rim he went down swiftly. The inner side of the cliffs was more broken, not quite so sheer. In less than half the time it had taken him to ascend the outer side, he dropped to the swarded valley floor.

With one hand on his sword, he looked alertly about him. There was no reason to suppose men lied when they said that Alkmeenon was empty and deserted, haunted only by the ghosts of the dead past. But it was Conan's nature to be suspicious and wary. The silence was primordial; not even a leaf quivered on a branch. When he bent to peer under the trees, he saw nothing but the marching rows of trunks, receding and receding into the blue gloom of the deep woods.

Nevertheless he went warily, sword in hand, his restless eyes combing the shadows from side to side, his springy tread making no sound on the sward. All about him he saw signs of an ancient civilization; marble fountains, voiceless and crumbling, stood in circles of slender trees whose patterns were too symmetrical to have been a chance of nature. Forest-growth and underbrush had invaded the evenly planned groves, but their outlines were still visible. Broad pavements ran away under the trees, broken, and with grass growing through the wide cracks. He glimpsed walls with ornamental copings, lattices of carven stone that might once have served as the walls of pleasure pavilions.

Ahead of him, through the trees, the domes gleamed and the bulk of the structure supporting them became more apparent as he advanced. Presently, pushing through a screen of vine-tangled branches, he came into a comparatively open space where the trees straggled, unencumbered by undergrowth, and saw before him the wide, pillared portico of the palace.

As he mounted the broad marble steps, he noted that the building was in far better state of preservation than the lesser structures he had glimpsed. The thick walls and massive pillars seemed too powerful to crumble before the assault of time and the elements. The same enchanted quiet brooded over all. The cat-like pad of his sandaled feet seemed startlingly loud in the stillness.

Somewhere in this palace lay the effigy or image which had in times past served as oracle for the priests of Keshan. And somewhere in the palace, unless that indiscreet priest had babbled a lie, was hidden the treasure of the forgotten kings of Alkmeenon.

Conan passed into a broad, lofty hall, lined with tall columns, between which arches gaped, their door long rotted away. He traversed this in a twilight dimness, and at the other end passed through great double-valved bronze doors which stood partly open, as they might have stood for centuries. He emerged into a vast domed chamber which must have served as audience hall for the kings of Alkmeenon.

It was octagonal in shape, and the great dome up to which the lofty ceiling curved obviously was cunningly pierced, for the chamber was much better lighted than the hall which led to it. At the farther side of the great room there rose a dais with broad lapis-lazuli steps leading up to it, and on that dais there stood a massive chair with ornate arms and a high back which once doubtless supported a cloth-of-gold canopy. Conan grunted explosively and his eyes lit. The golden throne of Alkmeenon, named in immemorial legendry! He weighed it with a practised eye. It represented a fortune in itself, if he were but able to bear it away. Its richness fired his imagination concerning the treasure itself, and made him burn with eagerness. His fingers itched to plunge among the gems he had heard described by story-tellers in the market squares of

Keshia, who repeated tales handed down from mouth to mouth through the centuries – jewels not to be duplicated in the world, rubies, emeralds, diamonds, bloodstones, opals, sapphires, the loot of the ancient world.

He had expected to find the oracle-effigy seated on the throne, but since it was not, it was probably placed in some other part of the palace, if, indeed, such a thing really existed. But since he had turned his face toward Keshan, so many myths had proved to be realities that he did not doubt that he would find some kind of image or god.

Behind the throne there was a narrow arched doorway which doubtless had been masked by hangings in the days of Alkmeenon's life. He glanced through it and saw that it let into an alcove, empty, and with a narrow corridor leading off from it at right angles. Turning away from it, he spied another arch to the left of the dais, and it, unlike the others, was furnished with a door. Nor was it any common door. The portal was of the same rich metal as the throne, and carved with many curious arabesques.

At his touch it swung open so readily that its hinges might recently have been oiled. Inside he halted, staring.

He was in a square chamber of no great dimensions, whose marble walls rose to an ornate ceiling, inlaid with gold. Gold friezes ran about the base and the top of the walls, and there was no door other than the one through which he had entered. But he noted these details mechanically. His whole attention was centered on the shape which lay on an ivory dais before him.

He had expected an image, probably carved with the skill of a forgotten art. But no art could mimic the perfection of the figure that lay before him.

It was no effigy of stone or metal or ivory. It was the actual body of a woman, and by what dark art the ancients had preserved that form unblemished for so many ages Conan could not even guess. The very garments she wore were intact – and Conan scowled at that, a vague uneasiness stirring at the back of his mind. The arts that preserved the body should not have affected the garments. Yet there they were – gold breast-plates set with concentric circles of small gems, gilded sandals, and a short silken skirt upheld by a jeweled girdle. Neither cloth nor metal showed any signs of decay.

Yelaya was coldly beautiful, even in death. Her body was like alabaster, slender yet voluptuous; a great crimson jewel gleamed against the darkly piled foam of her hair.

Conan stood frowning down at her, and then tapped the dais with his sword. Possibilities of a hollow containing the treasure occurred to him, but the dais rang solid. He turned and paced the chamber in some indecision. Where should he search first, in the limited time at his disposal? The priest he had overheard babbling to a courtesan had said the treasure was hidden in the palace. But that included a space of considerable vastness. He wondered if he should hide himself until the priests had come and gone, and then renew the search. But there was a strong chance that they might take the jewels with them when they returned to Keshia. For he was convinced that Thutmekri had corrupted Gorulga.

Conan could predict Thutmekri's plans from his knowledge of the man. He knew that it had been Thutmekri who had proposed the conquest of Punt to the kings of Zembabwei, which conquest was but one move toward their real goal – the capture of the Teeth of Gwahlur. Those wary kings would demand proof that the treasure really existed before they made any move. The jewels Thutmekri asked as a pledge would furnish that proof.

With positive evidence of the treasure's reality, the kings of Zembabwei would move. Punt would be invaded simultaneously from the east and the west, but the Zembabwans would see to it that the Keshani did most of the fighting, and then, when both Punt and Keshan were exhausted from the struggle the Zembabwans would crush both races, loot Keshan and take the treasure by force, if they had to destroy every building and torture every living human in the kingdom.

But there was always another possibility: if Thutmekri could get his hands on the hoard, it would be characteristic of the man to cheat his employers, steal the jewels for himself and decamp, leaving the Zembabwan emissaries holding the sack.

Conan believed that this consulting of the oracle was but a ruse to persuade the king of Keshan to accede to Thutmekri's wishes – for he never for a moment doubted that Gorulga was as subtle and devious as all the rest mixed up in this grand swindle. Conan had not approached the high priest himself, because in the game of bribery he would have no chance against Thutmekri, and to attempt it would be to play directly into the Stygian's hands. Gorulga could denounce the Cimmerian to the people, establish a reputation for integrity, and rid Thutmekri of his rival at one stroke. He wondered how Thutmekri had corrupted the high priest, and just what could be offered as a bribe to a man who had the greatest treasure in the world under his fingers.

At any rate he was sure that the oracle would be made to say that the gods willed it that Keshan should follow Thutmekri's wishes, and he was sure, too, that it would drop a few pointed remarks concerning himself. After that Keshia would be too hot for the Cimmerian, nor had Conan had any intention of returning when he rode away in the night.

The oracle chamber held no clue for him. He went forth into the great throne-room and laid his hands on the throne. It was heavy, but he could tilt it up. The floor beneath, a thick marble dais, was solid. Again he sought the alcove. His mind clung to a secret crypt near the oracle. Painstakingly he began to tap along the walls, and presently his taps rang hollow at a spot opposite the mouth of the narrow corridor. Looking more closely he saw that the crack between the marble panel at that point and the next was wider than usual. He inserted a dagger-point and pried.

Silently the panel swung open, revealing a niche in the wall, but nothing else. He swore feelingly. The aperture was empty, and it did not look as if it had ever served as a crypt for treasure. Leaning into the niche he saw a system of tiny holes in the wall, about on a level with a man's mouth. He peered through, and grunted understandingly. That was the wall that formed the partition between the alcove and the oracle chamber. Those holes had not been visible in the chamber. Conan grinned. This explained the mystery of the oracle, but it was a bit cruder than he had expected.

Gorulga would plant either himself or some trusted minion in that niche, to talk through the holes, and the credulous acolytes would accept it as the veritable voice of Yelaya.

Remembering something, the Cimmerian drew forth the roll of parchment he had taken from the mummy and unrolled it carefully, as it seemed ready to fall to pieces with age. He scowled over the dim characters with which it was covered. In his roaming about the world the giant adventurer had picked up a wide smattering of knowledge, particularly including the speaking and reading of many alien tongues. Many a sheltered scholar would have been astonished at the Cimmerian's linguistic abilities, for he had experienced many adventures where knowledge of a strange language had meant the difference between life and death.

These characters were puzzling, at once familiar and unintelligible, and presently he discovered the reason. They were the characters of archaic Pelishtim, which possessed many points of difference from the modern script, with which he was familiar, and which, three centuries ago, had been modified by conquest by a nomad tribe. This older, purer script baffled him. He made out a recurrent phrase, however, which he recognized as a proper name: Bît Yakin. He gathered that it was the name of the writer.

Scowling, his lips unconsciously moving as he struggled with the task, he blundered through the manuscript, finding much of it untranslatable and most of the rest of it obscure.

He gathered that the writer, the mysterious Bît Yakin, had come from afar with his servants, and entered the valley of Alkmeenon. Much that followed was meaningless, interspersed as it was with unfamiliar phrases and characters. Such as he could translate seemed to indicate the passing of a very long period of time. The name of Yelaya was repeated frequently, and toward the last part of the manuscript it became apparent that Bît Yakin knew that death was upon him. With a slight start Conan realized that the mummy in the cavern must be the remains of the writer of the manuscript, the mysterious Pelishtim, Bît Yakin. The man had died, as he had prophesied, and his servants, obviously, had placed him in that open crypt, high up on the cliffs, according to his instructions before his death.

It was strange that Bît Yakin was not mentioned in any of the legends of Alkmeenon. Obviously he had come to the valley after it had been deserted by the original inhabitants – the manuscript indicated as much – but it seemed peculiar that the priests who came in the old days to consult the oracle had not seen the man or his servants. Conan felt sure that the mummy and this parchment were more than a hundred years old. Bît Yakin had dwelt in the valley when the priests came of old to bow before dead Yelaya. Yet concerning him the legends were silent, telling only of a deserted city, haunted only by the dead.

Why had the man dwelt in this desolate spot, and to what unknown destination had his servants departed after disposing of their master's corpse?

Conan shrugged his shoulders and thrust the parchment back into his girdle – he started violently, the skin on the backs of his hands tingling. Startlingly, shockingly in the slumberous stillness, there had boomed the deep strident clangor of a great gong!

He wheeled, crouching like a great cat, sword in hand, glaring down the narrow corridor from which the sound had seemed to come. Had the priests of Keshia arrived? This was improbable, he knew; they would not have had time to reach the valley. But that gong was indisputable evidence of human presence.

Conan was basically a direct-actionist. Such subtlety as he possessed had been acquired through contact with the more devious races. When taken off guard by some unexpected occurrence, he reverted instinctively to type. So now, instead of hiding or slipping away in the opposite direction as the average man might have done, he ran straight down the corridor in the direction of the sound. His sandals made no more sound than the pads of a panther would have made; his eyes were slits, his lips unconsciously asnarl. Panic had momentarily touched his soul at the shock of that unexpected reverberation, and the red rage of the primitive that is wakened by threat of peril always lurked close to the surface of the Cimmerian.

He emerged presently from the winding corridor into a small open court. Something glinting in the sun caught his eye. It was the gong, a great gold disk, hanging from a gold arm extending from the crumbling wall. A brass mallet lay near, but there was no sound or sight of humanity. The surrounding arches gaped emptily. Conan crouched inside the doorway for what seemed a long time. There was no sound or movement throughout the great palace. His patience exhausted at last, he glided around the curve of the court, peering into the arches, ready to leap either way like a flash of light, or to strike right or left as a cobra strikes.

He reached the gong, stared into the arch nearest it. He saw only a dim chamber, littered with the debris of decay. Beneath the gong the polished marble flags showed no footprints, but there was a scent in the air – a faintly fetid odor he could not classify; his nostrils dilated like those of a wild beast as he sought in vain to identify it.

He turned toward the arch – with appalling suddenness the seemingly solid flags splintered and gave way under his feet. Even as he fell he spread wide his arms and caught the edges of the aperture that gaped beneath him. The edges crumbled off under his clutching fingers. Down into utter darkness he shot, into black icy water that gripped him and whirled him away with breathless speed.

2

A Goddess Awakens

The Cimmerian at first made no attempt to fight the current that was sweeping him through lightless night. He kept himself afloat, gripping between his teeth the sword, which he had not relinquished, even in his fall, and did not even seek to guess to what doom he was being borne. But suddenly a beam of light lanced the darkness ahead of him. He saw the surging, seething black surface of the water, in turmoil as if disturbed by some monster of the deep, and he saw the sheer stone walls of the channel curved up to a vault overhead. On each side ran a narrow ledge, just below the arching roof, but they were far out of his reach. At one point this roof had been broken, probably fallen in, and the light was streaming through the aperture. Beyond that shaft of light was utter blackness, and panic assailed the Cimmerian as he saw he would be swept on past that spot of light, and into the unknown blackness again.

Then he saw something else: bronze ladders extended from the ledges to the water's surface at regular intervals, and there was one just ahead of him. Instantly he struck out for it, fighting the current that would have held him to the middle of the stream. It dragged at him as with tangible, animate slimy hands, but he buffeted the rushing surge with the strength of desperation and now drew closer and closer inshore, fighting furiously for every inch. Now he was even with the ladder and with a fierce, gasping plunge he gripped the bottom rung and hung on, breathless.

A few seconds later he struggled up out of the seething water, trusting his weight dubiously to the corroded rungs. They sagged and bent, but they held, and he clambered up onto the narrow ledge which ran along the wall scarcely a man's length below the curving roof. The tall Cimmerian was forced to bend his head as he stood up. A heavy bronze door showed in the stone at a point even with the head of the ladder, but it did not give to Conan's efforts. He transferred his sword from his teeth to its scabbard, spitting blood – for the edge had cut his lips in that fierce fight with the river – and turned his attention to the broken roof.

He could reach his arms up through the crevice and grip the edge, and careful testing told him it would bear his weight. An instant later he had drawn himself up through the hole, and found himself in a wide chamber, in a state of extreme disrepair. Most of the roof had fallen in, as well as a great section of the floor, which was laid over the vault of a subterranean river. Broken arches opened into other chambers and corridors, and Conan believed he was still in the great palace. He wondered uneasily how many chambers in that palace had underground water directly under them, and when the ancient flags or tiles might give way again and precipitate him back into the current from which he had just crawled.

And he wondered just how much of an accident that fall had been. Had those rotten flags simply chanced to give way beneath his weight, or was there a more sinister explanation? One thing at least was obvious: he was not the only living thing in that palace. That gong had not sounded of its own accord, whether the noise had been meant to lure him to his death, or not. The silence of the palace became suddenly sinister, fraught with crawling menace.

Could it be someone on the same mission as himself? A sudden thought occurred to him, at the memory of the mysterious Bît-Yakin. Was it not possible that this man had found the Teeth of Gwahlur in his long residence in Alkmeenon – that his servants had taken them with them when they departed? The possibility that he might be following a will-o'-the-wisp infuriated the Cimmerian.

Choosing a corridor which he believed led back toward the part of the palace he had first entered, he hurried along it, stepping gingerly as he thought of that black river that seethed and foamed somewhere below his feet.

His speculations recurrently revolved about the oracle chamber and its cryptic occupant. Somewhere in that vicinity must be the clue to the mystery of the treasure, if indeed it still remained in its immemorial hiding-place.

The great palace lay silent as ever, disturbed only by the swift passing of his sandaled feet. The chambers and halls he traversed were crumbling into ruin, but as he advanced the ravages of decay became less apparent. He wondered briefly for what purpose the ladders had been suspended from the ledges over the subterranean river, but dismissed the matter with a shrug. He was little interested in speculating over unremunerative problems of antiquity.

He was not sure just where the oracle chamber lay, from where he was, but presently he emerged into a corridor which led back into the great throne-room under one of the arches. He had reached a decision; it was useless for him to wander aimlessly about the palace, seeking the hoard. He would conceal himself somewhere here, wait until the Keshani priests came, and then, after they had gone through the farce of consulting the oracle, he would follow them to the hiding-place of the gems, to which he was certain they would go. Perhaps they would take only a few of the jewels with them. He would content himself with the rest.

Drawn by a morbid fascination, he re-entered the oracle chamber and stared down again at the motionless figure of the princess who was worshipped as a goddess, entranced by her frigid beauty. What cryptic secret was locked in that marvelously molded form?

He started violently. The breath sucked through his teeth, the short hairs prickled at the back of his scalp. The body still lay as he had first seen it, silent, motionless, in breast-plates of jeweled gold, gilded sandals and silken skirt. But now there was a subtle difference. The lissom limbs were not rigid, a peach-bloom touched the cheeks, the lips were red—

With a panicky curse Conan ripped out his sword.

'Crom! She's alive!'

At his words the long dark lashes lifted; the eyes opened and gaped up at him inscrutably, dark, lustrous, mystical. He glared in frozen speechlessness.

She sat up with a supple ease, still holding his ensorceled stare. He licked his dry lips and found voice.

'You – are – are you Yelaya?' he stammered.

'I am Yelaya!' The voice was rich and musical, and he stared with new wonder. 'Do not fear. I will not harm you if you do my bidding.'

'How can a dead woman come to life after all these centuries?' he demanded, as if skeptical of what his senses told him. A curious gleam was beginning to smolder in his eyes.

She lifted her arms in a mystical gesture.

'I am a goddess. A thousand years ago there descended upon me the curse of the greater gods, the gods of darkness beyond the borders of light. The mortal in me died; the goddess in me could never die. Here I have lain for so many centuries, to awaken each night at sunset and hold my court as of yore, with specters drawn from the shadows of the past. Man, if you would not view that which will blast your soul for ever, get hence quickly! I command you! Go!' The voice became imperious, and her slender arm lifted and pointed.

Conan, his eyes burning slits, slowly sheathed his sword, but he did not obey her order. He stepped closer, as if impelled by a powerful fascination – without the slightest warning he grabbed her up in a bear-like grasp. She screamed a very ungoddess-like scream, and there was a sound of ripping silk, as with one ruthless wrench he tore off her skirt.

'Goddess! Ha!' His bark was full of angry contempt. He ignored the frantic writhings of his captive. 'I thought it was strange that a princess of Alkmeenon would speak with a Corinthian accent! As soon as I'd gathered my wits I knew I'd seen you somewhere. You're Muriela, Zargheba's Corinthian dancing-girl. This crescent-shaped birthmark on your hip proves it. I saw it once when Zargheba was whipping you. Goddess! Bah!' He smacked the betraying hip contemptuously and resoundingly with his open hand, and the girl yelped piteously.

All her imperiousness had gone out of her. She was no longer a mystical figure of antiquity, but a terrified and humiliated dancing-girl, such as can be bought at almost any Shemitish market-place. She lifted up her voice and wept unashamedly. Her captor glared down at her with angry triumph.

'Goddess! Ha! So you were one of the veiled women Zargheba brought to Keshia with him. Did you think you could fool me, you little idiot? A year ago I saw you in Akbitana with that swine, Zargheba, and I don't forget faces – or women's figures. I think I'll—'

Squirming about in his grasp she threw her slender arms about his massive neck in an abandon of terror; tears coursed down her cheeks, and her sobs quivered with a note of hysteria.

'Oh, please don't hurt me! Don't! I had to do it! Zargheba brought me here to act as the oracle!'

'Why, you sacrilegious little hussy!' rumbled Conan. 'Do you not fear the gods? Crom! is there no honesty anywhere?'

'Oh, please!' she begged, quivering with abject fright. 'I couldn't disobey Zargheba. Oh, what shall I do? I shall be cursed by these heathen gods!'

'What do you think the priests will do to you if they find out you're an impostor?' he demanded.

At the thought her legs refused to support her, and she collapsed in a shuddering heap, clasping Conan's knees and mingling incoherent pleas for mercy and protection with piteous protestations of her innocence of any malign intention. It was a vivid change from her pose as the ancient princess, but not surprising. The fear that had nerved her then was now her undoing.

'Where is Zargheba?' he demanded. 'Stop yammering, damn it, and answer me.'

'Outside the palace,' she whimpered, 'watching for the priests.'

'How many men with him?'

'None. We came alone.'

'Ha!' It was much like the satisfied grunt of a hunting lion. 'You must have left Keshia a few hours after I did. Did you climb the cliffs?'

She shook her head, too choked with tears to speak coherently. With an impatient imprecation he seized her slim shoulders and shook her until she gasped for breath.

'Will you quit that blubbering and answer me? How did you get into the valley?'

'Zargheba knew the secret way,' she gasped. 'The priest Gwarunga told him, and Thutmekri. On the south side of the valley there is a broad pool lying at the foot of the cliffs. There is a cave-mouth under the surface of the water that is not visible to the casual glance. We ducked under the water and entered it. The cave slopes up out of the water swiftly and leads through the cliffs. The opening on the side of the valley is masked by heavy thickets.'

'I climbed the cliffs on the east side,' he muttered. 'Well, what then?'

'We came to the palace and Zargheba hid me among the trees while he went to look for the chamber of the oracle. I do not think he fully trusted Gwarunga. While he was gone I thought I heard a gong sound, but I was not sure. Presently Zargheba came and took me into the palace and brought me to this chamber, where the goddess Yelaya lay upon the dais. He stripped the body and clothed me in the garments and ornaments. Then he went forth to hide the body and watch for the priests. I have been afraid. When you entered I wanted to leap up and beg you to take me away from this place, but I feared Zargheba. When you discovered I was alive, I thought I could frighten you away.'

'What were you to say as the oracle?' he asked.

'I was to bid the priests to take the Teeth of Gwahlur and give some of them to Thutmekri as a pledge, as he desired, and place the rest in the palace at Keshia. I was to tell them that an awful doom threatened Keshan if they did not agree to Thutmekri's proposals. And, oh, yes, I was to tell them that you were to be skinned alive immediately.'

'Thutmekri wanted the treasure where he – or the Zembabwans – could lay hand on it easily,' muttered Conan, disregarding the remark concerning himself. 'I'll carve his liver yet – Gorulga is a party to this swindle, of course?'

'No. He believes in his gods, and is incorruptible. He knows nothing about this. He will obey the oracle. It was all Thutmekri's plan. Knowing the Keshani would consult the oracle, he had Zargheba bring me with the embassy from Zembabwei, closely veiled and secluded.'

'Well, I'm damned!' muttered Conan. 'A priest who honestly believes in his oracle, and can not be bribed. Crom! I wonder if it was Zargheba who banged that gong. Did he know I was here? Could he have known about that rotten flagging? Where is he now, girl?'

'Hiding in a thicket of lotus trees, near the ancient avenue that leads from the south wall of the cliffs to the palace,' she answered. Then she renewed her importunities. 'Oh, Conan, have pity on me! I am afraid of this evil, ancient place. I know I have heard stealthy footfalls padding about me – oh, Conan, take me away with you! Zargheba will kill me when I have served his purpose here – I know it! The priests, too, will kill me if they discover my deceit.

'He is a devil – he bought me from a slave-trader who stole me out of a caravan bound through southern Koth, and has made me the tool of his intrigues ever since. Take me away from him! You can not be as cruel as he. Don't leave me to be slain here! Please! Please!'

She was on her knees, clutching at Conan hysterically, her beautiful tear-stained face upturned to him, her dark silken hair flowing in disorder over her white shoulders. Conan picked her up and set her on his knee.

'Listen to me. I'll protect you from Zargheba. The priests shall not know of your perfidy. But you've got to do as I tell you.'

She faltered promises of explicit obedience, clasping his corded neck as if seeking security from the contact.

'Good. When the priests come, you'll act the part of Yelaya, as Zargheba planned – it'll be dark, and in the torchlight they'll never know the difference. But you'll say this to them: "It is the will of the gods that the Stygian and his Shemitish dogs be driven from Keshan. They are thieves and traitors who plot to rob the gods. Let the Teeth of Gwahlur be placed in the care of the general Conan. Let him lead the armies of Keshan. He is beloved of the gods."'

She shivered, with an expression of desperation, but acquiesced.

'But Zargheba?' she cried. 'He'll kill me!'

'Don't worry about Zargheba,' he grunted. 'I'll take care of that dog. You do as I say. Here, put up your hair again. It's fallen all over your shoulders. And the gem's fallen out of it.'

He replaced the great glowing gem himself, nodding approval.

'It's worth a room full of slaves, itself alone. Here, put your skirt back on. It's torn down the side, but the priests will never notice it. Wipe your face. A goddess doesn't cry like a whipped schoolgirl. By Crom, you do look like Yelaya, face, hair, figure and all! If you act the goddess with the priests as well as you did with me, you'll fool them easily.'

'I'll try,' she shivered.

'Good; I'm going to find Zargheba.'

At that she became panicky again.

'No! Don't leave me alone! This place is haunted!'

'There's nothing here to harm you,' he assured her impatiently. 'Nothing but Zargheba, and I'm going to look after him. I'll be back shortly. I'll be watching from close by in case anything goes wrong during the ceremony; but if you play your part properly, nothing will go wrong.'

And turning, he hastened out of the oracle chamber; behind him Muriela squeaked wretchedly at his going.

Twilight had fallen. The great rooms and halls were shadowy and indistinct; copper friezes glinted dully through the dusk. Conan strode like a silent phantom through the great halls, with a sensation of being stared at from the shadowed recesses by invisible ghosts of the past. No wonder the girl was nervous amid such surroundings.

He glided down the marble steps like a slinking panther, sword in hand. Silence reigned over the valley, and above the rim of the cliffs stars were blinking out. If the priests of Keshia had entered the valley there was not a sound, not a movement in the greenery to betray them. He made out the ancient broken-paved avenue, wandering away to the south, lost amid clustering masses of fronds and thick-leaved bushes. He followed it warily, hugging the edge of the paving where the shrubs massed their shadows thickly, until he saw ahead of him, dimly in the dusk, the clump of lotus-trees, the strange growth peculiar to the black lands of Kush. There, according to the girl, Zargheba should be lurking. Conan became stealth personified. A velvet-footed shadow, he melted into the thickets.

He approached the lotus grove by a circuitous movement, and scarcely the rustle of a leaf proclaimed his passing. At the edge of the trees he halted suddenly, crouched like a suspicious panther among the deep shrubs. Ahead of him, among the dense leaves, showed a pallid oval, dim in the uncertain light. It might have been one of the great white blossoms which shone thickly among the branches. But Conan knew that it was a man's face. And it was turned toward him. He shrank quickly deeper into the shadows. Had Zargheba seen him? The man was looking directly toward him. Seconds passed. That dim face had not moved. Conan could make out the dark tuft below that was the short black beard.

And suddenly Conan was aware of something unnatural. Zargheba, he knew, was not a tall man. Standing erect, his head would scarcely top the Cimmerian's shoulder; yet that face was on a level with Conan's own. Was the man standing on something? Conan bent and peered toward the ground below the spot where the face showed, but his vision was blocked by undergrowth and the thick boles of the trees. But he saw something else, and he stiffened. Through a slot in the underbrush he glimpsed the stem of the tree under which, apparently, Zargheba was standing. The face was directly in line with that tree. He should have seen below that face, not the tree-trunk, but Zargheba's body – but there was no body there.

Suddenly tenser than a tiger who stalks his prey, Conan glided deeper into the thicket, and a moment later drew aside a leafy branch and glared at the face that had not moved. Nor would it ever move again, of its own volition. He looked on Zargheba's severed head, suspended from the branch of the tree by its own long black hair.

3

The Return of the Oracle

Conan wheeled supplely, sweeping the shadows with a fiercely questing stare. There was no sign of the murdered man's body; only yonder the tall lush grass was trampled and broken down and the sward was dabbled darkly and wetly. Conan stood scarcely breathing as he strained his ears into the silence. The trees and bushes with their great pallid blossoms stood dark, still and sinister, etched against the deepening dusk.

Primitive fears whispered at the back of Conan's mind. Was this the work of the priests of Keshan? If so, where were they? Was it Zargheba, after all, who had struck the gong? Again there rose the memory of Bît-Yakin and his mysterious servants. Bît-Yakin was dead, shriveled to a hulk of wrinkled leather and bound in his hollowed crypt to greet the rising sun for ever. But the servants of Bît-Yakin were unaccounted for. There was no proof they had ever left the valley.

Conan thought of the girl, Muriela, alone and unguarded in that great shadowy palace. He wheeled and ran back down the shadowed avenue, and he ran as a suspicious panther runs, poised even in full stride to whirl right or left and strike death blows.

The palace loomed through the trees, and he saw something else – the glow of fire reflecting redly from the polished marble. He melted into the bushes that lined the broken street, glided through the dense growth and reached the edge of the open space before the portico. Voices reached him; torches bobbed and their flare shone on glossy ebon shoulders. The priests of Keshan had come.

They had not advanced up the wide, overgrown avenue as Zargheba had expected them to do. Obviously there was more than one secret way into the valley of Alkmeenon.

They were filing up the broad marble steps, holding their torches high. He saw Gorulga at the head of the parade, a profile chiseled out of copper, etched in the torch glare. The rest were acolytes, giant black men from whose skins the torches struck highlights. At the end of the procession there stalked a huge negro with an unusually wicked cast of countenance, at the sight of whom Conan scowled. That was Gwarunga, whom Muriela had named as the man who had revealed the secret of the pool-entrance to Zargheba. Conan wondered how deeply the man was in the intrigues of the Stygian.

He hurried toward the portico, circling the open space to keep in the fringing shadows. They left no one to guard the entrance. The torches streamed steadily down the long dark hall. Before they reached the double-valved door at the other end, Conan had mounted the other steps and was in the hall behind them. Slinking swiftly along the column-lined wall, he reached the great door as they crossed the huge throne-room, their torches driving back the shadows. They did not look back. In single file, their ostrich plumes nodding, their leopardskin tunics contrasting curiously with the marble and arabesqued metal of the ancient palace, they moved across the wide room and halted momentarily at the golden door to the left of the throne-dais.

Gorulga's voice boomed eerily and hollowly in the great empty space, framed in sonorous phrases unintelligible to the lurking listener; then the high priest thrust open the golden door and entered, bowing repeatedly from his waist, and behind him the torches sank and rose, showering flakes of flame, as the worshippers imitated their master. The gold door closed behind them, shutting out sound and sight, and Conan darted across the throne-chamber and into the alcove behind the throne. He made less sound than a wind blowing across the chamber.

Tiny beams of light streamed through the apertures in the wall, as he pried open the secret panel. Gliding into the niche, he peered through, Muriela sat upright on the dais, her arms folded, her head leaning back against the wall, within a few inches of his eyes. The delicate perfume of her foamy hair was in his nostrils. He could not see her face, of course, but her attitude was as if she gazed tranquilly into some far gulf of space, over and beyond the shaven heads of the black giants who knelt before her. Conan grinned with appreciation. 'The little slut's an actress,' he told himself. He knew she was shriveling with terror, but she showed no sign. In the uncertain flare of the torches she looked exactly like the goddess he had seen lying on that same dais, if one could imagine that goddess imbued with vibrant life.

Gorulga was booming forth some kind of a chant in an accent unfamiliar to Conan, and which was probably some invocation in the ancient tongue of Alkmeenon, handed down from generation to generation of high priests. It seemed interminable. Conan grew restless. The longer the thing lasted, the more terrific would be the strain on Muriela. If she snapped – he hitched his sword and dagger forward. He could not see the little trollop tortured and slain by these men.

But the chant – deep, low-pitched and indescribably ominous – came to a conclusion at last, and a shouted acclaim from the acolytes marked its period. Lifting his head and raising his arms toward the silent form on the dais, Gorulga cried in the deep, rich resonance that was the natural attribute of the Keshani priest: 'Oh, great goddess, dweller with the great one of darkness, let thy heart be melted, thy lips opened for the ears of thy slave whose head is in the dust beneath thy feet! Speak, great goddess of the holy valley! Thou knowest the paths before us; the darkness that vexes us is as the light of the midday sun to thee. Shed the radiance of thy wisdom on the paths of thy servants! Tell us, oh mouthpiece of the gods: what is their will concerning Thutmekri the Stygian?'

The high-piled burnished mass of hair that caught the torch-light in dull bronze gleams quivered slightly. A gusty sigh rose from the blacks, half in awe, half in fear. Muriela's voice came plainly to Conan's ears in the breathless silence, and it seemed, cold, detached, impersonal, though the Cimmerian winced at the Corinthian accent.

'It is the will of the gods that the Stygian and his Shemitish dogs be driven from Keshan!' She was repeating his exact words. 'They are thieves and traitors who plot to rob the gods. Let the Teeth of Gwahlur be placed in the care of the general Conan. Let him lead the armies of Keshan. He is beloved of the gods!'

There was a quiver in her voice as she ended, and Conan began to sweat, believing she was on the point of an hysterical collapse. But the blacks did not notice, any more than they identified the Corinthian accent, of which they knew nothing. They smote their palms softly together and a murmur of wonder and awe rose from them. Gorulga's eyes glittered fanatically in the torchlight.

'Yelaya has spoken!' he cried in an exalted voice. 'It is the will of the gods! Long ago, in the days of our ancestors, they were made taboo and hidden at the command of the gods, who wrenched them from the awful jaws of Gwahlur the king of darkness, in the birth of the world. At the command of the gods the teeth of Gwahlur were hidden; at their command they shall be brought forth again. Oh star-born goddess, give us your leave to go to the secret hiding-place of the Teeth to secure them for him whom the gods love!'

'You have my leave to go!' answered the false goddess, with an imperious gesture of dismissal that set Conan grinning again, and the priests backed out, ostrich plumes and torches rising and falling with the rhythm of their genuflexions.

The gold door closed and with a moan, the goddess fell back limply on the dais. 'Conan!' she whimpered faintly. 'Conan!'

'Shhh!' he hissed through the apertures, and turning, glided from the niche and closed the panel. A glimpse past the jamb of the carven door showed him the torches receding across the great throne-room, but he was at the same time aware of a radiance that did not emanate from the torches. He was startled, but the solution presented itself instantly. An early moon had risen and its light slanted through the pierced dome which by some curious workmanship intensified the light. The shining dome of Alkmeenon was no fable, then. Perhaps its interior was of the curious whitely flaming crystal found only in the hills of the black countries. The light flooded the throne-room and seeped into the chambers immediately adjoining.

But as Conan made toward the door that led into the throne-room, he was brought around suddenly by a noise that seemed to emanate from the passage that led off from the alcove. He crouched at the mouth, staring into it, remembering the clangor of the gong that had echoed from it to lure him into a snare. The light from the dome filtered only a little way into that narrow corridor, and showed him only empty space. Yet he could have sworn that he had heard the furtive pad of a foot somewhere down it.

While he hesitated, he was electrified by a woman's strangled cry from behind him. Bounding through the door behind the throne, he saw an unexpected spectacle in the crystal light.

The torches of the priests had vanished from the great hall outside – but one priest was still in the palace: Gwarunga. His wicked features were convulsed with fury, and he grasped the terrified Muriela by the throat, choking her efforts to scream and plead, shaking her brutally.

'Traitress!' Between his thick red lips his voice hissed like a cobra. 'What game are you playing? Did not Zargheba tell you what to say? Aye, Thutmekri told me! Are you betraying your master, or is he betraying his friends through you? Slut! I'll twist off your false head – but first I'll—'

A widening of his captive's lovely eyes as she stared over his shoulder warned the huge black. He released her and wheeled, just as Conan's sword lashed down. The impact of the stroke knocked him headlong backward to the marble floor, where he lay twitching, blood oozing from a ragged gash in his scalp.

Conan started toward him to finish the job – for he knew that the priest's sudden movement had caused the blade to strike flat – but Muriela threw her arms convulsively about him.

'I've done as you ordered!' she gasped hysterically. 'Take me away! Oh, please take me away!'

'We can't go yet,' he grunted. 'I want to follow the priests and see where they get the jewels. There may be more loot hidden there. But you can go with me. Where's the gem you wore in your hair?'

'It must have fallen out on the dais,' she stammered, feeling for it. 'I was so frightened – when the priests left I ran out to find you, and this big brute had stayed behind, and he grabbed me—'

'Well, go get it while I dispose of this carcass,' he commanded. 'Go on! That gem is worth a fortune itself.'

She hesitated, as if loth to return to that cryptic chamber; then, as he grasped Gwarunga's girdle and dragged him into the alcove, she turned and entered the oracle room.

Conan dumped the senseless black on the floor, and lifted his sword. The Cimmerian had lived too long in the wild places of the world to have any illusions about mercy. The only safe enemy was a headless enemy. But before he could strike, a startling scream checked the lifted blade. It came from the oracle chamber.

'Conan! Conan! She's come back!' The shriek ended in a gurgle and a scraping shuffle.

With an oath Conan dashed out of the alcove, across the throne dais and into the oracle chamber, almost before the sound had ceased. There he halted, glaring bewilderedly. To all appearances Muriela lay placidly on the dais, eyes closed as in slumber.

'What in thunder are you doing?' he demanded acidly. 'Is this any time to be playing jokes—'

His voice trailed away. His gaze ran along the ivory thigh molded in the close-fitting silk skirt. That skirt should gape from girdle to hem. He knew, because it had been his own hand that tore it as he ruthlessly stripped the garment from the dancer's writhing body. But the skirt showed no rent. A single stride brought him to the dais and he laid his hand on the ivory body – snatched it away as if it had encountered hot iron instead of the cold immobility of death.

'Crom!' he muttered, his eyes suddenly slits of bale-fire. 'It's not Muriela! It's Yelaya!'

He understood now that frantic scream that had burst from Muriela's lips when she entered the chamber. The goddess had returned. The body had been stripped by Zargheba to furnish the accouterments for the pretender. Yet now it was clad in silk and jewels as Conan had first seen it. A peculiar prickling made itself manifest among the short hairs at the base of Conan's scalp.

'Muriela!' he shouted suddenly. 'Muriela! Where the devil are you?'

The walls threw back his voice mockingly. There was no entrance that he could see except the golden door, and none could have entered or departed through that without his knowledge. This much was indisputable: Yelaya had been replaced on the dais within the few minutes that had elapsed since Muriela had first left the chamber to be seized by Gwarunga; his ears were still tingling with the echoes of Muriela's scream, yet the Corinthian girl had vanished as if into thin air. There was but one explanation that offered itself to the Cimmerian, if he rejected the darker speculation that suggested the supernatural – somewhere in the chamber there was a secret door. And even as the thought crossed his mind, he saw it.

In what had seemed a curtain of solid marble, a thin perpendicular crack showed, and in the crack hung a wisp of silk. In an instant he was bending over it. That shred was from Muriela's torn skirt. The implication was unmistakable. It had been caught in the closing door and torn off as she was borne through the opening by whatever grim beings were her captors. The bit of clothing had prevented the door from fitting perfectly into its frame.

Thrusting his dagger-point into the crack, Conan exerted leverage with a corded forearm. The blade bent, but it was of unbreakable Akbitanan steel. The marble door opened. Conan's sword was lifted as he peered into the aperture beyond, but he saw no shape of menace. Light filtering into the oracle chamber revealed a short flight of steps cut out of marble. Pulling the door back to its fullest extent, he drove his dagger into a crack in the floor, propping it open. Then he went down the steps without hesitation. He saw nothing, heard nothing. A dozen steps down, the stair ended in a narrow corridor which ran straight away into gloom.

He halted suddenly, posed like a statue at the foot of the stair, staring at the paintings which frescoed the walls, half visible in the dim light which filtered down from above. The art was unmistakably Pelishtim; he had seen frescoes of identical characteristics on the walls of Asgalun. But the scenes depicted had no connection with anything Pelishtim, except for one human figure, frequently recurrent: a lean, white-bearded old man whose racial characteristics were unmistakable. They seemed to represent various sections of the palace above. Several scenes showed a chamber he recognized as the oracle chamber with the figure of Yelaya stretched upon the ivory dais and huge black men kneeling before it. And there were other figures, too – figures that moved through the deserted palace, did the bidding of the Pelishtim, and dragged unnamable things out of the subterranean river. In the few seconds Conan stood frozen, hitherto unintelligible phrases in the parchment manuscript blazed in his brain with chilling clarity. The loose bits of the pattern clicked into place. The mystery of Bît-Yakin was a mystery no longer, nor the riddle of Bît-Yakin's servants.

Conan turned and peered into the darkness, an icy finger crawling along his spine. Then he went along the corridor, cat-footed, and without hesitation, moving deeper and deeper into the darkness as he drew farther away from the stair. The air hung heavy with the odor he had scented in the court of the gong.

Now in utter blackness he heard a sound ahead of him – the shuffle of bare feet, or the swish of loose garments against stone, he could not tell which. But an instant later his outstreched hand encountered a barrier which he identified as a massive door of carven metal. He pushed against it fruitlessly, and his sword-point sought vainly for a crack. It fitted into the sill and jambs as if molded there. He exerted all his strength, his feet straining against the door, the veins knotting in his temples. It was useless; a charge of elephants would scarcely have shaken that titanic portal.

As he leaned there he caught a sound on the other side that his ears instantly identified – it was the creak of rusty iron, like a lever scraping in its slot. Instinctively action followed recognition so spontaneously that sound, impulse and action were practically simultaneous. And as his prodigious bound carried him backward, there was the rush of a great bulk from above, and a thunderous crash filled the tunnel with deafening vibrations. Bits of flying splinters struck him – a huge block of stone, he knew from the sound, dropped on the spot he had just quitted. An instant's slower thought or action and it would have crushed him like an ant.

Conan fell back. Somewhere on the other side of that metal door Muriela was a captive, if she still lived. But he could not pass that door, and if he remained in the tunnel another block might fall, and he might not be so lucky. It would do the girl no good for him to be crushed into a purple pulp. He could not continue his search in that direction. He must get above ground and look for some other avenue of approach.

He turned and hurried toward the stair, sighing as he emerged into comparative radiance. And as he set foot on the first step, the light was blotted out, and above him the marble door rushed shut with a resounding reverberation.

Something like panic seized the Cimmerian then, trapped in that black tunnel, and he wheeled on the stair, lifting his sword and glaring murderously into the darkness behind him, expecting a rush of ghoulish assailants. But there was no sound or movement down the tunnel. Did the men beyond the door – if they were men – believe that he had been disposed of by the fall of the stone from the roof, which had undoubtedly been released by some sort of machinery?

Then why had the door been shut above him? Abandoning speculation, Conan groped his way up the steps, his skin crawling in anticipation of a knife in his back at every stride, yearning to drown his semi-panic in a barbarous burst of blood-letting.

He thrust against the door at the top, and cursed soulfully to find that it did not give to his efforts. Then as he lifted his sword with his right hand to hew at the marble, his groping left encountered a metal bolt that evidently slipped into place at the closing of the door. In an instant he had drawn this bolt, and then the door gave to his shove. He bounded into the chamber like a slit-eyed, snarling incarnation of fury, ferociously desirous to come to grips with whatever enemy was hounding him.

The dagger was gone from the floor. The chamber was empty; and so was the dais. Yelaya had again vanished.

'By Crom!' muttered the Cimmerian. 'Is she alive, after all?'

He strode out into the throne-room, baffled, and then, struck by a sudden thought, stepped behind the throne and peered into the alcove. There was blood on the smooth marble where he had cast down the senseless body of Gwarunga – that was all. The black man had vanished as completely as Yelaya.

4

The Teeth of Gwahlur

Baffled wrath confused the brain of Conan the Cimmerian. He knew no more how to go about searching for Muriela than he had known how to go about searching for the Teeth of Gwahlur. Only one thought occurred to him – to follow the priests. Perhaps at the hiding-place of the treasure some clue would be revealed to him. It was a slim chance, but better than wandering about aimlessly.

As he hurried through the great shadowy hall that led to the portico, he half expected the lurking shades to come to life behind him with rending fangs and talons. But only the beat of his own rapid heart accompanied him into the moonlight that dappled the shimmering marble.

At the foot of the wide steps he cast about in the bright moonlight for some sign to show him the direction he must go. And he found it – petals scattered on the sward told where an arm or garment had brushed against a blossom-laden branch. Grass had been pressed down under heavy feet. Conan, who had tracked wolves in his native hills, found no insurmountable difficulty in following the trail of the Keshani priests.

It led away from the palace, through masses of exotic-scented shrubbery where great pale blossoms spread their shimmering petals, through verdant, tangled bushes that showered blooms at the touch, until he came at last to a great mass of rock that jutted like a titan's castle out from the cliffs at a point closest to the palace, which, however, was almost hidden from view by vine-interlaced trees. Evidently that babbling priest in Keshia had been mistaken when he said the Teeth were hidden in the palace. This trail had led him away from the place where Muriela had disappeared, but a belief was growing in Conan that each part of the valley was connected with that palace by subterranean passages.

Crouching in the deep velvet-black shadows of the bushes, he scrutinized the great jut of rock which stood out in bold relief in the moonlight. It was covered with strange, grotesque carvings, depicting men and animals, and half-bestial creatures that might have been gods or devils. The style of art differed so strikingly from that of the rest of the valley, that Conan wondered if it did not represent a different era and race, and was itself a relic of an age lost and forgotten at whatever immeasurably distant date the people of Alkmeenon had found and entered the haunted valley.

A great door stood open in the sheer curtain of the cliff, and a gigantic dragon head was carved about it so that the open door was like the dragon's gaping mouth. The door itself was of carven bronze and looked to weigh several tons. There was no lock that he could see, but a series of bolts showing along the edge of the massive portal, as it stood open, told him that there was some system of locking and unlocking – a system doubtless known only to the priests of Keshan.

The trail showed that Gorulga and his henchmen had gone through that door. But Conan hesitated. To wait until they emerged would probably mean to see the door locked in his face, and he might not be able to solve the mystery of its unlocking. On the other hand, if he followed them in, they might emerge and lock him in the cavern.

Throwing caution to the winds, he glided silently through the great portal. Somewhere in the cavern were the priests, the Teeth of Gwahlur, and perhaps a clue to the fate of Muriela. Personal risks had never yet deterred the Cimmerian from any purpose.

Moonlight illumined, for a few yards, the wide tunnel in which he found himself. Somewhere ahead of him he saw a faint glow and heard the echo of a weird chanting. The priests were not so far ahead of him as he had thought. The tunnel debouched into a wide room before the moonlight played out, an empty cavern of no great dimensions, but with a lofty, vaulted roof, glowing with a phosphorescent encrustation, which, as Conan knew, was a common phenomenon in that part of the world. It made a ghostly half-light, in which he was able to see a bestial image squatting on a shrine and the black mouths of six or seven tunnels leading off from the chamber. Down the widest of these – the one directly behind the squat image which looked toward the outer opening – he caught the gleam of torches wavering, whereas the phosphorescent glow was fixed, and heard the chanting increase in volume.

Down it he went recklessly, and was presently peering into a larger cavern than the one he had just left. There was no phosphorus here, but the light of the torches fell on a larger altar and a more obscene and repulsive god squatting toad-like upon it. Before this repugnant deity Gorulga and his ten acolytes knelt and beat their heads upon the ground, while chanting monotonously. Conan realized why their progress had been so slow. Evidently approaching the secret crypt of the Teeth was a complicated and elaborate ritual.

He was fidgeting in nervous impatience before the chanting and bowing were over, but presently they rose and passed into the tunnel which opened behind the idol. Their torches bobbed away into the nighted vault, and he followed swiftly. Not much danger of being discovered. He glided along the shadows like a creature of the night, and the black priests were completely engrossed in their ceremonial mummery. Apparently they had not even noticed the absence of Gwarunga.

Emerging into a cavern of huge proportions, about whose upward curving walls gallery-like ledges marched in tiers, they began their worship anew before an altar which was larger, and a god which was more disgusting, than any encountered thus far.

Conan crouched in the black mouth of the tunnel, staring at the walls reflecting the lurid glow of the torches. He saw a carven stone stair winding up from tier to tier of the galleries; the roof was lost in darkness.

He started violently and the chanting broke off as the kneeling blacks flung up their heads. An inhuman voice boomed out high above them. They froze on their knees, their faces turned upward with a ghastly blue hue in the sudden glare of a weird light that burst blindingly up near the lofty roof and then burned with a throbbing glow. That glare lighted a gallery and a cry went up from the high priest, echoed shudderingly by his acolytes. In the flash there had been briefly disclosed to them a slim white figure standing upright in a sheen of silk and a glint of jewel-crusted gold. Then the blaze smoldered to a throbbing, pulsing luminosity in which nothing was distinct, and that slim shape was but a shimmering blue of ivory.

'Yelaya!' screamed Gorulga, his brown features ashen. 'Why have you followed us? What is your pleasure?'

That weird unhuman voice rolled down from the roof, re-echoing under that arching vault that magnified and altered it beyond recognition.

'Woe to the unbelievers! Woe to the false children of Keshia! Doom to them which deny their deity!'

A cry of horror went up from the priests. Gorulga looked like a shocked vulture in the glare of the torches.

'I do not understand!' he stammered. 'We are faithful. In the chamber of the oracle you told us—'

'Do not heed what you heard in the chamber of the oracle!' rolled that terrible voice, multiplied until it was as though a myriad voices thundered and muttered the same warning. 'Beware of false prophets and false gods! A demon in my guise spoke to you in the palace, giving false prophecy. Now harken and obey, for only I am the true goddess, and I give you one chance to save yourselves from doom!

'Take the Teeth of Gwahlur from the crypt where they were placed so long ago. Alkmeenon is no longer holy, because it has been desecrated by blasphemers. Give the Teeth of Gwahlur into the hands of Thutmekri, the Stygian, to place in the sanctuary of Dragon and Derketo. Only this can save Keshan from the doom the demons of the night have plotted. Take the Teeth of Gwahlur and go: return instantly to Keshia; there give the jewels to Thutmekri, and seize the foreign devil Conan and flay him alive in the great square.'

There was no hesitation in obeying. Chattering with fear the priests scrambled up and ran for the door that opened behind the bestial god. Gorulga led the flight. They jammed briefly in the doorway, yelping as wildly waving torches touched squirming black bodies; they plunged through, and the patter of their speeding feet dwindled down the tunnel.

Conan did not follow. He was consumed with a furious desire to learn the truth of this fantastic affair. Was that indeed Yelaya, as the cold sweat on the backs of his hands told him, or was it that little hussy Muriela, turned traitress after all? If it was—

Before the last torch had vanished down the black tunnel he was bounding vengefully up the stone stair. The blue glow was dying down, but he could still make out that the ivory figure stood motionless on the gallery. His blood ran cold as he approached it, but he did not hesitate. He came on with his sword lifted, and towered like a threat of death over the inscrutable shape.

'Yelaya!' he snarled. 'Dead as she's been for a thousand years! Ha!'

From the dark mouth of a tunnel behind him a dark form lunged. But the sudden, deadly rush of unshod feet had reached the Cimmerian's quick ears. He whirled like a cat and dodged the blow aimed murderously at his back. As the gleaming steel in the dark hand hissed past him, he struck back with the fury of a roused python, and the long straight blade impaled his assailant and stood out a foot and a half between his shoulders.

'So!' Conan tore his sword free as the victim sagged to the floor, gasping and gurgling. The man writhed briefly and stiffened. In the dying light Conan saw a black body and ebon countenance, hideous in the blue glare. He had killed Gwarunga.

Conan turned from the corpse to the goddess. Thongs about her knees and breast held her upright against a stone pillar, and her thick hair, fastened to the column, held her head up. At a few yards' distance these bonds were not visible in the uncertain light.

'He must have come to after I descended into the tunnel,' muttered Conan. 'He must have suspected I was down there. So he pulled out the dagger' – Conan stooped and wrenched the identical weapon from the stiffening fingers, glanced at it and replaced it in his own girdle – 'and shut the door. Then he took Yelaya to befool his brother idiots. That was he shouting a while ago. You couldn't recognize his voice, under this echoing roof. And that bursting blue flame – I thought it looked familiar. It's a trick of the Stygian priests. Thutmekri must have given some of it to Gwarunga.'

He could easily have reached this cavern ahead of his companions. Evidently familiar with the plan of the caverns by hearsay or by maps handed down in the priestcraft, he had entered the cave after the others, carrying the goddess, followed a circuitous route through the tunnels and chambers, and ensconced himself and his burden on the balcony while Gorulga and the other acolytes were engaged in their endless rituals.

The blue glare had faded, but now Conan was aware of another glow, emanating from the mouth of one of the corridors that opened on the ledge. Somewhere down that corridor there was another field of phosphorus, for he recognized the faint steady radiance. The corridor led in the direction the priests had taken, and he decided to follow it, rather than descend into the darkness of the great cavern below. Doubtless it connected with another gallery in some other chamber, which might be the destination of the priests. He hurried down it, the illumination growing stronger as he advanced, until he could make out the floor and the walls of the tunnel. Ahead of him and below he could hear the priests chanting again.

Abruptly a doorway in the left-hand wall was limned in the phosphorus glow, and to his ears came the sound of soft, hysterical sobbing. He wheeled, and glared through the door.

He was looking again into a chamber hewn out of solid rock, not a natural cavern like the others. The domed roof shone with the phosphorous light, and the walls were almost covered with arabesques of beaten gold.

Near the farther wall on a granite throne, staring for ever toward the arched doorway, sat the monstrous and obscene Pteor, the god of the Pelishtim, wrought in brass, with his exaggerated attributes reflecting the grossness of his cult. And in his lap sprawled a limp white figure.

'Well, I'll be damned!' muttered Conan. He glanced suspiciously about the chamber, seeing no other entrance or evidence of occupation, and then advanced noiselessly and looked down at the girl whose slim shoulders shook with sobs of abject misery, her face sunk in her arms. From thick bands of gold on the idol's arms slim gold chains ran to smaller bands on her wrists. He laid a hand on her naked shoulder and she started convulsively, shrieked, and twisted her tear-stained face toward him.

'Conan!' She made a spasmodic effort to go into the usual clinch, but the chains hindered her. He cut through the soft gold as close to her wrists as he could, grunting: 'You'll have to wear these bracelets until I can find a chisel or a file. Let go of me, damn it! You actresses are too damned emotional. What happened to you, anyway?'

'When I went back into the oracle chamber,' she whimpered, 'I saw the goddess lying on the dais as I'd first seen her. I called out to you and started to run to the door – then something grabbed me from behind. It clapped a hand over my mouth and carried me through a panel in the wall, and down some steps and along a dark hall. I didn't see what it was that had hold of me until we passed through a big metal door and came into a tunnel whose roof was alight, like this chamber.

'Oh, I nearly fainted when I saw! They are not humans! They are gray, hairy devils that walk like men and speak a gibberish no human could understand. They stood there and seemed to be waiting, and once I thought I heard somebody trying the door. Then one of the things pulled a metal lever in the wall, and something crashed on the other side of the door.

'Then they carried me on and on through winding tunnels and up stone stairways into this chamber, where they chained me on the knees of this abominable idol, and then they went away. Oh, Conan, what are they?'

'Servants of Bît-Yakin,' he grunted. 'I found a manuscript that told me a number of things, and then stumbled upon some frescoes that told me the rest. Bît-Yakin was a Pelishtim who wandered into the valley with his servants after the people of Alkmeenon had deserted it. He found the body of Princess Yelaya, and discovered that the priests returned from time to time to make offerings to her, for even then she was worshipped as a goddess.

'He made an oracle of her, and he was the voice of the oracle, speaking from a niche he cut in the wall behind the ivory dais. The priests never suspected, never saw him or his servants for they always hid themselves when the men came. Bît-Yakin lived and died here without ever being discovered by the priests. Crom knows how long he dwelt here, but it must have been for centuries. The wise men of the Pelishtim know how to increase the span of their lives for hundreds of years. I've seen some of them myself. Why he lived here alone, and why he played the part of oracle no ordinary human can guess, but I believe the oracle part was to keep the city inviolate and sacred, so he could remain undisturbed. He ate the food the priests brought as an offering to Yelaya, and his servants ate other things – I've always known there was a subterranean river flowing away from the lake where the people of the Puntish highlands throw their dead. That river runs under this palace. They have ladders hung over the water where they can hang and fish for the corpses that come floating through. Bît-Yakin recorded everything on parchment and painted walls.

'But he died at last, and his servants mummified him according to instructions he gave them before his death, and stuck him in a cave in the cliffs. The rest is easy to guess. His servants, who were even more nearly immortal than he, kept on dwelling here, but the next time a high priest came to consult the oracle, not having a master to restrain them, they tore him to pieces. So since then – until Gorulga – nobody came to talk to the oracle.

'It's obvious they've been renewing the garments and ornaments of the goddess, as they'd seen Bît-Yakin do. Doubtless there's a sealed chamber somewhere where the silks are kept from decay. They clothed the goddess and brought her back to the oracle room after Zargheba had stolen her. And by the way they took off Zargheba's head and hung it in a thicket.'

She shivered, yet at the same time breathed a sigh of relief.

'He'll never whip me again.'

'Not this side of hell,' agreed Conan. 'But come on. Gwarunga ruined my chances with his stolen goddess. I'm going to follow the priests and take my chance of stealing the loot from them after they get it. And you stay close to me. I can't spend all my time looking for you.'

'But the servants of Bît-Yakin!' she whispered fearfully.

'We'll have to take our chance,' he grunted. 'I don't know what's in their minds, but so far they haven't shown any disposition to come out and fight in the open. Come on.'

Taking her wrist he led her out of the chamber and down the corridor. As they advanced they heard the chanting of the priests, and mingling with the sound the low sullen rushing of waters. The light grew stronger above them as they emerged on a high-pitched gallery of a great cavern and looked down on a scene weird and fantastic.

Above them gleamed the phosphorescent roof; a hundred feet below them stretched the smooth floor of the cavern. On the far side this floor was cut by a deep, narrow stream brimming its rocky channel. Rushing out of impenetrable gloom, it swirled across the cavern and was lost again in darkness. The visible surface reflected the radiance above; the dark seething waters glinted as if flecked with living jewels, frosty blue, lurid red, shimmering green, an ever-changing iridescence.

Conan and his companion stood upon one of the gallery-like ledges that banded the curve of the lofty wall, and from this ledge a natural bridge of stone soared in a breath-taking arch over the vast gulf of the cavern to join a much smaller ledge on the opposite side, across the river. Ten feet below it another, broader arch spanned the cave. At either end a carven stair joined the extremities of these flying arches.

Conan's gaze, following the curve of the arch that swept away from the ledge on which they stood, caught a glint of light that was not the lurid phosphorus of the cavern. On that small ledge opposite them there was an opening in the cave wall through which stars were glinting.

But his full attention was drawn to the scene beneath them. The priests had reached their destination. There in a sweeping angle of the cavern wall stood a stone altar, but there was no idol upon it. Whether there was one behind it, Conan could not ascertain, because some trick of the light, or the sweep of the wall, left the space behind the altar in total darkness.

The priests had stuck their torches into holes in the stone floor, forming a semicircle of fire in front of the altar at a distance of several yards. Then the priests themselves formed a semicircle inside the crescent of torches, and Gorulga, after lifting his arms aloft in invocation, bent to the altar and laid hands on it. It lifted and tilted backward on its hinder edge, like the lid of a chest, revealing a small crypt.

Extending a long arm into the recess, Gorulga brought up a small brass chest. Lowering the altar back into place, he set the chest on it, and threw back the lid. To the eager watchers on the high gallery it seemed as if the action had released a blaze of living fire which throbbed and quivered about the opened chest. Conan's heart leaped and his hand caught at his hilt. The Teeth of Gwahlur at last! The treasure that would make its possessor the richest man in the world! His breath came fast between his clenched teeth.

Then he was suddenly aware that a new element had entered into the light of the torches and of the phosphorescent roof, rendering both void. Darkness stole around the altar, except for that glowing spot of evil radiance cast by the teeth of Gwahlur, and that grew and grew. The blacks froze into basaltic statues, their shadows streaming grotesquely and gigantically out behind them.

The altar was laved in the glow now, and the astounded features of Gorulga stood out in sharp relief. Then the mysterious space behind the altar swam into the widening illumination. And slowly with the crawling light, figures became visible, like shapes growing out of the night and silence.

At first they seemed like gray stone statues, those motionless shapes, hairy, man-like, yet hideously human; but their eyes were alive, cold sparks of gray icy fire. And as the weird glow lit their bestial countenances, Gorulga screamed and fell backward, throwing up his long arms in a gesture of frenzied horror.

But a longer arm shot across the altar and a misshapen hand locked on his throat. Screaming and fighting, the high priest was dragged back across the altar; a hammer-like fist smashed down, and Gorulga's cries were stilled. Limp and broken he sagged across the altar, his brains oozing from his crushed skull. And then the servants of Bît-Yakin surged like a bursting flood from hell on the black priests who stood like horror-blasted images.

Then there was slaughter, grim and appalling.

Conan saw black bodies tossed like chaff in the inhuman hands of the slayers, against whose horrible strength and agility the daggers and swords of the priests were ineffective. He saw men lifted bodily and their heads cracked open against the stone altar. He saw a flaming torch, grasped in a monstrous hand, thrust inexorably down the gullet of an agonized wretch who writhed in vain against the arms that pinioned him. He saw a man torn in two pieces, as one might tear a chicken, and the bloody fragments hurled clear across the cavern. The massacre was as short and devastating as the rush of a hurricane. In a burst of red abysmal ferocity it was over, except for one wretch who fled screaming back the way the priests had come, pursued by a swarm of blood-dabbled shapes of horror which reached out their red-smeared hands for him. Fugitive and pursuers vanished down the black tunnel, and the screams of the human came back dwindling and confused by the distance.

Muriela was on her knees clutching Conan's legs; her face pressed against his knee and her eyes tightly shut. She was a quaking, quivering mold of abject terror. But Conan was galvanized. A quick glance across at the aperture where the stars shone, a glance down at the chest that still blazed open on the blood-smeared altar, and he saw and seized the desperate gamble.

'I'm going after that chest!' he grated. 'Stay here!'

'Oh, Mitra, no!' In an agony of fright she fell to the floor and caught at his sandals. 'Don't! Don't! Don't leave me!'

'Lie still and keep your mouth shut!' he snapped, disengaging himself from her frantic clasp.

He disregarded the tortuous stair. He dropped from ledge to ledge with reckless haste. There was no sign of the monsters as his feet hit the floor. A few of the torches still flared in their sockets, the phosphorescent glow throbbed and quivered, and the river flowed with an almost articulate muttering, scintillant with undreamed radiances. The glow that had heralded the appearance of the servants had vanished with them. Only the light of the jewels in the brass chest shimmered and quivered.

He snatched the chest, noting its contents in one lustful glance – strange, curiously shapen stones that burned with an icy, non-terrestrial fire. He slammed the lid, thrust the chest under his arm, and ran back up the steps. He had no desire to encounter the hellish servants of Bît-Yakin. His glimpse of them in action had dispelled any illusion concerning their fighting ability. Why they had waited so long before striking at the invaders he was unable to say. What human could guess the motives or thoughts of these monstrosities? That they were possessed of craft and intelligence equal to humanity had been demonstrated. And there on the cavern floor lay crimson proof of their bestial ferocity.

The Corinthian girl still cowered on the gallery where he had left her. He caught her wrist and yanked her to her feet, grunting: 'I guess it's time to go!'

Too bemused with terror to be fully aware of what was going on, the girl suffered herself to be led across the dizzy span. It was not until they were poised over the rushing water that she looked down, voiced a startled yelp and would have fallen but for Conan's massive arm about her. Growling an objurgation in her ear, he snatched her up under his free arm and swept her, in a flutter of limply waving arms and legs, across the arch and into the aperture that opened at the other end. Without bothering to set her on her feet, he hurried through the short tunnel into which this aperture opened. An instant later they emerged upon a narrow ledge on the outer side of the cliffs that circled the valley. Less than a hundred feet below them the jungle waved in the starlight.

Looking down, Conan vented a gusty sigh of relief. He believed that he could negotiate the descent, even though burdened with the jewels and the girl; although he doubted if even he, unburdened, could have ascended at that spot. He set the chest, still smeared with Gorulga's blood and clotted with his brains, on the ledge, and was about to remove his girdle in order to tie the box to his back, when he was galvanized by a sound behind him, a sound sinister and unmistakable.

'Stay here!' he snapped at the bewildered Corinthian girl. 'Don't move!' And drawing his sword, he glided into the tunnel, glaring back into the cavern.

Halfway across the upper span he saw a gray deformed shape. One of the servants of Bît-Yakin was on his trail. There was no doubt that the brute had seen them and was following them. Conan did not hesitate. It might be easier to defend the mouth of the tunnel – but this fight must be finished quickly, before the other servants could return.

He ran out on the span, straight toward the oncoming monster. It was no ape, neither was it a man. It was some shambling horror spawned in the mysterious, nameless jungles of the south, where strange life teemed in the reeking rot without the dominance of man, and drums thundered in temples that had never known the tread of a human foot. How the ancient Pelishtim had gained lordship over them – and with it eternal exile from humanity – was a foul riddle about which Conan did not care to speculate, even if he had had opportunity.

Man and monster; they met at the highest arch of the span, where, a hundred feet below, rushed the furious black water. As the monstrous shape with its leprous gray body and the features of a carven, unhuman idol loomed over him, Conan struck as a wounded tiger strikes, with every ounce of thew and fury behind the blow. That stroke would have sheared a human body asunder; but the bones of the servant of Bît-Yakin were like tempered steel. Yet even tempered steel could not wholly have withstood that furious stroke. Ribs and shoulder-bone parted and blood spouted from the great gash.

There was no time for a second stroke. Before the Cimmerian could lift his blade again or spring clear, the sweep of a giant arm knocked him from the span as a fly is flicked from a wall. As he plunged downward the rush of the river was like a knell in his ears, but his twisted body fell halfway across the lower arch. He wavered there precariously for one blood-chilling instant, then his clutching fingers hooked over the farther edge, and he scrambled to safety, his sword still in his other hand.

As he sprang up, he saw the monster, spurting blood hideously, rush toward the cliff-end of the bridge, obviously intending to descend the stair that connected the arches and renew the feud. At the very ledge the brute paused in mid-flight – and Conan saw it too – Muriela, with the jewel chest under her arm, stood staring wildly in the mouth of the tunnel.

With a triumphant bellow the monster scooped her up under one arm, snatched the jewel chest with the other hand as she dropped it, and turning, lumbered back across the bridge. Conan cursed with passion and ran for the other side also. He doubted if he could climb the stair to the higher arch in time to catch the brute before it could plunge into the labyrinth of tunnels on the other side.

But the monster was slowing, like clockwork running down. Blood gushed from that terrible gash in his breast, and he lurched drunkenly from side to side. Suddenly he stumbled, reeled and toppled sidewise – pitched headlong from the arch and hurtled downward. Girl and jewel chest fell from his nerveless hands and Muriela's scream rang terribly above the snarl of the water below.

Conan was almost under the spot from which the creature had fallen. The monster struck the lower arch glancingly and shot off, but the writhing figure of the girl struck and clung, and the chest hit the edge of the span near her. One falling object struck on one side of Conan and one on the other. Either was within arm's length; for the fraction of a split second the chest teetered on the edge of the bridge, and Muriela clung by one arm, her face turned desperately toward Conan, her eyes dilated with the fear of death and her lips parted in a haunting cry of despair.

Conan did not hesitate, nor did he even glance toward the chest that held the wealth of an epoch. With a quickness that would have shamed the spring of a hungry jaguar, he swooped, grasped the girl's arm just as her fingers slipped from the smooth stone, and snatched her up on the span with one explosive heave. The chest toppled on over and struck the water ninety feet below, where the body of the servant of Bît-Yakin had already vanished. A splash, a jetting flash of foam marked where the Teeth of Gwahlur disappeared for ever from the sight of the man.

Conan scarcely wasted a downward glance. He darted across the span and ran up the cliff stair like a cat, carrying the limp girl as if she had been an infant. A hideous ululation caused him to glance over his shoulder as he reached the higher arch, to see the other servants streaming back into the cavern below, blood dripping from their bared fangs. They raced up the stair that wound from tier to tier, roaring vengefully; but he slung the girl unceremoniously over his shoulder, dashed through the tunnel and went down the cliffs like an ape himself, dropping and springing from hold to hold with breakneck recklessness. When the fierce countenances looked over the ledge of the aperture, it was to see the Cimmerian and the girl disappearing into the forest that surrounded the cliffs.

'Well,' said Conan, setting the girl on her feet within the sheltering screen of branches, 'we can take our time now. I don't think those brutes will follow us outside the valley. Anyway, I've got a horse tied at a water-hole close by, if the lions haven't eaten him. Crom's devils! What are you crying about now?'

She covered her tear-stained face with her hands. and her slim shoulders shook with sobs.

'I lost the jewels for you,' she wailed miserably. 'It was my fault. If I'd obeyed you and stayed out on the ledge, that brute would never have seen me. You should have caught the gems and let me drown!'

'Yes, I suppose I should,' he agreed. 'But forget it. Never worry about what's past. And stop crying, will you? That's better. Come on.'

'You mean you're going to keep me? Take me with you?' she asked hopefully.

'What else do you suppose I'd do with you?' He ran an approving glance over her figure and grinned at the torn skirt which revealed a generous expanse of tempting ivory-tinted curves. 'I can use an actress like you. There's no use going back to Keshia. There's nothing in Keshan now that I want. We'll go to Punt. The people of Punt worship an ivory woman, and they wash gold out of the rivers in wicker baskets. I'll tell them that Keshan is intriguing with Thutmekri to enslave them – which is true – and that the gods have sent me to protect them – for about a houseful of gold. If I can manage to smuggle you into their temple to exchange places with their ivory goddess, we'll skin them out of their jaw teeth before we get through with them!'

BEYOND THE BLACK RIVER

1

Conan Loses His Ax

The stillness of the forest trail was so primeval that the tread of a soft-booted foot was a startling disturbance. At least it seemed so to the ears of the wayfarer, though he was moving along the path with the caution that must be practised by any man who ventures beyond Thunder River. He was a young man of medium height, with an open countenance and a mop of tousled tawny hair unconfined by cap or helmet. His garb was common enough for that country – a coarse tunic, belted at the waist, short leather breeches beneath, and soft buckskin boots that came short of the knee. A knife-hilt jutted from one boot-top. The broad leather belt supported a short, heavy sword and a buckskin pouch. There was no perturbation in the wide eyes that scanned the green walls which fringed the trail. Though not tall, he was well built, and the arms that the short wide sleeves of the tunic left bare were thick with corded muscle.

He tramped imperturbably along, although the last settler's cabin lay miles behind him, and each step was carrying him nearer the grim peril that hung like a brooding shadow over the ancient forest.

He was not making as much noise as it seemed to him, though he well knew that the faint tread of his booted feet would be like a tocsin of alarm to the fierce ears that might be lurking in the treacherous green fastness. His careless attitude was not genuine; his eyes and ears were keenly alert, especially his ears, for no gaze could penetrate the leafy tangle for more than a few feet in either direction.

But it was instinct more than any warning by the external senses which brought him up suddenly, his hand on his hilt. He stood stock-still in the middle of the trail, unconsciously holding his breath, wondering what he had heard, and wondering if indeed he had heard anything. The silence seemed absolute. Not a squirrel chattered or bird chirped. Then his gaze fixed itself on a mass of bushes beside the trail a few yards ahead of him. There was no breeze, yet he had seen a branch quiver. The short hairs on his scalp prickled, and he stood for an instant undecided, certain that a move in either direction would bring death streaking at him from the bushes.

A heavy chopping crunch sounded behind the leaves. The bushes were shaken violently, and simultaneously with the sound, an arrow arched erratically from among them and vanished among the trees along the trail. The wayfarer glimpsed its flight as he sprang frantically to cover.

Crouching behind a thick stem, his sword quivering in his fingers, he saw the bushes part, and a tall figure stepped leisurely into the trail. The traveler stared in surprise. The stranger was clad like himself in regard to boots and breeks, though the latter were of silk instead of leather. But he wore a sleeveless hauberk of dark mesh-mail in place of a tunic, and a helmet perched on his black mane. That helmet held the other's gaze; it was without a crest, but adorned by short bull's horns. No civilized hand ever forged that head-piece. Nor was the face below it that of a civilized man: dark, scarred, with smoldering blue eyes, it was a face untamed as the primordial forest which formed its background. The man held a broadsword in his right hand, and the edge was smeared with crimson.

'Come on out,' he called, in an accent unfamiliar to the wayfarer. 'All's safe now. There was only one of the dogs. Come on out.'

The other emerged dubiously and stared at the stranger. He felt curiously helpless and futile as he gazed on the proportions of the forest man – the massive iron-clad breast, and the arm that bore the reddened sword, burned dark by the sun and ridged and corded with muscles. He moved with the dangerous ease of a panther; he was too fiercely supple to be a product of civilization, even of that fringe of civilization which composed the outer frontiers.

Turning, he stepped back to the bushes and pulled them apart. Still not certain just what had happened, the wayfarer from the east advanced and stared down into the bushes. A man lay there, a short, dark, thickly-muscled man, naked except for a loin-cloth, a necklace of human teeth and a brass armlet. A short sword was thrust into the girdle of the loin-cloth, and one hand still gripped a heavy black bow. The man had long black hair; that was about all the wayfarer could tell about his head, for his features were a mask of blood and brains. His skull had been split to the teeth.

'A Pict, by the gods!' exclaimed the wayfarer.

The burning blue eyes turned upon him.

'Are you surprised?'

'Why, they told me at Velitrium and again at the settlers' cabins along the road, that these devils sometimes sneaked across the border, but I didn't expect to meet one this far in the interior.'

'You're only four miles east of Black River,' the stranger informed him. 'They've been shot within a mile of Velitrium. No settler between Thunder River and Fort Tuscelan is really safe. I picked up this dog's trail three miles south of the fort this morning, and I've been following him ever since. I came up behind him just as he was drawing an arrow on you. Another instant and there'd have been a stranger in Hell. But I spoiled his aim for him.'

The wayfarer was staring wide-eyed at the larger man, dumfounded by the realization that the man had actually tracked down one of the forest-devils and slain him unsuspected. That implied woodsmanship of a quality undreamed, even for Conajohara.

'You are one of the fort's garrison?' he asked.

'I'm no soldier. I draw the pay and rations of an officer of the line, but I do my work in the woods. Valannus knows I'm of more use ranging along the river than cooped up in the fort.'

Casually the slayer shoved the body deeper into the thickets with his foot, pulled the bushes together and turned away down the trail. The other followed him.

'My name is Balthus,' he offered. 'I was at Velitrium last night. I haven't decided whether I'll take up a hide of land, or enter fort-service.'

'The best land near Thunder River is already taken,' grunted the slayer. 'Plenty of good land between Scalp Creek – you crossed it a few miles back – and the fort, but that's getting too devilish close to the river. The Picts steal over to burn and murder – as that one did. They don't always come singly. Some day they'll try to sweep the settlers out of Conajohara. And they may succeed – probably will succeed. This colonization business is mad, anyway. There's plenty of good land east of the Bossonian marches. If the Aquilonians would cut up some of the big estates of their barons, and plant wheat where now only deer are hunted, they wouldn't have to cross the border and take the land of the Picts away from them.'

'That's queer talk from a man in the service of the Governor of Conajohara,' objected Balthus.

'It's nothing to me,' the other retorted. 'I'm a mercenary. I sell my sword to the highest bidder. I never planted wheat and never will, so long as there are other harvests to be reaped with the sword. But you Hyborians have expanded as far as you'll be allowed to expand. You've crossed the marches, burned a few villages, exterminated a few clans and pushed back the frontier to Black River; but I doubt if you'll even be able to hold what you've conquered, and you'll never push the frontier any further westward. Your idiotic king doesn't understand conditions here. He won't send you enough reinforcements, and there are not enough settlers to withstand the shock of a concerted attack from across the river.'

'But the Picts are divided into small clans,' persisted Balthus. 'they'll never unite. We can whip any single clan.'

'Or any three or four clans,' admitted the slayer. 'But some day a man will rise and unite thirty or forty clans, just as was done among the Cimmerians, when the Gundermen tried to push the border northward, years ago. They tried to colonize the southern marches of Cimmeria: destroyed a few small clans, built a fort-town, Venarium – you've heard the tale.'

'So I have indeed,' replied Balthus, wincing. The memory of that red disaster was a black blot in the chronicles of a proud and war-like people. 'My uncle was at Venarium when the Cimmerians swarmed over the walls. He was one of the few who escaped that slaughter. I've heard him tell the tale, many a time. The barbarians swept out of the hills in a ravening horde, without warning, and stormed Venarium with such fury none could stand before them. Men, women and children were butchered. Venarium was reduced to a mass of charred ruins, as it is to this day. The Aquilonians were driven back across the marches, and have never since tried to colonize the Cimmerian country. But you speak of Venarium familiarly. Perhaps you were there?'

'I was,' grunted the other. 'I was one of the horde that swarmed over the hills. I hadn't yet seen fifteen snows, but already my name was repeated about the council fires.'

Balthus involuntarily recoiled, staring. It seemed incredible that the man walking tranquilly at his side should have been one of those screeching, blood-mad devils that had poured over the walls of Venarium on that long-gone day to make her streets run crimson.

'Then you, too, are a barbarian!' he exclaimed involuntarily.

The other nodded, without taking offence.

'I am Conan, a Cimmerian.'

'I've heard of you.' Fresh interest quickened Balthus' gaze. No wonder the Pict had fallen victim to his own sort of subtlety. The Cimmerians were barbarians as ferocious as the Picts, and much more intelligent. Evidently Conan had spent much time among civilized men, though that contact had obviously not softened him, nor weakened any of his primitive instincts. Balthus' appre-hension turned to admiration as he marked the easy cat-like stride, the effortless silence with which the Cimmerian moved along the trail. The oiled links of his armor did not clink, and Balthus knew Conan could glide through the deepest thicket or most tangled copse as noiselessly as any naked Pict that ever lived.

'You're not a Gunderman?' It was more assertion than question.

Balthus shook his head. 'I'm from the Tauran.'

'I've seen good woodsmen from the Tauran. But the Bossonians have sheltered you Aquilonians from the outer wildernesses for too many centuries. You need hardening.'

That was true; the Bossonian marches, with their fortified villages filled with determined bowmen, had long served Aquilonia as a buffer against the outlying barbarians. Now among the settlers beyond Thunder River there was growing up a breed of forestmen capable of meeting the barbarians at their own game, but their numbers were still scanty. Most of the frontiersmen were like Balthus – more of the settler than the woodsman type.

The sun had not set, but it was no longer in sight, hidden as it was behind the dense forest wall. The shadows were lengthening, deepening back in the woods as the companions strode on down the trail.

'It will be dark before we reach the fort,' commented Conan casually; then: 'Listen!'

He stopped short, half crouching, sword ready, transformed into a savage figure of suspicion and menace, poised to spring and rend. Balthus had heard it too – a wild scream that broke at its highest note. It was the cry of a man in dire fear or agony.

Conan was off in an instant, racing down the trail, each stride widening the distance between him and his straining companion. Balthus puffed a curse. Among the settlements of the Tauran he was accounted a good runner, but Conan was leaving him behind with maddening ease. Then Balthus forgot his exasperation as his ears were outraged by the most frightful cry he had ever heard. It was not human, this one; it was a demoniacal caterwauling of hideous triumph that seemed to exult over fallen humanity and find echo in black gulfs beyond human ken.

Balthus faltered in his stride, and clammy sweat beaded his flesh. But Conan did not hesitate; he darted around a bend in the trail and disappeared, and Balthus, panicky at finding himself alone with that awful scream still shuddering through the forest in grisly echoes, put on an extra burst of speed and plunged after him.

The Aquilonian slid to a stumbling halt, almost colliding with the Cimmerian who stood in the trail over a crumpled body. But Conan was not looking at the corpse which lay there in the crimson-soaked dust. He was glaring into the deep woods on either side of the trail.

Balthus muttered a horrified oath. It was the body of a man which lay there in the trail, a short, fat man, clad in the gilt-worked boots and (despite the heat) the ermine-trimmed tunic of a wealthy merchant. His fat, pale face was set in a stare of frozen horror; his thick throat had been slashed from ear to ear as if by a razor-sharp blade. The short sword still in its scabbard seemed to indicate that he had been struck down without a chance to fight for his life.

'A Pict?' Balthus whispered, as he turned to peer into the deep-ening shadows of the forest.

Conan shook his head and straightened to scowl down at the dead man.

'A forest devil. This is the fifth, by Crom!'

'What do you mean?'

'Did you ever hear of a Pictish wizard called Zogar Sag?'

Balthus shook his head uneasily.

'He dwells in Gwawela, the nearest village across the river. Three months ago he hid beside this road and stole a string of pack-mules from a pack-train bound for the fort – drugged their drivers, somehow. The mules belonged to this man' – Conan casu-ally indicated the corpse with his foot – 'Tiberias, a merchant of Velitrium. They were loaded with ale-kegs, and old Zogar stopped to guzzle before he got across the river. A woodsman named Soractus trailed him, and led Valannus and three soldiers to where he lay dead drunk in a thicket. At the importunities of Tiberias, Valannus threw Zogar Sag into a cell, which is the worst insult you can give a Pict. He managed to kill his guard and escape, and sent back word that he meant to kill Tiberias and the five men who captured him in a way that would make Aquilonians shudder for centuries to come.

'Well, Soractus and the soldiers are dead. Soractus was killed on the river, the soldiers in the very shadow of the fort. And now Tiberias is dead. No Pict killed any of them. Each victim – except Tiberias, as you see – lacked his head – which no doubt is now ornamenting the altar of Zogar Sag's particular god.'

'How do you know they weren't killed by the Picts?' demanded Balthus.

Conan pointed to the corpse of the merchant.

'You think that was done with a knife or a sword? Look closer and you'll see that only a talon could have made a gash like that. The flesh is ripped, not cut.'

'Perhaps a panther—' began Balthus, without conviction.

Conan shook his head impatiently.

'A man from the Tauran couldn't mistake the mark of a panther's claws. No. It's a forest devil summoned by Zogar Sag to carry out his revenge. Tiberias was a fool to start for Velitrium alone, and so close to dusk. But each one of the victims seemed to be smitten with madness just before doom overtook him. Look here; the signs are plain enough. Tiberias came riding along the trail on his mule, maybe with a bundle of choice otter pelts behind his saddle to sell in Velitrium, and the *thing* sprang on him from behind that bush. See where the branches are crushed down.

'Tiberias gave one scream, and then his throat was torn open and he was selling his otter skins in Hell. The mule ran away into the woods. Listen! Even now you can hear him thrashing about under the trees. The demon didn't have time to take Tiberias' head; it took fright as we came up.'

'As *you* came up,' amended Balthus. 'It must not be a very terrible creature if it flees from one armed man. But how do you know it was not a Pict with some kind of a hook that rips instead of slicing? Did you see it?'

'Tiberias was an armed man,' grunted Conan. 'If Zogar Sag can bring demons to aid him, he can tell them which men to kill and which to let alone. No, I didn't see it. I only saw the bushes shake as it left the trail. But if you want further proof, look here!'

The slayer had stepped into the pool of blood in which the dead man sprawled. Under the bushes at the edge of the path there was a footprint, made in blood on the hard loam.

'Did a man make that?' demanded Conan.

Balthus felt his scalp prickle. Neither man nor any beast that he had ever seen could have left that strange, monstrous three-toed print, that was curiously combined of the bird and the reptile, yet a true type of neither. He spread his fingers above the print, careful not to touch it, and grunted explosively. He could not span the mark.

'What is it?' he whispered. 'I never saw a beast that left a spoor like that.'

'Nor any other sane man,' answered Conan grimly. 'It's a swamp demon – they're thick as bats in the swamps beyond Black River. You can hear them howling like damned souls when the wind blows strong from the south on hot nights.'

'What shall we do?' asked the Aquilonian, peering uneasily into the deep blue shadows. The frozen fear on the dead countenance haunted him. He wondered what hideous head the wretch had seen thrust grinning from among the leaves to chill his blood with terror.

'No use to try to follow a demon,' grunted Conan, drawing a short woodsman's ax from his girdle. 'I tried tracking him after he killed Soractus. I lost his trail within a dozen steps. He might have grown himself wings and flown away, or sunk down through the earth to Hell. I don't know. I'm not going after the mule, either. It'll either wander back to the fort, or to some settler's cabin.'

As he spoke Conan was busy at the edge of the trail with his ax. With a few strokes he cut a pair of saplings nine or ten feet long, and denuded them of their branches. Then he cut a length from a serpent-like vine that crawled among the bushes near by, and making one end fast to one of the poles, a couple of feet from the end, whipped the vine over the other sapling and interlaced it back and forth. In a few moments he had a crude but strong litter.

'The demon isn't going to get Tiberias' head if I can help it,' he growled. 'We'll carry the body into the fort. It isn't more than three miles. I never liked the fat fool, but we can't have Pictish devils making so cursed free with white men's heads.'

The Picts were a white race, though swarthy, but the border men never spoke of them as such.

Balthus took the rear end of the litter, onto which Conan unceremoniously dumped the unfortunate merchant, and they moved on down the trail as swiftly as possible. Conan made no more noise laden with their grim burden than he had made when unencumbered. He had made a loop with the merchant's belt at the end of the poles, and was carrying his share of the load with one hand, while the other gripped his naked broadsword, and his restless gaze roved the sinister walls about them. The shadows were thickening. A darkening blue mist blurred the outlines of the foliage. The forest deepened in the twilight, became a blue haunt of mystery sheltering unguessed things.

They had covered more than a mile, and the muscles in Balthus' sturdy arms were beginning to ache a little, when a cry rang shuddering from the woods whose blue shadows were deepening into purple.

Conan started convulsively, and Balthus almost let go the poles.

'A woman!' cried the younger man. 'Great Mitra, a woman cried out then!'

'A settler's wife straying in the woods,' snarled Conan, setting down his end of the litter. 'Looking for a cow, probably, and – stay here!'

He dived like a hunting wolf into the leafy wall. Balthus' hair bristled.

'Stay here alone with this corpse and a devil hiding in the woods?' he yelped. 'I'm coming with you!'

And suiting action to words, he plunged after the Cimmerian. Conan glanced back at him, but made no objection, though he did not moderate his pace to accommodate the shorter legs of his companion. Balthus wasted his wind in swearing as the Cimmerian drew away from him again, like a phantom between the trees, and then Conan burst into a dim glade and halted crouching, lips snarling, sword lifted.

'What are we stopping for?' panted Balthus, dashing the sweat out of his eyes and gripping his short sword.

'That scream came from this glade, or near by,' answered Conan. 'I don't mistake the location of sounds, even in the woods. But where—'

Abruptly the sound rang out again – *behind them*; in the direction of the trail they had just quitted. It rose piercingly and pitifully, the cry of a woman in frantic terror – and then, shockingly, it changed to a yell of mocking laughter that might have burst from the lips of a fiend of lower Hell.

'What in Mitra's name—' Balthus' face was a pale blur in the gloom.

With a scorching oath Conan wheeled and dashed back the way he had come, and the Aquilonian stumbled bewilderedly after him. He blundered into the Cimmerian as the latter stopped dead, and rebounded from his brawny shoulders as though from an iron statue. Gasping from the impact, he heard Conan's breath hiss through his teeth. The Cimmerian seemed frozen in his tracks.

Looking over his shoulder, Balthus felt his hair stand up stiffly. Something was moving through the deep bushes that fringed the trail – something that neither walked nor flew, but seemed to glide like a serpent. But it was not a serpent. Its outlines were indistinct, but it was taller than a man, and not very bulky. It gave off a glimmer of weird light, like a faint blue flame. Indeed, the eery fire was the only tangible thing about it. It might have been an embodied flame moving with reason and purpose through the blackening woods.

Conan snarled a savage curse and hurled his ax with ferocious will. But the thing glided on without altering its course. Indeed it was only a few instants' fleeting glimpse they had of it – a tall, shadowy thing of misty flame floating through the thickets. Then it was gone, and the forest crouched in breathless stillness.

With a snarl Conan plunged through the intervening foliage and into the trail. His profanity, as Balthus floundered after him, was lurid and impassioned. The Cimmerian was standing over the litter on which lay the body of Tiberias. And that body no longer possessed a head.

'Tricked us with its damnable caterwauling!' raved Conan, swinging his great sword about his head in his wrath. 'I might have known! I might have guessed a trick! Now there'll be five heads to decorate Zogar's altar.'

'But what thing is it that can cry like a woman and laugh like a devil, and shines like witch-fire as it glides through the trees?' gasped Balthus, mopping the sweat from his pale face.

'A swamp devil,' responded Conan morosely. 'Grab those poles. We'll take in the body, anyway. At least our load's a bit lighter.'

With which grim philosophy he gripped the leathery loop and stalked down the trail.

2

The Wizard of Gwawela

Fort Tuscelan stood on the eastern bank of Black River, the tides of which washed the foot of the stockade. The latter was of logs, as were all the buildings within, including the donjon (to dignify it by that appellation), in which were the governor's quarters, overlooking the stockade and the sullen river. Beyond that river lay a huge forest, which approached jungle-like density along the spongy shores. Men paced the runways along the log parapet day and night, watching that dense green wall. Seldom a menacing figure appeared, but the sentries knew that they too were watched, fiercely, hungrily, with the mercilessness of ancient hate. The forest beyond the river might seem desolate and vacant of life to the ignorant eye, but life teemed there, not alone of bird and beast and reptile, but also of men, the fiercest of all the hunting beasts.

There, at the fort, civilization ended. Fort Tuscelan was the last outpost of a civilized world; it represented the westernmost thrust of the dominant Hyborian races. Beyond the river the primitive still reigned in shadowy forests, brush-thatched huts where hung the grinning skulls of men, and mud-walled enclosures where fires flickered and drums rumbled, and spears were whetted in the hands of dark, silent men with tangled black hair and the eyes of serpents. Those eyes often glared through the bushes at the fort across the river. Once dark-skinned men had built their huts where that fort stood; yes, and their huts had risen where now stood the fields and log cabins of fair-haired settlers, back beyond Velitrium, that raw, turbulent frontier town on the banks of Thunder River, to the shores of that other river that bounds the Bossonian marches. Traders had come, and priests of Mitra who walked with bare feet and empty hands, and died horribly, most of them; but soldiers had followed, and men with axes in their hands and women and children in ox-drawn wains. Back to Thunder River, and still back, beyond Black River the aborigines had been pushed, with slaughter and massacre. But the dark-skinned people did not forget that once Conajohara had been theirs.

The guard inside the eastern gate bawled a challenge. Through a barred aperture torchlight flickered, glinting on a steel head-piece and suspicious eyes beneath it.

'Open the gate,' snorted Conan. 'You see it's I, don't you?'

Military discipline put his teeth on edge.

The gate swung inward and Conan and his companion passed through. Balthus noted that the gate was flanked by a tower on each side, the summits of which rose above the stockade. He saw loopholes for arrows. The guardsmen grunted as they saw the burden borne between the men. Their pikes jangled against each other as they thrust shut the gate, chin on shoulder, and Conan asked testily: 'Have you never seen a headless body before?'

The face of the soldiers were pallid in the torchlight.

'That's Tiberias,' blurted one. 'I recognize that fur-trimmed tunic. Valerius here owes me five lunas. I told him Tiberias had heard the loon call when he rode through the gate on his mule, with his glassy stare. I wagered he'd come back without his head.'

Conan grunted enigmatically, motioned Balthus to ease the litter to the ground, and then strode off toward the governor's quarters, with the Aquilonian at his heels. The tousle-headed youth stared about him eagerly and curiously, noting the rows of barracks along the walls, the stables, the tiny merchants' stalls, the towering blockhouse, and the other buildings, with the open square in the middle where the soldiers drilled, and where, now, fires danced and men off duty lounged. These were now hurrying to join the morbid crowd gathered about the litter at the gate. The rangy figures of Aquilonian pikemen and forest runners mingled with the shorter, stockier forms of Bossonian archers.

He was not greatly surprised that the governor received them himself. Autocratic society with its rigid caste laws lay east of the marches. Valannus was still a young man, well knit, with a finely chiseled countenance already carved into sober cast by toil and responsibility.

'You left the fort before daybreak, I was told,' he said to Conan. 'I had begun to fear that the Picts had caught you at last.'

'When they smoke my head the whole river will know it,' grunted Conan. 'They'll hear Pictish women wailing their dead as far as Velitrium – I was on a lone scout. I couldn't sleep. I kept hearing drums talking across the river.'

'They talk each night,' reminded the governor, his fine eyes shadowed, as he stared closely at Conan. He had learned the un-wisdom of discounting wild men's instincts.

'There was a difference last night,' growled Conan. 'There has been ever since Zogar Sag got back across the river.'

'We should either have given him presents and sent him home, or else hanged him,' sighed the governor. 'You advised that, but—'

'But it's hard for you Hyborians to learn the ways of the out-lands,' said Conan. 'Well, it can't be helped now, but there'll be no peace on the border so long as Zogar lives and remembers the cell he sweated in. I was following a warrior who slipped over to put a few white notches on his bow. After I split his head I fell in with this lad whose name is Balthus and who's come from the Tauran to help hold the frontier.'

Valannus approvingly eyed the young man's frank countenance and strongly-knit frame.

'I am glad to welcome you, young sir. I wish more of your

people would come. We need men used to forest life. Many of our soldiers and some of our settlers are from the eastern provinces and know nothing of woodcraft, or even of agricultural life.'

'Not many of that breed this side of Velitrium,' grunted Conan. 'That town's full of them, though. But listen, Valannus, we found Tiberias dead on the trail.' And in a few words he related the grisly affair.

Valannus paled. 'I did not know he had left the fort. He must have been mad!'

'He was,' answered Conan. 'Like the other four; each one, when his time came, went mad and rushed into the woods to meet his death like a hare running down the throat of a python. *Something* called to them from the deeps of the forest, something the men call a loon, for lack of a better name, but only the doomed ones could hear it. Zogar Sag has made a magic that Aquilonian civilization can't overcome.'

To this thrust Valannus made no reply; he wiped his brow with a shaky hand.

'Do the soldiers know of this?'

'We left the body by the eastern gate.'

'You should have concealed the fact, hidden the corpse somewhere in the woods. The soldiers are nervous enough already.'

'They'd have found it out some way. If I'd hidden the body, it would have been returned to the fort as the corpse of Soractus was – tied up outside the gate for the men to find in the morning.'

Valannus shuddered. Turning, he walked to a casement and stared silently out over the river, black and shiny under the glint of the stars. Beyond the river the jungle rose like an ebony wall. The distant screech of a panther broke the stillness. The night pressed in, blurring the sounds of the soldiers outside the blockhouse, dimming the fires. A wind whispered through the black branches, rippling the dusky water. On its wings came a low, rhythmic pulsing, sinister as the pad of a leopard's foot.

'After all,' said Valannus, as if speaking his thoughts aloud, 'what do we know – what does anyone know – of the things that jungle may hide? We have dim rumors of great swamps and rivers, and a forest that stretches on and on over everlasting plains and hills to end at last on the shores of the western ocean. But what things lie between this river and that ocean we dare not even guess. No white man has ever plunged deep into that fastness and returned alive to tell us what he found. We are wise in our civilized knowledge, but our knowledge extends just so far – to the western bank of that ancient river! Who knows what shapes earthly and unearthly may lurk beyond the dim circle of light our knowledge has cast?

'Who knows what gods are worshipped under the shadows of that heathen forest, or what devils crawl out of the black ooze of the swamps? Who can be sure that all the inhabitants of that black country are natural? Zogar Sag – a sage of the eastern cities would sneer at his primitive magic-making as the mummery of a fakir; yet he has driven mad and killed five men in a manner no man can explain. I wonder if he himself is wholly human.'

'If I can get within ax-throwing distance of him I'll settle that question,' growled Conan, helping himelf to the governor's wine and pushing a glass toward Balthus, who took it hesitatingly, and with an uncertain glance toward Valannus.

The governor turned toward Conan and stared at him thoughtfully.

'The soldiers, who do not believe in ghosts or devils,' he said, 'are almost in a panic of fear. You, who believe in ghosts, ghouls, goblins, and all manner of uncanny things, do not seem to fear any of the things in which you believe.'

'There's nothing in the universe cold steel won't cut,' answered Conan. 'I threw my ax at the demon, and he took no hurt, but I might have missed, in the dusk, or a branch deflected its flight. I'm not going out of my way looking for devils; but I wouldn't step out of my path to let one go by.'

Valannus lifted his head and met Conan's gaze squarely.

'Conan, more depends on you than you realize. You know the weakness of this province – a slender wedge thrust into the un-tamed wilderness. You know that the lives of all the people west of the marches depend on this fort. Were it to fall, red axes would be splintering the gates of Velitrium before a horseman could cross the marches. His majesty, or his majesty's advisers, have ignored my plea that more troops be sent to hold the frontier. They know nothing of border conditions, and are averse to expending any more money in this direction. The fate of the frontier depends upon the men who now hold it.

'You know that most of the army which conquered Conajohara has been withdrawn. You know the force left me is inadequate, especially since that devil Zogar Sag managed to poison our water supply, and forty men died in one day. Many of the others are sick, or have been bitten by serpents or mauled by wild beasts which seem to swarm in increasing numbers in the vicinity of the fort. The soldiers believe Zogar's boast that he could summon the forest beasts to slay his enemies.

'I have three hundred pikemen, four hundred Bossonian archers, and perhaps fifty men who, like yourself, are skilled in woodcraft. They are worth ten times their number of soldiers, but there are so few of them. Frankly, Conan, my situation is becoming precarious. The soldiers whisper of desertion; they are low-spirited, believing Zogar Sag has loosed devils on us. They fear the black plague with which he threatened us – the terrible black death of the swamplands. When I see a sick soldier I sweat with fear of seeing him turn black and shrivel and die before my eyes.

'Conan, if the plague is loosed upon us, the soldiers will desert in a body! The border will be left unguarded and nothing will check the sweep of the dark-skinned hordes to the very gates of Velitrium – maybe beyond! If we can not hold the fort, how can they hold the town?

'Conan, Zogar Sag must die, if we are to hold Conajohara. You have penetrated the unknown deeper than any other man in the fort; you know where Gwawela stands, and something of the forest trails across the river. Will you take a band of men tonight and endeavour to kill or capture him? Oh, I know it's mad. There isn't more than one chance in a thousand that any of you will come back alive. But if we don't get him, it's death for us all. You can take as many men as you wish.'

'A dozen men are better for a job like that than a regiment,' answered Conan. 'Five hundred men couldn't fight their way to Gwawela and back, but a dozen might slip in and out again. Let me pick my men. I don't want any soldiers.'

'Let me go!' eagerly exclaimed Balthus. 'I've hunted deer all my life on the Tauran.'

'All right. Valannus, we'll eat at the stall where the foresters gather, and I'll pick my men. We'll start within an hour, drop down the river in a boat to a point below the village and then steal upon it through the woods. If we live, we should be back by daybreak.'

3

The Crawlers in the Dark

The river was a vague trace between walls of ebony. The paddles that propelled the long boat creeping along in the dense shadow of the eastern bank dipped softly into the water, making no more noise than the beak of a heron. The broad shoulders of the man in front of Balthus were a blur in the dense gloom. He knew that not even the keen eyes of the man who knelt in the prow would discern anything more than a few feet ahead of them. Conan was feeling his way by instinct and an intensive familiarity with the river.

No one spoke. Balthus had had a good look at his companions in the fort before they slipped out of the stockade and down the bank into the waiting canoe. They were of a new breed growing up in the world on the raw edge of the frontier – men whom grim necessity had taught woodcraft. Aquilonians of the western provinces to a man, they had many points in common. They dressed alike – in buckskin boots, leathern breeks and deerskin shirts, with broad girdles that held axes and short swords; and they were all gaunt and scarred and hard-eyed; sinewy and taciturn.

They were wild men, of a sort, yet there was still a wide gulf between them and the Cimmerian. They were sons of civilization, reverted to a semi-barbarism. He was a barbarian of a thousand generations of barbarians. They had acquired stealth and craft, but he had been born to these things. He excelled them even in lithe economy of motion. They were wolves, but he was a tiger.

Balthus admired them and their leader and felt a pulse of pride that he was admitted into their company. He was proud that his paddle made no more noise than did theirs. In that respect at least he was their equal, though woodcraft learned in hunts on the Tauran could never equal that ground into the souls of men on the savage border.

Below the fort the river made a wide bend. The lights of the outpost were quickly lost, but the canoe held on its way for nearly a mile, avoiding snags and floating logs with almost uncanny precision.

Then a low grunt from their leader, and they swung its head about and glided toward the opposite shore. Emerging from the black shadows of the brush that fringed the bank and coming into the open of the midstream created a peculiar illusion of rash exposure. But the stars gave little light, and Balthus knew that unless one were watching for it, it would be all but impossible for the keenest eye to make out the shadowy shape of the canoe crossing the river.

They swung in under the overhanging bushes of the western shore and Balthus groped for and found a projecting root which he grasped. No word was spoken. All instructions had been given before the scouting-party left the fort. As silently as a great panther Conan slid over the side and vanished in the bushes. Equally noise-less, nine men followed him. To Balthus, grasping the root with his paddle across his knee, it seemed incredible that ten men should thus fade into the tangled forest without a sound.

He settled himself to wait. No word passed between him and the other man who had been left with him. Somewhere, a mile or so to the northwest, Zogar Sag's village stood girdled with thick woods. Balthus understood his orders; he and his companion were to wait for the return of the raiding-party. If Conan and his men had not returned by the first tinge of dawn, they were to race back up the river to the fort and report that the forest had again taken its immemorial toll of the invading race. The silence was oppressive. No sound came from the black woods, invisible beyond the ebony masses that were the overhanging bushes. Balthus no longer heard the drums. They had been silent for hours. He kept blinking, unconsciously trying to see through the deep gloom. The dank night-smells of the river and the damp forest oppressed him. Somewhere, near by, there was a sound as if a big fish had flopped and splashed the water. Balthus thought it must have leaped so close to the canoe that it had struck the side, for a slight quiver vibrated the craft. The boat's stern began to swing, slightly away from the shore. The man behind him must have let go of the projection he was gripping. Balthus twisted his head to hiss a warning, and could just make out the figure of his companion, a slightly blacker bulk in tbe blackness.

The man did not reply. Wondering if he had fallen asleep, Balthus reached out and grasped his shoulder. To his amazement, the man crumpled under his touch and slumped down in the canoe. Twisting his body half about, Balthus groped for him, his heart shooting into his throat. His fumbling fingers slid over the man's throat – only the youth's convulsive clenching of his jaws choked back the cry that rose to his lips. His fingers encountered a gaping, oozing wound – his companion's throat had been cut from ear to ear.

In that instant of horror and panic Balthus started up – and then a muscular arm out of the darkness locked fiercely about his throat, strangling his yell. The canoe rocked wildly. Balthus' knife was in his hand, though he did not remember jerking it out of his boot, and he stabbed fiercely and blindly. He felt the blade sink deep, and a fiendish yell rang in his ear, a yell that was horribly answered. The darkness seemed to come to life about him. A bestial clamor rose on all sides, and other arms grappled him. Borne under a mass of hurtling bodies the canoe rolled sidewise, but before he went under with it, something cracked against Balthus' head and the night was briefly illuminated by a blinding burst of fire before it gave way to a blackness where not even stars shone.

4

The Beasts of Zogar Sag

Fires dazzled Balthus again as he slowly recovered his senses. He blinked, shook his head. Their glare hurt his eyes. A confused medley of sound rose about him, growing more distinct as his senses cleared. He lifted his head and stared stupidly about him. Black figures hemmed him in, etched against crimson tongues of flame.

Memory and understanding came in a rush. He was bound upright to a post in an open space, ringed by fierce and terrible figures. Beyond that ring fires burned, tended by naked, dark-skinned women. Beyond the fires he saw huts of mud and wattle, thatched with brush. Beyond the huts there was a stockade with a broad gate. But he saw these things only incidentally. Even the cryptic dark women with their curious coiffures were noted by him only absently. His full attention was fixed in awful fascination on the men who stood glaring at him.

Short men, broad-shouldered, deep-chested, lean-hipped, they were naked except for scanty loin-clouts. The firelight brought out the play of their swelling muscles in bold relief. Their dark faces were immobile, but their narrow eyes glittered with the fire that burns in the eyes of a stalking tiger. Their tangled manes were bound back with bands of copper. Swords and axes were in their hands. Crude bandages banded the limbs of some, and smears of blood were dried on their dark skins. There had been fighting, recent and deadly.

His eyes wavered away from the steady glare of his captors, and he repressed a cry of horror. A few feet away there rose a low, hideous pyramid: it was built of gory human heads. Dead eyes glared glassily up at the black sky. Numbly he recognized the countenances which were turned toward him. They were the heads of the men who had followed Conan into the forest. He could not tell if the Cimmerian's head were among them. Only a few faces were visible to him. It looked to him as if there must be ten or eleven heads at least. A deadly sickness assailed him. He fought a desire to retch. Beyond the heads lay the bodies of half a dozen Picts, and he was aware of a fierce exultation at the sight. The forest runners had taken toll, at least.

Twisting his head away from the ghastly spectacle, he became aware that another post stood near him – a stake painted black as was the one to which he was bound. A man sagged in his bonds there, naked except for his leathern breeks, whom Balthus recognized as one of Conan's woodsmen. Blood trickled from his mouth, oozed sluggishly from a gash in his side. Lifting his head as he licked his livid lips, he muttered, making himself heard with difficulty above the fiendish clamor of the Picts: 'So they got you, too!'

'Sneaked up in the water and cut the other fellow's throat,' groaned Balthus. 'We never heard them till they were on us. Mitra, how can anything move so silently?'

'They're devils,' mumbled the frontiersman. 'They must have been watching us from the time we left midstream. We walked into a trap. Arrows from all sides were ripping into us before we knew it. Most of us dropped at the first fire. Three or four broke through the bushes and came to hand-grips. But there were too many. Conan might have gotten away. I haven't seen his head. Been better for you and me if they'd killed us outright. I can't blame Conan. Ordinarily we'd have gotten to the village without being discovered. They don't keep spies on the river bank as far down as we landed. We must have stumbled into a big party coming up the river from the south. Some devilment is up. Too many Picts here. These aren't all Gwaweli; men from the western tribes here and from up and down the river.'

Balthus stared at the ferocious shapes. Little as he knew of Pictish ways, he was aware that the number of men clustered about them was out of proportion to the size of the village. There were not enough huts to have accommodated them all. Then he noticed that there was a difference in the barbaric tribal designs painted on their faces and breasts.

'Some kind of devilment,' muttered the forest runner. 'They might have gathered here to watch Zogar's magic-making. He'll make some rare magic with our carcasses. Well, a border-man doesn't expect to die in bed. But I wish we'd gone out along with the rest.'

The wolfish howling of the Picts rose in volume and exultation, and from a movement in their ranks, an eager surging and crowding, Balthus deduced that someone of importance was coming. Twisting his head about, he saw that the stakes were set before a long building, larger than the other huts, decorated by human skulls dangling from the eaves. Through the door of that structure now danced a fantastic figure.

'Zogar!' muttered the woodsman, his bloody countenance set in wolfish lines as he unconsciously strained at his cords. Balthus saw a lean figure of middle height, almost hidden in ostrich plumes set on a harness of leather and copper. From amidst the plumes peered a hideous and malevolent face. The plumes puzzled Balthus. He knew their source lay half the width of a world to the south. They fluttered and rustled evilly as the shaman leaped and cavorted.

With fantastic bounds and prancings he entered the ring and whirled before his bound and silent captives. With another man it would have seemed ridiculous – a foolish savage prancing meaninglessly in a whirl of feathers. But that ferocious face glaring out from the billowing mass gave the scene a grim significance. No man with a face like that could seem ridiculous or like anything except the devil he was.

Suddenly he froze to statuesque stillness; the plumes rippled once and sank about him. The howling warriors fell silent. Zogar Sag stood erect and motionless, and he seemed to increase in height – to grow and expand. Balthus experienced the illusion that the Pict was towering above him, staring contemptuously down from a great height, though he knew the shaman was not as tall as himself. He shook off the illusion with difficulty.

The shaman was talking now, a harsh, guttural intonation that yet carried the hiss of a cobra. He thrust his head on his long neck toward the wounded man on the stake; his eyes shone red as blood in the firelight. The frontiersman spat full in his face.

With a fiendish howl Zogar bounded convulsively into the air, and the warriors gave tongue to a yell that shuddered up to the stars. They rushed toward the man on the stake, but the shaman beat them back. A snarled command sent men running to the gate. They hurled it open, turned and raced back to the circle. The ring of men split, divided with desperate haste to right and left. Balthus saw the women and naked children scurrying to the huts. They peeked out of doors and windows. A broad lane was left to the open gate, beyond which loomed the black forest, crowding sullenly in upon the clearing, unlighted by the fires.

A tense silence reigned as Zogar Sag turned toward the forest, raised on his tiptoes and sent a weird inhuman call shuddering out into the night. Somewhere, far out in the black forest, a deeper cry answered him. Balthus shuddered. From the timbre of that cry he knew it never came from a human throat. He remembered what Valannus had said – that Zogar boasted that he could summon wild beasts to do his bidding. The woodsman was livid beneath his mask of blood. He licked his lips spasmodically.

The village held its breath. Zogar Sag stood still as a statue, his plumes trembling faintly about him. But suddenly the gate was no longer empty.

A shuddering gasp swept over the village and men crowded hastily back, jamming one another between the huts. Balthus felt the short hair stir on his scalp. The creature that stood in the gate was like the embodiment of nightmare legend. Its color was of a curious pale quality which made it seem ghostly and unreal in the dim light. But there was nothing unreal about the low-hung savage head, and the great curved fangs that glistened in the firelight. On noiseless padded feet it approached like a phantom out of the past. It was a survival of an older, grimmer age, the ogre of many an ancient legend – a saber-tooth tiger. No Hyborian hunter had looked upon one of those primordial brutes for centuries. Immemorial myths lent the creatures a supernatural quality, induced by their ghostly color and their fiendish ferocity.

The beast that glided toward the men on the stakes was longer and heavier than a common, striped tiger, almost as bulky as a bear. Its shoulders and forelegs were so massive and mightily muscled as to give it a curiously top-heavy look, though its hind-quarters were more powerful than that of a lion. Its jaws were massive, but its head was brutishly shaped. Its brain capacity was small. It had room for no instincts except those of destruction. It was a freak of carnivorous development, evolution run amuck in a horror of fangs and talons.

This was the monstrosity Zogar Sag had summoned out of the forest. Balthus no longer doubted the actuality of the shaman's magic. Only the black arts could establish a domination over that tiny-brained, mighty-thewed monster. Like a whisper at the back of his consciousness rose the vague memory of the name of an ancient god of darkness and primordial fear, to whom once both men and beasts bowed and whose children – men whispered – still lurked in dark corners of the world. New horror tinged the glare he fixed on Zogar Sag.

The monster moved past the heap of bodies and the pile of gory heads without appearing to notice them. He was no scavenger. He hunted only the living, in a life dedicated solely to slaughter. An awful hunger burned greenly in the wide, unwinking eyes; the hunger not alone of belly-emptiness, but the lust of death-dealing. His gaping jaws slavered. The shaman stepped back; his hand waved toward the woodsman.

The great cat sank into a crouch, and Balthus numbly remembered tales of its appalling ferocity: of how it would spring upon an elephant and drive its sword-like fangs so deeply into the titan's skull that they could never be withdrawn, but would keep it nailed to its victim, to die by starvation. The shaman cried out shrilly, and with an ear-shattering roar the monster sprang.

Balthus had never dreamed of such a spring, such a hurtling of incarnated destruction embodied in that giant bulk of iron thews and ripping talons. Full on the woodsman's breast it struck, and the stake splintered and snapped at the base, crashing to the earth under the impact. Then the saber-tooth was gliding toward the gate, half dragging, half carrying a hideous crimson hulk that only faintly resembled a man. Balthus glared almost paralysed, his brain refusing to credit what his eyes had seen.

In that leap the great beast had not only broken off the stake, it had ripped the mangled body of its victim from the post to which it was bound. The huge talons in that instant of contact had disemboweled and partially dismembered the man, and the giant fangs had torn away the whole top of his head, shearing through the skull as easily as through flesh. Stout rawhide thongs had given way like paper; where the thongs had held, flesh and bones had not. Balthus retched suddenly. He had hunted bears and panthers, but he had never dreamed the beast lived which could make such a red ruin of a human frame in the flicker of an instant.

The saber-tooth vanished through the gate, and a few moments later a deep roar sounded through the forest, receding in the distance. But the Picts still shrank back against the huts, and the shaman still stood facing the gate that was like a black opening to let in the night.

Cold sweat burst suddenly out on Balthus' skin. What new horror would come through that gate to make carrion-meat of his body? Sick panic assailed him and he strained futilely at his thongs. The night pressed in very black and horrible outside the firelight. The fires themselves glowed lurid as the fires of hell. He felt the eyes of the Picts upon him – hundreds of hungry, cruel eyes that reflected the lust of souls utterly without humanity as he knew it. They no longer seemed men; they were devils of this black jungle, as inhuman as the creatures to which the fiend in the nodding plumes screamed through the darkness.

Zogar sent another call shuddering through the night, and it was utterly unlike the first cry. There was a hideous sibilance in it – Balthus turned cold at the implication. If a serpent could hiss that loud, it would make just such a sound.

This time there was no answer – only a period of breathless silence in which the pound of Balthus' heart strangled him; and then there sounded a swishing outside the gate, a dry rustling that sent chills down Balthus' spine. Again the firelit gate held a hideous occupant.

Again Balthus recognized the monster from ancient legends. He saw and knew the ancient and evil serpent which swayed there, its wedge-shaped head, huge as that of a horse, as high as a tall man's head, and its palely gleaming barrel rippling out behind it. A forked tongue darted in and out, and the firelight glittered on bared fangs.

Balthus became incapable of emotion. The horror of his fate paralysed him. That was the reptile that the ancients called Ghost Snake, the pale, abominable terror that of old glided into huts by night to devour whole families. Like the python it crushed its victim, but unlike other constrictors its fangs bore venom that carried madness and death. It too had long been considered extinct. But Valannus had spoken truly. No white man knew what shapes haunted the great forests beyond Black River.

It came on silently rippling over the ground, its hideous head on the same level, its neck curving back slightly for the stroke. Balthus gazed with glazed, hypnotized stare into that loathsome gullet down which he would soon be engulfed, and he was aware of no sensation except a vague nausea.

And then something that glinted in the firelight streaked from the shadows of the huts, and the great reptile whipped about and went into instant convulsions. As in a dream Balthus saw a short throwing-spear transfixing the mighty neck, just below the gaping jaws; the shaft protruded from one side, the steel head from the other.

Knotting and looping hideously, the maddened reptile rolled into the circle of men who strove back from him. The spear had not severed its spine, but merely transfixed its great neck muscles. Its furiously lashing tail mowed down a dozen men and its jaws snapped convulsively, splashing others with venom that burned like liquid fire. Howling, cursing, screaming, frantic, they scattered before it, knocking each other down in their flight, trampling the fallen, bursting through the huts. The giant snake rolled into a fire, scattering sparks and brands, and the pain lashed it to more

337

frenzied efforts. A hut wall buckled under the ram-like impact of its flailing tail, disgorging howling people.

Men stampeded through the fires, knocking the logs right and left. The flames sprang up, then sank. A reddish dim glow was all that lighted that nightmare scene where the giant reptile whipped and rolled, and men clawed and shrieked in frantic flight.

Balthus felt something jerk at his wrists, and then, miraculously, he was free, and a strong hand dragged him behind the post. Dazedly he saw Conan, felt the forest man's iron grip on his arm.

There was blood on the Cimmerian's mail, dried blood on the sword in his right hand; he loomed dim and gigantic in the shadowy light.

'Come on! Before they get over their panic!'

Balthus felt the haft of an ax shoved into his hand. Zogar Sag had disappeared. Conan dragged Balthus after him until the youth's numb brain awoke, and his legs began to move of their own accord. Then Conan released him and ran into the building where the skulls hung. Balthus followed him. He got a glimpse of a grim stone altar, faintly lighted by the glow outside; five human heads grinned on that altar, and there was a grisly familiarity about the features of the freshest; it was the head of the merchant Tiberias. Behind the altar was an idol, dim, indistinct, bestial, yet vaguely man-like in outline. Then fresh horror choked Balthus as the shape heaved up suddenly with a rattle of chains, lifting long misshapen arms in the gloom.

Conan's sword flailed down, crunching through flesh and bone, and then the Cimmerian was dragging Balthus around the altar, past a huddled shaggy bulk on the floor, to a door at the back of the long hut. Through this they burst, out into the enclosure again. But a few yards beyond them loomed the stockade.

It was dark behind the altar-hut. The mad stampede of the Picts had not carried them in that direction. At the wall Conan halted, gripped Balthus and heaved him at arm's length into the air as he might have lifted a child. Balthus grasped the points of the upright logs set in the sun-dried mud and scrambled up on them, ignoring the havoc done his skin. He lowered a hand to the Cimmerian, when around a corner of the altar-hut sprang a fleeing Pict. He halted short, glimpsing the man on the wall in the faint glow of the fires. Conan hurled his ax with deadly aim, but the warrior's mouth was already open for a yell of warning, and it rang loud above the din, cut short as he dropped with a shattered skull.

Blinding terror had not submerged all ingrained instincts. As that wild yell rose above the clamor, there was an instant's lull, and then a hundred throats bayed ferocious answer and warriors came leaping to repel the attack presaged by the warning.

Conan leaped high, caught, not Balthus' hand but his arm near the shoulder, and swung himself up. Balthus set his teeth against the strain, and then the Cimmerian was on the wall beside him, and the fugitives dropped down on the other side.

5

The Children of Jhebbal Sag

'Which way is the river?' Balthus was confused.

'We don't dare try for the river now,' grunted Conan. 'The woods between the village and the river are swarming with warriors. Come on! We'll head in the last direction they'll expect us to go – west!'

Looking back as they entered the thick growth, Balthus beheld the wall dotted with black heads as the savages peered over. The Picts were bewildered. They had not gained the wall in time to see the fugitives take cover. They had rushed to the wall expecting to repel an attack in force. They had seen the body of the dead warrior. But no enemy was in sight.

Balthus realized that they did not yet know their prisoner had escaped. From other sounds he believed that the warriors, directed by the shrill voice of Zogar Sag, were destroying the wounded serpent with arrows. The monster was out of the shaman's control. A moment later the quality of the yells was altered. Screeches of rage rose in the night.

Conan laughed grimly. He was leading Balthus along a narrow

trail that ran west under the black branches, stepping as swiftly and surely as if he trod a well-lighted thoroughfare. Balthus stumbled after him, guiding himself by feeling the dense wall on either hand.

'They'll be after us now. Zogar's discovered you're gone, and he knows my head wasn't in the pile before the altar-hut. The dog! If I'd had another spear I'd have thrown it through him before I struck the snake. Keep to the trail. They can't track us by torchlight, and there are a score of paths leading from the village. They'll follow those leading to the river first – throw a cordon of warriors for miles along the bank, expecting us to try to break through. We won't take to the woods until we have to. We can make better time on this trail. Now buckle down to it and run as you never ran before.'

'They got over their panic cursed quick!' panted Balthus, complying with a fresh burst of speed.

'They're not afraid of anything, very long,' grunted Conan.

For a space nothing was said between them. The fugitives devoted all their attention to covering distance. They were plunging deeper and deeper into the wilderness and getting farther away from civilization at every step, but Balthus did not question Conan's wisdom. The Cimmerian presently took time to grunt: 'When we're far enough away from the village we'll swing back to the river in a big circle. No other village within miles of Gwawela. All the Picts are gathered in that vicinity. We'll circle wide around them. They can't track us until daylight. They'll pick up our path then, but before dawn we'll leave the trail and take to the woods.'

They plunged on. The yells died out behind them. Balthus' breath was whistling through his teeth. He felt a pain in his side, and running became torture. He blundered against the bushes on each side of the trail. Conan pulled up suddenly, turned and stared back down the dim path.

Somewhere the moon was rising, a dim white glow amidst a tangle of branches.

'Shall we take to the woods?' panted Balthus.

'Give me your ax,' murmured Conan softly. 'Something is close behind us.'

'Then we'd better leave the trail!' exclaimed Balthus.

Conan shook his head and drew his companion into a dense thicket. The moon rose higher, making a dim light in the path.

'We can't fight the whole tribe!' whispered Balthus.

'No human being could have found our trail so quickly, or followed us so swiftly,' muttered Conan. 'Keep silent.'

There followed a tense silence in which Balthus felt that his heart could be heard pounding for miles away. Then abruptly, without a sound to announce its coming, a savage head appeared in the dim path. Balthus' heart jumped into his throat; at first glance he feared to look upon the awful head of the saber-tooth. But this head was smaller, more narrow; it was a leopard which stood there, snarling silently and glaring down the trail. What wind there was was blowing toward the hiding men, concealing their scent. The beast lowered his head and snuffed the trail, then moved forward uncertainly. A chill played down Balthus' spine. The brute was undoubtedly trailing them.

And it was suspicious. It lifted its head, its eyes glowing like balls of fire, and growled low in its throat. And at that instant Conan hurled the ax.

All the weight of arm and shoulder was behind the throw, and the ax was a streak of silver in the dim moon. Almost before he realized what had happened, Balthus saw the leopard rolling on the ground in its death-throes, the handle of the ax standing up from its head. The head of the weapon had split its narrow skull.

Conan bounded from the bushes, wrenched his ax free and dragged the limp body in among the trees, concealing it from the casual glance.

'Now let's go, and go fast!' he grunted, leading the way southward, away from the trail. 'There'll be warriors coming after that cat. As soon as he got his wits back Zogar sent him after us. The Picts would follow him, but he'd leave them far behind. He'd circle the village until he hit our trail and then come after us like a streak. They couldn't keep up with him, but they'll have an idea as to our

341

general direction. They'd follow, listening for his cry. Well, they won't hear that, but they'll find the blood on the trail, and look around and find the body in the brush. They'll pick up our spoor there, if they can. Walk with care.'

He avoided clinging briars and low-hanging branches effortlessly, gliding between trees without touching the stems and always planting his feet in the places calculated to show least evidence of his passing; but with Balthus it was slower, more laborious work.

No sound came from behind them. They had covered more than a mile when Balthus said: 'Does Zogar Sag catch leopard-cubs and train them for bloodhounds?'

Conan shook his head. 'That was a leopard he called out of the woods.'

'But,' Balthus persisted, 'if he can order the beasts to do his bidding, why doesn't he rouse them all and have them after us? The forest is full of leopards; why send only one after us?'

Conan did not reply for a space, and when he did it was with a curious reticence.

'He can't command all the animals. Only such as remember Jhebbal Sag.'

'Jhebbal Sag?' Balthus repeated the ancient name hesitantly. He had never heard it spoken more than three or four times in his whole life.

'Once all living things worshipped him. That was long ago, when beasts and men spoke one language. Men have forgotten him; even the beasts forget. Only a few remember. The men who remember Jhebbal Sag and the beasts who remember are brothers and speak the same tongue.'

Balthus did not reply; he had strained at a Pictish stake and seen the nighted jungle give up its fanged horrors at a shaman's call.

'Civilized men laugh,' said Conan. 'But not one can tell me how Zogar Sag can call pythons and tigers and leopards out of the wilderness and make them do his bidding. They would say it is a lie, if they dared. That's the way with civilized men. When they can't explain something by their half-baked science, they refuse to believe it.'

The people on the Tauran were closer to the primitive than most Aquilonians; superstitions persisted, whose sources were lost in antiquity. And Balthus had seen that which still prickled his flesh. He could not refute the monstrous thing which Conan's words implied.

'I've heard that there's an ancient grove sacred to Jhebbal Sag somewhere in this forest,' said Conan. 'I don't know. I've never seen it. But more beasts *remember* in this country than any I've ever seen.'

'Then others will be on our trail?'

'They are now,' was Conan's disquieting answer. 'Zogar would never leave our tracking to one beast alone.'

'What are we to do, then?' asked Balthus uneasily, grasping his ax as he stared at the gloomy arches above him. His flesh crawled with the momentary expectation of ripping talons and fangs leaping from the shadows.

'Wait!'

Conan turned, squatted and with his knife began scratching a curious symbol in the mold. Stooping to look at it over his shoulder, Balthus felt a crawling of the flesh along his spine, he knew not why. He felt no wind against his face, but there was a rustling of leaves above them and a weird moaning swept ghostily through the branches. Conan glanced up inscrutably, then rose and stood staring somberly down at the symbol he had drawn.

'What is it?' whispered Balthus. It looked archaic and meaningless to him. He supposed that it was his ignorance of artistry which prevented his identifying it as one of the conventional designs of some prevailing culture. But had he been the most erudite artist in the world, he would have been no nearer the solution.

'I saw it carved in the rock of a cave no human had visited for a million years,' muttered Conan, 'in the uninhabited mountains beyond the Sea of Vilayet, half a world away from this spot. Later I saw a black witch-finder of Kush scratch it in the sand of a nameless river. He told me part of its meaning – it's sacred to Jhebbal Sag and the creatures which worship him. Watch!'

They drew back among the dense foliage some yards away and

waited in tense silence. To the east drums muttered and some-where to north and west other drums answered. Balthus shivered, though he knew long miles of black forest separated him from the grim beaters of those drums whose dull pulsing was a sinister overture that set the dark stage for bloody drama.

Balthus found himself holding his breath. Then with a slight shaking of the leaves, the bushes parted and a magnificent panther came into view. The moonlight dappling through the leaves shone on its glossy coat rippling with the play of the great muscles beneath it.

With its head held low it glided toward them. It was smell-ing out their trail. Then it halted as if frozen, its muzzle almost touching the symbol cut in the mold. For a long space it crouched motionless; it flattened its long body and laid its head on the ground before the mark. And Balthus felt the short hairs stir on his scalp. For the attitude of the great carnivore was one of awe and adoration.

Then the panther rose and backed away carefully, belly almost to the ground. With his hind-quarters among the bushes he wheeled as if in sudden panic and was gone like a flash of dappled light.

Balthus mopped his brow with a trembling hand and glanced at Conan.

The barbarian's eyes were smoldering with fires that never lit the eyes of men bred to the ideas of civilization. In that instant he was all wild, and had forgotten the man at his side. In his burning gaze Balthus glimpsed and vaguely recognized pristine images and half-embodied memories, shadows from Life's dawn, forgotten and repudiated by sophisticated races – ancient, primeval fantasms unnamed and nameless.

Then the deeper fires were masked and Conan was silently leading the way deeper into the forest.

'We've no more to fear from the beasts,' he said after a while, 'but we've left a sign for men to read. They won't follow our trail very easily, and until they find that symbol they won't know for sure we've turned south. Even then it won't be easy to smell us out without the beasts to aid them. But the woods south of the trail will be full of warriors looking for us. If we keep moving after daylight, we'll be sure to run into some of them. As soon as we find a good place we'll hide and wait until another night to swing back and make the river. We've got to warn Valannus, but it won't help him any if we get ourselves killed.'

'Warn Valannus?'

'Hell, the woods along the river are swarming with Picts! That's why they got us. Zogar's brewing war-magic; no mere raid this time. He's done something no Pict has done in my memory – united as many as fifteen or sixteen clans. His magic did it; they'll follow a wizard farther than they will a war-chief. You saw the mob in the village; and there were hundreds hiding along the river bank that you didn't see. More coming, from the farther villages. He'll have at least three thousand fighting-men. I lay in the bushes and heard their talk as they went past. They mean to attack the fort; when, I don't know, but Zogar doesn't dare delay long. He's gathered them and whipped them into a frenzy. If he doesn't lead them into battle quickly, they'll fall to quarreling with one another. They're like blood-mad tigers.

'I don't know whether they can take the fort or not. Anyway, we've got to get back across the river and give the warning. The settlers on the Velitrium road must either get into the fort or back to Velitrium. While the Picts are besieging the fort, war-parties will range the road far to the east – might even cross Thunder River and raid the thickly settled country behind Velitrium.'

As he talked he was leading the way deeper and deeper into the ancient wilderness. Presently he grunted with satisfaction. They had reached a spot where the underbrush was more scattered, and an outcropping of stone was visible, wandering off southward. Balthus felt more secure as they followed it. Not even a Pict could trail them over naked rock.

'How did you get away?' he asked presently.

Conan tapped his mail-shirt and helmet.

'If more borderers would wear harness there'd be fewer skulls hanging on the altar-huts. But most men make noise if they wear armor. They were waiting on each side of the path, without moving. And when a Pict stands motionless, the very beasts of the forest pass him without seeing him. They'd seen us crossing the river and got in their places. If they'd gone into ambush after we left the bank, I'd have had some hint of it. But they were waiting, and not even a leaf trembled. The devil himself couldn't have suspected anything. The first suspicion I had was when I heard a shaft rasp against a bow as it was pulled back. I dropped and yelled for the men behind me to drop, but they were too slow, taken by surprise like that.

'Most of them fell at the first volley that raked us from both sides. Some of the arrows crossed the trail and struck Picts on the other side. I heard them howl.' He grinned with vicious satisfaction. 'Such of us as were left plunged into the woods and closed with them. When I saw the others were all down or taken, I broke through and outfooted the painted devils through the darkness. They were all around me. I ran and crawled and sneaked, and sometimes I lay on my belly under the bushes while they passed me on all sides.

'I tried for the shore and found it lined with them, waiting for just such a move. But I'd have cut my way through and taken a chance on swimming, only I heard the drums pounding in the village and knew they'd taken somebody alive.

'They were all so engrossed in Zogar's magic that I was able to climb the wall behind the altar-hut. There was a warrior supposed to be watching at that point, but he was squatting behind the hut and peering around the corner at the ceremony. I came up behind him and broke his neck with my hands before he knew what was happening. It was his spear I threw into the snake, and that's his ax you're carrying.'

'But what was that – that thing you killed in the altar-hut?' asked Balthus, with a shiver at the memory of the dim-seen horror.

'One of Zogar's gods. One of Jhebbal's children that didn't remember and had to be kept chained to the altar. A bull ape. The Picts think they're sacred to the Hairy One who lives on the moon – the gorilla-god of Gullah.

'It's getting light. Here's a good place to hide until we see how close they're on our trail. Probably have to wait until night to break back to the river.'

A low hill pitched upward, girdled and covered with thick trees and bushes. Near the crest Conan slid into a tangle of jutting rocks, crowned by dense bushes. Lying among them they could see the jungle below without being seen. It was a good place to hide or defend. Balthus did not believe that even a Pict could have trailed them over the rocky ground for the past four or five miles, but he was afraid of the beasts that obeyed Zogar Sag. His faith in the curious symbol wavered a little now. But Conan had dismissed the possibility of beasts tracking them.

A ghostly whiteness spread through the dense branches; the patches of sky visible altered in hue, grew from pink to blue. Balthus felt the gnawing of hunger, though he had slaked his thirst at a stream they had skirted. There was complete silence, except for an occasional chirp of a bird. The drums were no longer to be heard. Balthus' thoughts reverted to the grim scene before the altar-hut.

'Those were ostrich plumes Zogar Sag wore,' he said. 'I've seen them on the helmets of knights who rode from the East to visit the barons of the marches. There are no ostriches in this forest, are there?'

'They came from Kush,' answered Conan. 'West of here, many marches, lies the seashore. Ships from Zingara occasionally come and trade weapons and ornaments and wine to the coastal tribes for skins and copper ore and gold dust. Sometimes they trade ostrich plumes they got from the Stygians, who in turn got them from the black tribes of Kush, which lies south of Stygia. The Pictish shamans place great store by them. But there's much risk in such trade. The Picts are too likely to try to seize the ship. And the coast is dangerous to ships. I've sailed along it when I was with the pirates of the Barachan Isles, which lie southwest of Zingara.'

Balthus looked at his companion with admiration.

'I knew you hadn't spent your life on this frontier. You've mentioned several far places. You've traveled widely?'

'I've roamed far; farther than any other man of my race ever wandered. I've seen all the great cities of the Hyborians, the Shemites, the Stygians and the Hyrkanians. I've roamed in the unknown countries south of the black kingdoms of Kush, and east of the Sea of Vilayet. I've been a mercenary captain, a corsair, a *kozak*, a penniless vagabond, a general – hell, I've been everything except a king, and I may be that, before I die.' The fancy pleased him, and he grinned hardly. Then he shrugged his shoulders and stretched his mighty figure on the rocks. 'This is as good a life as any. I don't know how long I'll stay on the frontier; a week, a month, a year. I have a roving foot. But it's as well on the border as anywhere.'

Balthus set himself to watch the forest below them. Momentarily he expected to see fierce painted faces thrust through the leaves. But as the hours passed no stealthy footfall disturbed the brooding quiet. Balthus believed the Picts had missed their trail and given up the chase. Conan grew restless.

'We should have sighted parties scouring the woods for us. If they've quit the chase, it's because they're after bigger game. They may be gathering to cross the river and storm the fort.'

'Would they come this far south if they lost the trail?'

'They've lost the trail, all right; otherwise they'd have been on our necks before now. Under ordinary circumstances they'd scour the woods for miles in every direction. Some of them should have passed within sight of this hill. They must be preparing to cross the river. We've got to take a chance and make for the river.'

Creeping down the rocks Balthus felt his flesh crawl between his shoulders as he momentarily expected a withering blast of arrows from the green masses about them. He feared that the Picts had discovered them and were lying about in ambush. But Conan was convinced no enemies were near, and the Cimmerian was right.

'We're miles to the south of the village,' grunted Conan. 'We'll hit straight through for the river. I don't know how far down the river they've spread. We'll hope to hit it below them.'

With haste that seemed reckless to Balthus they hurried east-ward. The woods seemed empty of life. Conan believed that all the Picts were gathered in the vicinity of Gwawela, if indeed, they had not already crossed the river. He did not believe they would cross in the daytime, however.

'Some woodsman would be sure to see them and give the alarm. They'll cross above and below the fort, out of sight of the sentries. Then others will get in canoes and make straight across for the river wall. As soon as they attack, those hidden in the woods on the east shore will assail the fort from the other sides. They've tried that before, and got the guts shot and hacked out of them. But this time they've got enough men to make a real onslaught of it.'

They pushed on without pausing, though Balthus gazed longingly at the squirrels flitting among the branches, which he could have brought down with a cast of his ax. With a sigh he drew up his broad belt. The everlasting silence and gloom of the primitive forest was beginning to depress him. He found himself thinking of the open groves and sun-dappled meadows of the Tauran, of the bluff cheer of his father's steep-thatched, diamond-paned house, of the fat cows browsing through the deep, lush grass, and the hearty fellowship of the brawny, bare-armed plowmen and herdsmen.

He felt lonely, in spite of his companion. Conan was as much a part of this wilderness as Balthus was alien to it. The Cimmerian might have spent years among the great cities of the world; he might have walked with the rulers of civilization; he might even achieve his wild whim some day and rule as king of a civilized nation; stranger things had happened. But he was no less a barbarian. He was concerned only with the naked fundamentals of life. The warm intimacies of small, kindly things, the sentiments and delicious trivialities that make up so much of civilized men's lives were meaningless to him. A wolf was no less a wolf because a whim of chance caused him to run with the watchdogs. Bloodshed and violence and savagery were the natural elements of the life Conan knew; he could not, and would never, understand the little things that are so dear to civilized men and women.

The shadows were lengthening when they reached the river and peered through the masking bushes. They could see up and down the river for about a mile each way. The sullen stream lay bare and empty. Conan scowled across at the other shore.

'We've got to take another chance here. We've got to swim the river. We don't know whether they've crossed or not. The woods over there may be alive with them. We've got to risk it. We're about six miles south of Gwawela.'

He wheeled and ducked as a bow-string twanged. Something like a white flash of light streaked through the bushes. Balthus knew it was an arrow. Then with a tigerish bound Conan was through the bushes. Balthus caught the gleam of steel as he whirled his sword, and heard a death scream. The next instant he had broken through the bushes after the Cimmerian.

A Pict with a shattered skull lay face-down on the ground, his fingers spasmodically clawing at the grass. Half a dozen others were swarming about Conan, swords and axes lifted. They had cast away their bows, useless at such deadly close quarters. Their lower jaws were painted white, contrasting vividly with their dark faces, and the designs on their muscular breasts differed from any Balthus had ever seen.

One of them hurled his ax at Balthus and rushed after it with lifted knife. Balthus ducked and then caught the wrist that drove the knife licking at his throat. They went to the ground together, rolling over and over. The Pict was like a wild beast, his muscles hard as steel strings.

Balthus was striving to maintain his hold on the wild man's wrist and bring his own ax into play, but so fast and furious was the struggle that each attempt to strike was blocked. The Pict was wrenching furiously to free his knife hand, was clutching at Balthus' ax, and driving his knees at the youth's groin. Suddenly he attempted to shift his knife to his free hand, and in that instant Balthus, struggling up on one knee, split the painted head with a desperate blow of his ax.

He sprang up and glared wildly about for his companion, expecting to see him overwhelmed by numbers. Then he realized the full strength and ferocity of the Cimmerian. Conan bestrode two of his attackers, shorn half asunder by that terrible broadsword. As Balthus looked he saw the Cimmerian beat down a thrusting shortsword, avoid the stroke of an ax with a cat-like sidewise spring which brought him within arm's length of a squat savage stooping for a bow. Before the Pict could straighten, the red sword flailed down and clove him from shoulder to mid-breastbone, where the blade stuck. The remaining warriors rushed in, one from either side. Balthus hurled his ax with an accuracy that reduced the attackers to one, and Conan, abandoning his efforts to free his sword, wheeled and met the remaining Pict with his bare hands. The stocky warrior, a head shorter than his tall enemy, leaped in, striking with his ax, at the same time stabbing murderously with his knife. The knife broke on the Cimmerian's mail, and the ax checked in midair as Conan's fingers locked like iron on the descending arm. A bone snapped loudly, and Balthus saw the Pict wince and falter. The next instant he was swept off his feet, lifted high above the Cimmerian's head – he writhed in midair for an instant, kicking and thrashing, and then was dashed headlong to the earth with such force that he rebounded, and then lay still, his limp posture telling of splintered limbs and a broken spine.

'Come on!' Conan wrenched his sword free and snatched up an ax. 'Grab a bow and a handful of arrows, and hurry! We've got to trust to our heels again. That yell was heard. They'll be here in no time. If we tried to swim now, they'd feather us with arrows before we reached midstream!'

6

Red Axes of the Border

Conan did not plunge deeply into the forest. A few hundred yards from the river, he altered his slanting course and ran parallel with it. Balthus recognized a grim determination not to be hunted away from the river which they must cross if they were to warn the men in the fort. Behind them rose more loudly the yells of the forest men. Balthus believed the Picts had reached the glade where the bodies of the slain men lay. Then further yells seemed to indicate that the savages were streaming into the woods in pursuit. They had left a trail any Pict could follow.

Conan increased his speed, and Balthus grimly set his teeth and kept on his heels, though he felt he might collapse any time. It seemed centuries since he had eaten last. He kept going more by an effort of will than anything else. His blood was pounding so furiously in his ear-drums that he was not aware when the yells died out behind them.

Conan halted suddenly. Balthus leaned against a tree and panted.

'They've quit!' grunted the Cimmerian, scowling.

'Sneaking – up – on – us!' gasped Balthus.

Conan shook his head.

'A short chase like this they'd yell every step of the way. No. They've gone back. I thought I heard somebody yelling behind them a few seconds before the noise began to get dimmer. They've been recalled. And that's good for us, but damned bad for the men in the fort. It means the warriors are being summoned out of the woods for the attack. These men we ran into were warriors from a tribe down the river. They were undoubtedly headed for Gwawela to join in the assault on the fort. Damn it, we're farther away than ever, now. We've got to get across the river.'

Turning east he hurried through the thickets with no attempt at concealment. Balthus followed him, for the first time feeling the sting of lacerations on his breast and shoulder where the Pict's savage teeth had scored him. He was pushing through the thick bushes that fringed the bank when Conan pulled him back. Then he heard a rhythmic splashing, and peering through the leaves, saw a dugout canoe coming up the river, its single occupant paddling hard against the current. He was a strongly built Pict with a white heron feather thrust in a copper band that confined his square-cut mane.

'That's a Gwawela man,' muttered Conan. 'Emissary from Zogar. White plume shows that. He's carried a peace talk to the tribes down the river and now he's trying to get back and take a hand in the slaughter.'

The lone ambassador was now almost even with their hiding-place, and suddenly Balthus almost jumped out of his skin. At his very ear had sounded the harsh gutturals of a Pict. Then he realized that Conan had called to the paddler in his own tongue. The man started, scanned the bushes and called back something, then cast a startled glance across the river, bent low and sent the canoe shooting in toward the western bank. Not understanding, Balthus saw Conan take from his hand the bow he had picked up in the glade, and notch an arrow.

The Pict had run his canoe in close to the shore, and staring up into the bushes, called out something. His answer came in the twang of the bow-string, the streaking flight of the arrow that sank to the feathers in his broad breast. With a choking gasp he slumped sidewise and rolled into the shallow water. In an instant Conan was down the bank and wading into the water to grasp the drifting canoe. Balthus stumbled after him and somewhat dazedly crawled into the canoe. Conan scrambled in, seized the paddle and sent the craft shooting toward the eastern shore. Balthus noted with envious admiration the play of the great muscles beneath the sun-burnt skin. The Cimmerian seemed an iron man, who never knew fatigue.

'What did you say to the Pict?' asked Balthus.

'Told him to pull into shore; said there was a white forest runner on the bank who was trying to get a shot at him.'

'That doesn't seem fair,' Balthus objected. 'He thought a friend was speaking to him. You mimicked a Pict perfectly—'

'We needed his boat,' grunted Conan, not pausing in his exertions. 'Only way to lure him to the bank. Which is worse – to betray a Pict who'd enjoy skinning us both alive, or betray the men across the river whose lives depend on our getting over?'

Balthus mulled over this delicate ethical question for a moment, then shrugged his shoulder and asked: 'How far are we from the fort?'

Conan pointed to a creek which flowed into Black River from the east, a few hundred yards below them.

'That's South Creek; it's ten miles from its mouth to the fort. It's the southern boundary of Conajohara. Marshes miles wide south of it. No danger of a raid from across them. Nine miles above the fort North Creek forms the other boundary. Marshes beyond that, too. That's why an attack must come from the west, across Black River. Conajohara's just like a spear, with a point nineteen miles wide, thrust into the Pictish wilderness.'

'Why don't we keep to the canoe and make the trip by water?'

'Because, considering the current we've got to brace, and the bends in the river, we can go faster afoot. Besides, remember Gwawela is south of the fort; if the Picts are crossing the river we'd run right into them.'

Dusk was gathering as they stepped upon the eastern bank. Without pause Conan pushed on northward, at a pace that made Balthus' sturdy legs ache.

'Valannus wanted a fort built at the mouths of North and South Creeks,' grunted the Cimmerian. 'Then the river could be patrolled constantly. But the Government wouldn't do it.

'Soft-bellied fools sitting on velvet cushions with naked girls offering them iced wine on their knees – I know the breed. They can't see any farther than their palace wall. Diplomacy – hell! They'd fight Picts with theories of territorial expansion. Valannus and men like him have to obey the orders of a set of damned fools. They'll never grab any more Pictish land, any more than they'll ever rebuild Venarium. The time may come when they'll see the barbarians swarming over the walls of the Eastern cities!'

A week before, Balthus would have laughed at any such preposterous suggestion. Now he made no reply. He had seen the unconquerable ferocity of the men who dwelt beyond the frontiers.

He shivered, casting glances at the sullen river, just visible through the bushes, at the arches of the trees which crowded close to its banks. He kept remembering that the Picts might have crossed the river and be lying in ambush between them and the fort. It was fast growing dark.

A slight sound ahead of them jumped his heart into his throat, and Conan's sword gleamed in the air. He lowered it when a dog, a great, gaunt, scarred beast, slunk out of the bushes and stood staring at them.

'That dog belonged to a settler who tried to build his cabin on the bank of the river a few miles south of the fort,' grunted Conan. 'The Picts slipped over and killed him, of course, and burned his cabin. We found him dead among the embers, and the dog lying senseless among three Picts he'd killed. He was almost cut to pieces. We took him to the fort and dressed his wounds, but after he recovered he took to the woods and turned wild— What now, Slasher, are you hunting the men who killed your master?'

The massive head swung from side to side and the eyes glowed greenly. He did not growl or bark. Silently as a phantom he slid in behind them.

'Let him come,' muttered Conan. 'He can smell the devils before we can see them.'

Balthus smiled and laid his hand caressingly on the dog's head. The lips involuntarily writhed back to display the gleaming fangs; then the great beast bent his head sheepishly, and his tail moved with jerky uncertainty, as if the owner had almost forgotten the emotions of friendliness. Balthus mentally compared the great gaunt hard body with the fat sleek hounds tumbling vociferously over one another in his father's kennel yard. He sighed. The frontier was no less hard for beasts than for men. This dog had almost forgotten the meaning of kindness and friendliness.

Slasher glided ahead, and Conan let him take the lead. The last tinge of dusk faded into stark darkness. The miles fell away under their steady feet. Slasher seemed voiceless. Suddenly he halted, tense, ears lifted. An instant later the men heard it – a demoniac yelling up the river ahead of them, faint as a whisper.

Conan swore like a madman.

'They've attacked the fort! We're too late! Come on!'

He increased his pace, trusting to the dog to smell out ambushes ahead. In a flood of tense excitement Balthus forgot his hunger and weariness. The yells grew louder as they advanced, and above the devilish screaming they could hear the deep shouts of the soldiers. Just as Balthus began to fear they would run into the savages who seemed to be howling just ahead of them, Conan swung away from the river in a wide semicircle that carried them to a low rise from which they could look over the forest. They saw the fort, lighted with torches thrust over the parapets on long poles. These cast a flickering, uncertain light over the clearing, and in that light they saw throngs of naked, painted figures along the fringe of the clearing. The river swarmed with canoes. The Picts had the fort completely surrounded.

An incessant hail of arrows rained against the stockade from the woods and the river. The deep twanging of the bow-strings rose above the howling. Yelling like wolves, several hundred naked warriors with axes in their hands ran from under the trees and raced toward the eastern gate. They were within a hundred and fifty yards of their objective when a withering blast of arrows from the wall littered the ground with corpses and sent the survivors fleeing back to the trees. The men in the canoes rushed their boats toward the river-wall, and were met by another shower of clothyard shafts and a volley from the small ballistas mounted on towers on that side of the stockade. Stones and logs whirled through the air and splintered and sank half a dozen canoes, killing their occupants, and the other boats drew back out of range. A deep roar of triumph rose from the walls of the fort, answered by bestial howling from all quarters.

'Shall we try to break through?' asked Balthus, trembling with eagerness.

Conan shook his head. He stood with his arms folded, his head slightly bent, a somber and brooding figure.

'The fort's doomed. The Picts are blood-mad, and won't stop until they're all killed. And there are too many of them for the men in the fort to kill. We couldn't break through, and if we did, we could do nothing but die with Valannus.'

'There's nothing we can do but save our own hides, then?'

'Yes. We've got to warn the settlers. Do you know why the Picts are not trying to burn the fort with fire-arrows? Because they don't want a flame that might warn the people to the east. They plan to stamp out the fort, and then sweep east before anyone knows of its fall. They may cross Thunder River and take Velitrium before the people know what's happened. At least they'll destroy every living thing between the fort and Thunder River.

'We've failed to warn the fort, and I see now it would have done no good if we had succeeded. The fort's too poorly manned. A few more charges and the Picts will be over the walls and breaking down the gates. But we can start the settlers toward Velitrium. Come on! We're outside the circle the Picts have thrown around the fort. We'll keep clear of it.'

They swung out in a wide arc, hearing the rising and falling of the volume of the yells, marking each charge and repulse. The men in the fort were holding their own; but the shrieks of the Picts did not diminish in savagery. They vibrated with a timbre that held assurance of ultimate victory.

Before Balthus realized they were close to it, they broke into the road leading east.

'Now run!' grunted Conan. Balthus set his teeth. It was nineteen miles to Velitrium, a good five to Scalp Creek beyond which began the settlements. It seemed to the Aquilonian that they had been fighting and running for centuries. But the nervous excitement that rioted through his blood stimulated him to Herculean efforts.

Slasher ran ahead of them, his head to the ground, snarling low, the first sound they had heard from him.

'Picts ahead of us!' snarled Conan, dropping to one knee and scanning the ground in the starlight. He shook his head, baffled. 'I can't tell how many. Probably only a small party. Some that couldn't wait to take the fort. They've gone ahead to butcher the settlers in their beds! Come on!'

Ahead of them presently they saw a small blaze through the trees, and heard a wild and ferocious chanting. The trail bent there, and leaving it, they cut across the bend, through the thickets. A few moments later they were looking on a hideous sight. An ox-wain stood in the road piled with meager household furnishings; it was burning; the oxen lay near with their throats cut. A man and a woman lay in the road, stripped and mutilated. Five Picts were dancing about them with fantastic leaps and bounds, waving bloody axes; one of them brandished the woman's red-smeared gown.

At the sight a red haze swam before Balthus. Lifting his bow he lined the prancing figure, black against the fire, and loosed. The slayer leaped convulsively and fell dead with the arrow through his heart. Then the two white men and the dog were upon the startled survivors. Conan was animated merely by his fighting spirit and an old, old racial hate, but Balthus was afire with wrath.

He met the first Pict to oppose him with a ferocious swipe that split the painted skull, and sprang over his falling body to grapple with the others. But Conan had already killed one of the two he had chosen, and the leap of the Aquilonian was a second late. The warrior was down with the long sword through him even as Balthus' ax was lifted. Turning toward the remaining Pict, Balthus saw Slasher rise from his victim, his great jaws dripping blood.

Balthus said nothing as he looked down at the pitiful forms in the road beside the burning wain. Both were young, the woman little more than a girl. By some whim of chance the Picts had left her face unmarred, and even in the agonies of an awful death it was beautiful. But her soft young body had been hideously slashed with many knives – a mist clouded Balthus' eyes and he swallowed chokingly. The tragedy momentarily overcame him. He felt like falling upon the ground and weeping and biting the earth.

'Some young couple just hitting out on their own,' Conan was saying as he wiped his sword unemotionally. 'On their way to the fort when the Picts met them. Maybe the boy was going to enter the service; maybe take up land on the river. Well, that's what will happen to every man, woman and child this side of Thunder River if we don't get them into Velitrium in a hurry.'

Balthus' knees trembled as he followed Conan. But there was no hint of weakness in the long easy stride of the Cimmerian. There was a kinship between him and the great gaunt brute that glided beside him. Slasher no longer growled with his head to the trail. The way was clear before them. The yelling on the river came faintly to them, but Balthus believed the fort was still holding. Conan halted suddenly, with an oath.

He showed Balthus a trail that led north from the road. It was an old trail, partly grown with new young growth, and this growth had recently been broken down. Balthus realized this fact more by feel than sight, though Conan seemed to see like a cat in the dark. The Cimmerian showed him where broad wagon tracks turned off the main trail, deeply indented in the forest mold.

'Settlers going to the licks after salt,' he grunted. 'They're at the edges of the marsh, about nine miles from here. Blast it! They'll be cut off and butchered to a man! Listen! One man can warn the people on the road. Go ahead and wake them up and herd them into Velitrium. I'll go and get the men gathering the salt. They'll be camped by the licks. We won't come back to the road. We'll head straight through the woods.'

With no further comment Conan turned off the trail and hurried down the dim path, and Balthus, after staring after him for a few moments, set out along the road. The dog had remained with him, and glided softly at his heels. When Balthus had gone a few rods he heard the animal growl. Whirling, he glared back the way he had come, and was startled to see a vague ghostly glow vanishing into the forest in the direction Conan had taken. Slasher rumbled deep in his throat, his hackles stiff and his eyes balls of green fire. Balthus remembered the grim apparition that had taken the head of the merchant Tiberias not far from that spot, and he hesitated. The thing must be following Conan. But the giant Cimmerian had repeatedly demonstrated his ability to take care of himself, and Balthus felt his duty lay toward the helpless settlers who slumbered in the path of the red hurricane. The horror of the fiery phantom was overshadowed by the horror of those limp, violated bodies beside the burning ox-wain.

He hurried down the road, crossed Scalp Creek and came in sight of the first settler's cabin – a long, low structure of ax-hewn logs. In an instant he was pounding on the door. A sleepy voice inquired his pleasure.

'Get up! The Picts are over the river!'

That brought instant response. A low cry echoed his words and then the door was thrown open by a woman in a scanty shift. Her hair hung over her bare shoulders in disorder; she held a candle in one hand and an ax in the other. Her face was colorless, her eyes wide with terror.

'Come in!' she begged. 'We'll hold the cabin.'

'No. We must make for Velitrium. The fort can't hold them back. It may have fallen already. Don't stop to dress. Get your children and come on.'

'But my man's gone with the others after salt!' she wailed, wringing her hands. Behind her peered three tousled youngsters, blinking and bewildered.

'Conan's gone after them. He'll fetch them through safe. We must hurry up the road to warn the other cabins.'

Relief flooded her countenance.

'Mitra be thanked!' she cried. 'If the Cimmerian's gone after them, they're safe if mortal man can save them!'

In a whirlwind of activity she snatched up the smallest child and herded the others through the door ahead of her. Balthus took the candle and ground it out under his heel. He listened an instant. No sound came up the dark road.

'Have you got a horse?'

'In the stable,' she groaned. 'Oh, hurry!'

He pushed her aside as she fumbled with shaking hands at the bars. He led the horse out and lifted the children on its back, telling them to hold to its mane and to one another. They stared at him seriously, making no outcry. The woman took the horse's halter and set out up the road. She still gripped her ax and Balthus knew that if cornered she would fight with the desperate courage of a she-panther.

He held behind, listening. He was oppressed by the belief that the fort had been stormed and taken; that the dark-skinned hordes were already streaming up the road toward Velitrium, drunken on slaughter and mad for blood. They would come with the speed of starving wolves.

Presently they saw another cabin looming ahead. The woman started to shriek a warning, but Balthus stopped her. He hurried to the door and knocked. A woman's voice answered him. He repeated his warning, and soon the cabin disgorged its occupants – an old woman, two young women and four children. Like the other woman's husband, their men had gone to the salt licks the day before, unsuspecting of any danger. One of the young women seemed dazed, the other prone to hysteria. But the old woman, a stern old veteran of the frontier, quieted them harshly; she helped Balthus get out the two horses that were stabled in a pen behind the cabin and put the children on them. Balthus urged that she herself mount with them, but she shook her head and made one of the younger women ride.

'She's with child,' grunted the old woman. 'I can walk – and fight, too, if it comes to that.'

As they set out, one of the women said: 'A young couple passed along the road about dusk; we advised them to spend the night at our cabin, but they were anxious to make the fort tonight. Did – did—'

'They met the Picts,' answered Balthus briefly, and the woman sobbed in horror.

They were scarcely out of sight of the cabin when some distance behind them quavered a long high-pitched yell.

'A wolf!' exclaimed one of the women.

'A painted wolf with an ax in his hand,' muttered Balthus. 'Go! Rouse the other settlers along the road and take them with you. I'll scout along behind.'

Without a word the old woman herded her charges ahead of her. As they faded into the darkness, Balthus could see the pale ovals that were the faces of the children twisted back over their shoulders to stare toward him. He remembered his own people on the Tauran and a moment's giddy sickness swam over him. With momentary weakness he groaned and sank down in the road; his muscular arm fell over Slasher's massive neck and he felt the dog's warm moist tongue touch his face.

He lifted his head and grinned with a painful effort.

'Come on, boy,' he mumbled, rising. 'We've got work to do.'

A red glow suddenly became evident through the trees. The Picts had fired the last hut. He grinned. How Zogar Sag would froth if he knew his warriors had let their destructive natures get the better of them. The fire would warn the people farther up the road. They would be awake and alert when the fugitives reached them. But his face grew grim. The women were traveling slowly, on foot and on the overloaded horses. The swift-footed Picts would run them down within a mile, unless— he took his position behind a tangle of fallen logs beside the trail. The road west of him was lighted by the burning cabin, and when the Picts came he saw them first – black furtive figures etched against the distant glare.

Drawing a shaft to the head, he loosed and one of the figures crumpled. The rest melted into the woods on either side of the road. Slasher whimpered with the killing lust beside him. Suddenly a figure appeared on the fringe of the trail, under the trees, and began gliding toward the fallen timbers. Balthus' bow-string twanged and the Pict yelped, staggered and fell into the shadows with the arrow through his thigh. Slasher cleared the timbers with a bound and leaped into the bushes. They were violently shaken and then the dog slunk back to Balthus' side, his jaws crimson.

No more appeared in the trail; Balthus began to fear they were stealing past his position through the woods, and when he heard a faint sound to his left he loosed blindly. He cursed as he heard the shaft splinter against a tree, but Slasher glided away as silently as a phantom, and presently Balthus heard a thrashing and a gurgling; then Slasher came like a ghost through the bushes, snuggling his great, crimson-stained head against Balthus' arm. Blood oozed from a gash in his shoulder, but the sounds in the wood had ceased for ever.

The men lurking on the edges of the road evidently sensed the fate of their companion, and decided that an open charge was preferable to being dragged down in the dark by a devil-beast they could neither see nor hear. Perhaps they realized that only one man lay behind the logs. They came with a sudden rush, breaking cover from both sides of the trail. Three dropped with arrows through them – and the remaining pair hesitated. One turned and ran back down the road, but the other lunged over the breastwork, his eyes and teeth gleaming in the dim light, his ax lifted. Balthus' foot slipped as he sprang up, but the slip saved his life. The descending ax shaved a lock of hair from his head, and the Pict rolled down the logs from the force of his wasted blow. Before he could regain his feet Slasher tore his throat out.

Then followed a tense period of waiting, in which time Balthus wondered if the man who had fled had been the only survivor of the party. Obviously it had been a small band that had either left the fighting at the fort, or was scouting ahead of the main body. Each moment that passed increased the chances for safety of the women and children hurrying toward Velitrium.

Then without warning a shower of arrows whistled over his retreat. A wild howling rose from the woods along the trail. Either the survivor had gone after aid, or another party had joined the first. The burning cabin still smoldered, lending a little light. Then they were after him, gliding through the trees beside the trail. He shot three arrows and threw the bow away. As if sensing his plight, they came on, not yelling now, but in deadly silence except for a swift pad of many feet.

He fiercely hugged the head of the great dog growling at his side, muttered: 'All right, boy, give 'em hell!' and sprang to his feet, drawing his ax. Then the dark figures flooded over the breastworks and closed in a storm of flailing axes, stabbing knives and ripping fangs.

7

The Devil in the Fire

When Conan turned from the Velitrium road he expected a run of some nine miles and set himself to the task. But he had not gone four when he heard the sounds of a party of men ahead of him. From the noise they were making in their progress he knew they were not Picts. He hailed them.

'Who's there?' challenged a harsh voice. 'Stand where you are until we know you, or you'll get an arrow through you.'

'You couldn't hit an elephant in this darkness,' answered Conan impatiently. 'Come on, fool; it's I – Conan. The Picts are over the river.'

'We suspected as much,' answered the leader of the men, as they strode forward – tall, rangy men, stern-faced, with bows in their hands. 'One of our party wounded an antelope and tracked it nearly to Black River. He heard them yelling down the river and ran back to our camp. We left the salt and the wagons, turned the oxen loose and came as swiftly as we could. If the Picts are besieging the fort, war-parties will be ranging up the road toward our cabins.'

'Your families are safe,' grunted Conan. 'My companion went ahead to take them to Velitrium. If we go back to the main road we may run into the whole horde. We'll strike southeast, through the timber. Go ahead. I'll scout behind.'

A few moments later the whole band was hurrying south-eastward. Conan followed more slowly, keeping just within ear-shot. He cursed the noise they were making; that many Picts or Cimmerians would have moved through the woods with no more noise than the wind makes as it blows through the black branches.

He had just crossed a small glade when he wheeled answering the conviction of his primitive instincts that he was being followed. Standing motionless among the bushes he heard the sounds of the retreating settlers fade away. Then a voice called faintly back along the way he had come: 'Conan! Conan! Wait for me, Conan!'

'Balthus!' he swore bewilderedly. Cautiously he called: 'Here I am.'

'Wait for me, Conan!' the voice came more distinctly.

Conan moved out of the shadows, scowling. 'What the devil are you doing here? – Crom!'

He half crouched, the flesh prickling along his spine. It was not Balthus who was emerging from the other side of the glade. A weird glow burned through the trees. It moved toward him, shimmering weirdly – a green witch-fire that moved with purpose and intent.

It halted some feet away and Conan glared at it, trying to

distinguish its fire-misted outlines. The quivering flame had a solid core; the flame was but a green garment that masked some animate and evil entity; but the Cimmerian was unable to make out its shape or likeness. Then, shockingly, a voice spoke to him from amidst the fiery column.

'Why do you stand like a sheep waiting for the butcher, Conan?'

The voice was human but carried strange vibrations that were not human.

'Sheep?' Conan's wrath got the best of his momentary awe. 'Do you think I'm afraid of a damned Pictish swamp devil? A friend called me.'

'I called in his voice,' answered the other. 'The men you follow belong to my brother; I would not rob his knife of their blood. But you are mine. Oh, fool, you have come from the far gray hills of Cimmeria to meet your doom in the forests of Conajohara.'

'You've had your chance at me before now,' snorted Conan. 'Why didn't you kill me then, if you could?'

'My brother had not painted a skull black for you and hurled it into the fire that burns for ever on Gullah's black altar. He had not whispered your name to the black ghosts that haunt the uplands of the Dark Land. But a bat has flown over the Mountains of the Dead and drawn your image in blood on the white tiger's hide that hangs before the long hut where sleep the Four Brothers of the Night. The great serpents coil about their feet and the stars burn like fire-flies in their hair.'

'Why have the gods of darkness doomed me to death?' growled Conan.

Something – a hand, foot or talon, he could not tell which, thrust out from the fire and marked swiftly on the mold. A symbol blazed there, marked with fire, and faded, but not before he recognized it.

'You dared make the sign which only a priest of Jhebbal Sag dare make. Thunder rumbled through the black Mountain of the Dead and the altar-hut of Gullah was thrown down by a wind from the Gulf of Ghosts. The loon which is messenger to the Four

Brothers of the Night flew swiftly and whispered your name in my ear. Your head will hang in the altar-hut of my brother. Your body will be eaten by the black-winged, sharp-beaked Children of Jhil.'

'Who the devil is your brother?' demanded Conan. His sword was naked in his hand, and he was subtly loosening the ax in his belt.

'Zogar Sag; a child of Jhebbal Sag who still visits his sacred groves at times. A woman of Gwawela slept in a grove holy to Jhebbal Sag. Her babe was Zogar Sag. I too am a son of Jhebbal Sag, out of a fire-being from a far realm. Zogar Sag summoned me out of the Misty Lands. With incantations and sorcery and his own blood he materialized me in the flesh of his own planet. We are one, tied together by invisible threads. His thoughts are my thoughts; if he is struck, I am bruised. If I am cut, he bleeds. But I have talked enough. Soon your ghost will talk with the ghosts of the Dark Land, and they will tell you of the old gods which are not dead, but sleep in the outer abysses, and from time to time awake.'

'I'd like to see what you look like,' muttered Conan, working his ax free, 'you who leave a track like a bird, who burn like a flame and yet speak with a human voice.'

'You shall see,' answered the voice from the flame, 'see, and carry the knowledge with you into the Dark Land.'

The flames leaped and sank, dwindling and dimming. A face began to take shadowy form. At first Conan thought it was Zogar Sag himself who stood wrapped in green fire. But the face was higher than his own and there was a demoniac aspect about it – Conan had noted various abnormalities about Zogar Sag's features – an obliqueness of the eyes, a sharpness of the ears, a wolfish thinness of the lips; these peculiarities were exaggerated in the apparition which swayed before him. The eyes were red as coals of living fire.

More details came into view: a slender torso, covered with snaky scales, which was yet man-like in shape, with man-like arms, from the waist upward; below, long crane-like legs ended in splay, three-toed feet like those of some huge bird. Along the monstrous limbs the blue fire fluttered and ran. He saw it as through a glistening mist.

Then suddenly it was towering over him, though he had not seen it move toward him. A long arm, which for the first time he noticed was armed with curving, sickle-like talons, swung high and swept down at his neck. With a fierce cry he broke the spell and bounded aside, hurling his ax. The demon avoided the cast with an unbelievably quick movement of its narrow head and was on him again with a hissing rush of leaping flames.

But fear had fought for it when it slew its other victims, and Conan was not afraid. He knew that any being clothed in material flesh can be slain by material weapons, however grisly its form may be.

One flailing talon-armed limb knocked his helmet from his head. A little lower and it would have decapitated him. But fierce joy surged through him as his savagely driven sword sank deep in the monster's groin. He bounded backward from a flailing stroke, tearing his sword free as he leaped. The talons raked his breast, ripping through mail-links as if they had been cloth. But his return spring was like that of a starving wolf. He was inside the lashing arms and driving his sword deep in the monster's belly – felt the arms lock about him and the talons ripping the mail from his back as they sought his vitals – he was lapped and dazzled by blue flame that was chill as ice – then he had torn fiercely away from the weakening arms and his sword cut the air in a tremendous swipe.

The demon staggered and fell sprawling sidewise, its head hanging only by a shred of flesh. The fires that veiled it leaped fiercely upward, now red as gushing blood, hiding the figure from view. A scent of burning flesh filled Conan's nostrils. Shaking the blood and sweat from his eyes, he wheeled and ran staggering through the woods. Blood trickled down his limbs. Somewhere, miles to the south, he saw the faint glow of flames that might mark a burning cabin. Behind him, toward the road, rose a distant howling that spurred him to greater efforts.

8

Conajohara No More

There had been fighting on Thunder River; fierce fighting before the walls of Velitrium; ax and torch had been piled up and down the bank, and many a settler's cabin lay in ashes before the painted horde was rolled back.

A strange quiet followed the storm, in which people gathered and talked in hushed voices, and men with red-stained bandages drank their ale silently in the taverns along the river bank.

There, to Conan the Cimmerian, moodily quaffing from a great wine-glass, came a gaunt forester with a bandage about his head and his arm in a sling. He was the one survivor of Fort Tuscelan.

'You went with the soldiers to the ruins of the fort?'

Conan nodded.

'I wasn't able,' murmured the other. 'There was no fighting?'

'The Picts had fallen back across the Black River. Something must have broken their nerve, though only the devil who made them knows what.'

The woodsman glanced at his bandaged arm and sighed.

'They say there were no bodies worth disposing of.'

Conan shook his head. 'Ashes. The Picts had piled them in the fort and set fire to the fort before they crossed the river. Their own dead and the men of Valannus.'

'Valannus was killed among the last – in the hand-to-hand fighting when they broke the barriers. They tried to take him alive, but he made them kill him. They took ten of the rest of us prisoners when we were so weak from fighting we could fight no more. They butchered nine of us then and there. It was when Zogar Sag died that I got my chance to break free and run for it.'

'Zogar Sag's dead?' ejaculated Conan.

'Aye. I saw him die. That's why the Picts didn't press the fight against Velitrium as fiercely as they did against the fort. It was strange. He took no wounds in battle. He was dancing among the

368

slain, waving an ax with which he'd just brained the last of my comrades. He came at me, howling like a wolf – and then he staggered and dropped the ax, and began to reel in a circle screaming as I never heard a man or beast scream before. He fell between me and the fire they'd built to roast me, gagging and frothing at the mouth, and all at once he went rigid and the Picts shouted that he was dead. It was during the confusion that I slipped my cords and ran for the woods.

'I saw him lying in the firelight. No weapon had touched him. Yet there were red marks like the wounds of a sword in the groin, belly and neck – the last as if his head had been almost severed from his body. What do you make of that?'

Conan made no reply, and the forester, aware of the reticence of barbarians on certain matters, continued: 'He lived by magic, and somehow, he died by magic. It was the mystery of his death that took the heart out of the Picts. Not a man who saw it was in the fighting before Velitrium. They hurried back across Black River. Those that struck Thunder River were warriors who had come on before Zogar Sag died. They were not enough to take the city by themselves.

'I came along the road, behind their main force, and I know none followed me from the fort. I sneaked through their lines and got into the town. You brought the settlers through all right, but their women and children got into Velitrium just ahead of those painted devils. If the youth Balthus and old Slasher hadn't held them up awhile, they'd have butchered every woman and child in Conajohara. I passed the place where Balthus and the dog made their last stand. They were lying amid a heap of dead Picts – I counted seven, brained by his ax, or disemboweled by the dog's fangs, and there were others in the road with arrows sticking in them. Gods, what a fight that must have been!'

'He was a man,' said Conan. 'I drink to his shade, and to the shade of the dog, who knew no fear.' He quaffed part of the wine, then emptied the rest upon the floor, with a curious heathen gesture, and smashed the goblet. 'The heads of ten Picts shall pay for his, and seven heads for the dog, who was a better warrior than many a man.'

And the forester, staring into the moody, smoldering blue eyes, knew the barbaric oath would be kept.

'They'll not rebuild the fort?'

'No; Conajohara is lost to Aquilonia. The frontier has been pushed back. Thunder River will be the new border.'

The woodsman sighed and stared at his calloused hand, worn from contact with ax-haft and sword-hilt. Conan reached his long arm for the wine-jug. The forester stared at him, comparing him with the men about them, the men who had died along the lost river, comparing him with those other wild men over that river. Conan did not seem aware of his gaze.

'Barbarism is the natural state of mankind,' the borderer said, still staring somberly at the Cimmerian. 'Civilization is unnatural. It is a whim of circumstance. And barbarism must always ultimately triumph.'